CW00932991

THE HOOKED CROSS

THE HOOKED CROSS

(Das Hakenkreuz)

Keith Vickery

Book Guild Publishing

Sussex, England

First published in Great Britain in 2007 by
The Book Guild Ltd
Pavilion View
19 New Road
Brighton BN1 1UF

Typesetting in Times by
Keyboard Services, Luton, Bedfordshire

Printed in Great Britain by
CPI Antony Rowe

A catalogue record for this book is available from
The British Library

ISBN 978 1 84624 103 1

To my wife Beverley without whose support and encouragement this book would not have been published.

FOREWORD

By the middle of 1942, German forces had successfully conquered and occupied virtually the whole of Europe. On the Russian Front, despite earlier setbacks, their Panzers were again sweeping across the vast Soviet Union and in the Western Desert the Afrika Korps were continuing to make major territorial gains over Allied forces. On every front the Nazi war machine rolled relentlessly onward and to the rest of the world their leader, Adolf Hitler, appeared invincible. Yet how could this have happened? How could a defeated nation, led by a poorly educated, one-time vagrant tramping the streets of Vienna, achieve such phenomenal political and military success?

Born of a doting mother and a bullying father, Hitler started life in the small village of Braunau am Inn on the Austro-German border. An academic failure at school, he finished his education without gaining a single qualification and even such talent he had as an artist failed to gain him entry into the Vienna Academy of Fine Arts. And whilst his military service in the Great War proved him a brave soldier, he again failed to gain any great success, achieving only the rank of *Gefreiter* (corporal).

Yet despite such an undistinguished background this seemingly insignificant individual was destined to become Chancellor of Germany, successfully uniting a disrupted and divided nation of eighty million people, the majority of whom willingly accepted him not only as their leader but also in his role as a dictator. After gaining power, the bitterness Hitler felt from what he perceived to be Germany's ignominious surrender in 1918, made him seek to redeem Germany's position and regain its former dignity by launching his country into the greatest war the world had ever known. Surprising and confounding his battle-experienced generals with daring and innovative planning, he achieved victory after victory and quickly became one of history's most successful military conquerors.

But how could all this have happened, given his political inexperience and military naivety? Was it simply a unique chain of circumstances? An accident of history? Or could there have been something else? Perhaps a hitherto unknown factor that brought about his success? If so, could that same factor in some perverse way have also caused the sudden reversal of his fortunes in the late autumn of 1942, when his much-vaunted armies suddenly began suffering defeat after defeat, a pattern that was to continue and ultimately lead to the destruction of his Nazi empire?

How *did* it happen? Perhaps this book will provide the answer...

PROLOGUE

MUNICH – NOVEMBER 1920

Flurries of snow skipped and danced merrily along the streets of the Bavarian capital, driven by a bitterly cold north-easterly wind that heralded the onset of the alpine winter.

It was early evening and the streets were filled with people hurrying about their business, either travelling home from their daily work, or engaged in some late shopping – albeit the shops had little to offer. For what goods were available were both limited and expensive, a consequence of the crippling war reparations imposed by the Allies under the terms of the detested Treaty of Versailles. Already two years had passed since the signing of the armistice in the railway wagon at Compiègne, yet the economic conditions in Germany had seen little signs of improvement during that time. Unemployment still ran at record levels and, with industry crippled by raging inflation, work was hard to find, and life for many had simply become a struggle for survival.

One such victim of this economic misery could be seen caught up in the rush and bustle of the crowded streets of Munich that cold November evening. At first glance he could easily have been taken for a vagrant with his shabby, well-worn overcoat and battered trilby hat, both looking as if they had seen far better days. Only his boots, a souvenir from the Army, were of any consequence. His manner and bearing too were different from those about him. His pace was much slower as he trudged along, head down, hands thrust deep

1

in the pockets of his threadbare overcoat. He seemed oblivious of the crowds of people pushing past, or of the swirling snow-flakes which blew into his face, save for the few which alighted on his black 'tooth-brush' moustache and which he would unconsciously brush away from time to time. He was in a world of his own, lost deep in thought as he slowly made his way along the street, stopping only occasionally to gaze absently into a shop window. Yet he had little interest in the sparse contents on display. How could he? Being one of the millions of unemployed, the little money he did have was strictly reserved for food and shelter.

He drew level with a dimly lit pawnbroker's window and stopped momentarily to gaze aimlessly at the jumbled bric-a-brac on display. Clocks and watches, old jewellery, chipped porcelain, items which had perhaps once been treasured possessions, now sacrificed for a pitiful sum to perpetuate the frugal existence of their former owners. He was about to move away when an object tucked away in a corner at the back of the window suddenly caught his attention. It was partially obscured by a gaudily painted vase, and he had to shift his position in order to gain a better view. As he stared at the object his eyes began to widen and for several moments his attention became totally focused. Then he abruptly turned and made for the shop entrance.

A small bell tinkled musically as he stepped inside, his eyes instantly darting nervously about the dim interior as he took in his surroundings. The shop was small and had that musty smell that always seemed to associate itself with old things. It was also very cramped, every available space taken up by items offered for sale, from the scuffed, leather-bound volumes stacked in untidy piles on the bare wooden floorboards, to the numerous musical instruments hanging from the ceiling – dusty violins and violas with broken strings, tarnished brass trumpets, even a huge base drum. Around the walls mounted heads of wild animals stared down – deer, boar, long-horned antelope – their glass eyes glaring evilly at anyone who dared enter.

A glass-topped counter ran the length of the shop, its surface abraded by the volume of coins that had passed across it over countless years, whilst under the misted surface a jumbled array of old gold and jewellery was displayed: personal items – perhaps gifts, given as tokens of love or affection – their individual identity now lost in the anonymity of the crowded display case.

The shop had no other customers that evening and the tramp-like figure lost no time in making his way across to the counter where he rapped his knuckles impatiently on the glass surface. Behind it a wizened old man sat in a rocking chair reading a newspaper. He looked up frowning his annoyance at the noisy summons, then heaved a sigh of resignation, carefully folded his newspaper, placed it on a nearby table and rose to his feet.

He was a frail-looking, diminutive man, standing no more than five feet six in height and dressed even more scruffily than his visitor. He wore a tattered red woollen cardigan several sizes too large and full of holes, his none-too-clean shirt had no collar and several buttons missing, whilst the coarse baggy trousers that covered his lower half were also far too big and looked as though they had been tied up with a piece of string.

Shuffling painfully up to the counter in well-worn carpet slippers, he placed his mitten-covered hands on the glass top for support and peered quizzically at his customer through a pair of steel-rimmed spectacles perched precariously on the tip of his aquiline nose. His overall appearance was comical, circus-like even, but no humour could be discerned on the face of his visitor, for his attention had become firmly focused on the faded skullcap clamped to the old man's head. His eyes narrowed as he stared contemptuously at the old Jew. In turn the old man looked with suspicion at his visitor,

3

wondering what a vagrant could possibly want in a pawnbroker's shop. He gave a cautious nod of greeting.

'Good evening, *Mein Herr*. What can I do for you?'

The man disdainfully ignored the greeting and simply nodded towards the window at the front of the shop.

'You have a *Hakenkreuz* in the window. I might be interested in buying it,' he announced gruffly.

'*Hakenkreuz?*' questioned the shopkeeper, momentarily puzzled. Then he suddenly remembered that he had put such an object in the window only days before. 'Ah, yes...' He smiled, pleased his memory hadn't entirely failed him. 'I remember, the *Hakenkreuz...*' But then the smile disappeared as he pondered what possible interest a tramp could have in such an object – and, more importantly, if he had money to buy it. He hesitated, tapping his fingers anxiously on the glass surface. 'You ... You would like to see it, I suppose?'

'Of course I want to see it, you old fool!' snarled the tramp impatiently. 'And hurry up. I don't have all night!'

The sudden and unexpected aggressiveness startled the old shopkeeper and he quickly hurried to the window, audibly bemoaning the lack of politeness in these 'modern' times before returning using both his hands to carry the weighty object.

'It's very heavy. Made of bronze, you know. Quite valuable.'

'Hmph... Really?' grunted the tramp, unimpressed by the pawnbroker's claims. 'Let me have a look at it.'

Again the old Jew hesitated, the doubts in his mind about this unkempt stranger increasing by the minute. He was also becoming a little frightened by the man's aggressive attitude. Yet, despite these fears, he refused to be browbeaten. He cleared his throat.

'Ahem... You must excuse me for asking, *Mein Herr*, but do you have money to buy an item such as this?'

'Of course I have money!' came the harsh reply. 'Now let me see it.'

4

He reached out and snatched the swastika from the old man's bony grasp.

'Please be careful,' begged the shopkeeper, his alarm increasing. 'It's very old... And I'm sure it's quite valuable.' The man ignored the shopkeeper, concentrating his attention on the metal object, turning it over and over in his hands. The old man was right: it was heavy, very heavy, and obviously solid metal. He held it up to the light. It measured some twenty centimetres high and fifteen centimetres across at its widest point, with a maximum depth of around five centimetres at the base. The swastika itself was plain, but the wreath of laurel leaves that encircled it had been carved with a beautiful symmetry, each leaf displaying minute detail, and the oblong base on which it was mounted had been painstakingly covered in neat rows of strangely carved characters. It was a thing of beauty yet at the same time it exuded a somewhat sinister aura.

'What makes you think it's very old?' demanded the man, tracing the outline of the swastika with his fingers as he spoke.

'The lady I bought it from ... a dear widow lady ... only a few days ago,' explained the old man. 'She said it had been in the family for many years. Her husband brought it back from Persia during one of his trips there. An archaeologist I believe...'

He hesitated with his explanation, wondering if he was saying too much about the object's possible value and wondering if the tramp might make a sudden bolt for the door.

'And...?' grunted the man, not bothering to look up from his examination of the swastika.

'Ah! Yes, well...' continued the old shopkeeper. 'She told me it dates back some two thousand years or more. Even claimed her husband told her it once belonged to Alexander III of Macedonia – Alexander the Great.'

'Rubbish!' snorted the tramp. 'Only a fool would believe that!'

'It could be true,' claimed the old man defiantly. 'That writing on the base... It's Koine, the language of ancient Greece.'

'How d'you know that?' grunted the tramp. 'You're making it up, just to boost the price.' He looked suspiciously at the object in his hands. 'Anyone can see it's a fake. Probably been made by the thousand. Worth a few marks, that's all.'

Anger appeared on the old Jew's face and he reached across the counter to retrieve the object.

'If that's what you think, then hand it back. I can't understand why someone like you would be interested in an old *Hakenkreuz* – and I don't believe you have got the money to pay for it. So hand it back and be on your way, otherwise I'll call the police.'

He again extended his hand for the swastika. But the tramp held it out of his reach.

'Bronze, you say?' he sneered, pointing at the base of the object where the surface showed signs of flaking. 'Bronze coloured paint you mean. Look at this!' He thrust it under the old Jew's nose and inserted his thumbnail under the flake of paint. As he peeled it back, a different coloured metal glinted dully in the gaslight. 'Look! What did I tell you? Brass, that's what it's made of... Common brass!'

The old Jew leaned forward to take a closer look. Then his eyes widened. He had been buying and selling jewellery all his adult life and knew gold when he saw it. His hand shot out to grab the swastika, but the tramp was too quick for him, and held it out of reach.

'That's not brass,' the old Jew exclaimed excitedly. 'That's gold. Give it back to me at once!'

'Gold?' replied the tramp in surprise. He stared at the bared metal, his eyes narrowing as he glanced back at the old Jew. 'You sure?'

'Of course I'm sure! I know gold when I see it. Now hand it over, or I'll call the police.'

Again he reached out to seize it, but only succeeded in grabbing one of the lapels of the man's tattered overcoat. He held on to it grimly.

'Let go of me, you filthy Jew!' snarled the man, stepping back and trying to break the old shopkeeper's grip.

'Not until you give me the *Hakenkreuz*,' yelled the old man, hanging on with fierce determination. 'Now give it to me!'

'Give it to you, you Jewish swine?' screamed the man, struggling to free himself. 'Give it to you?' His face became contorted with hatred. 'I'll give it to you!'

The hand holding the heavy swastika suddenly rose swiftly into the air and came down on the old man's skull. A crunching sound was heard. A second blow quickly followed, then a third...

Seconds later, a dishevelled man hurriedly left the shop. Snow was falling more heavily now. He pulled his hat well down over his eyes and wrapped the collar of his shabby overcoat around his neck before hastily making his way along Der Prinzenstrasse. Fellow pedestrians were elbowed to one side as he forced his way through the crowd and escaped into the evening darkness.

The adverse weather conditions favoured the murderer. No further customers called at the pawnbroker's and it wasn't until hours later that a patrolling policeman, curious to see lights still burning after normal closing time, entered the shop and found the battered body of the old man in a pool of blood behind the counter.

The investigating police team were baffled by the apparently motiveless murder, and though they carried out a major search of the surrounding area no trace could be found of the murder weapon. Numerous enquiries followed but with no leads or witnesses, the case was soon abandoned. Although technically still open, the file on the case joined the rest of the unsolved crimes for that year and eventually found its way into the archives of the Bavarian State Police Commission.

Thirteen years later, in 1933, coincidentally the same year the Nazi Party came to power, a mysterious fire occurred at these same offices. The only records destroyed, however, were those relating to unsolved crimes for the year 1920.

1

HAMPSHIRE, ENGLAND – AUGUST 1942

Tom Davey stood at the stable yard entrance gazing out over the green, undulating parkland shimmering in the afternoon heat. The cloudless sky gave free rein to the bright sun and though the peak of his cap provided some protection the brilliance nevertheless caused him to screw up his eyes as he scanned a stand of oaks on the skyline some six or seven hundred yards away. He knew that, if they followed the usual route, this would be the direction from which they would come.

He pulled a red and white spotted handkerchief from his jacket pocket, removed his cap and wiped the beads of sweat from his brow. Replacing his cap, he leaned against one of the red-brick pillars guarding the stable entrance, wincing as he adjusted his position to take the majority of his body weight onto his right leg. Most of the time he was able to ignore the pain, something he had learned to do ever since the German mortar bomb had exploded in his section's trench in 1917. It had been a messy wound, a chunk of shrapnel tearing away a section of muscle from the back of his thigh, leaving him with both a hideous scar and a limp which would dog him for the rest of his life. He nevertheless considered himself a lucky man. The same bomb had killed three of his comrades outright and crippled two others for life, one losing an arm and the other both legs. At least he was alive, he would tell himself, and able to hold down a job, something that had been vitally important in the 'twenties when Britain was bedevilled by unemployment.

He had his former battalion commander, Lieutenant Colonel Sir Geoffrey Hardwicke, to thank for giving him the job – a job that had proved dear to his heart. As stable manager for the Hardwicke estate, he couldn't have wished for better. Tending and caring for the family's horses, he looked after them as if they were his own and continued to find contentment working at the ancestral home in the New Forest. In truth, the job was far from demanding. Apart from Sir Geoffrey, now a retired General, together with a live-in butler and a cook, only the General's twenty-year-old daughter Daphne lived there, Lady Hardwicke having died from tuberculosis when Daphne was only five. Of course there were numerous visitors to Hardwicke Hall, most of whom would inevitably want to ride the General's fine string of Irish-bred horses, but it was never too much for Tom. He felt life had been good to him. After all, he might have been working in a grimy factory somewhere in the Midlands. No, he thought contentedly as he continued to gaze at the green fields, he was a very lucky man indeed.

His musings were suddenly interrupted as a movement in the distance caught his eye. Shielding his eyes from the bright glare, he picked out the figures of two riders as they cantered across his line of vision in front of the distant oak trees. A frown appeared on his weathered features as he watched the leading rider swing his mount in the direction of the stables and spur the horse into a fast gallop. The second rider also turned, but instead chose to follow at a steady canter.

Tom straightened up, the frown replaced by a look of anger as he watched the fast approaching rider. 'Bloody young fool,' he muttered to himself. 'Ought to know better!'

The object of his anger, a young man wearing the uniform of an army subaltern, made no attempt to slacken his pace as he grew nearer and old Tom's mouth clamped in a thin line. In fact it wasn't until almost the very last moment that the rider suddenly heaved hard on the reins bringing the chestnut gelding to a skidding halt only yards from where Tom was standing. As the mount reared up, thrashing the air with its forelegs, Tom was forced to step back to avoid the flailing hooves. The young rider, totally unperturbed by the horse's antics, laughed as the animal pranced around excitedly, its nostrils flared, its eyes staring wildly.

Unable to contain himself, Tom stepped forward and grabbed the horse's reins. 'You've ridden him too hard, Mr James,' he cried angrily. 'Just look at him.'

He would dearly have loved to give the rider a sharp dressing down, but the young officer was a guest at Hardwicke Hall and had to be treated with respect. Nevertheless, he felt something had to be said.

'It's too hot to gallop him like you have, Mr James. Now look at the state he's in!'

Shaking his head, he pulled the same red and white spotted handkerchief from his pocket once more and began wiping away foaming sweat from the horse's neck and around the breastplate of its martingale, at the same time speaking soothingly to the skittish animal, patting its neck and stroking its muzzle.

The young officer meanwhile dismounted with an athletic bound and stood, hands on his hips, a huge grin on his face. A fraction over six feet tall, lean and handsome, Lieutenant James Callendar was the epitome of an English army subaltern. He looked mockingly at the stable manager, his pale blue eyes filled with amusement.

'What's the matter, Tom?' he laughed, taking off his service cap to run his fingers through his short blond hair. 'You're an old fusspot. Major loves a good work-out, as well you know.'

'Not this weather, Mr James,' retorted Tom. 'You should

11

know that. You've ridden him often enough before. Now I'll have to give him a good rub down and cooling off before I can stable him.'

The young officer shrugged nonchalantly. 'You don't have to do it. You're the stable manager. Get young Harry on the job. After all, that's what stable boys are for.'

But Tom wasn't listening. He was staring at the horse's bridle, his anger deepening.

'And what bloody fool put this bridle on him? A snaffle bit's useless. Major always has a Pelham with curb chain. Everyone knows that. No wonder he's in this state.'

James Callendar's face reddened. 'Actually, *I* tacked him up,' he snapped. 'I had to do it because you weren't here.'

Tom ignored the criticism. He had other duties to perform around the estate and couldn't be in the stable yard all the time.

'Then you should have waited until I got here,' he retorted.

Blood rushed to Callendar's face. He wasn't used to being spoken to in this fashion and certainly not by someone he considered a mere servant.

'I rather think you're forgetting to whom you're talking, Tom,' he snapped.

Tom was about to open his mouth but common sense prevailed. He knew if he really gave vent to his feelings he could well find himself looking for another job. Sir Geoffrey had always expressed complete satisfaction with Tom's work on the estate, but if it came to a test he had no doubt where Sir Geoffrey's loyalties would lie. He would support his own kind – they always did. That was the way of things. The invidiousness of class distinction still pervaded society, despite the commonality of war.

It also didn't help that Old Tom had never liked James Callendar. He was one of society's 'hooray henrys', a young man who had never done a day's work, yet enjoyed all the privileges money could buy: public school education, university – it had even bought him a commission in a famous regiment of the line. Tom's eyes flicked to the silver badge adorning the young officer's cap – a grinning skull and crossbones bearing the legend *'or Glory'*, the regimental badge of the 17th/21st Lancers. Death or Glory. Such romanticism would appeal to someone like James Callendar he thought, the idea of being a daring young cavalry officer dashing into battle. But he had yet to experience the realities of war. The scream of incoming shells, the whine of bullets streaking past your head, the ear-splitting artillery airbursts sending red-hot metal fragments ripping into cowering human bodies; the noise of men screaming in agony, the sight of limbs being torn away – the blood, the pain, the stench of death. No, he had yet to learn, this arrogant young man. To learn there is no glory in battle, only pain and heartache and misery.

By this time the second rider had arrived, a pretty young woman in her early twenties riding a midnight black thoroughbred, her tailored riding jacket and jodhpurs bearing a film of reddish dust kicked up from the dry soil. She reined in beside the two men, dismounting immediately as she sensed the tension between them.

'What on earth's the matter?' she asked.

James Callendar laughed lightly, giving a dismissive wave of the hand. 'Nothing to worry about, Daphne. Nothing at all,' he said loftily. 'Just old Tom fretting unnecessarily. Thinks I rode Major too hard.'

Daphne Hardwicke looked at the agitated horse and pursed her lips. She turned to old Tom.

'He's all right, isn't he Tom?' she asked, stepping up to stroke the gelding on the side of the neck. 'Nothing wrong is there?'

The stable manager's face remained tense.

'You know Major, Miss Daphne. He'll run his heart out if you let him. That's why he should always have a Pelham with curb chain, just to keep him in check. Should never use a snaffle bit. Not on a spirited horse like Major.'

'As I said, Tom. That wouldn't have happened had you been here,' snapped Callendar defensively.

Tom clenched his jaw.

'I do have other duties, Mr James, as you well know,' he replied coldly. 'And as for your suggestion about young Harry attending to Major, that'd be a bit difficult considering he's somewhere in Aldershot right this minute, probably doing a bit of square bashing I shouldn't wonder.'

Callendar stared at him in surprise. 'Young Harry? Aldershot? You mean to tell me he's joined up?'

'Not joined up exactly. Got conscripted. Got his papers a couple of weeks ago. Left last Thursday. Joined the RASC.'

'RASC?' Callendar frowned. 'Good God, man! Why didn't you let me know? I could have got him into the Regiment – probably still working with horses. Look, I'm sure if I had a word with my Colonel, I could get him transferred. You'll have to let me know which unit he's in, Tom.' He glanced at his watch. 'We'd better get up to the house, Daphne. I expect your father's waiting for us.'

He handed Major's reins to the stable manager and turned to make his way towards the manor house. Daphne hesitated for a moment before following.

'Major *is* all right, isn't he Tom?'

Tom smiled reassuringly.

'Don't you worry, Miss. I'll walk him round for a bit, just to cool him down, then I'll give him a good rub down. He'll be all right.'

'Thanks, Tom.' She smiled gratefully and turned to follow Callendar. 'Oh, by the way, Tom! You won't forget to let Mr James know young Harry's unit, will you?'

Tom raised a bushy eyebrow and gave her an old-fashioned look.

14

'Do you really think young Harry would thank me for doing that, Miss?' he said softly.

Daphne Hardwicke smiled awkwardly. 'No... Perhaps not, Tom. But do give Harry my regards when you next see him, will you? And tell him we do miss him.'

'Of course I will, Miss. He'll appreciate that.'

He touched his cap respectfully as the young woman turned away and watched thoughtfully as she hurried to catch up with the young officer.

'There's no accounting for taste,' he muttered to himself. 'But you could do a lot better for yourself than that stuck-up young fool, Miss Daphne.'

Shaking his head, he led the two horses into the cobbled yard.

Daphne caught up with Callendar in the rose garden, as he headed toward the conservatory at back of the house. She fell in beside him, her face troubled.

'James, don't you think you were a little short with Tom just now? After all, he was only concerned about Major. You know how he feels about the horses.'

'Not the point, old girl,' replied Callendar offhandedly. 'The man's a paid servant. Should do as he's told – and certainly not talk to guests in the tone of voice he used to me!'

'Even so, Daddy has a high regard for Tom. He considers him to be the most knowledgeable stable manager in the county. I know we'd be lost without him.'

'Perhaps so,' Callendar agreed. 'And I'm sure your father's opinion is well placed. Nevertheless, one mustn't forget Tom is still a servant and should behave accordingly.'

Daphne shook her head with exasperation.

'Oh! For goodness' sake, James! There are times when you behave like a snob.'

Callendar held open the conservatory door for her to enter.

'Don't deny it, old girl,' he readily agreed. 'But we do

15

have a responsibility to maintain the status quo after all. Otherwise we might as well all become socialists and treat everybody as equals. Can you imagine that? Lowering ourselves to the standard of the working class?' He laughed loudly. 'Good Lord! The social structure of the whole country would collapse. Then where would we be?'

Passing through the conservatory, they entered the spacious lounge where an elderly grey-haired man was waiting.

'I trust you had an enjoyable ride, Mr James, Miss Daphne,' the butler enquired respectfully. 'May I take your things?'

Daphne gave the old retainer a friendly smile.

'Yes, we've had a marvellous afternoon, thank you, Clements,' she replied, removing her hat and handing it to him. 'Do you know where my father is?'

'The General is in the library, Miss. He's asked for you both to join him for tea, when you are ready.'

'That sounds heavenly. I'm just dying for a cup.' She looked at him hopefully. 'I don't suppose there's any chance of a cream cake, is there?'

Clements gave a knowing smile. 'I believe cook has been baking this afternoon, Miss. I'm sure we can manage to rustle up something.'

'By the way, Clements,' Callendar interrupted, 'what's on the menu for dinner this evening?'

'Roast haunch of venison with fresh vegetables, sir. Cook has managed to lay her hands on some late strawberries for dessert.'

'Absolutely marvellous!' Callendar enthused eagerly. He turned to Daphne. 'It'll make a change from the dreary food we get in the Mess.'

'Will that be all, sir? Miss?'

'Yes, thank you, Clements. We'll join father in the library,' Daphne replied.

'Very good, miss. I'll serve tea immediately.' The old man gave a slight bow and turned to make his way to the kitchen.

16

'Now that's what I mean!' exclaimed Callendar, as they left the lounge and headed for the library. 'Clements exemplifies how a servant should behave. Respectful and courteous and knows his place.'

'Oh, James! Don't let's get on to that again,' Daphne groaned. 'Come on, I'm dying for that cup of tea.'

She led the way into the library and crossed to where a grey-haired man sat reading a copy of *The Times*.

General Sir Geoffrey Hardwicke, DSO, MC, now retired, smiled and rose to greet his daughter. He was a tall man with short, neatly groomed hair, a handlebar moustache and blue eyes that seemed to miss nothing and an air of dignity which immediately commanded respect.

'Hello, you two.' He folded his newspaper and laid it on a table at the side of his armchair, then he kissed his daughter lightly on the cheek. 'Did you have a good ride?'

'Mmm... Yes, although it's jolly hot out there,' replied Daphne, returning her father's kiss. She sat down on the leather chesterfield whilst the General resumed his seat in the armchair.

'And how about you, my boy?' he asked, turning to Callendar.

'Excellent, sir,' replied James, addressing the old man as though he were his senior officer. 'Blew a few cobwebs away.' He joined Daphne on the settee. 'You know I really can't thank you enough, having me down for the weekend. It's a welcome relief to get away from the garrison for a few hours, what with the endless training, the drills and manoeuvres. It gets quite unbearable at times and all the chaps are saying the same thing: "When's the balloon going up?" or "When are we going to see some action?"'

'It'll come soon enough, James. Just be patient,' replied the General, smiling at his boyish enthusiasm. 'By the way, how's your father? Haven't spoken to him for some time.'

'Oh, he's quite well, thank you, sir. Although he finds

working at the War Office somewhat tame after all those years as Military Attaché in the Embassy in Berlin. Much preferred the glamour and intrigue of the international set.'

The General nodded understandingly. 'I can well imagine. Of course you were actually born there, weren't you, James? In Berlin, I mean.'

'Yes, in fact I attended infant school there, which is how I learned to speak German. It's a second language for me.'

'James?' interrupted Daphne. 'Whilst I think of it, you haven't forgotten about the twentieth, have you? Remember? You're taking me to the Hunt Ball.'

Callendar shifted uncomfortably, avoiding her gaze.

'Oh, James!' she cried. 'You'd forgotten, hadn't you? You promised.'

Callendar looked awkward. 'No, I hadn't forgotten Daphne. You see it's like this...'

His embarrassment was momentarily spared by the arrival of Clements bearing a large tray laden with a silver tea service, cups, saucers and a plate of chocolate éclairs. He placed the tray on the table at the side of Sir Geoffrey's chair and picked up the silver teapot.

'Oh, Clements. Thank you!' exclaimed a delighted Daphne, her attention now focused on the cream cakes. 'I really don't know how cook manages to produce such luxuries.' She turned to Callendar. 'You know, James, last week in the village I saw people actually queuing for basic items like bread and meat. Can you imagine it?'

'Do you wish me to pour the tea, Sir Geoffrey?' asked Clements.

'No, it's all right, Clements. I'm sure Miss Daphne will be happy to perform that function,' Sir Geoffrey replied, smiling in her direction.

'Very good, sir.' The butler replaced the teapot. 'Will there be anything further?'

'Thank you, no. I'll ring if I need you.'

18

'Very good, sir.' Clements gave a slight bow and left the room.

'Well, James,' said Daphne, lifting the teapot, 'what are you hiding from me? I hope your silence isn't an indication that there's a problem about your being my partner at the Ball?'

Callendar coughed and brushed an invisible speck of dust from the knee of his riding breeches. 'Well, actually, there *is* a bit of a problem. I'm afraid something's come up.'

A frown creased her pretty face. 'What d'you mean, something's come up? What can be more important than taking me to the Hunt Ball? I hope it's not some polo match or other.' She glared at him. 'Or is it?'

'Good Lord, no! Nothing like that,' he replied. 'It's... Well, it's something I'd completely forgotten about. It all began a few weeks ago. An item appeared on Regimental Orders asking for volunteers who spoke German and, preferably, had also spent some time in Berlin. Well, as you know, apart from Eton in England and of course Oxford, I virtually lived there for a number of years. Anyway, I put my name forward and had a brief interview with a Major from Military Intelligence, then promptly forgot all about it. Then, a few days ago, I received orders to report to some camp near Trowbridge.' He frowned. 'All a bit odd, really. I have to report tomorrow morning wearing civvies – no baggage, just my toilet things. I've been told I shall be more or less incommunicado for a while – several weeks in fact.'

'James! How could you?' exclaimed Daphne. 'You know how much I was looking forward to going. This really is too much! You're just as bad as Teddy Haversham. He's done exactly the same thing to Cynthia, going off to North Africa at a moment's notice.'

'You can't blame poor Teddy,' interjected her father, smiling at her frustration. 'He was ordered to go. He had no option.

19

There is a war on, after all.' He nodded towards Callendar. 'And the same goes for James. He has to obey orders too.'

'Well, it's not fair,' pouted Daphne. 'Why can't they postpone whatever it is, just for a few weeks.' She turned to her father. 'Could you do something, Daddy?' she pleaded. 'After all, you've got friends at the War Office.'

The General laughed. 'I'm sorry m'dear, but I doubt I could pull strings even if I wanted. Can't interfere with a soldier's duties.' He turned to Callendar. 'Sounds a bit odd, this civvies thing. What's it all about, James? Bit hush, hush?'

'Not really sure, sir,' he replied, taking a sip of tea. 'Probably something boringly simple, like interrogating prisoners of war. You know, intelligence gathering, that sort of thing.'

'Still seems a bit odd though, this civvies thing and being kept incommunicado. Still,' the General sighed, 'nothing surprises me about these Intelligence people. Odd bunch, get up to all sort of dirty tricks I understand.' He frowned at Callendar. 'Hope you're not going to be involved in that sort of thing, James. Hardly the behaviour of an officer and gentleman.'

Callendar laughed and tried to sound blasé. 'I rather doubt it. Probably just stuck in a Nissen hut in the wilds of somewhere or other, questioning a load of sorry-looking Huns. Nothing more romantic than that.' He waved a hand. 'Shall we change the subject? I have to say I'm especially looking forward to dinner this evening. Goodness knows when I shall be eating food like it again.' Then a thought struck him. 'Oh! By the way, there is just one other thing. Daphne, would you be an absolute angel and run me over to Wiltshire in the morning?'

Daphne stared at him in disbelief, then burst out laughing. 'James! You really are the limit!'

* * *

20

Later that same evening, the two of them stood on the terrace admiring the night sky, Daphne turned suddenly to the young officer.

'James,' she said thoughtfully. 'I know you think I'm an old fusspot at times...'

'*Young* fusspot surely, darling,' smiled Callendar teasingly.

'Do be serious for once,' she pleaded, laying an affectionate hand on his arm. 'I know you can't tell me what this is all about, or where you're going, but promise me you won't do anything stupid. You see I'm... I'm rather fond of you, and I don't want anything to happen...'

Callendar held her hands and, looking into her eyes, smiled softly. 'Don't worry, old girl. Nothing's going to happen to me, I promise. You'll see, I'll be back before you know it – and there *will* be other Hunt Balls.'

'Oh, James! I hope so. I really do hope so.'

WESTONZOYLAND, SOMERSET

Edna Thompson gave the pot of tripe and onions another stir and looked out of the cottage window to watch her husband playing football with their two children. The scene brought a contented smile to her face. It was good when Bill was home. Both Brian, who was coming up to his tenth birthday, and Mary, just turned seven, missed him terribly when he was away in the army, though they were proud their Dad was 'doing his bit' for the war effort.

As she busied herself preparing for the evening meal, she reflected on how much worse things could be. Being stationed only twenty-five miles away, Bill was able to get home almost every weekend, and working in the stores at the Royal Army Ordnance depot near Yeovil he was well away from any danger. It made her appreciate how lucky they were – particularly when she thought of the sailors on those vital convoys, crossing the U-boat strewn Atlantic, listening each day to radio reports of sinkings and the lives lost; or of the aircrews, flying bombing missions over Germany, listening to the daily news bulletins, almost all of which inevitably ended with those awful words: 'A number of our aircraft are missing'. Then there were the men fighting in North Africa and in the Far East, thousands of miles away from home, every day facing death and danger.

Inevitably her thoughts turned to Mrs Bartlett down at the village stores. It was only last week the poor woman had received one of those dreaded telegrams, saying her husband Fred had been posted missing in action, presumed killed. It made her shudder when she thought of the distraught woman and the four little children, one barely a year old. How on earth would they manage?

Her train of thought was suddenly interrupted by the sound of the pot boiling over on the wood-burning stove. She gave it another vigorous stir and moved it off the heat slightly, before her thoughts again returned to the war and the effect it was having on their lives. Thankfully she was able to take comfort in the fact that, being in the Ordnance Corps, Bill wouldn't see much action, not even when the Second Front came – or so he said. Then, when the war was over, Bill would be able to return to his old job as languages master at the grammar school in nearby Bridgwater and things would be back to normal.

The vision of peacetime brought a smile to her face – but it gradually faded when she recalled Bill saying something about a 'special job' he was going on. He hadn't said much about it at the time, apart from the fact that he wouldn't be able to get home for a few weeks, but she hadn't pressed him. She wasn't looking forward to his absence, but there had been the compensation of the unexpected seven days' leave he had been granted.

Again she looked out of the window at the small cottage

garden. Bill had always been a keen gardener and was particularly proud of the vegetable plot he had created to supplement the family's food rations. It had been a pity to lose the flowerbeds, she thought, with their colourful summer displays and the smell of the honeysuckle and the roses, but it couldn't be helped.

A small patch of lawn had managed to survive and this was currently the scene of the football match between Bill and the children. The yells of laughter coming through the open window made her feel happy. This was the way things should be – a happy family unit.

Later, when they were eating the evening meal, young Brian pestered his father with questions about his new posting.

'What're you going to be doing, Dad? Are you joining the Secret Service and parachuting out of a plane? I bet you're going on a secret mission to blow up ol' Hitler. Isn't that right, Dad?'

Bill Thompson laughed at the young boy's wild imagination.

'Don't get carried away, son. I'm just going on special duties for a few weeks. It's got something to do with the fact I speak German and that probably means interrogating prisoners of war captured in North Africa. Nothing to get alarmed or excited about.'

He patted the boy's head and gave a reassuring smile to his wife. He knew she worried, even though she hadn't said anything – which only served to increase his sense of guilt. In all their twelve years of marriage he had never lied to her, yet on this occasion he hadn't been entirely honest either. He had omitted to tell her that only volunteers had been selected for the work, knowing full well the word 'volunteer' would increase her anxiety, implying as it did that danger would be involved.

'Does that mean you'll be going to Africa, Dad?' persisted Brian, his excitement and enthusiasm unabated. 'Will you see lions and elephants and giraffes and...?'

Again his father laughed. 'I said North Africa – that's all sand and desert; no wild animals there – except for camels. And anyway, if it is for interrogation then I expect they'll be shipped to England. Makes more sense.'

'I don't want you to go anywhere!'

The sudden plaintive cry came from his daughter Mary, her little face puckering up and tears welling in her eyes.

'Let them send somebody else,' she sobbed. 'Why do you have to go?'

He tenderly stroked the long golden hair. 'Sorry, blossom. But there's a war on and Daddy has to do as he's told. Just like you have to at school.'

'I don't like this stupid war,' she wailed, finally succumbing to the threatened flood of tears. 'I just want my Daddy.' Choking with tears, she slipped off her chair and climbed onto her father's lap. Wrapping her arms tightly about his neck, she sobbed, 'I love you, Daddy. Please don't go away.'

'Now, now, Blossom,' he chided, trying to inject a note of cheerfulness into his voice. 'You're getting a big girl now and you've got to learn to be brave. Daddy won't be away very long and Mummy's going to need all the help she can get whilst I'm gone.' He gave her shaking form a big hug. 'Tell you what: I'll probably have another week's leave when I get back and then I'll take you all to Bristol Zoo. How's that for a promise?'

He pulled her arms from around his neck and gave her a big smile, reaching into his pocket for a handkerchief to wipe away her tears. She looked at him with uncertainty, her lower lip still quivering.

'Is that a real promise, Daddy? D'you mean it? You know you can't break a *real* promise.'

He kissed her on the forehead and gave her a hug. 'Yes! That's a real, *real* promise, Blossom.'

'Honest, Dad? Do you mean it?' cried Brian, his eyes shining at the prospect.

Their father solemnly licked his index finger and, holding it in the air, declared: 'See this wet?' Then, wiping away the moisture on his shirtfront, continued: 'See this dry? May I never go to heaven if I lie.'

'You shouldn't say things like that, Bill!' warned his wife, as she rose from her chair and began clearing the table. 'Now you children go out in the garden and play. Your father and me have got things to talk about. Go on now.'

Obediently, they both disappeared into the garden. Bill Thompson rose and lent a hand clearing the table.

'They're good kids, both of them. A lot better than some I had in the grammar school.'

His wife nodded absently. 'Yes... Yes, they are.' She began to wash the dishes.

Suddenly, she burst out, 'Bill? I know I shouldn't really ask. But this job they want you to do...' A worried look crossed her face. 'What young Brian said... It's not dangerous, is it, Bill? I mean, really dangerous?'

Her husband laid down the plate he had been drying and slipped his arm around her shoulders.

'Don't be daft, woman! Do you think I'd do anything so stupid? Look, I'll show you.'

He went across to the corner of the kitchen where his battledress blouse hung on a coat hook. Unfastening the right hand breast pocket, he pulled out a folded document, took it back and held it up for her to read.

'Sorry, I can't let you see the top part,' he apologised. 'Bit secret and all that. But you can read the rest.'

His wife fumbled in her pinafore pocket for her reading glasses and peered closely at the document:

2. Accordingly you are ordered to report to Trencham Barracks, Warminster, at 10.00hrs Monday, 3rd Aug 1942.

25

3. You are required to report wearing civilian clothes. Do not bring any baggage or additional items except for your personal toiletries.

4. Do not forget to bring with you your AB64 Part I together with the enclosed Movement Order.

Signed: E. Ferguson, Major.

'There you are! I told you there's nothing to worry about, didn't I?' exclaimed Thompson, carefully re-folding the document and replacing it in his trousers pocket. 'You saw what it said. Civvies! Now that's got to mean a cushy number. And Warminster. That's not too far away, either.'

His wife laid her hand on her breast in that familiar womanly gesture and released a sigh of relief.

'Oh! Thank goodness for that, Bill. I've been out of my mind with worry.' She wrapped her arms around him. 'I really don't know what I'd do if anything were to happen to you. I really don't.'

He kissed her affectionately on the forehead.

'Come on, love! Nothing's going to happen. You saw the letter. I told you there's nothing to worry about, didn't I? Now stop fretting.' He gently eased himself away from her embrace. 'Now then, I'm off down the Red Lion for a pint. So why don't you go into the parlour, switch on the wireless and listen to ITMA – it'll be on in a few minutes.'

He kissed her briefly on the cheek then donned his battledress blouse and beret.

'I shan't be late. Tell the kids I'll be up to say goodnight before they go to sleep.'

He walked slowly as he made his way down the lane towards the pub, his brow furrowed. He could hardly have told his wife the truth. He stopped for a moment and glanced about, just to make sure no one was around, before retrieving the piece of paper from his trouser pocket. He read it again and again, as he had done so many times already, his attention riveted on the part he had deliberately concealed from his wife.

VOLUNTEERS FOR HAZARDOUS DUTY
1. *As you have not conveyed to your Commanding Officer your wish to withdraw your application for the above, I am pleased to confirm your selection.*

'HAZARDOUS DUTY' – what did it mean? He wasn't so naïve as to believe it really did have anything to do with interrogating prisoners of war – that was for sure. No, it had to be something more. Something connected with his ability to speak fluent German. But what? Some element of danger had to be involved – but exactly how dangerous? Life-threatening, or just slightly risky? He grimly shook his head. It had to be something serious. The Army, particularly Military Intelligence, didn't describe things as hazardous without due cause.

The realisation suddenly made him feel weak in the knees. Why had he been so stupid? Why had he put his name forward in the first place? He must have been mad. Nor had he withdrawn his name within the seven days' period of grace, even though he had been told it wouldn't be reflected on his record.

He was already regretting his impetuosity in volunteering – not for any cowardly reasons. It was the sense of guilt that racked him. He felt as if he had betrayed Edna and the kids. What was it she'd said? She didn't know how she'd manage if . . . He swallowed hard. He knew he shouldn't have done it. There were probably hundreds of other men who could do the job, perhaps better than he could. But then, if that was the case, why *had* they accepted *him*? They knew he was married with a young family – that had come out at the interview – but it apparently hadn't made any difference.

27

He slowly re-folded the paper, thrust it back into his pocket and gazed at the surrounding green fields. Would this be the last time he saw them, he wondered. But he knew it was too late for such thoughts; he had given his word – he couldn't back out now.

COVENTRY, WARWICKSHIRE

The fine drizzle drifting down from a leaden sky did little to relieve the depressing atmosphere in the graveyard of St Christopher's Church. Few people were about that late afternoon, despite the large number of brown patches scarring the neatly cut green sward – evidence of recently dug graves. But funerals were all too commonplace these days and relatives and friends didn't linger long in the graveyard once interment was over. Death was a frequent visitor; it touched most people's lives almost daily now: they quickly came to terms with their loss.

In one corner of the graveyard, in front of a grave that had recently received its headstone, knelt a solitary figure. Bare-headed and oblivious of the fine rain, the man stared silently at the block of granite, a khaki waterproof cape draped over his shoulders to protect his uniform. He was a sergeant in the Royal Army Service Corps. He had been there some time, the rain plastering his short, dark hair against his forehead, running down to mix with his tears. He struggled to control his grief, reading and re-reading the inscription carved in the grey stone:

In loving memory of Elizabeth Mary Sinclair aged 24 years and Penelope Anne Sinclair aged 2 years, killed by German bombs November 15th, 1940

The man rubbed the back of his hand across his eyes.

28

'Dearest Beth,' he whispered softly. 'My darling Penny. As God is my witness, I won't rest until I've avenged your deaths a hundred ... a thousand times. I'll make sure they pay dearly for taking you from me.'

His eyes dropped to the brown earth and to the bunch of flowers he had brought with him. Again the tears welled up.

He tried desperately to fill his thoughts with memories of happier times: of his youth in Montreal, of his first job as a motor mechanic in that same city and later, how proud he had been when he managed to get a job working for the mighty Daimler Benz company in Germany. But all that had come to an end when the Nazis came to power. What he saw frightened him and he knew that rumours of war would soon become reality. He fled to England where he quickly adopted British nationality and volunteered for the Army, determined to do what he could to combat the Nazi threat. He was accepted into the Royal Army Service Corps and, after basic training, posted to a unit based near Coventry. It was here he was destined to meet Elizabeth and fall instantly in love. After a whirlwind romance they were married and a year later, Penny was born and his life was complete. He took every opportunity to be with them, even dashing home for a few hours of an evening. But after war was declared training at the camp intensified and it became more and more difficult to get away. To make up for this he would write long letters to Beth each day, eagerly reading the replies that arrived no less frequently.

He was on manoeuvres in the Welsh mountains when news came of the Luftwaffe raid on the Midlands. Although BBC news bulletins carried reports of heavy casualties among the civilian population, his concerns were not immediate because Beth and Penny had moved out of the city to live with her parents, some thirty miles away in the country.

Even when he received an unexpected summons from the adjutant, he experienced no anxiety. The officer showed great sensitivity in breaking the tragic news, and granted him immediate compassionate leave. But Sinclair ignored the reports, convinced it was all a terrible mistake. They couldn't be dead; they were safe in the country. Even when he was told that positive identification had been made, he refused to accept the fact.

On arrival in Coventry, he had hurried to the street where they lived, only to be horrified by the chaos and devastation that greeted him. The musty smell of building debris hung in the air as he stood gazing in disbelief at the heaps of rubble that had once been rows of neat terraced houses. It seemed not a single house had escaped the attack and, with sinking heart, he began to pick his way through the debris-strewn street, towards where his home had once stood. He stared at the collapsed building, painfully recognising the pitiful remains of furniture poking through the pile of bricks and rubble. The wallpaper he and Beth had chosen to decorate the parlour still clung to one of the wall sections.

It was only when an ARP warden came up and spoke to him that he managed to tear his eyes away. The warden confirmed that the bodies of a young woman and baby girl had been pulled from the wreckage of number eight. 'Killed outright,' he said. Even then he could not believe they were dead. He telephoned Beth's mother from a nearby aid station. The sobbing voice of his mother-in-law confirmed the awful facts. How? Why? She explained how her daughter had returned with Penny that fateful day, simply to collect a few belongings, fully intending to return to the country cottage that same evening. It was a tragic coincidence that the Nazis had chosen that particular day to mount one of the heaviest raids of the war. Beth's father had undertaken the gruesome task of identifying the shattered bodies; Sinclair was at least spared that ordeal.

He had replaced the receiver and collapsed into a chair, the reality of the situation at last beginning to sink in. A kindly WVS lady brought him a strong cup of tea, but it went ignored on the table in front of him. At first a sort of numbness anaesthetised the pain and anguish, but this was short-lived. Suddenly, he collapsed onto the table, knocking over the cup of tea and bursting into uncontrollable tears. The WVS lady, her face full of concern, hurried back and tried to comfort him. But he pushed her away and ran out of the aid station into the street, sobbing hysterically. He ran and ran like a man demented, roughly pushing away those who tried to stop him, charging aimlessly from street to street.

Eventually, gasping for breath, he found himself in a small park where he collapsed exhausted on a bench, and still his tears flowed. How long he remained there he never knew. Passers-by looked at the forlorn figure and shook their heads knowingly.

He went to stay with Elizabeth's parents, but the family's grief served only to deepen his own depression and he made every excuse to get out of the house. After the funeral, he cut his leave short and returned to his unit. Back in the familiar surroundings of the camp he buried himself in his duties. But nothing could hide the dramatic change to his personality. Gone was the transatlantic openness, the ever ready smile, and the mischievous twinkle in his eye. He became morose and introverted. Now, filled with hatred and bitterness for the death of his wife and child, he resolved to wreak personal vengeance on those responsible. But he had to wait for almost two years, before fate gave him the opportunity to fulfil that resolve.

In early June of 1942, an item appeared on Battalion Part One Orders, seeking volunteers who spoke fluent German. Instinctively, he knew this was what he had been waiting for. His Commanding Officer, surprised by the alacrity and fervour of his application, endeavoured to dissuade him from his purpose, reminding him personal vendettas had no place in military operations. At first, he refused to forward Sinclair's name, but, faced with stubborn insistence, he finally relented. After attending a selection interview with an officer from the War Office, he was selected for training. Convinced Fate was presenting him with the opportunity he craved, his life developed a new purpose. Now, on the eve of reporting for his new duties, he paid this last visit to St Peter's cemetery. The drizzle persisted as he rose to his feet and replaced the beret on his head, tugging it into place with a defiant gesture.

'Sleep well, my darlings,' he whispered softly. 'I promise we'll be together again, real soon.'

In a final gesture, he placed the tips of his fingers against his lips, leant forward, and gently placed them on the cold headstone. Jaw set, he turned away and marched down the path.

THE ROSE AND CROWN PUBLIC HOUSE – LONDON'S EAST END

''Ere Linda! Where's my pint?' a strong cockney voice yelled, straining to be heard above the noise of the public bar. The customer, a young man in his early twenties, leaned across the polished surface of the bar trying to attract the barmaid's attention. He failed to see the pool of spilt beer lying on the polished surface and one sleeve of his khaki battledress blouse became saturated.

'Oh, my Gawd!' he exclaimed, as the cold liquid seeped through the thick serge. 'Look at my bleedin' uniform. Bloody soaked!' He held his arm up for general inspection by those around him. 'Look Linda,' he complained, as the barmaid came hurrying towards him.

'No use you yelling, young Bob Nicholson,' she retorted, ignoring the out-thrust arm. 'There's more than just you wanting a drink.' She waved a hand at the throng of drinkers crowded into the pub. 'You'll take your turn just like anyone else.'

'Aw, c'mon Linda,' Nicholson pleaded. ''Ere I am, ready to fight for King and Country an' dyin' of thirst in me own local.'

'Hah! Fight for King and Country, my Aunt Fanny!' the barmaid retorted, wiping up the beer spillage with a dishcloth. 'You Army types, stuck in cushy billets, free bed and board. Life of Riley, that's what you've got!' She held a mug under the best bitter spout and deftly drew the required pint with two expert strokes.

'Now if you was in the Air Force,' she continued, placing the full pint in front of her impatient customer, 'actually coming face to face with them Jerries, all alone in the wild blue yonder, then you could say you was a fighting man. Why, they see more action in five minutes than you've seen in all the time you've bin wearing khaki knickers.'

Her assessment of Nicholson's battle experience brought raucous laughter from the surrounding drinkers.

Unabashed, the young soldier paid for his beer and took a long pull at the fresh pint, before wiping his mouth with the back of his hand.

'You don't know what you're talking abaht, Linda me ol' love. For all you know, I could be abaht to go on a top-secret mission. Could even be a one-way ticket,' he added mysteriously.

'Aw, get on with you!' the barmaid laughed. 'You? On a top-secret mission? Lord love us, whatever next!' She turned away still laughing and walked back along the bar to serve another customer. Nicholson good-humouredly ignored her jibe and carried on supping his beer, but his enjoyment received a rude interruption.

'Top secret job, eh, Nicholson? Bit dodgy pickin' you for it, don't you fink?'

The comment, loud enough for surrounding customers to hear, caused the buzz of conversation suddenly to dwindle.

All eyes turned to a soldier standing with two others a few feet away at the end of the bar. For a moment Nicholson stood motionless, the glass of beer at his lips. Then his eyes narrowed dangerously as he slowly lowered the glass and placed it back on the bar.

'What's that s'posed to mean, Curtiss?'

Nicholson hadn't needed to turn his head to see who had made the comment. The voice was all too familiar.

'I said: What's that s'posed to mean?' This time the words came through clenched teeth.

Curtiss, a self-satisfied smirk on his face, found he was enjoying being the centre of attention.

'Well it's like this,' he sneered. 'The problem with sending you on any sort of secret mission, Nicholson, is that they wouldn't know whose side you was on. I mean, havin' a Jerry for a mother.'

The few feet separating the protagonists Nicholson covered in two rapid strides. His speed caught both Curtiss and his companions by surprise and before anyone could stop him, Nicholson's fist had landed a tremendous blow squarely on Curtiss' jaw, sending the man crashing backwards onto the floor. His blood well and truly up, Nicholson immediately whirled round to face Curtiss' companions, fists still clenched, face contorted with anger and ready to do battle. But both men, stunned by the speed and violence of the onslaught, quickly backed away.

The noise of the scuffle brought Linda charging down the bar.

'What in the 'ell's going on?' she demanded, looking down at Curtiss who was sitting in the sawdust rubbing his jaw. She wheeled round on Nicholson. 'You responsible for this?' she asked. 'If so, you can clear out now. I'll have no fighting in my pub.'

Fists still clenched, Nicholson didn't take his eyes off Curtiss.

'He asked for it, saying what he did about my Mum.'

Everyone in the neighbourhood knew about Nicholson's German mother, not that there had ever been any ill feelings towards her, or the Nicholson family. John Nicholson had met her in France in 1918, a refugee fleeing from the Fatherland. He had married her in Lyons and brought her back to England where they had settled down in the East End. She had proved both a good wife and mother and had been accepted by the majority of the community as one of their own. Only the slightest trace of an accent betrayed her former nationality. But since the outbreak of hostilities there were some, like the Curtiss family, who were all too ready to stir up trouble.

Linda nodded her head. She could guess the sort of comment Curtiss would have made.

'So that's what it's all about, is it?' She turned to Curtiss and his two companions. 'Right, you three, drink up and clear out.'

For a brief moment Curtiss, who had by now clambered back onto his feet, looked ready to retaliate.

'Now!' thundered Linda. 'Or I'll call the law on you.'

Curtiss hesitated for a moment, then turned back to the bar, drained his glass in one choking gulp and said to his two companions, 'C'mon, let's get out of this lousy place. It's full o' Jerry lovers.'

Truculently he strode towards the door, closely followed by the other two.

'You'll get yours one of these days, Nicholson,' he shouted as he opened the door. 'Stinkin' Jerry!'

The parting insult had Nicholson charging towards the doorway, but he was stopped by a number of customers who blocked his way, telling him it wasn't worth it. Breathing heavily, he gave up struggling and allowed himself to be guided back to the bar.

'You want to watch that temper of yours, young Bob,'

Linda reproved, shaking her head. 'Get you in a lot of trouble one day.'

'I don't care. No-one's goin' to say things like that about my Mum. No-one! Particularly not little shits like him!'

'Get on with you, Bob. You don't want to take any notice of the likes of Jack Curtiss,' said Linda pacifically. 'Nasty piece of work, just like the rest of his family. Born troublemakers. C'mon, I'll give you a pint on the 'ouse.'

'Yeah, maybe. But I'll show 'em. Just you wait an' see,' he replied darkly. 'You fink I was kiddin' abaht them special duties, don't you? Well, I wasn't. Got to report to a new camp tomorrow.'

He picked up his free pint of best bitter and gave the barmaid a meaningful look.

'Jus' you wait an' see, Linda. I'll show 'em just whose side the Nicholsons are on.'

2

TRENCHAM BARRACKS, WILTSHIRE, ENGLAND
THURSDAY, AUGUST 13th, 1942

Private Johnson hated the army. He hated the discipline and the early morning working parades. He hated the incessant drilling, the shouting of the officers and NCOs and he hated the spit and polish. What was the point, he would ask himself, in spending hours and hours 'bulling' his boots and 'blancoing' his kit and polishing his brass buckles and badges, only to undergo training exercises the following morning, plodding across muddy fields? It was all so stupid. Private Johnson had concluded very early on in his military career, that there was nothing about the army he did like.

But of all his pet hates and miseries, there was one thing he hated most of all – guard duty at the main gate. Being on sentry, he would complain bitterly to his mates, put you in the spotlight which meant giving all the officers and NCOs passing in and out of the camp the ideal opportunity to pick fault with everything you did – or didn't – do. In Private Johnson's case this was reflected in the fact that his Company Conduct Sheet boasted more 252s than that of any other man at the depot.

He would argue that he hadn't *asked* to join up and would have much preferred remaining in his civilian job, driving for a firm of wholesale newsagents. Now there, he would declare to everyone, he'd been happy, really happy. With the job of delivery driver, he could always skive off for an hour or so, blaming the traffic and the customers for his subsequent

37

lateness and using the time to do odd jobs for friends – and gain that extra bit of cash. There was also the added bonus of taking the van home each night, which proved invaluable in pursuing his courtship with his girlfriend, Molly.

Ah, yes! Those were the days, he sighed to himself, as he stood on sentry duty at the main gate of Trencham Barracks that bright August morning. With plenty of ready cash and someone as pretty as Molly for his girlfriend, what more could a man want? He closed his eyes for a moment, imagining she was right there, in his arms. They were kissing passionately, feverishly even, his hand edging ever closer to her swelling bosom...

'Not goin' to sleep are we, Johnson?'

The raucous voice of Sergeant Wilson bellowed from the doorway of the guardroom a few feet away, forcing him out of his pleasant reverie. He quickly pulled himself together and snapped smartly to attention.

'No, Sarn't!'

'I'm pleased to 'ear it,' replied the guard commander, picking up his clipboard and stepping out into the bright sunlight. 'So let me see you march your beat occasionally, you idle little man. Otherwise, I might think your size tens 'ave rooted themselves to the tarmac!'

Johnson raised his eyes to the heavens, praying some evil misfortune might suddenly befall his guard commander and allow him some peace and quiet, but his prayers went unanswered.

'Come on! Look lively, you lazy soldier!'

Taking a deep breath, Johnson reluctantly threw his rifle up the right side of his body and caught it by the upper sling swivel with his left hand and the small of the butt with his right. After the regulation pause of 'two, three', he moved the weapon smartly across his chest, laying the stock on his left shoulder. In the same movement he released his left hand, which received the butt into the palm with an audible 'thwack'. Another regulation pause and the right hand whipped smartly away to his side. A look of surprise appeared on the sergeant's face.

'Ve-ry good, Johnson! Very good!' he beamed. 'Who knows? We might make a soldier of you yet.'

'No you bleedin' won't!' muttered Johnson under his breath, as he executed a smart right turn and commenced to march his beat up and down in front of the barrier. The critical eye of the guard commander followed his progress as he marched the regulation eight paces across the gateway, about turned, marched eight paces back, about turned and carried on repeating the monotonous exercise, praying the sergeant would quickly tire of his performance and disappear back into the relative comfort of the guardroom. Unfortunately the sergeant showed no such inclination and instead came forward, ducked under the arm of the barrier and walked to the edge of the road, where he stood looking up and down, as though expecting someone.

He had been there barely a matter of seconds before the sound of a powerful engine could be heard approaching. The noise gradually increased changing to a sudden roar as a dark green, open-top Bentley Tourer came screaming round the bend in the road and careered crazily across the carriageway. For a moment it looked as though the driver had lost control as the car's nose headed towards the wooden fence on the opposite side of the road. But somehow the driver managed to straighten up, accelerating forward for a brief moment before braking hard and coming to a screeching halt barely inches away from the highly polished toecaps of Sergeant Wilson's boots.

'That was quite a drive, Daphne old girl!' laughed the blond-haired young man sitting in the front passenger seat. He wiped his hand in mock horror across his brow. 'We'll have to get you down to Brand's Hatch for a spin sometime.' He leaned across and gave the girl an affectionate peck on the cheek. 'Now I really must fly. Late enough as it is.'

39

Gripping the top of the dashboard with one hand and clamping the other on top of the low door, he vaulted athletically from the open Bentley, landing perilously close to Sergeant Wilson's gleaming toecaps. Unconcerned, he reached into the dickey seat and pulled out a smart pigskin-leather grip.

'Thanks again, Daphne. Be in touch as soon as I can.' With that he stepped back and waved his hand in farewell.

'Bye James. And don't forget to write!'

'I won't, that's a promise. Bye!'

He stood and watched the Bentley pull away and roar off at the same breakneck speed, his eyes following its progress until the green vehicle disappeared in the distance. Then he turned to the waiting NCO.

'Morning, Sergeant,' he said crisply, adopting a more formal attitude. 'The name's Callendar. Lieutenant Callendar. I am expected. Perhaps you'd kindly point me in the direction of the Officers' Mess.'

Sergeant Wilson, his face the colour of beetroot, took a deep breath, clamped his lips together and glowered ferociously at the newcomer. Unabashed, the young officer waited impatiently for the sergeant to respond. Recovering his composure, Sergeant Wilson removed a pencil from his breast pocket and, with some deliberation, referred to the clipboard he was holding. Not that there was any need for this procedure – Lieutenant Callendar J, was the only name remaining unchecked on his list. He looked back at the young officer.

'Could I see some identification, please ... sir?'

Callendar frowned. The distinct pause between 'please' and 'sir' had been all too obvious. An 'old sweat' trying to score points over a young officer, he decided. He had come across this attitude many times in his career, so he said nothing as he withdrew his pay book and Movement Order from the inside pocket of his Harris Tweed jacket and handed them to the sergeant.

The deliberately slow and tedious examination of the documents that followed served only to exasperate Callendar further.

'Come, come, Sergeant,' he said testily. 'What's the problem? You are expecting me, are you not?'

Unhurriedly, the sergeant carefully re-folded the movement order, slipped it between the covers of Callendar's blue pay book and handed it back to him.

'Yes, Mr Callendar, sir. You *are* expected. In fact...' he made a great show of deliberately looking at his wrist-watch, 'you were expected over half an hour ago, at ten hundred hours to be precise. I understand they're getting a bit impatient.'

This time it was Callendar's turn to suffer a reddening complexion.

'They? They?' he snapped irritably. 'And just who are "they", Sergeant?'

Sergeant Wilson's expression didn't change. 'Why, sir, the other fifteen members of your party. They all arrived some time ago. In fact, well *before* the ten hundred hours reporting time.'

Callendar's face became an even deeper shade of red. He glared at the NCO.

'In that case, Sergeant, we'd better not waste any more time, had we? Now, if you'd kindly tell me where I'm to report....'

'Why, of course, sir,' Wilson replied politely. 'You're to report to Hut 3C, where the rest of your party are waiting. You'll find it easy enough.' He turned and pointed along the road leading into the camp. 'Just follow the main road here and take the third turning on your right. That's Row C. You'll find Hut 3 on your left.'

'*Thank* you, Sergeant!' replied Callendar through clenched teeth and giving the sergeant a murderous glare as he picked up his grip.

'Lift the barrier for the h'officer,' instructed Sergeant Wilson to a grinning Johnson.

As he watched the red-faced young man duck under the raised barrier and walk smartly away, the Sergeant felt a deep sense of satisfaction.

'There you are, Johnson,' he said to the sentry with a smug smile. 'Your first lesson in how to deal with a young upstart of an officer ... the toffee-nosed git!'

He shook his head as his eyes followed Callendar's diminishing figure.

'You know,' he murmured, more to himself than to the sentry, 'with young pricks like 'im in charge, there are times when I really do wonder if we'll ever win this bleedin' war.'

'Dunno about that, Sarge,' replied Johnson, not the least bit interested in the guard commander's opinion of young officers. 'But that tart 'e 'ad with 'im in that car. Gawd! She was a bit of all right, weren't she? Classy dame she were an' no mistake. Always fancied a girl like 'er.' He grinned. 'Nice motor an' all.'

Sergeant Wilson looked despairingly at the sentry.

'Don't you ever think of anythin' else, Johnson? Get on with your beat, for Gawd's sake!' And with a resigned shake of his head, he returned to the guardroom.

Callendar set off at a brisk pace, aware of his lateness. But he refused to run, for that would be undignified. Nevertheless, the exertions of his fast walk found him somewhat out of breath by the time he arrived at Hut 3C and he stopped for a few brief moments to recover before entering. As he stood outside he noticed a charabanc parked nearby painted in the usual mottled camouflage of dull greens, browns and black. At first, he didn't pay it too much attention, until he realised that all the windows had also been covered with the camouflage paint, the only exceptions being those surrounding the driver's cab.

Suddenly he realised he was being watched. A lance

corporal stood leaning against the radiator of the coach smoking a cigarette and looking at him with undisguised curiosity. Suspecting the coach had something to do with why he was there and that his lateness was the reason for the corporal's unwelcome interest, he quickly picked up his grip and made his way into the hut.

After the bright morning sunlight, the darkness inside the wooden building made it difficult to see anything at first, although the murmur of voices told him he was not alone. As his eyes gradually adjusted to the dim interior, he saw several small groups of men, all dressed in civilian clothes, sitting down and staring in his direction. The room had fallen silent as he entered and he was left standing awkwardly until a booming voice thundered from the far end of the room.

'*Mister* Callendar, I presume?'

Whipping his head round, Callendar saw the bulky figure of a company sergeant major bearing down on him.

'Ah, Sarn't Major. Morning. Sorry I'm a little late. Damn convoys on the road.'

'Yes, yes. I'm sure, Mr Callendar,' snapped the CSM loudly, sweeping Callendar's apologies to one side with a dismissive wave of his hand. 'Except it's a bit strange that everyone else can get here on time, convoys or not. You do realise you're over half an hour late and consequently have made everyone else late in the process?'

'Now just a moment, Sarn't Major,' Callendar protested, his face reddening with embarrassment. 'I think we need to establish our respective ranks...'

'No we don't!' interrupted the warrant officer tersely. 'My instructions are to treat you all the same. I don't know, nor do I wish to know, your rank. All of you are just plain "Mr" as far as I'm concerned – whether you're a brigadier or a bombardier – it makes no difference.'

Blocking any further attempted protests from Callendar he turned to address the whole room.

'Right, gentlemen! Please pay attention. Now that you're all here, perhaps we can get things moving onto the next stage of the proceedings.' He paused, looking round at the sea of faces to ensure everyone was paying attention. 'I'm sure you're all wondering what's happening next. Well, first of all, I can tell you this is not your final destination, merely an assembly point. There's transport waiting outside which will take you on to the next stage. Now don't ask me where that is, because I don't know, so you'd be wasting your breath.' He looked round the room. 'I trust no one has brought any kit with them, any luggage at all? No? Good.'

He spotted the grip at Callendar's feet and took a deep breath.

'That yours, Mr Callendar?'

Callendar's face reddened even more. 'Well, yes, as a matter of fact it is. I . . .'

The CSM shook his head in despair. 'You were specifically instructed *not* to bring any luggage, were you not?'

'Now just a moment, Sergeant Major,' Callendar objected hotly, 'they're just a few essential items.'

'They'll have to stay here,' decided the CSM brusquely, scribbling a note on his clipboard. 'Can't send 'em back to your home address. It'd risk a breach of security.'

Any further protests from Callendar were prevented by the sound of the coach's engine starting up outside.

'Right, gentlemen!' the CSM continued, walking quickly to the door and glancing outside. 'The transport's ready. Would you all make your way onto the coach in an orderly fashion and, please, no further talking until you're all on board. Quickly as you please, gentlemen.'

The assembled men rose to their feet and made their way towards the exit. Callendar, smarting from the rebukes handed out by the CSM, deliberately hung back and allowed everyone else to precede him. When he did eventually reach the doorway he silently surrendered his grip to the CSM without protest, inwardly resolving to lodge the strongest of protests about the warrant officer's attitude when they arrived at their final destination.

Aboard the coach, the thick camouflage paint covering the windows effectively blocked all daylight. The few dimly lit bulbs set in the roof of the charabanc gave barely sufficient illumination for people to find their seats. As he settled into his place, he noticed the partition window separating the driver's cab from the rest of the coach had been masked by a thick curtain – further evidence that someone had taken a lot of trouble to make sure the passengers wouldn't be able to see out, nor anyone else to see in.

He had barely settled in his seat, when the lance corporal appeared in the doorway to make a quick head count of those on board. Apparently satisfied with the result, he disappeared just as quickly, slamming the door behind him. When the sound of the key being turned in the lock was heard, a ginger-haired lad sitting at the front of the coach jumped up and tried the door. It refused to open.

''Ere! What d'you fink of that? They've gorn and locked us in,' he exclaimed in broad cockney. 'They're takin' us on a bleedin' mystery tour.'

His comments generated some smiles and laughter, but Callendar found the red-haired lad's remarks far from amusing. The sound of the Londoner's loud guffawing, particularly at his own humour, had Callendar cringing in his seat as he shot the cockney a disdainful look. Someone certainly to be avoided, he decided, leaning back and making himself as comfortable as the hard seats would allow. The driver wasted little time in getting under way and was soon passing the hapless Johnson at the main gate before turning out onto the main road. With nothing to see and no one to talk to, Callendar quickly dozed off.

His sleep seemed to have lasted barely minutes before he was awakened by a violent lurch as the bus turned off the metalled road onto what proved to be little more than a track. The driver slowed to little more than walking pace, as the coach bounced from one pothole to another, forcing the passengers to hang on grimly, and the sides and windows were continuously lashed by trees and bushes lining the track.

Their discomfort seemed endless, yet in reality it lasted only a few minutes before the coach came to a halt with one final rebellious jolt. The engine still running, the driver jumped down from his cab and unlocked the passenger door, allowing muted sunlight to flood in.

'Right, gentlemen!' he announced. 'We've arrived. So would you all please disembark as quickly as you can?'

Full of curiosity, the sixteen men rose and filed down the aisle to alight from the bus. They were all surprised to find themselves in a grassy clearing surrounded on three sides by mature trees and thick undergrowth. Overhead the branches of the trees were so thickly intertwined they created a dense, leafy canopy, through which a bare minimum of sunlight wanly filtered. Behind them, they could see the narrow track along which they had travelled meandering back through the trees towards the main road, its gravelled surface sprouting tufts of grass, indicative of infrequent use.

But it was the imposing stone wall rising in front of them, which seized their attention. Constructed of huge granite blocks and standing over twelve feet high, its top was festooned with gleaming coils of shiny barbed wire, whilst set in its base at ground level, stood a pair of stout, wooden gates, their surfaces covered in flaking green paint and discoloured by reddish streaks from rusting hinges and ornate iron handles. Massive stone pillars, rising slightly above the height of the wall and topped by lions rampant, flanked the gates.

'What the bleedin' 'ell's all this abaht?' demanded the redheaded cockney, as he took in his surroundings. He turned to the driver. 'Where in the 'ell are we?'

'Sorry, mate. Can't tell you.' The driver shrugged as he slammed the coach door shut. 'More'n my life's worth. I was just told to drop you 'ere. Don't fret, I expect someone'll be along in a minute.'

Before any further questions could be asked, he had leapt nimbly back into his cab and revved the engine. Clouds of blue grey smoke belched from the exhaust, as he manoeuvred the cumbersome vehicle around and sent it lurching back along the track.

'All seems a bit odd,' someone ventured. 'I wonder what we're expected to do now?'

'I would have thought that rather obvious,' commented Callendar dryly. 'I think you'll find we're expected to go through there.'

He pointed to the dilapidated-looking green gates.

'Nah! No chance!' snorted the red-haired cockney scornfully. 'Nuffin's bin through that gate in years. Anyone can see that. Look, I'll show yer.'

Stepping forward, the Londoner placed his shoulder against the aging doors and heaved as hard as he could. To his surprise the heavy wooden gate swung easily inwards, moving on silent, well-greased hinges. Quickly recovering from his surprise, he boldly led the way through the opening.

Once through the gateway, they found themselves in a belt of oak, beech and elm, which extended some thirty or so feet in front of them. Beyond the trees open meadowland sloped gently upwards, the green sward scarred by a gravelled track disappearing over the skyline. Between the trees and the grassland, and stretching as far as the eye could see, stood a formidable-looking fence. Built to a similar height as the wall behind them, it was constructed of upright pine log posts, some ten feet apart and strung with an impenetrable mesh of barbed wire. Directly in front of them, and forming part of the fence, was another gate, also constructed of timber poles and covered in the same dense barbed wire mesh.

47

Beyond this gate a corridor had been formed with further poles and wire, which terminated in a second gate some five yards distant. Closer inspection revealed a line of stakes, approximately eighteen inches high, had been inserted in the ground, level with this second gate and running parallel with the main fence. A single strand of wire ran along the top of the stakes, with signs hanging from it at measured distances. Each sign bore the same menacing legend: 'Achtung! Minen!'

'Christ!' exclaimed the red-headed cockney. 'Looks like we've arrived at a bleedin' prisoner o' war camp.'

But before anyone could respond, the shrill blast of a whistle pierced the air and a dozen or so armed men dressed in camouflaged combat uniforms appeared from behind the surrounding trees and quickly encircled the group, menacingly pointing their weapons. Another man emerged, dressed in the uniform of an SS officer and carrying a pistol in his right hand. His eyes wandered over the group.

'Handen hoch! Schnell, schnell!' he yelled, waving the pistol at the sixteen men.

At first they were all too stunned to move; then slowly, one by one, each man raised his hands above his head – except for the red-headed cockney. He remained with his hands on his hips and truculently faced his would-be aggressors.

'Piss off!' he snorted. 'This is bleedin' England. Ain't no one gonna tell me to stick me hands up 'ere!'

'Handen hoch!' the officer screamed again, taking deliberate aim with his pistol.

'Get stuffed, Fritz! You can go an'...'

Before he could finish the sentence, one of the troopers leapt forward and drove the butt of his Mauser rifle hard into the unsuspecting cockney's midriff. He doubled up, sinking to his knees, groaning and clutching his stomach. The stormtrooper raised his weapon ready to deliver another blow.

'Nein!' snapped the officer, waving the man away with his pistol.

48

He immediately lowered his weapon and stepped back, keeping the muzzle of his rifle aimed at the groaning man. The rest of the group looked on with disbelief, stunned by the brutality of the assault.

'What the hell d'you think you're doing?' angrily demanded a tall, muscular man with a distinct transatlantic accent. 'Who are you? And what's this all about?'

'Schweigen!' snarled the officer, swinging the muzzle of his pistol in the man's direction. 'Handen hoch!'

Callendar, despite his dislike of the cockney, was similarly incensed at the rough treatment meted out to his fellow soldier. He stepped forward, fists clenched.

'Well?' he challenged, looking round at the others. 'Are we just going to stand here or are we going to take these bullies on? I doubt very much those guns are loaded!'

The SS officer snapped his head round and nodded towards one of the troopers carrying a machine pistol. The man swung the muzzle of his weapon around and pointed it at a nearby oak. The rural tranquillity was abruptly shattered by the staccato sound of machine-gun fire, as a stream of bullets tore into the tree-trunk, sending chips of bark flying in all directions. The trooper's face remained impassive as he swung the smoking muzzle back to cover the group.

Callendar stared at the damaged oak. 'My God!' he ejaculated in horror. 'You must be mad!'

'Silence!' snapped the officer. 'Stand still, all of you.'

His eyes flicked to each man in turn, challenging anyone to defy his orders. No one moved. The demonstration had achieved its purpose.

Turning away, he drew a whistle from his jacket pocket, put it to his lips and gave three sharp blasts. Almost immediately two vehicles appeared over the crest of the rise, heading towards them on the gravelled track. The first was a German Opel-Blitz, 3-ton truck with a canvas canopy, closely followed by the second, an open top Kubelwagon.

Both vehicles had been painted in the usual black, brown and green camouflage paint but, additionally, each carried a sinister-looking German black cross on their doors.

As soon as they had both stopped, shouts of 'Schnell! Schnell!' accompanied a vigorous waving of his pistol as the SS officer indicated they should all board the three-tonner. He pointed his pistol at Callendar and the broad-shouldered Canadian. 'You two, help him onto the truck,' he ordered, nodding at the still doubled-up form of the cockney.

Together they got the injured man to his feet and helped him climb onto the waiting truck, where they moved as far down the vehicle as they could. Once the last man was aboard, two armed troopers climbed in and sat on the tailboard, keeping their machine pistols trained threateningly on their passengers.

'You OK?' the Canadian asked, as the truck pulled away.

'Yeah. I'm OK,' came the hoarse reply, as he massaged his bruised abdomen. He nodded angrily towards the back of the truck. 'Who in the hell are these bastards?'

'No idea. But I guess we'll find out shortly. By the way, my name's Sinclair.'

'Mine's Nicholson,' replied the cockney. 'And thanks.'

'Callendar,' added Callendar briefly.

They all shook hands but said nothing further as the truck pulled away for what proved a relatively short journey. When it came to a halt, skidding slightly on the gravelled surface, the two guards jumped out and dropped the tailboard.

'Raus! Raus!' they shouted as, one by one, the occupants disembarked leaving Callendar, Sinclair, Nicholson and one other, an older man, the last to dismount.

'Do you want a hand, or can you manage?' enquired the fourth man.

Callendar shook his head. 'Thanks, but I think we can manage.'

Once off the truck, they found themselves standing at the

foot of a flight of steps leading up to the entrance of an eighteenth-century manor house. Waiting to greet them at the top of the steps, stood another officer, this one reassuringly dressed in the uniform of a British Army major. The SS officer, now speaking in English, called his troopers to attention and saluted. Callendar recognised the hawk-like features and narrow frame of the British officer.

'I know him,' he murmured, nodding towards the major. 'His name's Ferguson. He's one of the officers who interviewed me for this operation.'

Sinclair nodded. 'Me too.'

They watched as Ferguson responded to the salute.

'Thank you, Sarn't Major. I'll take it from here.' He turned to the bemused faces of the sixteen men. 'Good afternoon, gentlemen. Welcome to Jackdaw's Nest. This will be your home for the next few weeks, so if you would kindly follow me.'

Swinging on his heel he strode into the house.

3

As the 'SS officer' marched the stormtroopers away, the sixteen bewildered men mounted the steps and followed Ferguson into the manor house. Nicholson, who had more or less recovered from his rough treatment, stubbornly declined further assistance and made his way independently up the steps. The three of them, together with the older man, brought up the rear as the group crossed a marble-flagged hallway and entered a large and lofty room.

From the empty bookshelves around the wall it was evident it had once been a library, although it was now in a poor decorative state, with paint flaking from both the ceiling and walls and with a thin layer of dust covering the empty bookcases. Despite this, and the recent addition of drab, brown, utility linoleum on the floor, the room still conveyed an impression of graceful and comfortable living. The original furniture had long since disappeared, to be replaced by a collapsible trestle table set close to the right-hand wall, together with two fold-up chairs, whilst in front and facing the table a further sixteen chairs had been placed in two rows of eight with a gap in the centre of the rows, effectively creating four groups of four chairs.

A ruddy-faced, grey-haired figure dressed in a Royal Navy uniform was sitting on one of the chairs positioned behind the table. Callendar recognised him immediately: Commodore Ernest Surridge RN, the officer who, together with Ferguson, had conducted their initial interviews. Ferguson had taken the other chair alongside the Commodore and was speaking urgently into his ear. The naval officer listened intently to

52

what Ferguson was saying, but broke off when the men entered the room and stood up, a smile on his face.

'Welcome gentlemen and please be seated.' He indicated the assembled chairs. 'Sit wherever you feel most comfortable. Smoke if you wish. There should be a few ashtrays dotted around.'

By the time Callendar, Sinclair, Nicholson and the older man had entered the room the only chairs still vacant were four at the front. Once they and the others were settled, the Commodore came to the front of the table and perched on its edge.

'First of all, gentlemen, may I welcome you all to the Jackdaw's Nest.' He gave a slightly mischievous smile. 'I trust our "welcoming committee" didn't cause too much alarm or distress although I do realise what happened may have appeared a little brutal. But it was not without purpose. You will understand better as matters progress.'

'Now the name Jackdaw's Nest is not the real name of the house, simply one we've come up with for the purpose of this operation. It may sound a little odd but it does have a certain significance, although just what that is must remain secret for the time being. I can tell you the house and the surrounding grounds are part of an establishment operated and controlled by the Special Operations Executive. I don't expect many of you will have heard of that organisation, but don't concern yourselves too much. Suffice to say that, much like us, their work is top secret, and therefore the security arrangements already in place here suit us admirably. Having said that, the particularly sensitive and secret nature of what *we* shall be doing does require us to operate entirely separately and within our own segregated area. Which, of course, begs the question: why have you been brought here?'

He scrutinised the sixteen men.

'Before I tell you as much as I am able, I must remind you that you all *volunteered* for this operation which, as you

53

are aware, comes under the heading of Hazardous Duty. During the past three months, Major Ferguson and I have interviewed a great number of chaps like yourselves and you sixteen have been selected to undergo some rather specialist training for a particularly important and crucial task. A task which, if successful, could bring this war to a swift and early conclusion.' He paused momentarily. 'Unfortunately, owing to the need for *absolute* secrecy, I am unable to divulge the exact nature of the task until your training is complete. And even then that information will be given only to the four men who are finally selected to undertake the mission itself.'

'What I can tell you, because it's going to be all too obvious once training commences, is that you are all going to become Nazis.'

The murmurs of surprise following this piece of news brought a slight smile to his face.

'And not just Nazis,' he continued. 'You are in fact to become members of the Nazi Waffen SS. Now for those of you who haven't heard of the Waffen SS, they are not soldiers in the strict sense of the word, but members of an élite force, highly trained, tough and ruthless – probably the toughest and most ruthless in the world. So you can imagine, gentlemen, the training you will be undertaking will be equally tough and equally ruthless – hence the nature of the your reception committee. It will be far tougher than anything the British Army can offer, and over the next six weeks you will do nothing but eat, sleep and breathe SS, so that by the time your training is finished you will be as close to the genuine article as we can possibly make you.' He paused again, to allow his words to sink in.

'Now, you all speak, or in the past have spoken, fluent German. Some of you are, understandably, a little rusty. Don't worry, that will improve. As from 06.00 hours tomorrow morning, you will speak German and only German. *Englisch ist verboten aller Zeit! Verstehen Sie?'* The question received a muted *Jawohl.*

'Good,' acknowledged the Commodore nodding. He took a deep breath. 'Gentlemen, it's important, *vitally* important, that you don't unconsciously lapse into English. It would prove fatal. And just to ensure you adhere absolutely to this requirement, I must tell you that microphones have been installed in your quarters in order that we shall hear everything you say. Not that I shall be concerned if you make adverse comments about myself, or any other member of staff, in your private moments – just as long as you say them in German. We also need to know if anyone talks in their sleep – which could prove embarrassing.'

He glanced at his notes, then looked up.

'Although I am unable to give too many details away, I can at least tell you this.' He paused for a moment, knowing full well how his next words would be received. 'In order to carry out the exercise, it is necessary to infiltrate four of you into the guard of Hitler's Reichs Chancellery in Berlin.'

There were incredulous looks and astonished mutterings from the assembly.

'Excuse me, sir,' interposed one, shaking his head. 'I know we've all volunteered. But what you suggest is impossible. You don't honestly expect any of us to get away with something like that, surely?'

The Commodore held his hands up. 'Believe me, gentlemen. If we didn't think it was achievable, it wouldn't even be contemplated. Rest assured, everything has been planned down to the last detail. All we need now is the right team to carry it out.'

Another man raised his hand. 'But this is almost like spying. Isn't it the sort of job to be done by these SOE people?'

'Yes, you're quite right,' the Commodore said, nodding his head. 'It *is* the sort of thing they do. But for this job

55

they lack the most important and singularly vital qualification. They have not had the training in military discipline that you chaps have. They are not used to responding to words of command instantly, nor do they know what it's like to stand to attention on guard for hours at a time. Nor do they know how to march, or how to salute – although a very different type of salute will be required for this job. No gentlemen, only chaps like you, trained soldiers, stand any chance of carrying this off.' He shook his head. 'Those SOE types would fall at the first hurdle.'

'Do I take it this job doesn't carry a return ticket?'

The blunt question, delivered in a soft transatlantic drawl, momentarily threw the Commodore and a frown clouded his face. He glared at Sinclair.

'What's that supposed to mean?' he snapped irritably.

Sinclair shrugged. 'Sounds to me, you're looking for an assassination squad. Someone to kill Hitler. And that's gotta mean a one-way ticket.'

Surridge shook his head vehemently. 'I can assure you that is *not* the purpose of the mission,' he averred. 'What we have planned doesn't even require Hitler to be anywhere near Berlin. So you can forget any ideas about assassination.'

He again referred to his notes, this time simply to cover his annoyance at Sinclair's suggestion.

'Now, returning to the matter of security,' he continued. 'As I have indicated, it will be of the highest order and from now until the successful completion of the mission, *no-one* with the exception of myself, will be allowed to leave Jackdaw's Nest. Not for any reason. Not even Major Ferguson.'

He glanced round at the Major, whose surprised face indicated he had been unaware of the impending restriction.

'Sorry Teddy. But I'm sure you will understand the necessity.'

He turned back to the men.

'And just to show you we mean business, you will have

noticed the area we occupy is surrounded by two high fences. The inner fence, I must warn you, is charged with some forty thousand volts of electricity. Not that anyone is likely to get near it, because the area between the fence and the trip wire is heavily mined and the gate, through which you entered the compound, has now been sealed off. Which leaves only one way in or out, and that is the gate leading into the main area of SOE's operations. This will be guarded twenty-four hours a day by an armed sentry. Those guards have been instructed to shoot anyone attempting to leave.' He looked grimly at the sixteen men. 'So you see, gentlemen, you are all virtually prisoners here. No one can get in or out. Any questions so far?'

There was a brief hesitation before the man next to Callendar spoke.

'Sir, you've made it obvious we are to be under severe restrictions here, but what about writing home? Will letters be allowed?'

'Yes! Of course. Thompson, isn't it? As far as your families and friends are concerned, you're now stationed somewhere in the Highlands of Scotland, far from civilisation and certainly too far to make any trips home on the weekend. Consequently, any letters you write will be sent to Scotland for posting, to ensure the appropriate postmark appears on the envelope. And incidentally,' he added, 'all letters will be censored. So be careful what you write. Any further questions?'

This time Callendar spoke. 'Sir. Infiltrating Hitler's Headquarters in Berlin isn't going to be easy. From what I know of the Germans, they're a damn thorough lot. Surely their security system will instantly pick up whoever goes?'

Surridge gave an enigmatic smile. 'You've no need to worry on that score. That's all been taken care of.'

'Which must mean you've already got someone on the inside,' suggested Sinclair quietly.

'No comment,' retorted Surridge, quickly moving on to

57

another subject. 'You may also be wondering why you were asked to report in civvies. Again there is purpose in this. Success during training and also during the mission depends on all of you working together as a team and I don't wish any differences in rank to prejudice that. Therefore you will all be treated as equals.'

For a moment it looked as though Callendar would say something, but he obviously thought better of it and satisfied himself with a withering look at Nicholson, one which did not go unnoticed by the Commodore.

'Major Ferguson will be in overall charge of training,' Surridge continued, 'ably assisted by two instructors, one of whom has had practical experience in SS training.'

He nodded to Ferguson who rose and opened the door. Two men dressed in SS combat uniform stepped smartly into the room, threw their right arms up in the Nazi salute and shouted, 'Heil Hitler'.

'Gentlemen, may I introduce SS Hauptscharführer Keppler and SS Hauptscharführer Walters, alias, I hasten to add, Colour Sergeant Jack Keppler of the 1st Battalion Duke of York's Regiment and Sergeant Tom Walters of the 2nd Battalion Grenadier Guards.' The two 'SS men' turned about to face the group and immediately Callendar felt Nicholson tense beside him.

'You've already met Hauptscharführer Keppler,' Surridge continued. 'He was in charge of the reception committee we laid on for you.'

The cockney rose to his feet, fists clenched.

'Sit down Nicholson,' snapped Surridge brusquely. 'I've heard what happened. The treatment you received may have been a little rough, but it is all part of your training.'

Nicholson hesitated for a moment before slowly sinking down onto his chair, still staring venomously at Keppler.

'Now listen to me, all of you...' The Commodore's voice was firm. 'You all witnessed what happened to your colleague earlier, and you may feel he was hard done by. But we are not playing games, gentlemen. You probably think discipline in the British Army is tough, but I can assure you it's nothing compared with the SS. Their training is carried out with ruthless efficiency. They obey orders instantly and without question – and you will learn to do the same. As I have already said, you will eat, drink and sleep as SS men. The pressure will be intense and the slightest infraction of the rules, or failure to perform, will incur penalties.' He didn't clarify what was meant by 'penalties'.

'Now, before I continue, are there any further questions?'

'Yes sir,' said Thompson hesitantly. 'As you rightly say, we did all volunteer for this. But...' He glanced round as if seeking support. 'What if any of us feel we can't... Well, make the grade, so to speak. Is it possible to ... drop out?'

The Commodore gave Thompson a long, withering look.

'Do I take it you're having second thoughts already, Thompson?' he asked icily. Thompson shifted uncomfortably in his chair.

'It's not so much that, sir. I ... I just wonder if I'll measure up to the job. I don't want to let anyone down,' he added.

'That particular judgment will be left to Major Ferguson and your instructors,' Surridge responded curtly. He turned to the whole group. 'As I have already said, if we feel any of you don't measure up, you won't be selected.' Then he added after a pause, 'Of course, if any of you do feel you want to withdraw at any stage, then I am bound to respect your wishes. You are, after all, volunteers. But I have to say, I shall personally be disappointed if that happens.'

The tone of contempt was all too obvious.

'However,' he continued in a more measured voice, 'in the event anyone does wish to withdraw, then the individual concerned will be assigned to other duties within the compound.' A broad smile appeared on his face and he clapped his hands together. 'But let's not talk negatively.

Let's keep a positive attitude.' He glanced at his watch. 'Now if there are no further questions, I believe lunch is ready. After lunch, you'll all be issued with uniforms and equipment and shown to your quarters.

'Oh! There's just one final thing,' he added. 'The plan calls for a four-man team to be sent, which means you need to be allocated into groups of four in order that you can train together, live together and thoroughly get to know each other. Now let's see...' He glanced round at Major Ferguson. 'As they're already sat in groups of four, I don't see any reason why they shouldn't stay in those groups. That is, unless you have any objections.'

Ferguson shook his head.

'Good!' exclaimed the Commodore and moved in front of the two left-hand rows. 'Shall we say that on this side, the front row will be Jackdaw One and the rear, Jackdaw Two, and on this side...' He moved across the room to the other two rows. 'The front row will be Jackdaw Three and the rear Jackdaw Four. Any questions? No? Good.'

He glanced at his wristwatch.

'Now I have to get back to London, but rest assured I shall be making frequent visits to see how you're all progressing. Meanwhile, I'll hand you over to Major Ferguson.' He glanced at the Major. 'Time for lunch, I think.' Turning to the two instructors he said, 'Would you kindly escort our guests to the dining room please? Thank you.'

Entering the dining room was like stepping into another world for the sixteen men and drew a typically characteristic comment from red-haired Nicholson.

'What the bleedin' 'ell!' he exclaimed.

Any resemblance to the dining room of an English manor house had completely disappeared. No paintings adorned the room, no landscapes, no seascapes, not even any portraits, although lighter patches on the oak panelled walls betrayed their former presence. In their place hung huge red Nazi

60

banners, their centres emblazoned with black swastikas on a white circle. At the far end of the room, positioned between two of the banners, was the only portrait in the room, a vast picture of Adolf Hitler in characteristic pose, whilst at the opposite end, an equally huge German eagle glowered down with a wreathed swastika clutched in its talons. On the side walls hung black flags bearing the SS symbol in white runic lettering, together with a shield bearing the same symbol and the legend *'Meine Ehre Heisst Treue'*. (Loyalty is My Honour)

Equally spaced around the room five round tables had been laid for lunch, each with four place settings. White cards had been set on four of the tables identifying them as Jackdaw One, Jackdaw Two, Jackdaw Three and Jackdaw Four, whilst the fifth table had been set apart and positioned directly under the picture of Hitler.

'Please be seated, gentlemen,' invited Ferguson, taking his own place with the two instructors at the fifth table. 'You will see your table is identified with your group number.'

Callendar, Sinclair, Nicholson and Thompson made their way to the table bearing the number 3 and took their seats. Two mess orderlies appeared and began serving lunch. The room quickly filled with the buzz of conversation, but a strange silence prevailed at table three. Thompson was the first to speak, shifting uncomfortably in his seat as he did so.

'I suppose you all think me a bit spineless – asking about quitting, I mean.'

Callendar looked at him with thinly-veiled contempt.

'Well, since you asked, yes I do. I can't understand why in heaven's name you volunteered in the first place, if you haven't got the guts to see it through?'

The icy tone cut deep, and Thompson fidgeted uneasily on his chair.

'You wouldn't understand,' the older man muttered quietly.

'You married?' interjected Sinclair almost accusingly.

Thompson nodded.

'Kids?' The question drew a further affirmative nod from Thompson.

'Then why the frigging 'ell did you volunteer?' exclaimed Nicholson frowning. 'I thought they only took single blokes for this sort o' thing.'

Thompson opened his mouth to reply, then closed it again as a white-jacketed orderly approached their table carrying plates of food. They all watched silently as he laid a plate of pickled cabbage and sausage in front of each of them.

Mystified, Nicholson stared at his plate. 'What the friggin' 'ell's this supposed to be?' he demanded, looking up at the orderly.

'Sauerkraut and bratwurst,' interrupted Callendar. 'Which,' he added condescendingly, 'happens to be a typical German meal. And, by the way, I would appreciate you moderating your language. Particularly at the meal table.'

Nicholson raised his eyebrows and pulled a face. 'Oh! Mister Hoity-Toity, is it?'

Callendar's face reddened.

'How dare you speak to me like that?' he snapped, his voice rising. 'Why, if you were in my...'

He was cut short by Sinclair.

'Let's all calm down, shall we? We're being watched.'

They looked up to see the rest of the room staring at them with curiosity, including Ferguson and the two instructors.

'Might as well scratch that lot straight away,' muttered Keppler, picking up a forkful of sauerkraut. 'They're going to be a disaster from the start.'

Ferguson's gaze remained on the four men. 'We'll see,' he replied quietly. 'It's early days yet. But I have to agree, they don't appear to be a particularly compatible bunch.'

Back at table three, the conversation continued in a more subdued tone.

'All right, so why did you volunteer?' Nicholson persisted.

Thompson shrugged, toying with his food.

'Not really sure. Sense of duty, I suppose.' He shook his head. 'I honestly didn't think it would involve the sort of thing the Commodore described.'

'Good God, man! What on earth do you think "Hazardous Duty" means?' demanded an exasperated Callendar. 'A garden party?'

Thompson shook his head.

'You haven't got a wife and kids, so you wouldn't understand,' he replied quietly.

'I wouldn't worry too much, if I were you,' interposed Sinclair calmly. 'From our performance so far, I don't think those up there are too impressed.' He nodded towards the top table. 'Chances are, we'll finish bottom of the selection list anyway.'

'Not if I have anything to do with it,' retorted Callendar. 'I've never come bottom at anything.'

'Nah. You wouldn't, would you!' grunted Nicholson, his mouth full of sausage and cabbage.

'For God's sake! Shut up, the pair of you,' snapped Sinclair tersely. 'You're behaving like a couple of school kids! Just remember, this isn't a game, it's for real. And whoever goes on this mission will need to work as a team, each relying on the other. Which we ain't exactly doing at this moment.' He looked around the room at the other groups. 'And whoever goes, they're goin' to need one helluva lot of luck. One helluva lot!'

After the meal had finished, Callendar turned towards Thompson. 'Look,' he began awkwardly, 'I think perhaps I ought to apologise. I was a bit selfish saying what I did. It's just that... well, I've always been taught not to accept second best. Always to give maximum effort, never quit at anything.'

'It's not for me, you understand. I'm not a coward, even if it looks that way. It's my wife Edna ... and the kids. If anything should happen...'

'Why don't you have a word with Ferguson,' suggested Sinclair. 'I'm sure he'll understand. There's no disgrace in backing down.' He stared at the back of his hands as if examining his fingernails. 'If I was in your position... Hell! I wouldn't hesitate.' He raised his head and looked Thompson in the eyes. 'And I mean that!'

'Yeah,' Nicholson chimed in. 'I'd jack it in meself, only I'm stayin' to meet up with that bastard who bashed me with his bleeding' rifle. I got a score to settle wiv 'im.'

Thompson gave a wry smile.

'Thanks!' He took a deep breath. 'But I can't back down.' He looked at Callendar. 'Like you, I wouldn't be able to look at myself in the mirror every morning if I were to renege on my word. I'll carry on. And I won't let you down.'

4

'C'mon, move yourselves!' stormed Hauptscharführer Keppler, slapping his swagger cane into the palm of his hand. 'We haven't got all day.'

Lunch over, the two instructors had marched the sixteen men to the Quartermaster's Stores to be issued with their new uniforms and equipment. Surprisingly, each man's issue had already been made up for him, right down to the correct collar, chest, inside leg and boot size.

'I'm impressed,' mused Sinclair, checking through his kit. 'Someone's taken a lot of trouble.'

'You can say that again,' agreed Nicholson, trying on the bucket-shaped steel helmet. 'First time I was issued wiv a uniform it was two sizes too big, an' when I complained, some bleedin' comedian told me I'd 'ave to grow into it.'

His eyes suddenly caught sight of a black SS dress uniform hung on a nearby wall.

'Now this looks a bit tidy,' he said, stepping forward and taking it down from its hook. 'I can jus' imagine meself wearing this.' He held it up for the others to see.

'Put that back,' roared Keppler, striding forward and angrily snatching the uniform from Nicholson's grasp. 'You'll be issued one of those *when* you've earned the right to wear it. Which in *your* case, will never happen. Now grab your kit and get outside.'

Nicholson pulled a face as he gathered up his equipment.

'For some reason I don't fink that man likes me,' he muttered to himself.

'Yeah? Well, maybe it's because he don't like loud-mouthed cockney gits,' grinned one of the store men.

Nicholson's fiery temper ignited instantly and he whirled round to face the grinning man. Despite the absence of a helmet, and combat uniform, the red-haired cockney immediately recognising him as the 'stormtrooper' who had rammed a rifle butt into his stomach. His eyes narrowed evilly.

'Oh, it's you is it? Well, you'd better watch yourself, my ole mate. I already owe you one, and us Nicholsons don't forget fings in a hurry.'

'Stop talking and keep moving.'

This time it was Walters who spoke, his soft, level tone contrasting sharply with that of the noisy Keppler. 'When you've got your kit, form up again outside in two ranks.'

Kit issue completed, the sixteen men were marched back to the manor house clutching their equipment to their chests and taken upstairs to the first floor where they were shown their new quarters.

Each Group had been allocated a separate room each with the same sparse furnishings: four iron beds, four metal cabinets to serve as wardrobes and a full-length mirror attached to the back of the door.

'You'll find the ablutions and toilets at the end of the corridor,' said Walters. 'Just dump your kit on the beds for the time being and get changed into your combat uniforms. When you're ready, reassemble outside. You've got five minutes.'

'And not a second longer,' yelled Keppler, stomping up and down the corridor, slapping his cane against the doorframe of each room. 'Then we're going to pay a visit to the camp barber for a haircut – and I mean a real haircut. So move yourselves!'

'I'm beginning to 'ate that man,' muttered Nicholson,

dropping his equipment onto one of the beds. 'Someone's goin' to do for 'im one day.'

'He does seem to find it difficult to do anything but shout and yell,' agreed Thompson. 'But the other instructor, what's his name? Walters? He seems OK.'

'Let's wait and see,' said Sinclair, dragging on his combat trousers. 'Don't be fooled by that soft exterior. He's got a job to do, same as the other guy. And I got a feeling he'll be just as tough when the time comes.'

Callendar had been taking in their Spartan surroundings. 'The accommodation leaves something to be desired,' he observed sourly. 'Hardly The Savoy.'

'Wouldn't know abaht that,' replied Nicholson, struggling with his heavy boots, 'The only Savoy I know is the flicks dahn the East End.'

Callendar cast a disdainful look at Nicholson's bowed back.

'Yes ... quite!' he murmured.

When they had reassembled outside, Keppler took command, walking up and down the two ranks, critically inspecting their new uniforms and making adjustments here and there. Then he took up position facing the sixteen men, standing with hands on hips.

'Right. Well you may think you look like SS soldiers,' he sneered, 'but I doubt if any of you'll have the guts to make the grade. However, it's my job to try and train you – God help me! Now the first thing you're going to learn is how to march SS-style.'

He gave a quick demonstration then marched them off towards the camp barber's, their arms swinging across the chest, elbows bent, as opposed to the British way of straight arms swung forward and back. Inevitably, some found it difficult to adapt after months of being drilled and shouted at by British drill sergeants to 'get it right', which delighted

Keppler, giving him even greater opportunity to berate those unfortunate individuals who were struggling. Nicholson found it particularly difficult and consequently drew the most abuse. Fortunately, it was but a short distance to the barber's, a Nissen hut set behind the manor house.

Forming a single file outside the hut door, they were taken inside one at a time, reappearing after an incredibly short time with hair close cropped in true Wehrmacht fashion.

'Forty-five bleedin' seconds!' exclaimed Nicholson, staring with incredulity at his watch. 'Must be using a bleedin' lawnmower.'

'Quiet!' stormed Keppler, striding along the queue. He stopped at Nicholson. 'So it's you again, is it?' He thrust his face close to the cockney. 'Keep this up and I'll find something not so amusing for you. Got it?'

'Yes, Colour Sarn't,' replied the cockney with a resigned sigh.

'Yes, Hauptscharführer,' yelled Keppler, tapping his collar tab with his swagger stick. 'You're in the SS now. And don't forget it.'

'Yes, Herr Hauptscharführer,' replied Nicholson, more smartly this time.

'And stand to attention when you speak to me,' roared Keppler, his face reddening with anger.

Nicholson brought his heels smartly together and stood straight as a ramrod. 'Yes, Herr Hauptscharführer!'

Keppler glared at him for several seconds before the voice of the unseen barber called out.

'Nexta please!'

'That's me,' volunteered Sinclair, stepping forward and entering the hut.

'Sitta down, please,' instructed the barber, a little fat man of about forty years.

'Italiano?' queried Sinclair, taking his place in the chair.

'Si, Si, Angelo Capaldi,' he replied proudly. 'Late of Bond Street, London, but before that, La Via Turino, Roma.'

'What're you doing here?' Sinclair queried as the little man draped a sheet over his shoulders. 'Thought all you Eyties – sorry, Italians – were put into camps when the war started.'

Angelo nodded.

'Si, Si, I was interned,' he sighed, running his electric clippers up the sides and back of Sinclair's head. 'I don't do nothing. But your government, they say I'm security risk. So I asked them to let me go back to Italia – to my wife, my lovely Maria and my bambini. But they say "no, you stay in camp".' He stopped for a moment and stared through the window. 'Thats'a all I dream of all the time. To see my wife and bambini again.' He gave a deep sigh. 'One day, perhaps, my wisha come true.' He resumed his assault on Sinclair's locks. 'That pig Mussolini, that fascisti, he ruin my country. One day, he get his.'

'But what are you doing here? At this camp?' queried Sinclair, wincing as he saw volumes of hair falling to the floor.

Angelo shrugged.

'The British authorities they say "Angelo, you good hairdresser, you cut British soldiers' hair". So, I come here.' He tapped Sinclair's shoulder with his comb. 'Better than internment camp,' he confided.

Keppler appeared in the doorway. 'What's going on?' he demanded. You're taking a long time with this one, Angelo.'

The little Italian, unaffected by the intrusion, shrugged his shoulders nonchalantly.

'Justa finishing. There you are, signor.' He swept the protective sheet away and shook his head as he looked with disgust at his handiwork. 'When the war she is over, you come to my salon; I show you how good a hairdresser I am.'

'I'll do that, Angelo. That's a promise,' said Sinclair, bringing a beaming smile to the little man's face.

'That's enough chatter,' snapped the ever-impatient Keppler. 'Now join the others. Right, next!'

Callendar made to move forward, but Keppler held his arm up blocking the way.

'No, not you. It's the comedian's turn.'

Keppler grinned sadistically as he pointed at Nicholson with his swagger cane.

'A special for this man, Angelo,' he instructed the little Italian. 'You know what I mean.'

The 'special' proved to be a close crop over the entire scalp, which had Nicholson ruefully rubbing his head as he emerged.

'That man's got a grudge against me,' he complained, nodding his head towards Keppler. 'If my ol' Mum could see me now she'd 'ave a bleedin' fit.'

'Stop complaining,' ordered Keppler. 'At least you're beginning to look like an SS soldier. Now get back in line.'

Still rubbing his stubble, Nicholson took his place in the ranks.

On returning to the Manor House, they were taken to the lecture room where they found Major Ferguson now dressed in the uniform of an SS Sturmbahnführer, waiting for them.

'Thank you, gentlemen. Please keep the same seats you had before.' He turned to Keppler. 'Thank you, Hauptscharführer, that'll be all for the time being.' The SS man sprang to attention, threw up a Nazi salute and departed. Ferguson turned back to the assembled men, and looked at them with approval.

'Good. Already you're beginning to look the part. Now, I want to run over the programme that lies ahead of you. As you heard from the Commodore, only one group will be required to undertake the mission and, needless to say, that group will be the one we feel stands the greatest chance of

70

success. Once the selected group is on its way, the rest of you will remain here in reserve. However, whether a reserve team proves necessary or not, you will still remain here until the mission is completed. That's simply a security precaution.

'Your training here will last for six weeks. It will be highly intensive and extremely demanding. So much so in fact, that we anticipate half of you won't make the grade. To give a simple illustration of what I mean: as you are aware guard duty, in the British Army normally lasts for twelve hours, each man being required to be on duty for two hours, then have four hours' rest. An SS guard is required to remain on duty for the full *twelve* hours – with no breaks. And that is something you'll have to practise.' He paused for emphasis. 'Now although the majority of your training will be physical, there is also a great deal of mental study for you. You will have to learn and instantly recognise the rank insignia of both the Wehrmacht and the SS – particularly the SS. Additionally, you will have noticed the SS motto displayed on the shields in the dining room: "Meine Ehre Heisst Treue" – Loyalty is my Honour. Learn it and remember it. You will also have to learn the oath of the SS, Der Sippeneid. But above all...' He picked up a pile of manila folders from the table behind him. '...you will need to study the contents of these folders. Each one contains the personal history of the character you will assume. Date of birth, place of birth, who your father and mother were, where you have been serving, what company, division, etc. I suggest you adopt this as your evening entertainment, because there is little here to distract your attention, so employ your spare time usefully. Study the contents of these folders; learn them off by heart. Test each other, because we will test you, time and time again. In other words, we want you to *become* these characters. Any questions?'

There was a general shaking of heads.

'Good! Now, as I call your name, come forward and I'll

issue you with your appropriate file. And one other thing – forget your British names; from now on you will only be referred to by your new identity.'

After collecting his file Callendar found he had become SS Untersturmführer Hans Richter, Sinclair SS Untersturmführer Friedrich Steiner, Thompson SS Untersturmführer Karl Dietrich and Nicholson SS Untersturmführer Franz Stein.

'You will note you all bear the same rank, SS Untersturmführer,' Ferguson continued. 'This equates to a junior subaltern in the British Army.' He smiled. 'Which means a number of you have just received unexpected promotion. Now for the rest of the day I suggest you familiarise yourselves with your new equipment and to start absorbing the contents of your files. Dinner will be at nineteen hundred hours sharp. Any questions?'

He cast his eye over the assembled men. Sinclair glanced towards Thompson but seeing he showed no sign of raising any points he turned back to face Ferguson.

'There's one thing I find curious, sir,' he ventured.

'And what's that?' smiled Ferguson.

'Well I don't claim to know much about military intelligence, but surely you've got people specially trained for this type of work – espionage or whatever you might want to call it. So, why choose guys like us? Ordinary soldiers, so to speak?'

Ferguson frowned.

'I thought the Commodore had covered that point earlier. However, the fact of the matter is that, as I understand it, the type of operation that's in mind requires chaps who are used to military discipline. You're quite right, of course, we do have specialist people, but their training has wholly concentrated on subversive warfare, the dirty tricks department. They aren't capable of drilling and turning out in smart uniforms. They don't salute senior officers, or come to attention at the shout of a command. In other words, nothing like you chaps have done and which comes as second nature to you. As such it was felt that you would adapt more readily to the training required and stand a greater chance of success.'

Nicholson thought about this explanation for a moment.

'But what if we're found out, y'know caught, will we be treated as prisoners o'war?'

Ferguson compressed his lips into a thin line.

'There's no point in lying to you. The answer has to be an emphatic "No". As you won't be wearing British uniforms, you won't be protected by the terms of the Geneva Convention. In other words, you would be treated as spies, saboteurs, and be treated accordingly.'

'What exactly does that mean, sir?' asked another.

Ferguson took a deep breath.

'If you were lucky, you would be shot by firing squad. If you were unlucky, perhaps tortured beforehand.'

An ominous silence fell over the room.

'Which is why we asked for volunteers and made it clear that the duties would be hazardous. Of course,' he went on, 'none of you will be forced to go. You can withdraw at any time you wish.'

'I don't think the Commodore would be too pleased,' said Thompson quietly. 'He made that pretty clear.'

'I think you all should be made aware, the whole concept of the mission is the Commodore's baby, so to speak. He conceived it and it was he who sold the idea to Mr Churchill and got the go-ahead. Understandably, he is keen to see it progress and to achieve its objective. However, I don't think for one moment he would wish to see any man forced into the task and I do know that Mr Churchill has insisted that it is to be carried out by volunteers. Does that put your mind at rest?'

Nicholson shook his head.

'My ol' man always said, never volunteer. An' my Gawd, was 'e right!'

Ferguson smiled briefly at the cockney's words, then became more serious.

'Look, don't be too judgemental at this stage. Wait until your training is complete and then if at that time you wish to withdraw, any one or all of you, you have my assurance you will be able to do so without any reflection on your character. Is that fair enough?'

Callendar, eager to identify with Ferguson as a brother officer, felt he should offer support.

'I think that some of us are being rather hasty...' He hesitated when he saw the pained expression appear on Ferguson's face. 'Which is quite understandable, of course,' he added quickly, face reddening. 'But I'm sure we'll all be eager to go if ... if selected,' he ended lamely.

'Well, we'll have to wait and see, won't we?' Ferguson replied, sending Callendar a withering look. 'All right. Let's leave it there for the time being. Don't forget, dinner at nineteen hundred hours. And I suggest you get an early night – you've a busy day ahead of you tomorrow.'

They rose to their feet as Ferguson made for the door. When he had disappeared, Nicholson turned to Callendar.

'I'm sure we'll be eager to go, sir,' he mimicked. 'You got some sort of bleedin' death wish, mate?'

Callendar's face flushed.

'I'm not your "mate" and never likely to be. Heaven forbid!' he retorted.

Nicholson's fists instantly clenched and Sinclair swiftly stepped between them.

'Cut it out, the pair of you. Save your aggression for the training course. I've a feeling we're all going to need it.'

When they reached their room, Sinclair lost no time in again turning on the would-be protagonists who were still exchanging angry glares.

'I don't know the reasons why either of you volunteered for this exercise,' he said quietly. 'But I can tell you this:

74

I've got personal reasons why I'm here and I intend to put every effort into it, and I won't let either you two idiots spoil my chances. Is that clear?'

He turned to Thompson.

'And as for you, you've got too much to lose. Why don't you pack it in now?'

Thompson stared at him resolutely. 'You won't have anything to worry about as far as I'm concerned. I've already told you, I'm staying.'

Sinclair returned the stare for a few seconds then turned away shrugging his shoulders.

'I hope you won't live to regret that decision.'

'If I do, then at least I'll still be alive,' Thompson rejoined.

'And for that I'll be thankful.'

5

The following morning the four groups found themselves introduced into the harsh reality of SS-style training. Roused at five-thirty and constantly spurred by Keppler's incessant yelling, they were given just ten minutes to get dressed in combat fatigues and assemble on the driveway in front of the Manor House. Keppler, brimming with impatience, stood at the bottom of the steps thwacking his swagger stick against the side of his leg as he watched each man emerge and fall in line. The last man to emerge, a heavily-built individual from Jackdaw Two, was still struggling with the buttons of his jacket as he came stumbling down the steps.

'And where do you think you're going?' snarled Keppler, stepping forward and arresting the man's progress by placing his swagger stick across the man's chest.

'I was just getting fell in, Staff,' blurted the man. 'Sorry I'm late...'

Keppler's face turned purple.

'Staff? Staff?' he screamed. '*Herr Hauptscharführer* to you, you miserable toad! Now get down and give me fifty press-ups.'

The man looked at him in horror.

'Fifty!' he exclaimed.

'D'you want me to make it a hundred?' thundered Keppler.

'No, *Herr Hauptscharführer*,' spluttered the man, hurrying to the grass verge.

'Now where d'you think you're going?' roared Keppler.

'I was just...'

Keppler gave a mirthless smile and pointed the ferruled

end of his swagger stick at the gravelled surface of the driveway.

'Here,' he said softly. 'You'll do them here!'

The man stared at him for a moment then dropped his eyes to the sharp, flint-like stones glinting in the early morning sunlight. 'But...'

'Here!' snarled Keppler, once more stabbing his swagger stick at the driveway.

The man's jaw muscles tightened as he made his way back to the front of the group.

'And I want to hear you count them off,' snapped Keppler.

'*Jawohl*, Herr Hauptscharführer,' the man muttered as he adopted the prone position. '*Ja*-bloody-*wohl!*'

'For that you can make it sixty!' snarled Keppler. 'Now begin!'

'One ... two ... three...'

The big man began steadily thrusting his body up and down, forcing the numbers through clenched teeth as the sharp edges of the tiny stones cut into the palms of his hands. The rest of the men watched in silence, each mentally enduring the man's agony, as the pain etched itself on his face. As the count progressed, the pace slowed, the pain becoming more and more acute.

It took a long time to complete the sixty press-ups and when he had finished and got to his feet, blood could be seen oozing from numerous lacerations on the palms of his hands. Keppler pointedly ignored the man's injuries and simply ordered him to fall in.

'Bastard!' muttered Nicholson under his breath.

'Silence!' snarled Keppler, his eyes hovering, trying unsuccessfully to spot the dissenter. 'Be warned. That will happen every morning. Last man to come down the steps will get the same punishment. Now... Right turn... Quick march!'

Without a pause for the unfortunate individual to recover

from his ordeal, the squad commenced on what was to prove a gruelling forced march around the inside perimeter of the compound. With Keppler and Walters setting a relentless pace, the effects quickly told: even the fittest men were panting for breath after only ten minutes, and for those unused to such rigorous exercise leg muscles were soon aching and feet quickly becoming sore. Thompson, in particular, suffered. Too much time spent working in the Stores, with little or no physical exercise, meant he found himself struggling. But he was a stubborn man. Gritting his teeth against the pain, he forced himself to keep pace with the rest of the group.

Callendar on the other hand who had always been a fitness fanatic, marched easily, head high, determined not to display the slightest sign of weakness. Next to him, marched Nicholson. His only exercise in recent months had been propping up the bar at the camp NAFFI, or The Rose and Crown in the East End, with the result that he too suffered. But, like Thompson, he had a stubborn streak and pressed on without complaint. He also had the additional spur of not wanting to be outdone by Callendar. Sinclair, solid as ever, paced himself and concentrated on marching steadily, conserving energy. Nevertheless, he found time to throw the occasional concerned glance in Thompson's direction, guessing he was suffering.

By the time they had finished, they had marched a distance of almost five miles and, on arrival back at the Manor House, several men collapsed exhausted on the grass verge. In contrast, Keppler and Walters still looked reasonably fresh, a tribute to their own fitness. Keppler stared at the collapsed men with cynical contempt.

'You lot, SS soldiers? Someone's got to be joking,' he sneered. 'You wouldn't survive the first hour in a proper SS training camp. Get up, the lot of you. No one gave you permission to sit down.'

Slowly they dragged themselves back onto their feet and reassembled in their squad positions.

Keppler shook his head.

'So you think that was tough, do you?' He pointed his swagger stick towards an assault course a hundred yards or so away. 'By the end of the next six weeks, I'll have you doing the same march in full kit, *and* have you across that assault course in record time. And if anyone can't make it, I'll fail them. Is that clear?'

The question brought only a tired, muted response.

'I said, "Is that clear?"' screamed Keppler.

The harshness of his voice made them jump. '*Jawohl, Herr Hauptscharführer*,' they responded loudly.

Keppler nodded begrudgingly.

'That's better. Now fall out, get washed and shaved and get your breakfasts. And afterwards...' he smiled sadistically. 'You can have your first taste of that.' He again pointed to the assault course. 'Now move!'

The assault course at Jackdaw's Nest commenced with a number of fairly straightforward obstacles, the first of which consisted of a ramp requiring each man to run up at speed before leaping out over coils of barbed wire and dropping some ten feet into a sandpit below. A fifteen-foot wide, water-filled ditch followed and this brought the first casualties. It looked simple enough, being traversed by means of a rope suspended from overhead scaffolding poles. But it had been cunningly conceived, requiring the full impetus of the rope swing to gain dry land on the other side. As a result, five of the men miscalculated the swing and earned themselves an impromptu cold bath. After that came a twelve-foot wall constructed of the already familiar pine logs. Here again, a single rope had been provided to scale the wall but many still found it difficult and it was only by working together in twos and threes that all sixteen eventually managed to get over the obstacle.

After that the tasks became more demanding. The next obstacle had them crawling twenty feet through a drainage pipe, barely two feet in diameter, oozing mud and more than half filled with dirty rainwater. The hesitancy shown by a few was quickly dispelled by Keppler's screaming threats and the calmer yet equally insistent voice of Walters. By the time they were all through each was soaked to the skin. But getting wet in the drain was but a prelude for the next task, a swim in the lake. This required each man to swim out to a yellow and red marker buoy some fifty yards out from the shore, turn and make their way back, collecting a mandatory number of yellow rubber rings floating on the surface. Those failing to round the buoy, or returning with less than the required number of rings, found themselves performing the task all over again.

Back on dry land, a hundred and fifty yards run up a steep grassy slope to a clump of tall pine trees followed and the next obstacle – an intimidating rope bridge slung between two tall fir trees, some fifty feet apart and thirty feet above the ground.

The antagonism that had sprung up between Callendar and Nicholson had developed the exercise into a personal battle between the two men, each trying to outdo the other. Keppler had been quick to spot the situation and capitalised on it by needling whichever of them was lagging behind. By the time they reached the clump of pines, Nicholson, who had proved to be a particularly strong swimmer, had gained some considerable distance over Callendar. But as he stood at the foot of the tall trees, the cockney faltered, staring up as if mesmerised at the frail-looking structure. He was still staring when Callendar caught up and overtook him.

Only when he saw Callendar scaling the rope ladder into the first of the tall firs, did he seem to recover his composure.

He quickly chased after him, but his progress up the swaying ladder proved slow and by the time he reached the wooden platform his rival was already halfway across the rope-bridge and making swift headway. Nicholson gazed out over the flimsy-looking bridge and again hesitated, his face pale, his mouth dry.

'Come on, move yourself!' Keppler's voice roared with impatience from below. 'What's the matter with you?'

It took several moments of further hesitation before Nicholson, taking a deep breath, closed his eyes and reached out to grasp the two ropes forming the handrails. Another moment's hesitation followed before his right foot edged slowly forward, gingerly feeling for the two-inch thick manila rope forming the footway. His progress was agonisingly slow and inspired further yells from the increasingly impatient Keppler thirty feet below.

But no matter how much verbal abuse, no matter how many dire threats the instructor screamed up at him, it had little or no effect on Nicholson, whose slow progress continued until he had reached halfway, the point where the swaying of the bridge reached its peak. There he froze, refusing to move another step.

Keppler's reaction was predictable. 'Come on, *dummkopf*!' he yelled. 'What are you waiting for? Someone to hold your hand? Move yourself!'

But Nicholson couldn't, or wouldn't, move and those watching from below could see his face was pale and tense, his eyes screwed tightly shut, his whole body trembling.

'Come on, Bob. You can do it,' encouraged Sinclair, shouting above the voices of the others. 'Take it one step at a time.'

'And don't look down,' added Walters. 'Just look straight ahead, feel for the rope with your feet. Come on, you'll make it!'

But despite the friendly advice and encouragement, the

81

red-haired cockney remained frozen. Perspiration was trickling down his ashen face and his trembling intensified as every muscle in his body locked solid.

'Come on, I said "move"!' screamed Keppler.

'You're wasting your time,' said Thompson, quietly. 'I think you'll find he's got vertigo. He'll never be able to move by himself and if someone doesn't hurry up and help him, he's likely to fall.'

Sinclair shot a brief glance at Thompson, then returned his gaze to the petrified Nicholson. 'I'll go,' he announced, making his way to the rope ladder hanging from the second tree.

'Stay where you are!' thundered Keppler, pointing his swagger stick at the Scots-Canadian. 'He can get down on his own. He doesn't need a nursemaid.'

'The man's got bloody vertigo. He can't get down,' retorted Sinclair angrily. 'So stuff you, Keppler. I'm going up to help him!'

'Stay where you are! And that's an order!' screamed Keppler, raising his swagger stick. It seemed as if he intended to strike the Scots-Canadian and Sinclair instinctively dropped into a crouch, arms raised defensively, his fists clenched. Suddenly there was a shout and both men turned to see Callendar climbing the second rope ladder with the rest of the men yelling encouragement.

'Get back down here,' screamed Keppler, throwing his swagger stick to the ground in frustration.

Callendar ignored him, continuing to climb rapidly upward. Reaching the top of the ladder, he heaved himself onto the platform and began to move slowly along the bridge towards the terrified Nicholson. Conscious excessive swaying of the bridge would only intensify the problem, Callendar moved forward cautiously, keeping up a ceaseless dialogue of reassurance in an endeavour to calm the petrified man.

His deliberately slow progress made it seem like an eternity before he at last reached a point where he thought he could reach out and grasp Nicholson's arm. But he had miscalculated and as he stretched forward, he suddenly lost his balance and one of his feet slipped from the two-inch rope, throwing him to one side and leaving him hanging by one hand from the rope handrail. Nicholson let out a whimper of fear as the rope bridge swung violently from side to side.

'It's OK ... It's OK,' assured Callendar hastily, struggling to regain his foothold. 'Sorry about that. Now listen. Don't worry, just try and keep calm. I'll have you down on the ground in no time at all. Just do as I say and you'll be perfectly all right.'

'I ... I ... I can't move. I'll bleedin' fall! I know I will.'

'No you won't,' Callendar insisted, keeping his voice calm. 'Just take it steady. Open your eyes and look at me. Don't look down, keep looking at me.'

Nicholson opened his eyes and gazed fixedly at Callendar's face.

'That's it. Just keep looking at me. Now, move one hand forward on the hand rope. Come on, you can do it.'

It took several moments before Nicholson could summon the courage to loosen the grip of his right hand and slowly slide it a foot or so along the rope, before again clamping his fingers tightly around its circumference.

'Good! That's good. Now, the other hand,' encouraged Callendar. 'Slowly, there's no rush. Keep looking at me, whatever you do, *don't* look away.'

Again it took a couple of moments before Nicholson's left hand had traversed a similar distance along the other hand rope.

'That's great! Now your feet. One at a time move them along the rope. Your right foot's in front, so move that one first.'

As he tentatively slid his foot along the rope, Nicholson's gaze automatically dropped down.

'Don't look down!' snapped Callendar sharply. 'Keep looking at me. Good ... that's good. Now the other foot.'

Thirty feet below, the watchers held their breath as the two men slowly edged along the rope bridge until at last they arrived at the platform of the second tree. Then, with Callendar in the lead and guiding the petrified Nicholson's feet onto each rung, they slowly descended the rope ladder. As soon as his feet touched the ground, Nicholson's knees buckled and he collapsed onto the grass amid the sound of cheering voices. Sinclair, who had moved across to the foot of the ladder to meet them, slapped his hand on Callendar's shoulder.

'Well done,' he murmured. 'That took some guts and patience.'

Callendar's face reddened.

'I'll say it did,' echoed Thompson, as he joined them.

Callendar turned away, hiding his embarrassment.

'It was nothing,' he muttered. 'Nothing at all.'

'Oh yes it bleedin' was,' interjected Nicholson, struggling to a kneeling position, his face still pale from the ordeal. 'If it wasn't for you, I'd still be stuck up there. I owe you one. Thanks!'

He held out his hand in gratitude. There was no mistaking the sincerity in his voice and the proffered hand served to increase Callendar's embarrassment. He mumbled inaudibly as he awkwardly shook hands.

But whilst Callendar's face was red with embarrassment, Keppler's had become purple with anger. Roughly he elbowed his way through the throng of men to where Callendar was standing.

'You,' he yelled, 'are on report for disobeying an order. And I'll make sure you're dropped from training before the day's out! Now get fell in, all of you.'

With mutterings of resentment, the sixteen men formed up in their two ranks, urged on by Keppler's ranting. Sinclair, seething at the treatment Callendar had received, was all for having a showdown with the Hauptscharführer there and then, but Thompson's powers of reasoning prevailed.

'Leave it, or you'll join him on report. Let's wait and see what happens before any of us say anything.'

Sinclair nodded. He knew Thompson was right. It would be stupid to give the bullying Keppler further reason to discipline them and it was left to Nicholson to sum up their joint feelings, which he did in characteristic fashion.

'Bastard!'

The rest of that first day was spent in the lecture room with Major Ferguson where they were shown film, obtained from Pathe Gazette and various other sources, of the elite Nazi SS both in training and in battle – the latter taken from a German cameraman captured in North Africa. They were also shown photographic slides of prominent members of the Nazi Party, whom they were required to identify and then commit the image to memory.

This was followed by instruction on identifying the various rank insignia of the SS and learning how to perform the Nazi salute correctly.

'Remember gentlemen, and remember it well,' Ferguson stressed, 'as opposed to the rest of the German armed forces, the Wehrmacht, the SS, *never*, repeat *never*, give the recognised military type of salute. In other words, they never raise their right hand to their caps when they salute a senior officer. When the SS salute it is always the fascist salute: the extending of the right arm at an angle halfway between horizontal and vertical.'

He turned to Keppler and Walters who were both standing to one side.

'Perhaps you would kindly demonstrate.'

Both instructors immediately came to attention, clicked their heels and threw their arms smartly into the air, accompanied by a cry of, '*Heil Hitler!*'

'Thank you.' Ferguson turned back to the class. 'Now we'll get you practising it. It's vitally important that you get it right. I understand recruits in the Waffen SS are required to practise this a hundred or more times a day during their training and I see no reason why we shouldn't follow their example. Right. Let's have Jackdaw Three first.' He looked across to the two instructors. 'Would you check points and correct them where they go wrong.'

The next half hour was spent practising the Nazi salute, at the end of which time arms had begun to ache. Sometimes it was done in front of a full-length mirror and sometimes saluting each other, but always with a noisy '*Heil Hitler*'.

'All right, all right, that's enough,' Ferguson called out above the noise. 'Please resume your seats.'

He waited until everyone was settled.

'Good. You seem to be getting the hang of it, but practice is the key to success. I'll arrange for a number of Nazi flags to be dotted around the place and I expect you to salute each time you pass them. Is that clear?'

They all chorused '*Jawohl!*'

The major nodded. 'Very good. Now there's just one other point where you need to be careful. As I said, the Wehrmacht, the regular German Army, always use the formal cap salute when saluting officers, even when they salute SS officers. The SS officers on the other hand, will always respond with a Nazi salute. So be extra vigilant. A silly slip, like responding with the wrong salute, will undoubtedly give the game away.'

'Good. Now let's get on with recognising the various rank insignia, so that you'll know who and who not, to salute...'

At the end of the afternoon's session they were dismissed for the day – except for Callendar. He was ordered to stay behind and received a severe dressing-down from Ferguson for deliberately disobeying Keppler's orders.

'As a result of your behaviour, Hauptscharführer Keppler has asked me to suspend you from training,' continued

86

Ferguson. 'However, that is something I am not prepared to do. You did after all display a quality that would be essential in any group to ensure the success of the mission. I refer of course to teamwork and what you did exemplifies teamwork at its best. That's all. Dismissed!'

Callendar, taken completely by surprise at the unexpected turn of events, stood rooted to the spot. Quickly recovering his composure he saluted, remembering, just in time, to make it a Nazi salute.

'*Danke, Herr Sturmbannführer. Heil Hitler!*'

Ferguson smiled to himself as he watched Callendar close the door behind him. They were learning.

6

'I 'ate that bastard Keppler,' opined Nicholson, displaying his feelings by viciously brushing his combat boots. 'Walters is all right, but that bastard Keppler...'

It was the evening of the first day and the four members of Jackdaw Three were in their room, engaged in various domestic chores: Nicholson and Sinclair cleaning the grime and mud from their equipment, Thompson darning a hole in a sock and Callendar, ever the perfectionist, practising his fascist salute in front of the full-length mirror. They were also discussing the first day's events.

'Don't let him get to you,' advised Thompson, painfully trying to thread a length of oversized wool through the eye of an undersized needle. 'I've met his type before, a bully, who uses his position to belittle others. I shouldn't lose any sleep over the likes of him.'

Nicholson pulled a face. 'Maybe. Trouble is, 'e could make it difficult, an' stop our group being picked for this job they got lined up.'

Thompson gave up on the needle and looked quizzically across at the young cockney. 'Is it that important to you? To be selected, I mean?'

'Yeah. Yeah, it is.' Nicholson sounded thoughtful as he looked up from his polishing. 'See, I got something to prove. My ol' lady ... well, she's German, see. Least she was born in Germany. That's 'ow I come to speak German. My Dad met 'er in Belgium just after the last war in 1918. After they was married, 'e brought 'er back to England. Well, didn't make no difference where we lived, in the East End, 'er being

German. We had lots a different nationalities – Polish, French, Irish, even some blacks. That was until bleedin' 'itler started this lot, an' that changed everything. People started pointing fingers, saying things behind her back.'

'What sort of things?' asked Sinclair.

Nicholson's jaw tightened. 'It wasn't everybody, jus' a few nasty-minded bastards. Said we was all Nazi sympathisers, 'aving a German mother. Broke her 'eart it did. That's why I volunteered for this lot. Just to show them friggin' busybodies, the Nicholsons is as British as they come.' He looked at Thompson. 'Anyway, 'ow about you? What are you doin' 'ere when you got a wife an' kids? As I said before, this sort o' lark is supposed to be for single men.'

The blunt comment made Thompson flinch.

'Stupid really,' the older man admitted, shaking his head. He laid aside the glass he'd been using to repair the damaged sock. 'Bloody stupid in fact. I was... I still am, I suppose ... a sergeant in the Ordnance Corps. Had a pretty cushy number too, running the Company stores and, what with being stationed only fifteen miles from home, I got to see Edna and the kids nearly every weekend. In fact, life wasn't much different from when I was languages master at the local grammar school.' He sighed. 'Trouble is, I've got a conscience. I kept seeing all those lads being sent out to North Africa, kitting them out, wishing them luck. It made me feel what a fraud I was. So when the notice appeared on Part One Orders, I put my name forward, thinking there wouldn't be anything really dangerous.' He sighed again. 'But now, here I am.'

He picked up a photo-frame resting on his bedside locker. The photograph showed the whole family standing in front of the railings outside Buckingham Palace, he was wearing his sergeant's uniform. He'd taken them all to London for a couple of days; they'd stayed at his brother's house in Paddington. He smiled.

'My lad, Brian, he's proud of his Dad. Thinks I'm going to win the war all by myself.'

'You can still back out, you know,' Sinclair reminded him, holding out his hand for the photograph. The picture brought back memories of his own short-lived family life. He passed the photograph to Callendar who had tired of practising saluting and now sat listening to the conversation.

'Look,' he began awkwardly, passing the photograph on to Nicholson. 'I ... I don't wish to appear rude, but ... well, aren't you a little old for this sort of thing? I mean ... it's a job for younger men surely.'

Thompson smiled. 'The Commodore and the Major obviously don't think so. Anyway, you don't have to worry. I won't let you down. I'll pull my weight and keep up with the best of you.'

'I didn't mean... I wasn't saying you're too old ... well, not exactly...'

'What he's trying to say,' interrupted Sinclair, coming to Callendar's rescue, 'is that he agrees with Nicholson and me. You should jack it in and go back home to your wife and kids. This is no place for a married man with a family.'

Thompson set his jaw stubbornly. 'I don't renege. I'll see this training through and if by some strange quirk of fate our group does get selected then I'll see the mission through as well. So, please, can we leave it at that?' He looked challengingly at Callendar. 'I suppose in your case, it's a question of family honour. Military traditions, all that sort of thing. Am I right?'

'Sort of,' acknowledged Callendar, embarrassed by Thompson's perceptiveness. 'You're right, I do come from a military family. My father was a regular soldier. He served in the last war and was later appointed military attaché at the British Embassy in Berlin. That's where I was born. My grandfather served in South Africa, against the Zulus, and my great-grandfather served with Wellington at Waterloo. So,

90

yes, I feel I do have a tradition to maintain and I suppose that's why I volunteered.' He turned to Sinclair. 'What about you? What's a Canadian doing in the British Army anyway?'

The big man lowered his head and continued brushing dried mud from his combat trousers.

'It's a long story,' he said quietly. 'You wouldn't be interested. Let's just say I'm here for personal reasons.'

'Come on,' encouraged Nicholson. 'We're s'posed to be a team, remember. You heard our reasons, it's only fair we hear yours. Ain't that right?'

He turned to the others for support.

'All right,' Sinclair sighed reluctantly. 'You're right. We should know about each other.'

He dropped his muddied combat trousers onto the bed and leaned over to open the drawer of his bedside cabinet. He withdrew his wallet and from it extracted a dog-eared photograph of an attractive young woman holding a pretty little girl in her arms.

'That's my wife Elizabeth and my daughter Penelope,' he announced, handing the photograph to Thompson.

The older man frowned. 'You're married?' he challenged. '*And* have a daughter? You're a fine one telling me I shouldn't be here, what about you?'

Sinclair stared at his big hands.

'They're the reason I am here. They were both killed two years ago. A German bomb scored a direct hit on our house in Coventry.'

'Shit!' exclaimed Nicholson, angrily punching the mattress of his bed. 'Friggin' bastards, bombing civilians.'

'I'm sorry,' murmured Thompson quietly. 'I...' He looked down at the photograph. 'You must have loved them very much.'

Sinclair nodded silently.

'And you must hate the Germans pretty badly,' added Callendar.

91

The Canadian shook his head. 'I don't hate the German people. It's the Nazis. They've corrupted the country and the minds of the people. I worked there for a number of years just before the war and I saw what the Nazis were doing. They're absolutely ruthless. They rule with an iron fist and anyone who disagrees with them gets beaten up or sent to a camp. I just reckon this madman Hitler's got to be stopped, otherwise the whole world will feel the Nazi jackboot.'

He took the photograph back from Nicholson, carefully returned it to his wallet, then glanced pointedly at the clock on the wall.

'I guess it's time we all got some sleep. I don't suppose for one minute Herr Keppler will let us have a lie-in in the morning – and I don't fancy the idea of being the next in line for fifty press-ups.'

'Come on! Come on! Hands off cocks and on with your socks! It's five-thirty. On your feet!'

Keppler's swagger stick whacked noisily on the foot-ends of the iron beds. He passed on to the next room, slamming the door behind him.

Sinclair, Callendar and Thompson were out of bed immediately and hurriedly dressing. Nicholson, on the other hand, was still heavy with sleep.

'Why don't someone kill that noisy, foul-mouthed bastard?' he groaned, burying his head under the pillow. 'It's still the middle of the bleedin' night.'

'You'd better move yourself if you don't want to be doing those fifty press-ups,' advised Sinclair, quickly buttoning his jacket, 'because if he sees it's you, who knows, he could even make it a hundred!'

The warning roused Nicholson to instant action. Kicking back the blankets, he leapt out of bed, dressed in record time and was soon leaping down the main stairway three at a time. Yet despite this sudden alacrity, he only just missed qualifying for the punishing press-ups. A member of Jackdaw One was the luckless individual. The disappointment was clearly etched on Keppler's face as he thrust it within inches of Nicholson's.

'Just made it this time, didn't you? Never mind, I'll have you one day. Now straighten up!' he snarled. 'Right, you!' He turned to the unfortunate latecomer and pointed his swagger stick at the gravel driveway. 'Fifty press-ups, here!'

With a look of resignation the man dropped to the ground.

The punishment completed, the morning's training session commenced. It proved to be a straightforward copy of the previous day, starting with the lung-bursting, leg-aching, forced march around the camp, both instructors demanding more and more effort. It was evident there would be no let-up.

'You OK?' Sinclair panted, glancing sideways at Thompson as they trudged along, side by side. 'You don't look too good.'

Thompson's face, though pale, was grimly set.

'I'm all right,' he replied tersely. 'You worry about yourself. I'll make it, never fear.'

He turned away, his face set with determination. The march continued in silence, each man conserving his breath and energy. Nevertheless, the Canadian's concern continued and he threw frequent glances at his companion, looking for any sign of deterioration in his condition. But, true to his word, Thompson acquitted himself manfully and arrived back at the House in surprisingly better condition than a number of the other men.

After their ablutions and a breakfast of cold meats, sausage and bread, they were marched across to where the assault course once again beckoned and, predictably, Nicholson and Callendar were quickly vying with each other for the lead. Having lagged behind the day before, and with the memory of his failure to negotiate the rope bridge still plaguing his mind, Nicholson put in an extraordinary effort, with the result that he had gained twenty or twenty-five yards on his companion by the time he plunged into the cold waters of the lake. Not one to give up, Callendar immediately followed, diving in and striking out energetically in the direction of the red hair bobbing some fifteen to twenty yards in front.

Despite the early morning sun, the water was particularly cold that morning and Callendar swam vigorously, summoning up all his energy in an effort to keep warm and to close the distance separating them. But Nicholson's aquatic superiority meant that his lead had increased even more by the time he reached the marker buoy. After rounding the bobbing float, he turned back towards the shore and to the floating rubber rings. Passing Callendar swimming the other way, he couldn't help noticing several other swimmers had overtaken his blond-haired colleague.

The bright yellow rings were always placed in the same area of the lake and on mornings when there was little or no wind they tended not to drift far, that is, until the swimmers got amongst them. Ironically, this meant the first men to arrive found it relatively easy to collect the required number of rings, whereas latecomers found the remainder had been scattered far and wide, making their task considerably more difficult. Today, Keppler had decreed each man should collect six rings and Nicholson soon had that number slipped over his arms and was on his way back to the shore. Dragging himself from the water, he counted off the six rings in the box lying at the feet of the glowering Hauptscharführer and set off towards the trees and the final phase of the assault course.

Sinclair and Thompson caught up with him at the clump of pines where they found him sitting at the foot of a tree, gathering his breath and staring up with morbid fascination at the rope bridge. Walters, who was standing nearby urging them on, had obviously accepted Nicholson would not again attempt the climb.

'Where's Callendar?' shouted Nicholson, as they trotted by. 'He missed a ring,' Sinclair breathlessly called back. 'Keppler's making him do it again.'

The thought of Callendar's misfortune brought a smug smile to the cockney's face and he stood up and walked to the top of a nearby grassy knoll, where he could look down and get a good view of the lake. Shading his eyes from the bright sunshine being reflected off the water, he saw the tail-enders struggling up the last stretch of sloping ground towards him. With them came the unmistakeable figure of Keppler, waving his swagger stick, but Nicholson couldn't see Callendar among them. He switched his gaze towards the lake, eyes straining against the glare. At first the expanse of water seemed empty. Then he thought he saw something bobbing up and down next to the marker buoy. His body stiffened, then with a sudden cry he was charging down the slope towards the lake running as fast as he could. His aching limbs forgotten, he ignored Keppler's shouts and drove himself unsparingly towards the lake's edge. As he got closer, he could see Callendar clinging to the buoy, one arm waving feebly in the air. Without checking his headlong flight, Nicholson dived headlong into the cold water and struck out strongly towards his troubled colleague.

'What's the matter?' he panted, swimming up to him.

'Cramp! Cramp in both legs!' came the agonised answer. 'I can't move.'

'OK, OK. Leave it to me, I'll soon 'ave you back to shore.'

Manoeuvring himself behind the stricken man, Nicholson slipped both arms under Callendar's armpits, locking his hands around his chest. 'Now, jus' let go of the buoy.'

But Callendar's fingers had become numb with cold, so Nicholson was forced to prise them open in order to release their grip. Once free, Callendar sank back against Nicholson's chest and the cockney began the slow task of towing his companion back to the shore.

It was energy-sapping work. With Callendar only semi-conscious he was a dead weight and by the time they reached halfway Nicholson was beginning to feel the strain. Nevertheless, he struggled on, but with the continuing loss of his own body heat in the chilly water he felt his strength ebbing away. Desperately, he struggled to stay afloat. He was almost at the end of his tether when he heard the welcome sound of voices close by.

'It's OK, we've got you, Bob!' came Sinclair's voice. 'Just a few more yards to go.'

The big Canadian, along with Thompson and a couple of others, dragged the two men onto the bank. Both were suffering from hypothermia. Surprisingly, it was Walters who took charge, quickly organising the rest of the men into relay teams to carry Callendar and Nicholson to the main building, where they were immediately taken to the medical room and the camp doctor summoned.

Swathed in blankets, together with hot water bottles, and plied with mugs of hot tea, it was not long before they began to recover. The MO gave them both a fairly lengthy examination before concluding neither would suffer any lasting effects. But he insisted they remain in bed for the rest of the day.

When Ferguson arrived outside the MI room, the doctor was just leaving. Grimly he listened to the doctor's report then turned to the two instructors demanding to know what had happened. Keppler, his face pale, explained how Callendar had failed to return with the required number of rings after the lake swim and how he had made him go back and do it again.

'But surely you were watching him,' frowned Ferguson. 'Don't tell me you just left him?'

Keppler stood stiffly to attention. 'I thought... I presumed he would be all right, sir. I didn't think...'

Suddenly aware the rest of the men were listening, the major stopped him.

'I think it would be better if we continued this conversation in my office.' He turned to Walters. 'Would you take over please, Hauptscharführer Walters?'

'Very good, sir,' Walters acknowledged, raising his hand to his cap in salute.

Ferguson gave him a baleful look.

'The rules on saluting also apply to instructors, Sturmscharfürer!' he rebuked sharply.

Walters snapped to attention, throwing his arm up in a Nazi salute. '*Jawohl, Herr Sturmbannführer!*'

Ferguson acknowledged the salute, turned and strode off, followed by a subdued-looking Keppler.

'Looks like our beloved Hauptscharführer's in for a right old bollocking,' one man observed happily. 'Couldn't happen to a nicer chap.'

'Shut up! And get fell in,' stormed Walters angrily. 'Otherwise I'll have you *all* doing press-ups.'

Back inside the Manor House, the two men continued to make rapid recovery from the effects of their prolonged immersion in the cold waters of the lake. Nicholson lay between the crisp white sheets dreamily enjoying this unexpected break from the rigorous training, whilst Callendar stared, deep in thought, at the numerous cracks in the flaking, whitewashed ceiling.

It was well known that he had never liked Nicholson. They were poles apart, both intellectually and socially. As far as he was concerned, the rope-bridge incident had changed nothing. The fact that he might well have saved Nicholson's life had not altered his feelings towards the man.

But now the situation had changed; the relationship had changed. This time it was he who owed a debt of gratitude and the knowledge made him distinctly uncomfortable. After all, how could he continue to dislike someone who had just saved his life? And, despite the prejudices that separated them, the courage displayed by Nicholson at the very least deserved respect, if not friendship. But how could he, how should he, bridge the gap? To say 'Thank you, for saving my life', seemed wholly inadequate. He moved restlessly in the camp bed, unable to relax.

'You OK?'

Callendar turned to see Nicholson, propped on one elbow, looking at him with a concerned expression. He gave him a weak smile and nodded his head.

'Yes. Yes, I'm fine.' He hesitated. 'Look ... um ... what happened ... back at the lake ... I ... uh ... I just wanted you to know... Well, perhaps we haven't always seen eye to eye on things and I know you probably think I'm an insufferable snob ... but I can't help being what I am. And whatever... I owe you my thanks for saving my life.'

'You don't owe me nothing,' Nicholson interrupted. 'I reckon it took a lot o' guts for you to say what you just did. An' while we're on the subject, I can't help being what I am, either. So we'll both have to learn to live with it.' He stuck out his right hand. 'Won't we ... mate!'

'Yes, I suppose we will...' He smiled awkwardly as he accepted the proffered hand. 'Mate!'

7

'Pay attention! Unless you want to get your stupid heads blown off,' snarled Hauptscharführer Keppler. His voice echoed eerily among the tall pine trees surrounding the weapons range.

They had reached their fourth week of training and were assembled at the weapons range. Their normal training dress of camouflaged combat uniform had today been supplemented by the addition of 'coal-scuttle' shaped steel helmets worn by the German Army. During the previous weeks the relentless physical demands of both Keppler and Walters had continued unabated. Even the lake incident involving Callendar's near drowning had failed to curb Keppler's ruthless style of training, although it was rumoured he had received a severe dressing down for failing to ensure adequate safety measures had been taken.

Additionally the incidents both at the lake and the rope bridge had brought a significant change in the relationship between Callendar and Nicholson. The bickering and arguing had disappeared to be replaced by a mutual, if grudging, respect. This change had been welcomed by both Sinclair and Thompson and even raised a rare smile on the Canadian's normally taciturn features. It also had a bonding effect on the four men: they became a close-knit team, rather than an assortment of ill-matched individuals. However, the change, though not lost on Ferguson, did little to improve the placing of Jackdaw Three in the weekly 'league table' of training results published on the notice board in the hallway of the Manor House. They found themselves consistently placed third or fourth, which Nicholson avowed was due to the ongoing feud between himself and Keppler, rather than a true reflection of their efforts. Undaunted, the four persevered, each day making every effort to achieve the near impossible standards demanded of them.

Assembled at the weapons range for the first time, they were formed into a semi-circle facing the targets at the small arms firing point. Keppler and Walters stood by a trestle table on which had been laid out an assortment of small arms, whilst under the trestle table lay a curious-looking bundle covered by waterproof capes.

'This morning,' announced Keppler. 'You're going to learn something about the weapons used by the SS.'

He picked up a machine pistol from the table and held it aloft for all to see.

'This is the MP40, more commonly known as a Schmeisser, and it is standard issue to all Waffen SS troops. It uses nine-millimetre continental rimless ammunition and can fire single shots, or be used as a fully automatic weapon with a rate of fire of five hundred rounds per minute.' He grinned. 'You ought to recognise it. It's one of the weapons we used to scare the shit out of you when you all arrived.'

'Yeah! I haven't forgotten, Keppler,' Nicholson muttered, more to himself than anyone in particular. 'I still owe you for that.'

'Quiet!' snapped Keppler, his eyes rapidly scanning the row of faces, trying to trace the individual who had spoken. He stared with suspicion at the red-headed cockney.

'No talking and pay attention,' he continued pointing the Schmeisser down the range. 'Now watch closely. First, single shots.' Taking aim, he fired off half a dozen shots at one of the man-shaped targets set some twenty-five yards away. Holes appeared in the target as each shot struck home. Still facing down the range, he lowered the Schmeisser to waist level.

'Now, on automatic.'

100

Firing in short bursts, he emptied the magazine and virtually disintegrated the target under the accurately aimed hail of bullets. Still pointing the weapon down the range, he removed the magazine, checked the breech, applied the safety catch and placed the weapon back on the trestle table.

'Right. Now it's your turn. You'll fire in your groups, starting with Jackdaw One.'

Each man fired one magazine from the Schmeisser, following the same pattern as Keppler: six single shots, then short bursts until the magazine was empty. Except for one individual, each man acquitted himself well enough, all the targets having been reduced to little more than matchwood by the time firing had ceased.

The one exception, a man in Jackdaw Two named Smith, had failed to score a single hit on his target! This wasn't surprising. Of the sixteen men selected for training at Jackdaw's Nest, Henry Smith was the least likely candidate to succeed on the course. A scholar of languages before the war, he had spent some time attending the University at Heidelberg, prior to returning to Oxford to read for a degree in German. His earlier than expected return to Britain at the start of hostilities had seen him recruited into the Royal Army Intelligence Corps as a translator. However, apart from wearing a uniform, all other aspects of military life were completely alien to Henry Smith and, along with Nicholson, he had become a natural target for Keppler's cynicism.

'Smith, next time I'll make sure there's a barn door around for you to aim at,' Keppler remarked acidly. 'You're bloody useless! Now get back in line.'

'As you can see,' continued Keppler, when the men had resumed their semi circular formation, 'the Schmeisser can be a formidable weapon – in the right hands, that is.'

He glared at Smith before turning to the trestle table where he picked up two handguns. He raised one in his right hand for all to see.

101

'This is a Walther P38 automatic, the personal side arm of all SS officers. Like the MP40 it fires nine-millimetre rimless ammunition, although with a shorter cartridge, and it has an eight round magazine capacity.' He held up his left hand. 'This one is a Walther PP. Again automatic, it's slightly smaller and fires 7.65-millimetre ammunition and also holds eight rounds.' He lowered his arm. 'The PP is favoured by the Gestapo, the Nazi secret police, because it fits snugly in the pocket of a coat.'

He replaced the two pistols on the trestle table.

'Ordinarily, at this stage you would practise firing both these weapons on the range. However, as the targets are now pretty useless, and because it's a close quarter weapon with which you can hardly miss...' He glanced at Smith with a sad shake of the head. 'Well, most of you anyway ... there's little point. Instead...' He reached under the trestle table, pulled out the odd shaped bundle and laid it on top of the trestle table. 'Instead, I've planned something a little different.'

He treated them to one of his sickly grins.

'Those of you who're a bit squeamish might find the next lesson somewhat distasteful. But it's something you're going to have to learn.'

Pulling away the groundsheets he revealed a tailor's dummy, the type that could be seen dressed in the latest fashionable suit and adorning the window of a Fifty Shilling Tailor's. This dummy, however, was headless and dressed rather incongruously in a dirty, threadbare jacket, a pair of torn, grey pin-striped trousers, and a dirty white shirt. The limbs, which could be swivelled into a variety of positions to emulate the various stances adopted by the human form, Keppler manipulated to get the dummy into a kneeling position on the ground. He then picked up a large turnip from under the trestle table, where it too had been hidden by groundsheets, and carefully balanced the vegetable on the dummy's shoulders to represent its head.

'Keppler,' interjected Walters frowning, 'you're not thinking of...?'

'*Hauptscharführer* Keppler, if you please,' Keppler snapped. 'And yes, I am. If you don't like it, then look the other way.'

'You can't,' protested Walters. 'This isn't in the training schedule. What's the point?'

'The point is *I'm* the senior instructor and I'll decide what's to be taught. Now you can either shut up or clear off back to the office. Please yourself. But don't interfere with what I'm doing. Got it?'

For a moment Walters stood his ground but eventually backed off and stood, tight-lipped behind the semi-circle of assembled men. Keppler, meanwhile, had picked up the Walther P38 and deftly loaded the magazine with ammunition. He slid the loaded magazine into the butt, applied the safety catch and tucked the weapon into his belt.

'The squeamish and faint-hearted can turn round and look away, if they want to. The rest of you, watch and learn.' He pointed a finger at the unfortunate Smith. 'Smith! Get yourself out here.'

'Oh Jesus! Not me,' Smith moaned, hauling himself to his feet.

'Come on, move yourself! I haven't got all day,' barked Keppler irritably.

Smith broke into a trot, stopping in front of the instructor.

'Kneel down,' ordered Keppler.

Smith dropped to his knees.

'What are you going to do, Herr Hauptscharführer?' he asked apprehensively.

'Don't worry, Smith. I'm not going to kill you. The army won't let me!'

He guffawed at his own humour.

'All right! Pay attention,' he continued, this time addressing the whole group. 'The SS and the Gestapo have a neat little way of disposing of people they don't like: Jews, gypsies, members of resistance groups and the like. Disposing of them, that is, after they've got all the information they want. Now how do they do this? Firing squad at dawn?' He shook his head. 'Too many bullets. Too many people involved.'

He picked up the small Walther PP from the trestle table, slipped out the magazine and placed it back on the table. After checking the breech was clear, he pressed the muzzle against the nape of the kneeling man's neck. The touch of cold metal made Smith jump.

'One bullet in the back of the neck, at the base of the skull. That's all it takes. Smashes the spinal column and severs the spinal cord. Death is instantaneous.' He removed the muzzle from Smith's neck. 'Right, you can get up.' He turned to the rest of the men. 'Quick, effective, economical. And second nature to any SS officer.'

He pulled the loaded P38 from his belt and handed it, butt first, to Smith.

'You're first, Smith. Show the others how it's done. Just place the muzzle against the "head". Even *you* can't miss at this range!'

Smith stared at the gun, then at the dummy, shaking his head.

'This is pointless. I know it's only a vegetable, but I could never kill anyone in cold blood. Not ... not like this. There's just no point in me doing it.'

'Place the muzzle against the head,' Keppler snarled. 'You're supposed to be an SS officer. You don't question orders.'

But Smith still couldn't bring himself to do it and an infuriated Keppler grabbed him by the arm and dragged him across to the kneeling dummy.

'This is a stinking Jewish pig! An enemy of the Reich! And I'm ordering you to kill him. So do it! Do it NOW!'

Swallowing hard, Smith raised the pistol and pointed it at

the turnip. He was shaking so badly, he had to use both hands to steady his aim. As he squeezed the trigger, he turned his head away disturbing his aim and causing the bullet simply to scour a groove along one side of the vegetable.

'Fool!' screamed Keppler, grabbing hold of Smith's head. 'Do it again! And this time, keep your bloody head still!'

This time the bullet struck the turnip in the centre, sending it toppling from the shoulders of the dummy.

'Not bad,' he commented grudgingly. 'Bit high, but it'll do. Right, you can sit down. Who's going to be next?'

One by one, each man was called forward to carry out the same mock execution, some, like Smith, having to repeat the task. The four members of Jackdaw Three completed their individual 'executions' without the need for secondary shots, although Callendar, who fired last, loudly and firmly averred that *he* could never carry out such an act on a fellow human being, no matter who they were, or what they had done.

'So, it offends your gentlemanly instincts, does it Herr Untersturmführer?' sneered Keppler mockingly. 'That's a pity. Because by the time this war is over your so-called gentlemanly instincts will no longer exist. No one will care a damn who shot who or why or how. Survival. That's what war is all about.' He turned to face the rest of the men. 'Personal survival – that's all that matters. Whoever goes on this damn mission will have to do exactly as they are told. Even if it means shooting your own grandmother! Because, if you don't – if you hesitate for one instant in carrying out an order – you'll either be dead, or headed toward the Russian front!' He turned back to Callendar. 'Now sit down!'

'I told you the bastard ain't human,' muttered Nicholson shaking his head. 'Shoot my ole granny? No chance! My muvver would string me up by me balls!'

A grim-faced Sinclair shook his head. 'Sadly, he's right. Whatever we think of Keppler, I believe he knows what he's talking about. Mind you...' He turned to Callendar. 'Like you, I don't think I could do it for real – not kill someone like that. Unless... Unless he was a Nazi. So we'd all better hope we're never put to the test.'

'Amen to that,' agreed Thompson.

'Stop talking!' thundered Keppler. 'Save your breath, 'cause you're going to need it.' He turned and pointed to his left. 'Over there, a hundred yards away, is the grenade range. That's where we're going next. At least, I am. You lot...' he pointed in the opposite direction, 'are also going to the grenade range, but via that oak tree.' He indicated a large oak some hundred yards away. 'Hauptscharführer Walters! You will wait here and make sure every man goes around that tree. Anyone who doesn't gets sent back to do it again. And the last man to arrive at the grenade range gets fifty press-ups. Wait for it,' he cautioned, as a few men started to get to their feet. 'GO!'

As the men set off en masse, Keppler glanced at Walters.

'I'll leave you to collect this lot,' he said, nodding at the weapons on the trestle table. 'And I'll see you over at the grenade pits.'

'I still say you were wrong,' challenged Walters, his face set. 'That charade was completely unnecessary.'

'Unnecessary, was it? Charade?' sneered the senior instructor. 'Listen! We're supposed to be teaching them to be SS officers and that's exactly what I'm doing. Don't forget I was in the SS for over a year before the war and it taught me to be a heartless, cruel bastard. And if any of these lily-livered recruits are to survive a trip into Nazi Germany, then better they learn now and not when it's too late. It's for their own good – and their survival. So keep your nose OUT!'

They stared at each other face to face for several moments, until Walters shook his head and turned away to watch the men rounding the tall oak tree in the distance.

106

'You're mad,' he muttered softly. 'Utterly mad.'

But Keppler didn't hear. He was already making his way towards the grenade pits.

8

The grenade range had been carefully sited within a secluded clearing surrounded on all sides by tall pine trees, their density having a muffling effect on the noise of the exploding bombs. In the centre of the clearing a wall, approximately twenty feet long and twelve feet high, had been constructed with pine logs. Thirty yards in front of the wall, a concrete-reinforced slit trench ran parallel for a distance of twenty yards or so before swinging at right angles for another twenty yards to form an 'L' shape. At each end of the 'L' a small concrete bunker provided refuge for those personnel waiting their turn to throw, or those who had finished the exercise.

Panting and gasping, Callendar and Nicholson were the first to arrive at the trench.

'Beat you!' panted the cockney, collapsing to the ground, chest heaving but with a big grin on his freckled features.

'This time perhaps,' gasped Callendar as he too fell to his knees. 'But I'll get you next time.'

'Get up, the pair of you!' snapped the irascible Keppler, slapping his swagger cane into the palm of his hand. 'No one said you could lie down.'

Dragging themselves to their feet, they watched the straggling line of men as they approached the grenade pits, yelling encouragement to Sinclair and Thompson, each man desperate to avoid the punishment imposed by Keppler. In the end the unfortunate runner turned out to be a heavy-set man from Jackdaw Four, who hobbled in with a twisted ankle, the result of an unseen rabbit hole. Characteristically, Keppler displayed no sympathy for the man's misfortune and pain.

'Should have been looking where you're going,' he said tersely. 'Now give me fifty.'

Meanwhile the rest of the men were ordered into the slit trench accompanied by Walters, who momentarily disappeared into one of the concrete bunkers and re-emerged carrying a small wooden crate. This he set down on the parapet of the trench before disappearing back into the bunker to collect a second crate, which he placed alongside the first.

'Right, get fell in,' snapped Keppler to the luckless man who had now completed his fifty press-ups. He watched without a shred of emotion as the man hobbled painfully into the trench then took up a stance above the trench where he could look down on the assembled men.

'Right, now pay attention. Before we get started on the grenades, just a word about safety. For those of you who haven't been on a grenade range before you'll have noticed there are holes in the floor of the trench, about eighteen inches deep. No, they're not rabbit holes for some clumsy clod to stick his foot in. They're for clumsy clods with butterfingers who drop a grenade onto the floor of the trench after they've pulled out the pin! If it happens you simply kick the grenade into the hole and dive flat on your face. Got it?'

He looked down at them and gave a deep sigh.

'Why is it I've got a feeling we're going to need that hole?'

'Right, let's get on with the lesson. There are just two types of grenade we're going to be dealing with: the Stielgranate, or stick grenade and the Eiergranate, or egg grenade.' He knelt down and prised open both boxes with a lever Walters had also brought from the bunker. From one he withdrew an object looking something like a tin can on the end of a short piece of broom handle.

'This is the stick grenade,' he announced, standing up and holding it aloft for all to see, 'affectionately referred to by

British troops as the Potato Masher. It's been in use in the German Army since the First World War and, although slightly bulky for carrying around, the handle provides for a good throwing action, giving it a range of around forty yards. It contains approximately twenty ounces of explosive, has a five second fuse and a killing radius of about seventeen yards. To activate the grenade, you first unscrew this cap on the end of the handle...' He removed the cap as he was talking. 'Pull the cord inside the handle and get rid of it pretty damn quick!'

Replacing the cap he returned the stick grenade to its crate and reached into the second box. This time the shape proved more familiar.

'The egg grenade is smaller and is similar in shape to a British Mills 36. It contains just twelve ounces of explosive but can be thrown up to a distance of fifty yards with an effective radius of about fifteen yards. Again it has a five second fuse.' He treated them to one of his rare smiles. 'Now I'm sure you've all seen Errol Flynn using these at the pictures, but in case you haven't it's activated by withdrawing this pin.' He slipped his forefinger through the ring attached to the pin and pulled. 'Although I've pulled the pin out, nothing will happen because I'm still holding down the striker lever. When you throw the bomb, the striker lever flies off and the fuse is ignited.'

He looked along the row of upturned faces.

'Any questions? No? Good. All of you out of the trench and Sturmscharführer Walters will demonstrate how the two grenades are thrown.'

Walters moved forward in the trench and removed a haversack he had slung over his shoulder. From it he produced one each of the two types of grenade displayed by Keppler, with one major difference – both were white in colour.

'You'll notice the grenades Sturmscharführer Walters is demonstrating have been painted white. That's to show they're only practice grenades and contain no fuse or explosive,' explained Keppler as Walters made ready to throw.

He had clearly practised the exercise often, because both grenades sailed over the log wall with room to spare. Smith was sent to collect the practice grenades and each man then took it in turn to throw them – with mixed results. Some failed miserably and were required to throw several times; even then, only a few managed to hit the wall itself – including the unfortunate Smith.

'Smith! Why do I bother?' muttered Keppler shaking his head.

'I don't know, Herr Hauptscharführer,' replied Smith weakly.

'No! Neither do I. You're excused throwing the live grenades, Smith. It'd be a bloody waste!'

'Excuse me, Hauptscharführer Keppler,' interjected Walters quietly. 'The training schedule calls for every man to throw – there are to be no exceptions. That has been emphasised.'

Walters received a murderous glare from Keppler, who knew his fellow instructor to be right. Ferguson had made it clear each man had to take part in all aspects of every exercise. The rope bridge incident involving Nicholson hadn't been forgotten and remained as a 'black mark' against his name.

When it came time to use the live grenades, they were all sent to the nearby bunker and brought out one at a time for their individual throwing practice, each man accompanied in the trench by either Keppler or Walters. Having completed their throws, they were sent to the second bunker from where, through the observation slits in the concrete walls, it was possible to watch the grenades exploding.

When it came to Nicholson's turn, he was relieved to find Walters had been allocated as his instructor, rather than his arch-enemy Keppler.

'Right, you know what to do,' said Walters, handing him a live egg-shaped grenade. 'Now remember, lob it rather than throw it. Bring your arm right back and try and get it over the wall. If you *don't* clear the wall, then for Christ's sake get down quick! Understand?'

Nicholson nodded and prepared himself to throw. It was the first time he had handled a live grenade. Nervously holding it very tightly in his right hand, he slipped the forefinger of his left hand through the ring and jerked out the pin. Beads of sweat formed on his brow and the palms of his hands became damp as he drew back his arm ready to lob the grenade. Whether it was nerves, or because his mind was totally preoccupied by the grenade he was clutching so tightly, he failed to notice he was standing close to one of the holes in the trench floor. As he stepped back to throw, his foot slipped into the hole, throwing him off balance. Struggling to keep on his feet, he fell backwards; the hand holding the grenade striking the rough concrete surface of the trench wall and his fingers to lost their grip; the striker lever made a distinct 'ping' as it flew off, followed by the audible crack of the percussion cap igniting the four second fuse. The grenade dropped to the floor of the trench.

Nicholson stared in horror as the black metal sphere spun towards Walter's feet. As if paralysed, his body refused to react and he stood frozen to the spot. Walters, on the other hand, moved with lightning speed. Grabbing the front of Nicholson's tunic he unceremoniously threw him to the ground, at the same time kicking the grenade into the hole. Nicholson had the breath knocked out of him as Walters landed on top of him.

'Stay down!' yelled Walters as Nicholson began to struggle. A split second later the grenade exploded, sending flame, smoke and shrapnel flying skywards.

Back in the bunker, Keppler had heard Walters' yell and the subsequent explosion. Leaping out of the bunker, he raced along the trench towards the two figures motionless on the floor. By the time he got there the smoke had almost

112

cleared; only the cloying smell of spent explosive lingered in the air.

'Tom! Are you OK?' he demanded anxiously.

'Yes. Yes, I'm fine,' replied Walters, raising his head and slowly shaking it from side to side. 'How about him?'

'I'm all right,' Nicholson groaned, trying to push Walters' weight off him. 'Christ you're bleedin' heavy.'

Keppler helped them to their feet. 'What the hell happened?' he demanded, as the rest of the men arrived on the scene.

'It's all right,' muttered Walters, still shaking his head to try and stop the ringing in his ears. 'Just an accident, no harm done.'

'It was my fault,' admitted Nicholson sheepishly. 'Didn't realise I was standing so close to the bleedin' hole in the ground. Put me foot in it an' fell over. Dropped the bleedin' grenade.' He looked at Walters. 'Good job you was there, otherwise I'd have been a gonner!'

Keppler glared at the cockney. 'I might have guessed,' he snarled. 'It just had to be you, didn't it? You careless, bloody fool! Get yourself into the other bunker. You're finished with grenades. You're too much of a danger to yourself and to others. Now get out of my sight. You've let your team down yet again.'

Nicholson's jaw tensed. Keppler's insults didn't bother him, but the accusation of having let down Sinclair, Thompson and Callendar, cut deep. Quietly he turned to Walters.

'Sorry for what happened. I know I could've killed both of us. Instead, you saved my life. Thanks.'

Without waiting for a response, he turned and silently made his way to the far bunker.

The remainder of the exercise continued without further incident and when each man had thrown Keppler brought them from the far bunker and had them again assemble in the slit trench, whilst he stood several yards away in deep and somewhat agitated conversation with Walters.

'I wonder what that's all about,' mused Thompson.

'No idea,' responded Sinclair. 'But my guess is Keppler's up to something, and Walters isn't too happy about it.'

'Nothing can go wrong,' Keppler was insisting, his voice low to avoid the men from hearing. 'Just as long as we're careful. Anyway, it'll be a good exercise for them. See if they've got the balls.' He grinned.

Walters remained reluctant. 'I'm not sure. Could be dangerous. What if something did go wrong?'

'Nothing can go wrong!' repeated Keppler. 'Look!' He held up the 'egg' grenade he was holding. 'This is the one from which I've removed the detonator. I've painted the base plug with some white paint I found in the bunker, so there won't be any mistakes. What d'you say?'

Walters looked far from convinced. 'I'm still not happy. The idea of it alone will scare the hell out of them. And if anything should go wrong...'

'I've told you. Nothing can go wrong,' insisted Keppler irritably.

'All right, but on *your* head be it.'

Turning back to the group assembled in the trench, Keppler took up his usual stance, hands on hips, legs astride. Walters dropped back in the trench to join the men, choosing to stand quietly to one side.

'Right. Pay attention!' said Keppler. 'Now you've heard me say it before, that SS officer recruits are required to go through the toughest training imaginable, probably the toughest in the world. Not only do they have to prove themselves physically, but they also undergo severe tests of courage.'

'Here it comes,' murmured Sinclair.

'One of the most demanding of these is the grenade test,' Keppler continued. 'And if any recruit refuses to take the test, or any test come to that, he is automatically rejected as officer material.' He grinned as he looked along the row of upturned faces and watched the apprehension start to grow.

'The test is quite simple. The officer cadet is required to stand at attention and balance a live grenade on top of his steel helmet. Then he withdraws the pin, releases the striker lever, and stands perfectly still whilst the grenade explodes harmlessly above his head.'

'You've got to be joking!' exclaimed Thompson. 'You don't seriously expect us to do that?'

'No way!' protested another man.

'Not on your Nellie!' said a third.

'Of course,' continued Keppler grinning. 'If the man gets nervous and moves his head, the grenade is likely to topple off and then ... Boom! No more recruit!'

He bent down and retrieved a helmet from one of the men's heads.

'Actually it's not so dangerous as it sounds. The German helmet has a reasonably flat surface on the top and the base plug of a grenade balances very well.'

'Herr Hauptscharführer,' called Thompson. 'You're not seriously proposing we take this "test", are you?'

Keppler grinned evilly. 'Smith. Get up here.'

'Oh, no! Not me again,' moaned the luckless Smith, displaying obvious reluctance to climb out of the trench.

'Get up here, I said,' snapped Keppler.

Smith clambered out of the trench and stood to attention in front of Keppler. 'Don't worry. All I want you to do is to balance the grenade on top of your helmet just to show the others how easy it is. Don't worry, I'm not asking you to take the pin out.'

He handed Smith the egg-shaped grenade who took it with shaking hands and, after several attempts, managed to balance it precariously on top of his helmet, Keppler insisting he stand there for a full minute.

'There!' exclaimed the instructor triumphantly. 'Nothing to it.' He looked questioningly along the file of men. 'Now then, is there anyone among you who's got the guts to do the real thing? Anyone?' He walked along the top of the trench studying the upturned faces, eventually arriving where Nicholson was standing. 'How about you? Our grenade throwing "expert" who can't walk a rope bridge. Fancy your chances, do you?'

'Don't do it,' murmured Callendar, nudging his companion. 'The man's mad!'

'Well? Lost your bottle completely?' sneered Keppler.

Nicholson, his jaw set, began to clamber out of the trench.

'Don't be a fool,' urged Thompson. 'He's just trying to needle you. Don't do it!'

But Nicholson wasn't listening. Hauling himself up over the parapet he stood in front of Keppler.

'Well,' greeted Keppler with a sarcastic smirk. 'Maybe you've got some balls after all!'

He turned to the rest of the men.

'Watch carefully – because, afterwards, I'll expect you all to take a turn.'

He handed Nicholson the same grenade Smith had used. 'Pull the pin, carefully release the striker lever, drop your hands to your sides and stand perfectly still. Got it?'

Nicholson nodded.

'The rest of you, when I say "Duck" get yourselves below the parapet PDQ. Because anyone entering the Mess this evening minus his head will be improperly dressed!'

He dropped down into the trench and turned to watch Nicholson as he made his way to the wall.

'Shit! If anything goes wrong...' murmured Sinclair.

'That's far enough,' called Keppler, when Nicholson had reached a point about twenty-five yards from the trench. 'Now don't panic and you'll be OK.'

Nicholson turned towards the trench, his face pale and tense as he lifted the grenade to the top of his helmet. Still holding it firmly, he carefully withdrew the pin. His fingers firmly holding the striker lever in place, he moved the grenade around trying to find exactly where on the top of his helmet it balanced safely. This took some time, but eventually he seemed satisfied and they watched dry-mouthed as he steadied himself before releasing the lever and dropping both arms to his sides.

'Everybody down!' roared Keppler who obstinately remained standing, gazing out at Nicholson's lonely figure. The men ducked below the level of the parapet.

'One ... two ... three...'

Someone could be heard counting off the seconds. When the count got to five and nothing happened, looks of stunned surprise appeared on their faces. Keppler burst into laughter.

'Fooled the lot of you, didn't I?' he guffawed, beckoning Nicholson to rejoin the group. 'You don't really think I'd let him use a live grenade, do you?' He gave Nicholson a look of grudging respect as he arrived back. 'Well! Well! So you have got some balls after all. Who knows, we may even see you crossing the rope bridge before long.'

Nicholson refused to rise to the bait as he handed Keppler the grenade and retaining pin.

'Where's the striker lever? No matter, there're plenty of spare levers lying around. Here Smith...'

He tossed the grenade towards the bespectacled Smith standing in the trench.

'See if you can re-prime this – without a detonator,' he grinned, comfortable in the knowledge that all the spare detonators were secure in the first bunker. 'OK. Who's next?'

One by one, each man followed Nicholson's example, acting out Keppler's charade until only Smith remained.

'C'mon Smith. You're last.'

'But Sturmscharführer, I've already done it,' Smith protested weakly.

'No you haven't – not properly that is. Now get yourself up here.'

Reluctantly Smith hauled himself out of the trench, took

117

the grenade from Keppler and started making his way toward the wall.

'That's far enough, Smith,' bellowed Keppler. 'Hurry up, we haven't got all day.'

Smith took an inordinate length of time to balance the grenade on his helmet. Eventually he appeared satisfied and withdrew the retaining pin, allowing the striker lever to fly off.

The unexpected sound of the detonator exploding inside the grenade shook everyone, including Smith. Startled, he moved his head. The grenade tumbled from his helmet landing on the ground less than a yard in front of him.

Keppler was the first to recover.

'Get down!' he screamed at Smith. 'For Christ's sake, get down!'

But Smith simply stared stupefied at the lump of metal lying in front of him.

'Down, Smith! Get down!'

By now everyone was yelling at him. At last something seemed to trigger a reaction in Smith's brain, but instead of dropping flat to the ground, he panicked and turned to run towards the trench. He had barely covered two yards before the grenade exploded.

Everyone in the trench automatically ducked as the explosion rent the air. When they stood up again, they could see Smith lying face down on the ground. Walters was the first out of the trench and raced across towards the motionless form.

'How is he?' Keppler demanded desperately. 'Is he alive?'

But the holes in Smith's camouflage jacket told their own story. Blood seeped from four wounds in his back where fragments of the grenade had struck him. The decisive wound, however, was in the back of his head, where the grenade's base plug had entered leaving a neat hole the size of half-a-crown.

'Dead!' Walters announced. 'Probably died instantly from that head wound.'

'Shit!' exclaimed Keppler, his face white as a sheet. 'How could it have happened? It was impossible. The grenade had a white base plug to show it was a dummy.'

'You mean like this one,' Sinclair said quietly, holding out the grenade with its base plug painted white. 'I found it lying in the bottom of the trench when we all ducked down.'

Keppler stared at it bewildered. 'I ... I don't understand...'

'It was an accident. A mix-up,' said Walters. 'A tragic mix-up. Come on, we'd better get transport over here to collect the body.'

'What the hell d'you think you were playing at?' demanded Ferguson. 'Playing games with live grenades. You're a bloody fool, Keppler. D'you realise what this means?'

Ferguson, informed of the accident as soon as they returned to the Lodge, had quickly made arrangements to recover Smith's body before summoning both instructors to his office for a full report on the incident. Once apprised of the facts, he had shown Keppler no mercy.

'First of all there'll be a Court of Enquiry, which no doubt will be followed by a civil inquest and, whether or not civil charges will be made against you, you will certainly face military justice. Then there's Smith's family. How his death is going to be explained to them, Heaven only knows. And finally, you've probably placed this whole operation in jeopardy. I hardly need to remind you that Smith, for all his drawbacks, was a member of Jackdaw Two, the team at the top of the performance table and therefore the team most likely to be chosen for the mission.' He took a deep breath and fixed Keppler with a steely glare. 'Thanks to you that is now highly unlikely.'

119

'Sir. I...'

'Save it, Keppler,' snapped Ferguson. 'Save it for your Court Martial.' He stood up and moved towards the window. 'I've advised the Commodore of the situation and he'll be here tomorrow morning. No doubt he'll take the appropriate action when he arrives. Meanwhile, you're relieved of all duties and you may consider yourself under open arrest. Is that clear?'

'Sir!'

'Dismissed.'

9

'There will be no Court of Enquiry, nor will there be any civil inquest,' insisted Commodore Surridge firmly.

'But, sir,' protested Ferguson, 'a man has been killed under questionable circumstances and for which Staff Sergeant Keppler is entirely to blame. We can't possibly ignore the situation.'

Surridge gazed at him steadily. 'Teddy, I still don't think you've quite grasped just how important all this is. Nothing, but nothing, can be allowed to jeopardise this exercise – and those are Churchill's words, not mine. What happened to Smith was a tragic accident, just that. It happens all the time during training. Premature explosions, faulty fuses – it's all part of war. Smith's body will be taken to the nearest military morgue where it will be kept until the mission is completed. After that, Smith's family will be informed of his death with the official records showing he was killed in action. We might even manage a medal for him.'

'So there's going to be a cover-up? And what about Keppler?'

'What about him? He'll carry on with training as normal – except, of course, in future there will be strictly no deviation from the prescribed programme.'

'And what about the men? After all, they did see one of their...'

'The men will do as they are told,' Surridge snapped irritably. 'Let's not forget they *are* subject to both military discipline and the Official Secrets Act, so there's an end to it. Now... ' He picked up Ferguson's performance report. 'Are these the latest results?'

The major nodded. 'They were drawn up last Friday by Keppler and Walters.'

'It's a pity Smith was part of Jackdaw Two. They were the most promising. Who's running second at the moment?'

'We could easily transfer a man from one of the other teams to Jackdaw Two,' suggested Ferguson, sidestepping the Commodore's question. 'To replace Smith I mean.'

'No, I don't think that would be a good idea. Team spirit wouldn't be the same.' He looked up. 'By the way, did you hear the eight o'clock news this morning?'

'You mean the new Stalingrad offensive? Yes, yes I did. Rather worrying to say the least. If the Germans make a concerted push this time, it'll finish the Russians. They can't hold out for ever.'

'I agree.' Surridge sat thoughtfully in one of the easy chairs in front of Ferguson's desk. 'It may mean we'll have to bring forward the start date of our little show. Otherwise, we might be just too late.'

'Too late for what? How d'you mean, "too late"?'

Surridge shook his head as he opened the report and began to read. 'Can't explain at the moment. Sorry, but you'll know soon enough. Good God!' He looked up at Ferguson in surprise. 'Is this right?'

The major shrugged. 'You mean Jackdaw Three?' He nodded. 'Both instructors are of a like mind. On overall performance, they put them in second place.'

'But damn it man!' retorted Surridge irascibly. 'I thought you said they weren't getting it together. Rows, arguments, that sort of thing.'

'That *was* true, but they appear to have overcome their differences, and I must say they're putting more effort into the training than any other group.'

A sceptical frown remained on Surridge's face as he

continued scanning the report. 'Hmmph! I see Nicholson hasn't been able to conquer his vertigo. Still unable to tackle the rope bridge.' He closed the report. 'Pity really. Spoils it for the others.'

'I don't think we need to concern ourselves too much, Commodore. Only Staff Sergeant Keppler chose to include that criticism. In any event, I rather doubt they'll find too many rope bridges stretched across the streets of Berlin.'

The sarcasm wasn't lost on Surridge.

'You're missing the point, Major,' he said angrily. 'Staff Keppler is right to include it in the report. A real SS officer is afraid of nothing. *Nothing!* Nicholson has shown a weakness, and he may have others, ones we don't yet know about.'

He got to his feet and strode to the window, hands clasped behind his back. When he spoke again, his voice was calmer.

'Teddy, we have to be absolutely damned sure of the men we send. We can't afford a weak member in the team. The success of this mission is so important, so vital, the slightest risk of failure is unacceptable!' He looked out of the window at the four groups, who were undergoing rigorous physical training in front of the house. 'We cannot... We *must* not fail!'

The final words were uttered so softly Ferguson hardly heard them.

The Major pursed his lips. 'My apologies if I sounded flippant. I didn't intend it that way. It would of course help if I knew just what the job is all about...'

Surridge turned away from the window shaking his head. 'No, I can't. Not yet. Sorry, Teddy – all in good time. Now, let's get back to young Nicholson. He really does need to overcome this silly fear of heights. Get the two instructors to harry him. I'm sure he can do it if he really tries.'

Ferguson looked dubious. 'Vertigo isn't something overcome that easily.' He looked at the Commodore. 'You don't propose to discount Jackdaw Three if he fails, do you?'

123

Surridge thought for a moment.

'No, I don't suppose I do,' he replied slowly. 'Particularly if they maintain their present form. Nevertheless, it'll do no harm for him not to know that. Give him a bit of incentive, don't you think?' Not waiting for an answer, he stood up. 'Now then. I'm due back in London for a meeting this afternoon. The Prime Minister wants to go over a few points regarding the exercise.'

Over the following week there was a noticeable intensification in the training. The tragic death of Smith seemed to have made little impact on Keppler who, together with the normally milder Walters, subjected the remaining fifteen men to even harsher treatment. Rumours ran rife among the four teams regarding the reasons for the sudden increase in training and these only ended when one evening, while they were busily engaged on equipment cleaning, the four members of Jackdaw Three were unexpectedly summoned to the Lecture Room.

Happily abandoning the wax polish, Brasso and cleaning utensils, they quickly made themselves reasonably presentable and hurried downstairs to the Lecture Room where, each filled with a mixture of excitement and apprehension, they trooped into the room where Commodore Surridge, Ferguson and the two instructors were waiting for them.

'Thank you gentlemen,' the Commodore said smiling. 'Please take a seat, would you.'

He indicated the front row of four chairs that had become their customary seats.

'Well, gentlemen I have some splendid news for you. You'll be pleased to hear that your training has now come to an end and, in the opinion of both instructors, Jackdaw Three has proven to be the most resourceful and successful of the four teams with the result that you four have been selected to undertake the mission. That opinion, incidentally, has been endorsed by Major Ferguson.' He gave a glazed smile to Nicholson. 'Despite a minor problem with the rope bridge.' The cockney's face remained expressionless.

'Sorry, no questions at the moment,' Surridge continued, holding up a restraining hand as Keppler began to open his mouth. 'Security is still paramount.' He looked down at the clipboard he was holding. 'From now on things will start to move rather quickly. First of all, tomorrow morning at 0900 hours, the four of you will report to the barber who, I can assure you, is a skilled tattooist, and he will tattoo a blood group number on the underside of your left arms. The number will not be *your* blood group, but that of the SS officer you are impersonating.' He smiled apologetically. 'Sorry about this, but it has to be done. We can't take any chances – a careless moment in the shower for instance. All SS personnel carry their blood group on that part of their arm, and if it wasn't there, then the game would be up. But we'll soon have it removed when you get back.' He referred again to his clipboard. 'After that, at ten hundred, you'll report to Major Ferguson who will fill you in on your itinerary for the next few days, which, incidentally, starts with dinner tomorrow evening.'

He looked apologetically at the two instructors.

'I'm sorry, gentlemen, but for security reasons the dinner has to be restricted to myself, Major Ferguson and the four members of the group. I'm sure you understand.'

Turning back to the four men, he continued.

'After dinner, I'll be able to brief you on the operation. After that, you will be kept incommunicado with the other groups, until the time comes for you to leave. That could be in as little as twenty-four hours, so be prepared.' He rose to his feet. 'That'll be all for now, thank you gentlemen. I look forward to seeing you at dinner tomorrow evening when I shall be able to answer all your questions.'

The two instructors and the four men respectfully rose to

their feet as Surridge and Ferguson made their way to the door. On reaching it, Surridge turned back to face them.

'One other thing. Dinner tomorrow evening. Dress is formal. Mess uniforms will be made available to you from the stores. Thank you.'

He disappeared through the door, Ferguson in tow.

Immediately they had gone, Keppler turned on Nicholson.

'Well, how about it?' he challenged. 'You heard what the Commodore said. Don't you reckon you ought to make one last attempt to overcome this stupid fear of yours? At least *try* to prove you're a man.'

Nicholson leapt to his feet, but Sinclair quickly pulled him back.

'He doesn't have to prove anything,' the big Canadian said softly. 'I haven't any problems about it, neither have Thompson nor Callendar. So leave him alone, Keppler.'

Keppler, who had been leaning against the wall, immediately straightened up, fists clenched. He glared menacingly at Sinclair who responded by swiftly rising from his chair and taking up an aggressive stance.

For a moment it looked as though the situation would turn nasty but Walters quickly stepped between the two antagonists.

'Let's all calm down, shall we? No point in arguing over something that's not that important,' he said quietly.

He turned to the four members of Jackdaw Three. 'You four had better save your energy. I think you'll all be needing it before long. Now cut along to your billet.'

126

10

Callendar opened his eyes to a blinding shaft of early morning sunlight flooding through a chink in the blackout curtains onto his face. He was invariably the first to wake each morning but today, as he turned his head away from the bright sunlight, he noticed Nicholson's bed was empty. It had been neatly made up as usual, ready for inspection, but of the red-haired cockney there was no sign. Callendar glanced at his watch. The hands showed five-thirty, still half an hour to go before reveille. He frowned as he contemplated the empty camp bed. It was so out of character. Normally Nicholson was last to get up, usually only after he had been tipped out by one or more of the others.

Sliding his legs out from under the blankets, Callendar padded over to where Sinclair lay, snoring softly. A gentle shake of the shoulder was all that was necessary to rouse the big man.

'What's wrong?' he asked, instantly alert.

'It's Nicholson. He's not in his bed.'

Sinclair glanced over at the empty bed then looked at Callendar. 'You don't think...?'

'Christ Almighty! The bloody fool! Come on, let's move. Give Thompson a shake, will you?'

The three men dressed hurriedly and were soon running across the sun-drenched meadowland towards the distant cluster of Douglas firs forming part of the assault course. They were panting breathlessly by the time they approached the tall conifers, slowing their pace to a walk as they headed to where the rope bridge was located. Only the sound of birds in morning chorus disturbed the rural tranquillity.

'Maybe I'm wrong,' panted Callendar. 'Maybe...'

'I hope to God you are,' interrupted Thompson, pointing a finger. 'Look!'

It was all too obvious something was not right. The bridge still linked the two tall Douglas firs, except that it now hung drunkenly to one side. Sinclair was the first to spot Nicholson. He was lying on his back, eyes staring sightlessly at the sky, his head twisted at an unnatural angle.

As he sank to the soft earth he knew he had no real need to feel for a pulse, but he did so anyway. Looking up at the others he slowly shook his head.

'Oh, Christ no! No!' yelled Callendar, his legs suddenly weak. 'Why? Why did he have to do it? There was no need!' He sank to his knees. 'Why did you do it?' he demanded of the lifeless form, as tears welled up in his eyes. 'You bloody, bloody fool!'

Sinclair looked up between the two trees.

'Perhaps we should also be asking how it happened,' he said quietly.

'What d'you mean?' asked Thompson, who had been kneeling beside Callendar. 'It was an accident. It has to be, surely?'

'Was it?' the big man replied. He looked again at the rope bridge. 'I'm not so sure. Don't you think it a bit strange? Fifteen of us used this bridge nearly every day for the past month with no problems. Then Nicholson comes out here on his own, when no-one's around and suddenly the bridge collapses. I don't buy it.'

He looked back at the trees for a moment.

'Look, why don't you two shoot off and report to the Major? While you're gone, I'll have a nosey around. See what I can find.'

Thompson pulled Callendar to his feet, giving him a

128

reassuring pat on the back. 'Come on, old son. There's nothing we can do for him now. Let's get going.' They both set off back to the Lodge.

After they had gone, Sinclair wandered across to the second tree and carefully climbed the rope ladder to the platform. It had been well constructed from thick planks of hardwood and showed no signs of damage, other than the wear and tear caused by the men's boots. A strong eyebolt had been sunk into the supporting members underneath the platform, to which the footrope remained firmly secured; neither the rope, nor the bolt showed any signs of damage or interference. Next he turned his attention to the two eyebolts embedded in the trunk of the tree securing the two rope handrails. One handrail rope remained firmly attached, but the other appeared to have snapped where it passed through the eye. The eye of the bolt was still closed, indicating that the rope could not have slipped out. Then he examined the metal bolts more closely, cautiously sniffing each in turn. He frowned, dropped to his knees and sniffed the platform directly under each of the eyebolts, where the timber carried slight staining. The frown deepened. He had recognised the smell.

'You bastard, Keppler!' he muttered. 'This time you've gone too far.'

The sound of approaching voices made him look up and, not wishing to be seen taking too much of an interest in the damaged bridge, he quickly slid down the rope ladder and was on the ground by the time the group arrived.

Callendar and Thompson were in the lead, Major Ferguson close behind, accompanied by the Camp Medical Officer with two medical orderlies carrying a stretcher and, bringing up the rear, Keppler and Walters. Whilst the MO busied himself examining Nicholson's body, Sinclair moved quietly across to where Keppler was standing at the back of the group.

'Are you satisfied?' he hissed through clenched teeth,

thrusting his face within inches of the instructor's. 'He's dead and it's your bloody fault, you murdering bastard!'

His pent-up emotions suddenly boiled over. Unable to contain himself any longer, he let fly with both fists. The first blow, a right to the solar plexus, knocked the wind out of Keppler, making him double over. As his head dropped down, it met a crisp left hook on the side of his face. Finally, the *coup de grâce*, a powerful right uppercut, almost lifting the man off his feet, sent him flying backwards to land in a crumpled heap. It was over in seconds, before anyone had a chance to intervene.

'What the hell's going on?' yelled Ferguson, turning from Nicholson's corpse and glaring at Sinclair. 'Stop it! Stop it at once!'

He strode across to the Scots-Canadian. 'Consider yourself under arrest!' Then, turning to Callendar and Thompson. 'You two, take him to my office and stay with him until I get there. That's an order!'

Keppler was on his knees, massaging a sore face and jaw. 'Doc! I think your services are more urgently needed here.'

'What the hell was that all about?' demanded Thompson, throwing a puzzled glance at Sinclair as the three men marched off towards Ferguson's office.

The big man stared straight ahead, his face set in a mask. 'I told you something was wrong. The rope bridge *had* been tampered with. Some form of acid had been poured on the handrail ropes at the point where they pass through the securing eyebolts. Hydrochloric or sulphuric, I'm not sure which. But whatever it was, it was probably poured on last night, which would give it enough time to weaken the ropes so the next time someone walked across their body weight would finish the job.'

'But that's murder!' exclaimed Callendar. 'Why should anyone want to kill Bob?'

'I don't think the intention was to kill him. Taunting him

130

as he did, Keppler knew Nicholson would rise to the bait, particularly after the Commodore's comment last night. No, he just wanted to scare the shit out of him even more. Only it all went horribly wrong, just as it did when Smith was killed on the grenade range.' He shook his head. 'The man's mad.'

Thompson looked thoughtful. 'What if you're right? About the acid, I mean. How are you going to prove it?'

'You can still smell it. The rope stinks of it.'

'But that doesn't mean Keppler was responsible.'

'Who else?' retorted Sinclair tersely. He lengthened his stride, indicating the conversation closed.

'Whatever your reasons,' thundered Ferguson, slamming his fist on the desk, 'there can be no justification for your unprovoked assault on Staff Sergeant Keppler. None whatsoever!'

He glared angrily at Sinclair, standing stiffly at attention in front of his desk, flanked by Callendar and Thompson. The major had kept them waiting for almost two hours before he had eventually returned to his office. Yet the time-lapse had done little to dissipate his anger.

'Under normal circumstances, this would have been a matter for a Court Martial. You do realise that?'

Sinclair's face remained impassive. 'Yes, sir.'

'Well? What have you got to say for yourself? Am I to presume you blame Staff Keppler for Nicholson's death?'

The Scots-Canadian said nothing.

'Well?' insisted Ferguson, impatience creeping into his voice.

'Sir? May I say something?' interjected Callendar respectfully.

Ferguson sighed. 'Yes, if it's relevant.'

'Sir, we have reason to believe the rope bridge was tampered with ... and that Nicholson was set up.'

131

'What?' retorted Ferguson. 'What on earth are you talking about?'

'The handrail ropes, sir,' said Thompson. 'We believe acid was deliberately poured on them. That's why they snapped.'

'And I suppose you think Staff Sergeant Keppler had something to do with it. Is that it?'

'He's had it in for Nicholson ever since we arrived here. Everyone knows that.' This time it was Sinclair who spoke.

'Utter nonsense!' exclaimed the major. 'Staff Sergeant Keppler had nothing to do with the failure of the bridge. The Royal Engineers were responsible for building that assault course, including the rope bridge, and they've already been across to have a look at the damaged section. That's what delayed me in getting here. Oh, yes! Acid was present on the ropes and, indeed, probably caused their failure. But the acid was contained in a compound applied to the *eyebolts*, not to the *ropes*. Applied, incidentally, by the Royal Engineers themselves. Some sort of long-term corrosion inhibitor they're experimenting with.' He paused to take a breath. 'Unfortunately, no one seemed to appreciate the effect the acid content would have on the rope. Hence the accident and poor Nicholson's death. And, gentlemen, it *was* an accident!'

He stared hard at the three of them, before wearily gesturing with his hand. 'Sit down, all of you.'

The brusque manner disappeared.

'Look, I know how you must feel about young Nicholson and I'm sorry. I know how close all of you had become.' He picked up a report sheet on his desk. 'The four of you had a rocky start when you first joined, but you've surprised us all. Over the past weeks, you developed into a close-knit team, which was precisely what we were looking for and why your group was selected as the final choice.' He laid the report back down on the desk. 'It also may surprise you to know that your group was strongly recommended, not only by Staff Sergeant Walters, but by Staff Keppler as well. He has a very high opinion of all of you – and that included Nicholson.'

He drummed his fingers on the desk.

'Which brings me on to another point. With Nicholson ... gone, the team is obviously now incomplete. I've spoken to Commodore Surridge and he is adamant that we can't go with only three men. Which leaves us with a problem.' He took a deep breath. 'It appears a degree of urgency has now crept into the situation, which means we can't afford any delays. So, we're left with two alternatives. Firstly, you three can step down if you wish, in which case we send in another group. Or, alternatively, we make up your number by transferring someone from one of the other groups. It's up to you.'

The three men exchanged glances, both Sinclair and Callendar looking expectantly at Thompson. The older man pursed his lips. It was a heaven-sent opportunity to escape his commitment and do so with dignity. Seconds passed. Then he seemed to make up his mind.

'Speaking for myself,' he said quietly, 'I came here to do a job. That hasn't changed.'

His response surprised Ferguson, who looked questioningly at the other two. After a brief glance at each other, both nodded their agreement

'There is a third alternative,' continued Ferguson, tapping his fingers on the desk. 'Both instructors have expressed a willingness to take Nicholson's place.' He quickly held up his hand. 'Now, don't dismiss the idea too readily. It could have some merit. After all, Staff Keppler is half German and spent a short time in the SS before the war and, therefore, has valuable practical experience and Staff Walters worked in Berlin for a number of years and knows the geography of the place like the back of his hand. The choice is yours, gentlemen. If you want time to think about it, then you'll have to be quick. There's little time to spare.'

133

'There's no way any of us would accept Keppler on the team,' replied Sinclair quietly. 'Not after what's happened to Nicholson.'

'*Staff Sergeant* Keppler, I think you mean,' said Ferguson coldly.

The Scots-Canadian made no comment.

'All right. Who is to be? A volunteer from one of the other groups, or Staff Walters? That is, of course, if you don't have any violent objections to his inclusion.'

Sinclair shrugged. 'He's OK as far as I'm concerned. But I can't speak for the others.'

'How about you two?'

'His knowledge of Berlin could be useful,' Callendar admitted. 'I only spent my holidays there. My memories of the place are a bit sketchy to say the least.'

'I've no objections to the man,' responded Thompson. 'He seems reasonable enough.'

'Good. Then that's settled.'

He glanced at his watch and stood up. The three men followed suit.

'Now you'd better cut along to the barber's and get those numbers tattooed. You'll also have to have photographs taken for your SS Identity Cards. I'll arrange for that to be done later on this afternoon. Meanwhile, I'll let Staff Walters know of your decision and I'll inform the Commodore. Which reminds me, I'll have to pick out an identity to suit Staff Walters. Thank you, gentlemen. Dismiss.'

The three men came smartly to attention, automatically gave the Nazi salute with the customary 'Heil Hitler' and marched from the room. Ferguson smiled to himself. Keppler and Walters had done a good job.

'Now keepa your arm still, if you don't wanna me to make da mistake,' instructed Angelo, frowning with concentration

134

as he worked away with his needle, pricking the skin and injecting bluish dye to the underside of Sinclair's left arm.

'Sorry, Angelo. The arm's aching a bit, holding it in this position,' apologised Sinclair.

The little Italian nodded. 'It'sa OK. Nearly finished now. Are you the lasta one?'

'No, one more to come. Staff Sergeant Walters. He'll be over later on.'

'There, all finished,' announced Angelo proudly, standing back to admire his handiwork.

Sinclair peered at the row of neatly applied bluish grey characters etched into the white skin under his upper arm. The skin around the lettering was already turning a blotchy pink, a sure sign of the soreness that would follow. He compared the number with the one written on the piece of paper he had given to the barber. They matched.

'Why you wanna me to do this?' questioned the Italian, a puzzled frown on his chubby face. 'Why you want Nazi numbers on your arms? Better I give you picture of lovely mermaid, or naked lady. Yes?'

He smiled hopefully at Sinclair.

'Sorry, Angelo, can't tell you. "It'sa bigga da secret",' he mimicked. 'And no, you can't give me a mermaid or a naked lady. Major Ferguson wouldn't approve.'

'OK, OK,' the little Italian replied sadly, heaving a great sigh. Then a big smile appeared on his face. 'When dis war, she is over, you come to Italia, si? To Roma. I do special tattoo for you. OK? No charge!'

He looked hopefully at Sinclair, but before the Scots-Canadian could reply, the smile slipped from the Italian's face. Clearly, the sudden thought of his lovely Italy was too much for him. He turned away and stared out of the window.

'Roma! My heart, she aches for to see my wife and bambini,' he murmured softly. 'It'sa not right for a man to be kept from his family.' He turned round again, his lower lip quivering. 'It'sa been three years since I saw them. I don'ta know how much longer I can stand it. I have to get back to Italia.' He looked pleadingly at Sinclair, holding both hands in supplication. 'Can you help me? Please help me! Speaka to da Majori for me. He listen to you.'

Sinclair knew only too well how the poor little Italian was suffering. The mention of family brought memories of his own dead wife and child flooding back. He closed his eyes, clenching his fists. He felt genuine sorrow for the little man, but there was nothing he could do or say to help him.

'Sorry, Angelo,' he replied tersely. 'Nothing I can do. You'll see your family again, never fear. Just be patient. The war will end one day.'

Unable to bear the sight of the tears running down the Italian's chubby cheeks, Sinclair left the room abruptly, rejoining the other two who were waiting outside.

'Come on, let's get out of here,' he grunted, and walked rapidly away through the murky rain.

'What's the hurry?' queried Callendar, as he and Thompson hastened to catch up.

'That poor bastard in there, tearing himself to pieces because he's missing his family.' He looked across at Thompson. 'I hope you know what you're doing!'

'I've told you before,' he retorted stonily. 'You don't have to worry about me.'

'Come on, you two. Let's get back to the billet before we get soaked,' urged Callendar. 'It's already been a long day and it's not over yet. Anyway, there's something I want to do. I don't know if it'll do any good, but I think I'd like to write a letter to Nicholson's family.'

When they arrived at the Lodge they found Ferguson waiting for them. He ushered them into the lecture room where a sergeant in the Intelligence Corps was waiting to take their identity photographs. For this they were required to don a Waffen SS jacket and cap.

'You'll be given your photos just before you leave,' said Ferguson. 'Whenever the Commodore decides that's to be.'

The three men spent the afternoon writing letters home – Thompson to his wife and children, Sinclair to his folks back in Canada, Callendar to Daphne, to his own family, and, finally, a difficult one to Nicholson's. They all knew it was the last chance they would have of putting pen to paper before leaving the Jackdaw's Nest.

The rain, which had started to fall shortly after their meeting with Ferguson, had continued throughout the day, accompanied by occasional flashes of lightning and noisy rumbles of thunder. By early evening, the clouds had thickened so much they had to switch on the lights in the billet. At about six o'clock a particularly intense flash of lightning suddenly illuminated the room, followed by a noise like an express train, as the ensuing thunder rolled around the heavens. At the same time, the lights in the billet dimmed almost to extinction for a brief second, before recovering their normal power.

'That was close,' Thompson commented wryly. 'Must have affected the power lines.'

11

'Thank you Simpson, that'll be all for the time being. I'll ring if there's anything else. Meanwhile, we're not to be disturbed under any circumstances. *Any* circumstances whatsoever! Is that clear?'

The Commodore's tone left the orderly in no doubt he meant exactly what he said and, after hurriedly clearing the last of the dishes onto the dinner trolley, Simpson headed swiftly towards the door. When the door had closed behind him, Surridge turned back to his dinner guests.

As requested, they had all donned mess uniform for the occasion. The Commodore himself was in naval dress, Ferguson wore that of the Coldstream Guards and the other four, Walters, Sinclair, Callendar and Thompson, were attired in the black mess uniforms of the Waffen SS.

'First of all, gentlemen, may I thank you for taking the trouble to wear mess dress this evening, which I feel is entirely appropriate for the occasion and, I have to say, the four of you look entirely convincing.' He turned to Walters. 'Staff, you and Colour Sergeant Keppler are to be congratulated. You've done an excellent job.' Then, turning to the others, 'And as for you three, well done. I know you've all worked jolly hard to achieve what you have and I've every confidence you'll carry through the task that lies before you.'

He paused, his face sombre. 'Before I divulge details of that task, however, it would be remiss of me not to express regret for today's tragic accident.' He shook his head. 'It's ironic; there was no need for him to attempt that rope bridge. But he did and I, for one, can't help but admire the man's

138

determination to conquer his fear. I don't really want to say any more. It was simply a dreadful accident, so let's leave it at that.'

Both Thompson and Callendar glanced at Sinclair, but the big man said nothing. He sat impassively watching the Commodore, who had reached forward and picked up one of the small Nazi flags adorning the table.

'Gentlemen, the time has come when I can at last reveal the purpose of all the training you have had to endure and why security has been necessarily strict. But first, we must start with a history lesson. How much do any of you know about the swastika?' He held up the flag and looked questioningly around the table. 'Apart from its being the symbol of the Nazi Party, that is,' he added quickly, before anyone stated the obvious.

The question brought blank stares from all but Ferguson.

'I seem to recall reading somewhere that it's quite an ancient design. Is that right?' the Major ventured.

'Absolutely right,' nodded the Commodore. 'In fact, and contrary to the popular belief that Adolf Hitler created the swastika, evidence of its existence goes back as far as the Palaeolithic period. In other words, gentlemen, not just thousands of years, but tens of thousands. Indeed, the earliest discovery so far comes from a site in the Ukraine, where a swastika was found etched on the underside of a bird's wing, which itself had been carved on a mammoth's tusk. And, gentlemen, the last mammoth existed over ten thousand years ago!'

He replaced the flag.

'Apart from this find in the Ukraine,' the Commodore continued, 'evidence of the swastika's early existence has been found in China, India, Persia, Scandinavia and even among the red Indian tribes of North America. It was used variously as a religious artefact, a good luck symbol, or simply as a decorative design. Indeed, many notable figures before Hitler adopted the swastika as a symbol of good luck, perhaps the most famous of these being Alexander the III of Macedonia – Alexander the Great, as he is better known. You will doubtless recall from your schooldays that he was the youngest and most successful military commander the world has ever known. Educated by Aristotle, he became King of Macedonia at the age of twenty, after the murder of his father Philip and having disposed of a number of his rivals.'

The Commodore sipped his brandy.

'As with all monarchs of years ago, Alexander led his armies personally and, on the eve of his famous battle with the Persians, his old mentor, Aristotle, presented him with a newly-designed personal standard, the central motif of which happened to be a swastika.

'The overwhelming success of his Persian campaign left Alexander convinced his new standard had brought him good luck and had been responsible for his victory. Thereafter, he refused to travel anywhere without it. Unfortunately, shortly after he had defeated Darius the standard was destroyed by fire and Alexander immediately ordered a swastika to be cast using gold taken from the vast treasure his armies had captured from the Persian king at Persepolis. He employed the most skilful of the Persian goldsmiths and had the base of the swastika inscribed with a record of his victory over the Persians.

'From then on he always took the gold swastika with him, convinced it held some mystical power which was the source of his triumph and good fortune. His subsequent victories seemed to confirm that belief. So much so that he became obsessed with the fear of losing it, or having it stolen, and it was therefore guarded day and night by his personal guards.

'Despite this high level of security, one day it went missing from his tent. Its loss sent him berserk and he immediately ordered every member of his personal guard be slain as punishment. An exhaustive search followed which lasted for days, but the swastika was never found. Angry and feeling betrayed, Alexander sought solace in drink. Night after night he drank until, after a night of particularly heavy indulgence, he died, probably from alcoholic poisoning. It was 323 BC and Alexander was just thirty-two years of age.

'The thief was never discovered and the swastika disappeared for well over two thousand years. Then, in 1909, a German archaeologist named Helmut Diels uncovered a hoard of artefacts at an ancient site in Persia. He brought a number of these items back to Germany for further study. Amongst them was a golden swastika.'

At this point the Commodore reached behind him to pick up a large brown manila envelope. Pulling open the flap, he inverted the envelope, allowing a number of sepia photographs to spill onto the polished surface of the dining table. They all carried the same picture: a gold swastika, surrounded by a laurel wreath and mounted on a base of the same metal. As they studied the photographs, the Commodore continued his narration.

'Diels was an expert on ancient Greece and therefore was able to translate the ancient Koine writing on the base of the swastika. Realising the significance of his find and its probable value, Diels decided to keep it for himself, but disguised it with a covering of bronze coloured paint. The problem was, like all the other artefacts that had been uncovered, it had been photographed at the time of its discovery. That's a copy of the original photograph you're all looking at.

'On his return to Germany, Diels was questioned on its whereabouts by the museum who had funded the expedition. He pleaded ignorance, claiming he had no idea what had happened to it; he suggested it had probably been lost or stolen in transit from Persia. The museum's directors had no idea of its famous origins and with so many other interesting items brought back by Diels they were not unduly concerned at its loss. However, Professor Diels was destined not to benefit from his dishonesty, for he had contracted a mysterious illness whilst in Persia which was to prove fatal. Believing it to be a punishment for his wrongdoing, Diels made a deathbed confession to his wife and told her the whole story. The dear lady, frightened of what the authorities might do, hid the swastika and kept silent about the whole affair.

'But her husband's death brought hardship for Frau Diels and her situation worsened with Germany's economic decline after the Great War. Eventually, in 1920, she was forced to start selling her possessions, including her personal jewellery. It was whilst rummaging through the house she once more came across the bronze-coloured swastika. Remembering what her husband had said about its value, and possibly reassured by the passage of ten years or so, she sold it to a pawnbroker in Munich, the same one to whom she had also sold her jewellery.

'A week or so later, she read in the local newspaper of the pawnbroker's murder. Although horrified by the killing, she didn't attach any particular meaning to his death. Not at the time, that is.' The Commodore again paused and reached behind him for a second manila envelope. 'It was also about this time,' he continued, clearing his throat, 'that Hitler and his new Nazi Party were becoming noticed in Munich, attracting publicity with their Nationalistic and anti-Semitic views. A right-wing newspaper, the *Völkischer Beobachter*, carried a report on one of their meetings held at the Hofbrauhaus, together with a photograph. The photograph showed Hitler and his cronies sitting around a table, and on the table stood a gold swastika which, apart from its colour, was recognised by Frau Diels as the same one she had sold to the murdered pawnbroker a week or so earlier.' He inverted the second envelope and more pictures slid out, this time copies of the newspaper photograph.

142

'Are you suggesting Hitler had something to do with the murder?' interrupted Thompson.

'Possibly,' replied the Commodore, 'but that's not the point of the story. It's the swastika that's important, Alexander's swastika. Up to the time he acquired the artefact in 1920, Hitler had been nothing. A nonentity. Few people had even heard of him. Then, suddenly, it all began to change. People started listening to his speeches. Membership of his party, the NSDAP, increased rapidly and soon his followers numbered thousands. Flushed with success, he made an attempted *coup d'état* in Munich in 1923. It failed, but it taught him a number of lessons and from then on his popularity and success grew until the Nazis took power in the Reichstag in 1933.' He surveyed his guests. 'Some politicians take a lifetime to achieve something as simple as junior minister. Yet, in the relatively short time-span of thirteen years, Adolf Hitler rose from being a nobody to becoming the leader of eighty million people!'

Ferguson looked sceptical. 'Commodore, surely you're not suggesting that Hitler's rise to power was due simply to his possession of this gold swastika?'

'Don't be too quick to judge, Major. Many intensive studies have been made of Adolf Hitler and it's accepted by all those who carried out those studies that he fervently believes in Destiny. That Destiny made him leader of the German people and that same Destiny has turned him into a military genius, just as Alexander was before him. Like Alexander, he really believes his success is due to the ancient swastika. Indeed, some researchers are of the opinion that Hitler considers himself the reincarnation of Alexander. It doesn't matter a hoot whether or not you and I believe the swastika has supernatural power; the important thing is that Hitler believes it. He also shares Alexander's fear of losing it. That's why his office in the Chancellery is guarded twenty-four hours a day by armed members of the Liebstandarte SS, his own personal body-guard.'

He picked up the photograph of the swastika and stared at it.

'Hitler is as fanatical about it as Alexander was. He treasures it more than life itself and is paranoid about its being stolen or lost. And that, gentlemen, is Hitler's Achilles heel. If he loses the swastika he'll be finished, destroyed by his own irrational beliefs.' He looked at the faces of the four men. 'This is precisely what you've been trained for. You're going to infiltrate the Liebstandarte, be picked to guard Hitler's office in the Reichs Chancellery, steal his ancient gold swastika right from under his nose and bring it back to England.'

The silence was broken only by the loud tick of the clock on the wall. Thompson was the first to speak.

'I'm sorry, sir, but I find it all rather incredible. Too fantastic to be true.'

'So do I,' said Ferguson.

'Of course it sounds incredible,' Surridge conceded without hesitation. 'Exactly that. It does sound too fantastic to be true. But these predictions of Hitler's reaction to the loss of his beloved swastika, or rather *Hakenkreuz*, as the Germans call it, have been arrived at by the best psychiatric people available. They're convinced its loss will destroy him – and so is the Prime Minister. This whole operation has his full personal backing.'

He stared down at his fingers before again looking up.

'I know it sounds unbelievable. And it's a hell of a lot to expect from you: to ask to risk your lives simply to steal an ancient lump of gold. When we had our first briefing I stressed that this operation would be undertaken purely on a voluntary basis. Mr Churchill himself insisted on that. If any one of you wants to withdraw, even at this stage, he is free to do so.'

The Commodore's gaze wandered round the table, fixing

144

each man in turn, seeking their individual response. First was Callendar, still suffering from Nicholson's death – his appetite at dinner had been noticeably lacking.

'If it has the backing of Churchill, then it must be important. I'm still ready to go,' he said quietly.

'Good man!' exclaimed the Commodore. He turned to Sinclair. The big Scots-Canadian also nodded.

'Crazy it may be, but if it means it'll shorten the war, if only by a few days, that's reason enough. Sure, I'm still willing.'

'Excellent!'

Surridge turned to Walters. 'It didn't apply to you at the time, Colour. Nevertheless, you have the option now.'

Walters grinned. 'That's why I volunteered, sir. I've a few scores to settle. I just hope I get the opportunity.'

'I'm sure you will. I knew I could rely on you.'

Finally, he looked at Thompson. 'I know you had some misgivings right from the start. How do you feel now? You know you can back out if you want to. I promise there'll be no recriminations.'

Everyone's eyes fell on the older man, trying to read his mind. The faintest of smiles appeared on his face. 'At least we know now why you chose the name Jackdaw's Nest for this place – that particular bird has a propensity for stealing bright objects.'

'Exactly so. And your response to the question?'

Thompson sighed. 'I can't let these idiots go on their own. They'll only get themselves into trouble if I'm not there. You've got yourself a team, sir.'

'Excellent, excellent!' exclaimed Surridge, slamming his hand down on the table in excitement. 'What d'you think now, eh Teddy?'

The major shrugged his shoulders. 'Who can argue? Nevertheless, I still find the whole affair utterly bizarre.'

'Never mind that. Let's get on with the details.'

He reached behind him for yet another manila folder, which he opened up and started reading.

'Now, you'll all leave here at 0700 hours tomorrow morning and be taken by car to a nearby military airfield. From there you will fly to Scotland where you will board one of His Majesty's submarines. The sub will take you across the North Sea and into the Skagerrak, where you will rendezvous with a Swedish cargo ship, the *Hilversund*, which will take you to Rostock on the north German coast. There you'll leave the ship disguised as Swedish seamen out on an evening's drinking and head for a tavern called *Das Wildschwein* – one of the sailors will give you directions. There you must order your drinks from the landlord, a man named Josef.' He wagged a finger. 'No one else but the landlord. That's important. And you must say, "Do you sell Schwanstein beer here?" He will reply, "No, that is a Bavarian beer. We only sell local beer in this tavern." Now it's important you get this right. It will identify you to the landlord and he will arrange for you to meet your contact. From there on, it's up to you. Any questions?'

'Just one,' responded Thompson. 'You haven't yet mentioned how we're supposed to get back to England.'

'Good question,' Surridge acknowledged. 'Don't worry, it's all been arranged by your contact. I won't go into details here, but you'll all be coming back via Switzerland. Now, let's drink a toast to a successful operation.'

As he stood up a knock came at the door. Frowning irritably he called out, 'Yes! Come in.'

The steward entered nervously.

'Simpson, I thought I said...'

'Sorry, sir,' interrupted the steward. 'Urgent message from Staff Sergeant Keppler.'

He handed the Commodore a folded sheet of notepaper.

Surridge unfolded it. As he read the message his face blanched. He looked at the steward.

146

'You know about this?'

'Yes, sir.'

'All right, Simpson. That'll be all.'

He waited until the door had closed. 'I'm sorry to have to tell you there's been another accident. The Italian barber, Capaldi. The perimeter guard found him ten minutes ago, lying near the electrified fence. I'm afraid he's dead, electrocuted. It would appear he was trying to break out of the camp.'

'Oh, my God!' exclaimed Ferguson, casting his eyes towards the ceiling. 'What a bloody fool!'

'Poor sod!' Walters commented. 'He was only saying to me this afternoon how much he wanted to get home to his wife and kids. Christ! He must have been desperate.'

'Yeah, he was. Said the same thing to me a couple of times,' observed Sinclair.

'But he knew the fence was electrified,' protested Callendar. 'Why in heaven's name would he try something so stupid?'

'You'd have to have a wife and kids and love them as much as he did, to understand,' replied Thompson softly. 'Perhaps he couldn't bear the separation any longer. Now he'll never see them, God rest his soul.'

'But...'

'Let's just leave it there shall we?' the Commodore said firmly, interrupting Callendar's protest. 'I'm afraid it's rather academic why he tried. Suffice it to say, the poor man paid an awful price for his foolishness.' He looked across at Ferguson. 'Would you make sure his wife is informed. Through the usual Red Cross channels of course.'

Surridge turned back to the four men. His voice was terse.

'Gentlemen, don't let today's tragic events deter you. We're all grown men and, heaven knows we've all seen many tragic deaths during the past three years. You four have a unique opportunity to be instrumental in bringing this war to a rapid conclusion. Make a success of your mission and I promise you hostilities will end quickly.'

He reached forward and picked up his brandy glass, but before he could propose the toast, Sinclair spoke.

'Excuse me, Commodore, sir. If you're about to propose a toast to the success of this mission, then you'd better know I won't be joining in.' The transatlantic drawl was soft, but the tone brooked no argument. He pushed his glass away from him towards the centre of the table. After a moment's hesitation both Thompson and Callendar followed suit. Ferguson and Walters, who had started to raise their glasses, awkwardly lowered them.

'What's the problem?' demanded Surridge. 'Why do you object to toasting a successful mission?'

Sinclair stared at the polished surface of the table. 'I haven't any problem, sir.' He raised his head and looked the Commodore directly in the eye. 'It's just that we ain't had a great deal of success so far and so I'd prefer to toast the mission *after* it's been successful, if it all the same to you, sir.'

For several long moments a heavy silence hung in the room. Eventually Surridge took a deep breath, stuck his jaw out truculently and rose to his feet.

'Very well. If that's the way you want it, so be it. I will respect your wishes. Now, you have an early start tomorrow. I suggest you all get some sleep.'

He strode to the door and summoned the orderly.

'Simpson will show you to your new accommodation where you will be confined until tomorrow morning. I'll see you all at 0600. Goodnight, gentlemen.'

The Commodore's clipped tones signalled an abrupt end to the dinner party. The four men stood up and, following Simpson, filed silently out of the room.

After they had gone, Ferguson drained his glass and looked across at Surridge. 'Pity it had to end like that, on a sour note. Particularly after the day's other unfortunate incidents.'

148

Surridge sought to make light of it. 'Only to be expected. Nerves. Makes them edgy. But I don't care about that, as long as they do the job and bring back that swastika. That's all that matters.'

Then he flopped back down onto his chair.

'Meanwhile, we've got yet another body to deal with ... and a load of damned paperwork.'

12

TUESDAY, SEPTEMBER 22nd, 1942

The four men awoke the following morning to mugs of hot tea provided by Simpson. At the insistence of the Commodore they had spent the night in a separate part of the Lodge, in a locked room guarded by an armed sentry outside the door.

'What time is it?' muttered Callendar, staring bleary-eyed at the orderly.

'0600, sir,' replied Simpson, annoyingly bright and cheerful. 'Breakfast will be served in the dining room at 0630. I've laid out the kit you'll be wearing today and there's plenty of hot water in the jug on the washstand for washing and shaving. As soon as you're dressed, gentlemen, I suggest you get down to breakfast. Transport to the airfield will be leaving at 0715 sharp.'

'What's the weather like?' asked Walters, swinging his feet to the floor.

'Not too clever, sir. Still overcast, with a bit of a wind. Wouldn't fancy flying meself today.'

'Thanks,' interposed Thompson dryly. 'This'll be the first time I've flown!'

After washing and shaving, the four quickly dressed in nondescript clothing provided by Simpson: coarse wool trousers, rough woven shirts, thick sweaters, thick woollen socks, rubber gum boots and, finally, dark blue reefer jackets and knitted hats. Carrying the reefer jackets, the hat stuffed into one of the pockets, they all stumped down the stairs and made their way to the dining room where they found

150

Ferguson already tucking into bacon and eggs. He laid down his knife and fork as they entered and nodded a greeting.

''Morning. Do sit down. Simpson'll be along shortly to take your orders.' He looked at them critically. 'They've done a good job. You really do look like merchant seamen. Well done. Ah, Simpson...'

The orderly appeared bearing a pot of tea in one hand and coffee pot in the other, and took their orders. Sinclair noticed the table had only been laid for five.

'The Commodore not joining us?'

'Unfortunately not,' replied Ferguson, dabbing egg from his mouth with a napkin. 'He's ... ah ... he's been summoned back to the War Office rather suddenly. Left about an hour ago. He did ask me to make his apologies.'

Sinclair gave a wry smile, but made no comment.

They all ate a substantial breakfast, their appetites undaunted by prospects of what lay ahead. Afterwards they assembled in the hallway of the lodge, where Ferguson subjected them to a rigorous search.

'Just to make sure you're not carrying anything which might compromise you,' he explained with a thin smile.

Then he handed them each a manila envelope containing their identity photographs.

'You will also find a small cellophane packet in your envelopes. It contains what is euphemistically referred to as an "L" pill – just in case things go awry.' The four men exchanged glances; they knew full well the implication of Ferguson's words.

The major walked with them to the compound gate where they boarded the Bedford 3-ton TCV waiting for them outside. They were surprised to find they were to be accompanied by an armed guard, a sergeant in the Military Police, carrying a Sten gun across his knees. He ushered them into the vehicle, telling them to move right down to the front, whilst he took up a seat at the tailgate.

151

He declined to answer their questions or say anything, save to warn them that he had orders to prevent anyone trying to leave the vehicle before they arrived at the airfield.

'Comforting thought,' observed Callendar sarcastically, deliberately keeping his voice low so that the guard wouldn't hear. 'Does Ferguson think we're likely to have a last minute change of mind and go AWOL?'

'I don't think it's Ferguson's doing,' commented Sinclair, also keeping his voice low. 'My guess is it's the Commodore. He's been obsessed with security ever since we got here – almost to the point of paranoia.'

'Not surprising though, is it?' interjected Walters. 'When you think what we've been asked to do. Perhaps we should take comfort in his obsession.'

'Yes. Perhaps we should,' Thompson said, 'because whatever lies ahead of us, the last thing we want is for someone to cock it up from this end.'

Conversation faded as the truck headed towards the airfield at Lyneham, some fifteen miles away.

After seeing them safely aboard the truck, Ferguson made his way back to the Lodge where the figure of Commodore Surridge appeared at the top of the steps.

'Everything go off all right?' he asked.

'Yes. They all seemed fairly relaxed.' He cast a sideways glance at the senior officer as they walked back into the house towards his office. 'I'm a little puzzled why you chose not to see them off yourself. I think they would rather have appreciated it.'

'You're right, Teddy. I should have.' He looked straight ahead, avoiding the gaze of his junior officer. 'But I have this terrible fear the whole thing will be a disaster and we shan't see any of those men again. That's why I didn't want to face them this morning.' As they reached Ferguson's office, he turned and faced him. 'I suppose you think that's pretty gutless, eh?'

152

Ferguson waited until they were both seated before replying. 'I don't understand this sudden concern, Commodore. The men have all been thoroughly trained – you've seen the reports. They're fully aware of the risks and they knew they could back out, right up to the last minute, but none of them did. With the personal support of Churchill the job must be important and therefore worth the risk. It is important, isn't it? I mean *really* important, this swastika?'

'Oh yes! Y-y-es! Of course, most certainly,' Surridge stammered hastily. 'No doubt about it. Absolutely!' He stood up, looking suddenly uncomfortable. 'Look... I ... ah ... I'd better be off. Due at the War Office. Must report to Churchill that things are under way. I'll see you in a few days' time.'

He made his way to the door.

'Oh, by the way, security remains tight, Teddy,' he added. 'No one leaves the compound without my permission. And no other form of contact with the outside either. Is that clear?'

'Yes. But what happens if there's an emergency? How do I contact you?'

'Same as before.' He pointed at the telephone. 'The direct line to the War Office is still open. It's the only number you'll get with that phone.'

'I understand,' Ferguson said resignedly.

He stared at the door as it closed behind Surridge, then stood up and crossed to the huge window overlooking the front of the Lodge. As he watched his superior officer trudging his way along the gravelled driveway towards the security gate, he thoughtfully rubbed his chin.

'There's something you're not telling me, Commodore. I wonder what it is...'

The TCV halted briefly at the entrance to Lyneham airfield whilst the driver's papers were checked, and an armed sentry

153

peered into the back of the vehicle to confirm the number of passengers. Then it jerked into motion once again, not stopping until it drew alongside a twin-engined Dakota parked on the apron in front of one of the huge hangars with its engines running.

Still clutching his Sten gun, their guard climbed over the tailboard and leapt down onto the tarmac. Unfastening the retaining catches, he dropped the tailboard with a bang.

'OK. You can get out now,' he announced, standing back and warily glancing around the apron as if expecting to be attacked at any moment. 'Straight on the aircraft, if you would, please, gentlemen.'

He waved the muzzle of his Sten towards the open doorway in the side of the aircraft.

'Christ!' exclaimed Callendar. 'It feels like we're prisoners already.'

'No talking! Straight onto the aircraft!' barked the sergeant.

The four men silently made their way on board, Sinclair bringing up the rear. Just as he was about to disappear inside the fuselage, the RMP sergeant broke his silence.

'Whatever you're doing, mate, it must be important – all this security and all. So good luck!'

Sinclair smiled and acknowledged the farewell wave, then made his way to join the others. A member of the aircrew immediately closed the door.

They were the only passengers on board, the rest of the available space being taken up by a cargo of wooden crates. They had barely settled themselves onto uncomfortable wooden seats and strapped themselves in before they heard the sound of the aircraft's twin engines develop into a deep roar as it rolled out towards the runway.

The flight to Scotland took just over two hours. None of the aircrew made any attempt at conversation, further confirming the blanket of security that had been thrown over the whole operation.

154

'Feels like we're being sent to Coventry, not Scotland,' observed Thompson.

Sinclair smiled briefly at the mention of his home town; memories of his wife and daughter occupied his thoughts. Callendar and Walters had their eyes closed, each leaning their heads on the canvas covered headrest. Thompson too closed his eyes and dozed off.

They were woken by the sudden change in engine noise as the Dakota dipped its nose and began its descent towards a remote RAF aerodrome located somewhere in the lowlands of Scotland. The landing was a bumpy affair, caused by heavy cross winds, and they were relieved when the aircraft reached the end of the runway and taxied across to where a camouflaged Royal Navy utility stood waiting for them. The strong winds were accompanied by driving rain and, as soon as they disembarked, they were hustled into the rear of the waiting vehicle, by an armed naval rating wearing a crash helmet and motorcycle weatherproofs.

Their arrival had attracted the attention of a number of RAF ground personnel working in a nearby hangar, but no attempt was made to approach them.

Once his passengers were ensconced in the rear of the utility, the driver immediately set off. With the naval rating following as escort on his motorcycle, they rapidly made their way through the security gate and onto the main highway. The journey to Rosyth took another hour. On arrival they were waved through after the briefest inspection of the driver's documents, their arrival clearly expected.

After a tortuous drive through the dockyard complex, the utility halted on a quayside, alongside a Royal Navy 'T' Class submarine. The motorcyclist waved with his hand, indicating they should go aboard immediately. With rain lashing down and the wind whipping at the canvas sides of the utility, the promised warmth and protection of the submarine acted as a spur and the four men wasted little time in

155

descending the gangway to the glistening deck. A further rating, suitably clad in weatherproofs, led them to an open hatch where they descended into the bowels of the craft.

A young lieutenant wearing the zigzag bars of the RNVR on his epaulettes met them at the foot of the ladder. He gave them a welcoming grin.

'Welcome aboard the *Triton*, gentlemen. The name's Seymour.' He held up his hand. 'It's OK, I shan't ask your names. I've been briefed on the drill. If you haven't been aboard a sub before, you'll find things a little cramped at first, but we've managed to get you installed in one of the larger cabins, so you shouldn't be too uncomfortable.' He glanced around. 'No luggage I see. That'll ease things considerably. If you'll follow me...'

The smell of lubricating oils and diesel permeated the comforting warmth of the submarine. Seymour led them along the narrow passageway, ducking through the watertight bulkhead doors and occasionally squeezing past members of the crew going about their duties. He stopped in front of a canvas sheet hanging against one of the steel bulkheads. Pulling it to one side he announced, 'This is it. Not exactly The Ritz, I'm afraid. But you'll soon settle in.'

The four men peered into their new quarters. It was really no bigger than a large cupboard, most of the available space being taken up by two-tier bunks fitted on either side with a gap some eighteen inches between them.

'I'm afraid you'll have to take turns in climbing into the bunks,' Seymour commented apologetically. 'But you shouldn't have to put up with it for too long.'

'Just how long will the trip take?' asked Callendar, casting a rueful eye over the Spartan accommodation.

'At this moment, I haven't the faintest idea,' Seymour replied. He grinned at the surprise on their faces. 'It's OK. It's just that, until I open my sealed orders, I've no idea where I'm taking you – and I can't open those until we've

156

cleared Rosyth and heading for open sea.' He glanced at his watch. 'That'll be in about an hour. I'll drop back and see you then. Meanwhile, I'll try to organise some hot cocoa for you.'

With that he quickly disappeared back along the corridor.

'More bloody secrecy,' observed Thompson, after they had each managed to clamber into one of the bunks and make themselves as comfortable as the conditions allowed. He glanced across at Sinclair in the opposite bunk. 'You're right. Our beloved Commodore *is* paranoid when it comes to security.'

'Don't criticise him for that,' commented Walters. 'As I said before, considering where we're going, the tighter the security is, the happier I am.'

Sinclair looked thoughtful. 'Yeah! I guess you're right ... maybe. But I can't help feeling Bill may have a point. Security's one thing, but you'd think the captain of the submarine would have been briefed on the rendezvous with the *Hilversund*. After all, he is responsible for his ship and crew and would need to know more than that.'

Callendar frowned. 'I might seem a bit dense but what exactly are you saying? Are you suggesting Surridge hasn't been entirely honest with us?'

Sinclair pursed his lips. 'Not too sure. Not yet, anyhow. But one thing's for certain: if there is any funny business goin' on, then we're goin' to find out, 'cause there ain't any backing out now!'

13

FRIDAY, SEPTEMBER 25th, 1942

Thirty-four hours after leaving the Rosyth dockyards HMS *Triton* arrived at the designated rendezvous point, just fifteen minutes ahead of schedule, a credit to the young lieutenant's seamanship and navigation.

The greater part of the voyage had taken place submerged, the craft venturing to the surface only during the hours of darkness to re-charge her batteries and vent the stale air from within the confines of the cramped vessel.

As zero hour approached the atmosphere inside the control room became tense. Seymour brought the submarine to periscope depth. With the craft lying motionless in the water there was little danger of the section of periscope protruding above the surface showing any tell-tale wash, yet the crew knew their situation was vulnerable.

'Up 'scope!'

The shiny cylinder rose slowly from the depths of the vessel. Carrying out a rapid three hundred and sixty degree sweep of the sea above, Seymour satisfied himself there was no immediate danger and began to rotate the instrument more slowly, staying within the quadrant which embraced the anticipated course of the SS *Hilversund*. Disappointingly, there was no sign of the Swedish cargo ship.

'That's a pity,' murmured Seymour, lifting the handles into the upright position. 'Down 'scope.'

'Down 'scope,' echoed the operating seaman.

The young lieutenant glanced at his wristwatch. 'We'll give it ten minutes and try again.'

The control room remained quiet as the minutes ticked by. The taut expressions on the faces of the crew, the white knuckles of the hydroplane operators, Seymour's clipped, almost terse, voice as he snapped orders: all betrayed the increasing tension building up inside the craft. Lying just below the surface of the sea, smack in the middle of one of the enemy's busiest shipping lanes, was not the healthiest place to be.

Meanwhile, waiting in their cramped quarters, Sinclair, Callendar, Walters and Thompson listened intently as Seymour's commands were relayed over the craft's intercom system. Disappointment increased as they heard Seymour give the order to take the submarine down to a depth of one hundred feet.

'No joy, by the sound of it,' muttered Thompson, nervously twiddling his fingers.

Sinclair swung his feet up onto the bunk, tucked his hands behind his head and closed his eyes. 'Relax guys. There's nothing we can do, except wait.'

'Easier said than done,' murmured Callendar. 'Be glad when we get out of this tin can.'

He had had a rough crossing and it was only when they were halfway into the voyage he had revealed he suffered with claustrophobia.

Walters gave him a concerned glance. 'You OK?'

Struggling to overcome the fear numbing his brain, Callendar simply nodded.

Suddenly the canvas curtain was drawn to one side and Seymour's head appeared in the doorway. He looked relaxed, but they could see the smile was forced.

'Sorry about this. Bit of a delay. Our Swedish friends haven't put in an appearance yet. But not to worry – always was a bit of a tall order, making this sort of rendezvous on a moonless night, right on Jerry's doorstep. I'll give it fifteen minutes, then take her up for another look-see. If she's still not sighted, we'll keep repeating the operation until she does show. Meanwhile, try and relax – saves oxygen.'

He grinned and disappeared.

Exactly fifteen minutes later, Seymour's voice was heard over the intercom repeating the order: 'Take her up to periscope depth', and, shortly after, 'Up 'scope!'

Silently they waited. When it came it was like an explosion over the loudspeaker.

'Got her!' they heard Seymour exclaim. 'She's coming in off the port quarter, range about a thousand yards. Four green navigation lights set in a diamond pattern on her starboard beam.' He swung the periscope through three hundred and sixty degrees to confirm no hostile craft were in the vicinity, then swept the two handles upwards and stood back. 'Down 'scope. Standby to surface... Surface!'

The submarine buzzed with activity. The four men left their bunks and stood waiting. When the first officer appeared in the doorway of the cabin, his attitude was sharp and business-like.

'This is it, gentlemen. Please follow me and be as quick as you can. We're about to surface and the captain wants to be on top for as little time as possible, for obvious reasons. We'll be taking you out on deck through the same hatch you came in by.'

Hurriedly he led the way along the corridor, the four following as quickly as their heavy sea boots would allow. When they reached the foot of a vertical steel ladder they waited until the command to open hatches came over the PA system. Deftly spinning the handle wheel, the young officer quickly unlocked the hatch and pushed the heavy metal cover upwards. A shower of seawater drenched their upturned faces, leaving a salty tang on their lips. The first officer slid back down the ladder and stood aside for them to climb up and out onto the deck.

Thankfully it was a moonless night, making it difficult for any hostile surface craft to pick out the submarine's low-lying silhouette. A gentle south-westerly breeze brushed their faces, welcome relief from the stuffy conditions below. Seymour was already on deck, having made his way through another hatch, together with two ratings, busy inflating a rubber dinghy by means of a compressed air line.

'Quickly as you can, chaps,' he said. 'Into the dinghy. Get yourselves balanced. You'll find four paddles in the bottom.'

Once they were settled into the inflatable, he pointed to the outline of a cargo vessel visible some two hundred yards away.

'There she is. That's the *Hilversund*. We've already exchanged recognition signals, so they're expecting you. We haven't got time to get you launched in the conventional way, so we're going to submerge under you. We'll do it very slowly so that we don't drag you under with us. Be careful you don't foul the straining wires as we submerge.' He paused and took a deep breath. 'I think that's it. It just remains for me to wish you the best of luck and, if you're ever in Portsmouth, look me up and I'll buy you all a pint.'

With a wave of farewell he hurried away to the open hatch. As soon as they heard the hatch cover close, they knew they were on their own and from now on their lives would be in the hands of destiny.

As Seymour took the submarine down slowly water crept up over the bulbous sides of the craft, swirling onto the deck and lifting the inflatable dinghy clear. As soon as they were properly afloat, the four men vigorously paddled away from the sinking sub and headed for the Swedish vessel.

On land two hundred yards is a fairly insignificant distance. On water and in a sea swell, even one that's only moderate, it becomes a different situation. It took them almost ten minutes of hard paddling before they found themselves

161

alongside the rust-streaked, steel plates of the *Hilversund*'s hull. A rope ladder had been thrown down from the waist of the vessel and, though breathless from their exertions in the rubber dinghy, they wasted little time in clambering onto the cumbersome ladder to the deck. Sinclair was last to leave. As he was about to place his foot on one of the rungs, a rope snaked down and a Swedish voice called out in English, asking him to attach the rope to the rubber craft.

On deck they were greeted in excellent English by a heavily set individual who introduced himself as Erik Carrlson, the ship's mate. He led them down a companionway and into a surprisingly spacious cabin, equipped with four single beds – a welcome improvement on the cramped quarters of *Triton*.

'OK. Just to put you in the picture, as you English say, we are sailing with a normal compliment of crew: eight men, plus the Captain and myself. So I must ask you not to leave this cabin until I tell you it is OK, otherwise the Germans will get suspicious if they see too many men wandering about on deck – they operate patrols day and night, both by boat and aircraft.

'We shall be docking in Rostock at about four in the afternoon and we shall start unloading immediately. During the unloading, German sentries will be on board, but don't worry – they never come below decks. Unloading will stop for the night at around six o'clock. Then we can relax and have a meal.' He gave them all a broad smile. 'Double helping of bacon and eggs OK?'

The suggestion met with a chorus of approval.

'Good.'

He reached into his jacket pocket and withdrew four slim green books, about the size of passports.

'These are Swedish merchant navy documents, one for each of you. They do not contain photographs, just a simple description. The German customs police are used to seeing

162

Swedish seamen. We come here every week, so they will not examine the books. But...' His hand delved into his pocket again. This time he withdrew a wad of official looking forms.

'These are *Ausweisen.* German Customs and Emigration forms. Each time we go ashore, we have to fill in one of these and hand it into the Customs office on the docks. They are very simple to fill in. They require only the same details contained in these books. Normally, they are filled out when you get to the Customs office, but it would look suspicious if you were seen copying from the books, so I managed to obtain a few spare forms for you to fill in now and take ashore with you. Just switch them with the blank one the official hands you. Now, the form is in two parts. They will rubberstamp and number both parts, giving one back to you while they retain the other. The part you are given is simply to get you back on board ship after your evening ashore. So don't lose it!'

Walters frowned. 'We ... we aren't coming back. Weren't you aware of that?'

Carrlson nodded. 'Yes, I know that.'

'Won't the Customs officials be suspicious if the second part isn't handed back in?' asked Thompson.

'Don't worry,' the Swede smiled. 'They *will* be handed back in, and by people wearing your clothes. Jews escaping from the Nazis.' His jaw tightened. 'Our country may be neutral but the Swedish people are well aware of what Hitler is doing to the Jews. We help where we can.

'One other thing. There is an eleven o'clock curfew – twenty-three hundred hours. Obviously it will not affect you, but you should be aware of it. The crew usually leave the ship for an evening's drinking at about seven-thirty. Four of them have volunteered to stay on board, to avoid drawing suspicion with too many men going ashore.' He took a deep breath. 'I think that's about all I have to say. Now I'd try

163

to get some rest if I were you. One of the crew will bring you breakfast.'

He was about to leave when Callendar piped up.

'Just a moment. From what you've said, it seems pretty damn obvious the whole crew knows about us. How can we be sure they can be trusted?'

Carrlson turned slowly and stared stonily at the blond-haired Englishman. When he spoke, his voice was thin and brittle. 'We have been doing this sort of work, smuggling people in and out of Germany, for over a year now. If there is a risk of betrayal, it will not be by a Swede. And you should remember, if we are ever caught, neutral or not, we too will face a Nazi firing squad. Our lives are just as much in your hands, as yours are in ours.'

He stepped out into the corridor, closing the door behind him.

For long moments no one spoke. Then Callendar exhaled noisily.

'Opened my big mouth again. I'll apologise when I see him.'

'Don't blame yourself too much,' muttered Sinclair. 'I was thinking much the same thing as you. It isn't surprising, when you consider the level of security they hit us with back in England.' He stared thoughtfully at the closed cabin door. 'Still, I don't think we've anything to worry about as far as the crew are concerned. Let's all get some shut-eye, shall we?'

SATURDAY, SEPTEMBER 26th

At around ten in the morning a late breakfast was brought in by one of the crew, a man in his fifties who said very little, but did manage a friendly, if toothless, smile. Having suffered the privations of rationing for over two years and

164

the obvious limitations imposed on the submarine's mess, what lay before them represented a banquet fit for a king: a mountain of bacon, eggs, sausages, sliced meats, even mushrooms, and, to top this bacchanalian offering, a jug of *real* rich dark coffee, its aroma wafting gently in the air, teasing nostrils and making mouths water. After the meal, and with Carlsson's consent, they took the opportunity to stretch their legs on deck, the exercise welcome after the cramped confines of the submarine.

The final leg of their voyage proved uneventful and it was late afternoon by the time the *Hilversund* tied up at her berth in Rostock harbour. An evening meal followed the initial unloading and the four men also took the opportunity to fill in the *Ausweisen* forms provided by the First Mate. At around seven-thirty they made preparations to leave the relative sanctuary of the ship.

Carlsson gave them a reassuring smile.

'There will be a number of seamen from this ship, as well as others who will be leaving the docks for a night in the taverns. So you will not be alone. But one word of warning the civil police, the *polizei*, and the secret police, the *Gestapo*, regularly patrol the taverns, so keep your documents handy.'

With these sobering words he wished them good luck and led the way up on deck and to the gangway leading down to the quay. On the quayside they joined several seamen from other ships, all making their way to the dock exit. Taking care not to get too close to these genuine Swedish seamen, in case they tried to engage them in conversation, the quartet soon found themselves waiting outside the Customs and Immigration office. This was quite small, and only three or four people were allowed in at a time.

Walters whispered to the other three, 'Let me go first. Then, if I make a mistake, I'll be better able to talk my way out of it. Watch what I do and if there are no problems then follow suit. I'll stay inside until all of you are through. Agreed?'

165

They all nodded, happy to let Walters take the lead.

But their fears were groundless. Deftly they switched their filled-in forms with the blank ones handed them by a bored-looking immigration official. The official rubber-stamped each form twice and handed back one half, repeating the same warning to each of them: 'Don't forget, you have to be back on board your ship by twenty-three hundred hours – and don't lose your *Ausweis!*'

Walters stayed behind until the other three had safely passed through, then joined them outside. Avoiding the temptation to hurry, they made their way through the dock gates, showing their *Ausweisen* to one of the armed *Kriegsmarine* on guard, and stepped out onto the streets of Rostock. With Walters and Sinclair in the lead they set off towards the town centre.

14

They found *Das Wildschwein* tucked away in a small side street in the old town, thanks to the directions given by the *Hilversund*'s first mate, although he had told them it wasn't a tavern normally frequented by Swedish seamen. Walters pushed open the glass-panelled door and the four men stepped into the smoky atmosphere.

It was crowded inside, mainly with *Wehrmacht* and *Kriegsmarine* personnel, but there were also a comforting number of merchant seamen, plus a scattering of civilians. Knowing that standing inside the entrance too long would draw unwelcome attention, they desperately looked round for an empty table. As luck would have it, a group of four soldiers were leaving and the four Englishmen quickly grabbed the vacant table and settled down on the wooden chairs. Trying to look calm and relaxed, they carefully took in their surroundings.

'For God's sake don't stare,' whispered Walters, 'or you'll attract attention. Just relax. Imagine you're back home in your own local.'

'You must be joking,' observed Thompson, matching his low tone. 'Talk about being in the lion's den.'

'Ssh!' hissed Sinclair. Catching Walters' eye, he inclined his head towards a table across the room occupied by two ominous-looking characters, dressed in long leather coats and wearing slouch hats. The slimmer of the two, a man with hawk-like features and rimless spectacles, appeared to have taken a keen interest in the four newcomers.

'Gestapo,' hissed Walters after a quick glance. 'For Christ's sake don't stare at them.'

167

'Too bloody late!' retorted Sinclair quietly. 'One of them is coming over.'

'Leave this to me,' murmured Walters. 'Just be ready to run like hell if anything goes wrong.'

Customers readily made way for the Gestapo agent as he made his way towards their table. He stood for several moments without saying a word, eyeing each man in turn through the thick pebble lenses of his spectacles as if mentally photographing their faces. Callendar found the palms of his hands were sweating and he thrust them out of sight under the table.

'Good evening, gentlemen.'

The voice was surprisingly high-pitched, almost like that of a young child. Under different circumstances it might have been comical. But in these strange surroundings, where everyone in the room was an enemy, it had a profoundly sinister tone.

'My name is Kramer, *Geheimestaatspolizei*,' he said crisply. 'Your papers.' He held out a gloved hand.

They delved into their pockets withdrawing and handing over their Swedish passports and *Ausweisen*. The Gestapo man's face seemed to adopt an almost cynical look as his long, thin fingers leafed carefully through each document, scrutinising it thoroughly. The procedure seemed to take for ever.

'So,' he said at last. 'You are all Swedish merchant seamen, *ja*?'

'*Ja*. That is correct,' confirmed Walters, backed up by nods of assent from the other three.

'*Gut!*' declared Gestapo Kramer, still maintaining his humourless smile. '*Alles ist in Ordnung.*' He handed back the passports and *Ausweisen*. 'Don't forget to return to your ship by twenty-three hundred hours, otherwise you will find yourselves in serious trouble. You understand?'

'*Ja, ja,*' they chorused, breathing silent relief as the Gestapo man turned away. They had almost relaxed when, quite unexpectedly, he whirled round to face them.

'Just one moment,' he said, frowning. 'There is something wrong here!'

They tensed, ready to flee from the tavern.

'You are not drinking,' he observed and turned towards the bar. 'Josef,' he shouted. 'You are neglecting our Swedish guests.'

'Yes, yes, all right, Herr Kramer. I'll be there shortly,' replied the harassed innkeeper.

Satisfied he had achieved something, the Gestapo officer gave a final nod to the group and made his way back to his table where his companion had risen from his seat. To the relief of the four Englishmen, both men made for the exit.

'My God!' breathed Thompson. 'That was a bit unnerving.'

Callendar nodded. 'Nasty piece of work. And his voice... I might forget his face, but I don't think I'd ever forget a voice like that.'

'Ssh! Here comes the landlord,' muttered Walters.

Josef, a plump, balding man in his fifties, wearing a white apron soiled with beer stains, hurried across to their table and laboriously wiped up the spillages left by the four soldiers.

'Good evening, gentlemen. What can I get you?'

'Four beers, please,' Walters replied.

'Four beers. Very good.' The landlord turned away.

'Oh, and do you sell Schwanstein beer here?'

The publican hesitated almost imperceptibly before he turned and casually replied, 'No, that is a Bavarian beer. We only sell local beer in this tavern.'

He hurried back to the bar.

'What d'you think?' whispered Thompson.

Walters stared at the retreating figure. 'Well, he gave the right response. We'll just have to wait and see, but be ready for a fast exit.'

After a few minutes had elapsed, Josef returned bearing two froth-capped *krugsteins* in each hand.

'Four beers, gentlemen,' he announced, setting the tankards down.

Then he drew a cloth from his apron pocket and again began unnecessarily wiping down the tabletop.

'When you have drunk your beer, one at a time, go through that door at the back, as if you were going to the toilet. You will find another door on your left marked "Private". Through there you will find some stairs. Go to the first floor and wait in the first room on your left. Someone will meet you.'

Josef was already on his way back to the bar before they had time to ask further questions.

'Well, it seems we've made contact,' breathed Walters. 'So far, so good. Now, as the man said, one at a time.' He nodded towards Sinclair. 'When you've finished your beer, you go first, followed by Callendar, then Thompson. I'll bring up the rear.'

'And if it's a trap?' queried the forever cautious Thompson.

Walters shrugged his shoulders. 'Unless anyone has got any better suggestion, I don't think we have much option. But let's keep our wits about us.' He looked at Sinclair. 'If you smell a trap, get the hell out of there, fast.'

Sinclair drained his beer and stood up. 'If I do find problems, I'll either be killing my first Jerries, or running the fastest race of my life. See you guys later.'

Placing his tankard on the table, he calmly made his way to the door indicated by Josef, opened it and stepped through.

Two doors faced him, one labelled *Herren*, the other *Damen*, obviously the toilets referred to by Josef, whilst on his left was the door marked *Privat*. He pushed it open to reveal the promised flight of stairs. Mounting two at a time, yet treading as softly as he could, he found himself facing a passageway. Thankfully, it was deserted.

On either side there were several doors off the passageway,

170

presumably leading to bedrooms. Tip-toeing to the first door on his left, he wiped his sweating palms on his donkey jacket and gently grasped the brass door handle. He placed his ear against the door panelling and listened for any noise from inside. There was none. Taking a deep breath, he gingerly eased the door open.

A single naked electric light bulb glowed from the ceiling, allowing him enough light to see the room was unoccupied. He breathed a sigh of relief and quickly stepped inside, quietly closing the door behind him. The room was small and sparsely furnished – just a double bed, a chest of drawers incorporating a washstand, a small wardrobe and a couple of chairs. A faded blue carpet covered most of the floor, leaving a border of bare wooden floorboards. On the wall facing him was the only window in the room, masked by thick, red curtains. On the right in the far corner was a door, connecting with the next room.

Walking as softly as he could, he moved over to it and tried the handle. It was locked. Going to the window, he eased away the edge of the curtain and tried to peer outside, but dusk had fallen and it was too dark to see what lay below. Suddenly, he heard the door open and whirled round on the balls of his feet. It was Callendar. Immediately Sinclair held a finger to his lips. Callendar nodded and made his way silently across to the window.

'Everything OK?' he queried softly.

'As far as I can tell.' He jerked his thumb toward the other door. 'I don't know where that leads, but it's locked and there's no sign of any key.' He turned back to the window. 'I was just trying to make out what's outside this window – in case we need to make a run for it. Turn off the light, will you. I want to see if it opens.'

Callendar went quietly to the light switch on the wall and flicked it off. Sinclair allowed a few moments for his eyes to adjust to the darkness, then slid back the curtains and examined the window. Surprisingly, it opened easily, sliding up and down on well-greased runners. They were obviously not the first to use this room. Thrusting his head through the open window, he peered out and found himself looking down into a small yard at the side of the tavern used for storing beer barrels. A pair of wooden gates opened out onto a narrow alleyway that appeared to connect with the main street. Withdrawing his head he closed the window and pulled the curtains.

'Lights,' he said softly.

Obligingly Callendar switched the light back on and sat on the edge of the bed to await the arrival of Thompson and Walters. Both appeared a few minutes later.

Thompson joined Callendar on the bed, whilst Walters and Sinclair took a chair each. Sinclair briefed them on what he had found: the locked communicating door and the possibilities the window held in the event they needed an emergency exit. The next few minutes were spent talking quietly amongst themselves, waiting for something to happen and wondering how long they would be kept in suspense. Even though they kept their voices low, they all failed to hear the barely audible sound of a key turning in a well-oiled lock, or notice the communicating door being opened on silent hinges.

'Stand up and raise your hands in the air!' barked an authoritative voice.

Four heads spun round to find a young woman standing in front of the communicating door, a Walther PP clenched in her right hand. She was surprisingly pretty, despite her blonde hair having been pulled back in a tight bun at the back of her head, which gave her a rather severe look. Her blue eyes too, which had melted the hearts of many men, now carried the hardness of steel. Less attractive was the grey uniform she was wearing, the silver SS logos on her collar tabs and the SD badge on her left forearm glinting dully in the electric light. Even more worrying was the way she was holding the pistol, the muzzle with its bulbous silencer pointed unwaveringly in their direction.

'I said stand up!' she repeated them. 'Raise your hands and don't try anything stupid.'

Slowly they rose to their feet and raised their arms in the air. The expression on the girl's face told them she wouldn't hesitate to shoot if she thought it necessary. She spent a few brief moments examining the face of each man in turn, during which time Sinclair eyed the distance separating them, wondering whether or not he could cover the intervening space before she would have time to use the gun. He was still thinking about it when Walters broke the silence.

'Who are you? What's this all about?' he demanded. 'We're just Swed...'

'Shut up!' she retorted. 'And do exactly as I tell you.' She waved the muzzle of the pistol. 'Now, form a line facing me ... and do it slowly.'

Not taking their eyes off the pistol they lined up to face her.

'Good,' she muttered. 'Now take off your jackets and toss them on the bed. Slowly!' she added sharply, as Sinclair moved with unexpected speed hoping she would be put off guard and give one of the others the opportunity to grab her gun. It didn't happen.

'Now, strip to the waist,' she ordered.

'What on earth for?' exclaimed Callendar indignantly.

She raised the pistol to shoulder height and took careful aim at his forehead. 'Do as you are told, NOW!'

The last word came like a pistol shot and Callendar, along with the others, hurriedly removed his jumper and shirt without further protest. The girl then fished a piece of paper from her left-hand jacket pocket, glanced at it, then looked up at the four men.

'You can lower your arms now, but keep perfectly still at all times, unless I tell you to do otherwise.' Gratefully, they lowered their arms. 'Now, let's not be stupid and waste time,' she continued. 'I know who you are and what you're doing here. So drop the charade of being Swedish seamen. Now you...' She pointed the pistol at Thompson standing at the end of the line on her right. 'Your rank, name and number?'

For a moment Thompson hesitated, not knowing whether he should give his real name, with British army rank and number, or his assumed identity. He stared back at the girl perplexed.

'Well?' she demanded, a note of irritation in her voice.

Thompson took a deep breath. '527487 Thompson, sergeant, British Army,' he blurted out truculently.

A brief smile flitted across her features. 'Thank you, Sergeant Thompson. Now would you please give me your other identity? Your *Schutzstaffel* identity.'

'Yes, of course,' he said. 'SS Untersturmführer Karl Dietrich, number SS768453.'

'Good. Now, turn around and raise your left arm in the air.'

Thompson complied.

'You!' She pointed the pistol at Callendar who was standing next to him. 'Read out the blood group tattooed under his arm.'

'AB-Rhesus Positive,' replied Callendar, reading the greyish-blue number indelibly etched into the skin of Thompson's underarm.

'Good. Now you.'

Callendar followed Thompson's example. 'SS Untersturmführer Hans Richter, number SS873654,' he announced.

'Raise your left arm. You...' The girl motioned to Thompson. 'Read out the blood group under his arm.'

'O-Rhesus Positive,' Thompson declared.

The girl nodded. 'You next.' She pointed to Walters.

'SS Untersturmführer Fritz Neuemuller, number SS579324.'

Like the others, Walters raised his left arm and the blood group was read out by Callendar.

'B-Rhesus Negative.'

Again the girl nodded. Sinclair was the last to go through the routine, his number being checked out by Walters.

'Good!'

Apparently satisfied with the results of her interrogation, she carefully re-folded the piece of paper with her free hand and returned it to her jacket pocket. Then she calmly raised her pistol and fired twice, in rapid succession.

15

'Morning, Teddy,' greeted Commodore Surridge breezily, as he strode into Ferguson's office. 'Give me an update on the latest situation, would you.' He casually tossed his briefcase into an easy chair. 'I saw the PM last night. Told him the team were away. He wants a daily briefing on how things are progressing...' His voice tailed off as he saw the grim expression on Ferguson's face. 'There's something wrong, isn't there? What's happened?'

'Two things, neither of them good, I'm afraid.'

The Commodore's face clouded as he sat down in one of the easy chairs. 'Well, you'd better get on with it. I've never known bad news to improve with age.'

Ferguson picked up a sheet of paper from his desk.

'We've had the result of the post-mortem on the Italian barber, Capaldi. It appears he didn't die by electrocution, despite where he was found and the burns on his clothing. The pathologist is adamant he was strangled to death, probably by a cord, or some other form of ligature. In other words, he was murdered.'

'Let me see.' The Commodore's hand shook slightly as he took the post-mortem report from Ferguson. 'Have the SIB been informed?'

'Not yet,' replied Ferguson. 'I thought it advisable to maintain absolute security. The body is being held in the morgue at the local hospital – unidentified, of course, pending further instructions from the War Office. I ... I assume you will be able to deal with the matter?'

'Yes. Yes, of course. Leave that to me. Any idea who was responsible?'

Ferguson picked up a second sheet of paper. 'I think this might well answer that question.' He paused before handing it over. 'Did you happen to see a report in *The Telegraph*, about ten days ago? About the naked body of a man having been found some twenty miles from here? At the time they said the body had been badly beaten and couldn't be identified.'

'Yes. I remember reading the article. Wasn't it suggested it was something to do with Black Marketeers falling out among themselves?'

'At the time, yes. But now they've identified the body, using dental records ... army medical records in fact.' Ferguson handed the sheet of paper to Surridge. 'This came in by special courier about an hour ago.'

The Commodore had been shocked by the news of Angelo's murder, but it was nothing compared to the wave of horror that coursed through him when he read the name on the sheet of paper. He looked up, his face white.

'Is there any doubt about this?'

Ferguson shook his head grimly.

'Then we must stop them. Abort the mission. Now ... at once!'

'Too late, I'm afraid. They boarded the SS *Hilversund* at twenty-three hundred the night before last. They've been out of contact for almost thirty-six hours.'

'Then it *is* too late. They're as good as dead ... all of them.' He stared at the floor for several moments then looked up. 'We can only hope they've had a chance to use their L pills.'

The first bullet took Walters in the heart. The second found its mark in the centre of his forehead, both shots striking with such force his body was catapulted backwards onto the bed behind.

It was all over in a split second, the noise of the two

177

shots reduced to a soft *Phut phut* by the effectiveness of the silencer. For several seconds no one moved or made a sound. Sinclair was the first to recover.

'What the bloody hell...'

'Shut up and no one move,' she snapped. The pistol pointed menacingly in his direction. 'You.' She waved the muzzle in Callendar's direction. 'Check to see he's dead.'

Hands shaking, Callendar knelt on the bed and felt for Walters' carotid artery. Nothing registered. He shook his head. The girl had expected no other response. Extensive practice on the pistol range had made her an excellent shot. She lowered the pistol.

'All right, the rest of you can relax. I don't intend to shoot anyone else ... unless you give me cause, that is.'

Callendar stared at the blonde. 'Why?' he blurted out, all his outrage and dismay compressed into the one word *'Why?'*

'Would you prefer to be lying there instead of him?' she replied calmly. 'Because that's what he had planned for you.'

'What in the hell are you talking about?' demanded Thompson. 'He was one of us. Staff Sergeant Tom Walters of the British Army.'

The girl unscrewed the silencer from the muzzle of her pistol and dropped it into the left-hand pocket of her jacket; the pistol disappeared into the right.

'Why don't you all put your clothes back on?' she suggested, pulling a packet of cigarettes from her breast pocket. She lit one and watched disinterestedly as they finished dressing.

'First of all, he isn't Sergeant Tom ... whoever you said he was. Nor was he ever in the British Army. The blood group you read from under his arm, B-Rhesus Negative, was wrong. SS Untersturmführer Fritz Neuemuller had the most common blood group – O-Rhesus Positive. This man is, or rather was, a Nazi spy, an SS officer. He was infiltrated into England at the time of Dunkirk and has been the SD's most successful agent for the past two years.'

'I hope you're bloody sure of that,' retorted Sinclair angrily. 'What if you've made a mistake and shot an innocent man?'

'I don't make mistakes,' replied the girl. 'I can't afford to.' She pulled nervously on her cigarette and blew the smoke upwards. 'His SS number didn't tally either. He was arrogant. He didn't use Neuemuller's number, he used his own.' She gave a hollow laugh. 'And that was stupid.'

Thompson, recovering from the shock, looked puzzled. 'What's the significance of the numbers? Why are they so important?'

The girl dropped the remains of her cigarette on the floor, sat down on one of the single chairs and crossed her legs. Her face wore a weary expression.

'Perhaps I'd better fill you in. Why don't you all sit down? But, before you do, put the body on the floor, on the other side of the bed. He'll be moved later.'

Sinclair and Thompson performed the unpleasant task. Then they joined Callendar on the edge of the bed and the girl continued.

'First of all, you'd better know who I am. My name is Anna Schenke. I'm an SS Unterscharführer employed in the SS Personnel section in the Reich Central Security Office. Incidentally, that's not my real name, but that's another story. As far as you are concerned, I am who I tell you I am. I'm also a British agent and a member of the Kreisau Circle here in Germany.' She paused. 'You would do well to remember, not all Germans are Nazis.'

She retrieved the packet of cigarettes from her pocket.

'I don't suppose you've brought any English cigarettes with you?'

They all shook their heads.

'No, of course you haven't. That would've been stupid. Pity though.'

She lit the fresh cigarette and went on.

'Some time ago I was asked by London to provide the

179

identities of sixteen genuine SS officers, all Untersturmführers, who could qualify for selection as guards at Hitler's office in the Reichs Chancellery. There was one qualification. They all had to be dead. I was told that four of the identities would be used as cover for a British team who intended to infiltrate the Reichs Chancellery. The four identities selected by your people, together with their SS identification numbers and blood groups, were signalled to our Resistance two days ago. However, there was a problem. Although all of the four names came from the original sixteen, in one instance the SS number and blood group didn't agree.' She carelessly tapped the ash from her cigarette onto the floor. 'It seemed strange. I couldn't understand why the number had been changed. So, out of curiosity, I checked that particular SS number in SS Personnel Records and, lo and behold, came up with the name of SS Hauptsturmführer Anton Stotz. Strangely, Stotz's file was missing from the records so, pretending I'd discovered its loss on a routine check, I reported the matter to my superior. At first he wouldn't comment. Then with some reluctance, he told me about Stotz's activities in England, even his code name, "Valkyrie". Then he must immediately have regretted giving me the information because he made me swear to keep my mouth shut and told me not ask any more questions. That's why we had to play out that little charade just now. I had to be sure before I shot him.'

She stood up. 'What I can't understand is why he used his own blood group number and his own SS number. If he'd used the numbers I supplied he'd never have been discovered.'

'Perhaps I can give you the answer,' suggested Thompson. 'The blood groups we were given were tattooed on by our camp barber, an Italian named Angelo Capaldi. If Walters — or rather Stotz — still had his original tattoo...'

'Obviously he did. It would have been difficult for him

to get it erased once he arrived in England. Too many questions would have been asked.'

'That must be it then,' Thompson concluded. 'He could hardly have gone to Angelo with a number already tattooed under his arm. It would have been a dead giveaway.'

'But he *did* go to see Angelo,' asserted Callendar. 'I saw him, the same day we had dinner at the lodge.'

'Which was the same day, or rather night, that Angelo supposedly tried to escape and got himself electrocuted,' said Sinclair. 'And that's too much of a coincidence.'

'Poor old Angelo,' Thompson murmured. 'He wouldn't have harmed a fly. Poor bastard.'

Sinclair grimaced. 'If Walters really was a German spy, and it very much looks that way, he wouldn't allow an insignificant little Italian to expose him. That's why he had to be killed.'

'We can't *know* he was murdered,' protested Callendar. 'Not for certain.'

'OK. Then why was Walters so desperate to get himself on this mission? D'you remember how quickly he volunteered when Bob Nicholson had his accident? He would have stopped at nothing to get included ... and now we know why. And another thing, Smith's death on the grenade range, Walters could have engineered that too. Don't forget Smith was in Jackdaw Two and they were the leading group at the time.'

'Just a minute,' interjected Thompson. 'Supposing Nicholson hadn't had his accident. How would Walters, or Stotz, how would he have managed to get included on the team? Or are you telling us he engineered Nicholson's accident!'

Sinclair shrugged. 'I've never been happy with Ferguson's explanation about the acid content of the grease. Oh, I'm sure he believes it himself, and maybe it does contain a small quantity – but not enough to eat through an inch-thick manila rope. No. I think Walters knew about the grease and

181

simply doctored the rope with undiluted acid the night before the accident, knowing Nicholson had been fired up by Keppler and would probably make one last attempt to cross the rope bridge, just to prove him wrong. Which makes me wonder if Keppler was also involved.'

Anna, who had been listening attentively to the conversation, asked what it had all been about. Thompson explained how Nicholson, having been selected for the mission, had felt a personal obligation to justify his inclusion by overcoming his fear of heights and negotiating the tree walk. Then, how he had fallen and broken his neck, and how Walters had volunteered to take his place.

'It makes sense,' she said. 'Stotz would have been an extremely resourceful character.'

'But why should he want to get on the mission?' asked Callendar. 'Apart from the obvious intention of frustrating it.'

The girl gave him a baleful glance. 'From the SS identities you were given, Stotz would have realised there was a spy working inside SS headquarters and by joining you he would have discovered it was me. He would have blown my cover, had me arrested and arranged for me to spend an extremely unpleasant session in the hands of those Gestapo thugs. As for you three, you would have been lucky. No need for questioning – "*Valkyrie*" already had all the answers. Just a quick firing squad for you.'

The three men exchanged glances; the reality of their position had suddenly been brought home to them.

'By the way,' Anna added, 'when you left the ship, was Stotz separated from you at any time? Even for a short while?'

'Well, he *was* the last of us to leave the bar just now, to come upstairs,' admitted Thompson.

The girl shook her head. 'No. You were all being watched. He couldn't have contacted anyone without us knowing. What about in the dockyard?'

182

Sinclair pursed his lips. 'Again, he was last to leave the customs and immigration office, despite being first in. I suppose he *could* have left a message, if that's what you're thinking, but it would have been brief – we weren't separated that long.'

'It doesn't take long to pass over a message,' she retorted tersely. 'Damn!'

She thought for a few moments.

'OK,' she announced briskly. 'Nothing we can do for the moment. Let me have your *Ausweisen* and Swedish passports. You'll not need them and we can put them to good use getting some people out of the country. And don't forget our friend, Herr Stotz – although in his case we'd better destroy them in case he did leave a message.'

The three men handed over their documents and Callendar leaned over the bed to extract Walters' from his dead body. The eyes of the corpse were open. He shivered involuntarily and placed his forefinger and thumb over Walters' eyelids, pulling them down to blot out the sightless stare. He handed the documents to Anna who casually flipped through them, then tossed them onto the bed.

'Let's go into the other room,' she suggested.

This proved to be much larger and was furnished with four single size beds. Neatly laid out on three of them were complete uniforms in the field grey of the Waffen SS, each bearing the badges of rank of an SS Untersturmführer. At the foot rested pairs of highly polished knee boots and a holdall each. These later proved to contain items of equipment which would normally form the luggage of an officer in transit: clean changes of underwear, shirts, socks, etc.

Sinclair looked at Anna in grudging admiration. 'You've been busy,' he commented.

'It's been done over a number of weeks. It wasn't easy. Look, I'm rather tired. Let's all sit down and I'll run through

183

the arrangements to get you to Berlin and then into Reich Central Security in Prinz Albrechtstrasse.'

She perched herself on the only chair in the room and crossed her legs.

'I thought we were supposed to report to the Chancellery,' said Callendar. 'Why go to Central Security?'

'You'll be billeted at Prinz Albrechtstrasse, right above Gestapo Headquarters. Don't worry. You couldn't be in a safer place. No one will suspect you.' She looked at Thompson who was staring at the empty bed. 'Something bothering you?'

'It's just occurred to me that we may have a slight problem. Berlin is expecting four of us, but now there's only three. Won't that cause some eyebrows to be raised?'

'Already taken care of,' she assured him. 'As soon as I realised what was happening, I selected a replacement – a genuine one this time. He'll be arriving the same time as you three.'

Thompson looked thoughtful. 'You said you knew about Walters before we left England.'

'So? What's the point?'

'I'm just curious. If that's the case, then why did you wait until we arrived here in Germany, before you ... before you took any action. You obviously have contact with London. Why didn't you inform our Intelligence people? They could easily have arrested him and it would've avoided an unnecessary death.'

'You fool!' she snorted. 'What in the hell are you doing here? You know nothing of what it's like here. Yes, I killed him, killed him without giving him a chance. Oh no, not the English way of doing things, I'm sure. But this isn't England. He would have killed me, you, all of us, without batting an eyelid. The only difference is that in my case they would've wanted information first, and they have some distinctly unpleasant ways of getting people to talk. I wasn't prepared to risk that – being forced to betray my comrades.'

She glared at Thompson with contempt.

'Yes, you're right,' she admitted, her voice a little calmer. 'I could have told London, but Stotz is ... was, a very resourceful character. He could easily have given your people the slip, contacted his wireless operator and had the information back to Berlin within twenty-four hours, and that would have put paid to your mission. Besides, I had my own self-preservation to think about. That's why he had to be killed.'

She lit another cigarette.

'You're right, of course,' Thompson conceded. 'You had no choice. I'm sorry.'

'Forget it,' she said absently. 'But I must say I find it hard to understand your attitude. OK, I've killed a man. But he *was* a Nazi and, after all, isn't that the reason you're here? To kill Hitler?'

'No ... that's not why we're here,' said Sinclair, surprised. 'We're not an assassination squad.'

'In God's name, what other reason could there be? Don't you realise, when it's discovered information has been leaked from SS records my cover will be blown and part of the Resistance Circle placed in jeopardy? For what? Why in the hell *are* you here?'

With help from Callendar and Thompson, Sinclair recounted the story of the ancient *Hakenkreuz*, how they had been instructed to steal it from under Hitler's nose and then smuggle it back to England.

'London believe Hitler places such value on it that to lose it would have so devastating an effect it would finish him,' Sinclair concluded.

Anna looked at them with incredulity.

'You're seriously telling me, all those clever people in London think that stealing an old lump of gold will bring about the downfall of the most powerful and evil dictator the world has ever known?' She laughed hollowly. 'You really want me to believe that?'

'It's the truth,' Callendar assured her, frowning at her scepticism. 'After all, I hardly think our people would go to all this trouble if they weren't convinced it would work.'

She looked at him with a mixture of sympathy and contempt.

'You fools. You poor bloody fools. What a waste!'

She walked to the window and peered out into the darkness. There was a silence of several minutes, eventually broken by Thompson.

'Does this mean you're not prepared to help us any further?' he demanded.

'It's all a bit academic now,' she replied. 'It doesn't make any difference whether I join in this idiotic venture or not. They're bound to find out about your true identities sooner or later and it'll not take them long to link you all with me. I'm already finished. The months of effort it took me to infiltrate the SS are all gone. Thrown away. And for what? Some hare-brained scheme dreamt up by an idiot. God! What a bloody waste!'

'You still haven't answered my question. Are you still prepared to help us?'

She looked at them and shook her head. 'You're mad. Completely mad. How do you know this so-called ancient *Hakenkreuz* still exists? If it ever did. I've never seen it, nor have I ever heard anyone mention it. And, even if it does, how can you be certain it's in the Reich Chancellery? If it means as much to him as you say it does, surely he wouldn't let it out of his sight? He'd take it with him wherever he went. Like now, when he's touring the Russian front.'

'Not so,' Sinclair assured her. 'Our information is that it never leaves the Chancellery and it's guarded twenty-four hours a day by at least two SS officers. Hence the reason we're here.'

Anna made a gesture of capitulation, moved over to one

of the beds and picked up three brown envelopes. Opening the first she withdrew a number of documents.

'These are what you'll need. SS Identity Card, Movement Orders and rail warrant. Now, be careful. You'll be carrying two Movement Orders. One to cover you on your journey from Rostock to Berlin, which you *must destroy* as soon as you arrive in Berlin. The second Movement Order is the one you'll hand in when you report to Reichs Central Security. Obviously, all the rail warrants are for Rostock to Berlin, but remember – you're all supposed to be coming from different directions. One of you from Lyons, one from Riga and one from Stalingrad. You did remember to bring your identity photographs I hope?'

They handed over the small manila envelopes given them by Ferguson.

'Good!'

Producing a small bottle of glue she carefully pasted each photograph into the appropriate identity card. She looked at one she was holding, then at Thompson.

'This is you, SS Untersturmführer Karl Dietrich.'

Thompson nodded.

'Just remember, you were awarded the Knights Cross for destroying three tanks single-handed on the Russian Front. Hitler awarded it personally to the real Dietrich, three months before he was run over by a Russian tank.'

'I think I would've preferred to be someone less conspicuous,' said Thompson. 'Heroes attract too much attention.'

Anna smiled wanly. 'Don't worry. They're commonplace at the Chancellery; Reichsmarschall Goering is a frequent visitor.' She handed Thompson the identity card together with the remaining contents of the envelope. 'You'll also find a few personal items, photographs, letters from wives or girlfriends, that sort of thing, to add to the authenticity. And some money, not that you should need much.'

She picked up the next card, checked the photograph and turned to Sinclair. 'This one's for you. SS Untersturmführer Friederich Steiner. You've been stationed at Lyons, working with the security service. Nothing too remarkable.' She picked up the last envelope.

'And this must be you. SS Untersturmführer Hans Richter.' She said to Callendar. 'You've come from Riga in Latvia, where you've been working with an *Einsatzkommando*, carrying out what are euphemistically referred to as "special duties". Have you any idea what those "special duties" were, Herr Untersturmführer?'

Callendar shook his head.

'The systematic liquidation of the Jewish population.'

'What on earth are you talking about?' exclaimed Thompson, looking up from examining his identity card.

'Exactly what I said. The deliberate murder of thousands of Jewish men, women and even children – and it's not limited to the Baltic States. Tens of thousands have been killed in Russia and Poland. The world doesn't want to know.'

'I don't believe you,' retorted Callendar, taking the envelope from her. 'We live in a civilised world. I know Nazis hate the Jews, but Hitler wouldn't dare...'

'Wouldn't he?' replied Anna mockingly. 'And who's going to stop him?'

'Jesus! I knew things were bad for the Jews,' Sinclair put in. 'But I hadn't realised it had gone this far.'

'Now you do know.' She turned back to Callendar.

'Well, Untersturmführer? *Could* you kill someone in cold blood? Place your pistol at the back of their head and pull the trigger? Because that's what Hans Richter had been doing – up to the time his vehicle was ambushed by a group of partisans.'

'It's incredible,' replied Callendar. 'Quite incredible. What sort of people would do that sort of thing?'

'Nazis,' she said simply. 'Let's get back to the matter in hand. Now listen carefully, this is what you will do. Obviously you'll sleep here tonight. Tomorrow morning Josef will guide you to the railway station. Don't be too concerned about the checkpoint at the station; SS officers are usually let through without question. In any event, your papers are quite genuine, so you have nothing to worry about.'

'Won't it seem rather strange, three SS officers passing through at the same time?' asked Sinclair.

'Fortunately, there's a transit camp just out of the city. Troop movements are commonplace here. Any more questions?'

They shook their heads.

'When you get to Berlin, for goodness' sake, don't all report at the Chancellery at the same time. I've put a suggested reporting time in each of your envelopes. These tie up with the arrival times of trains from your supposed departure points. Most importantly, for God's sake remember you don't know each other when you meet up again. You've never met before. Behave like total strangers to each other.'

'Yes, yes. We're aware of that,' declared Callendar irritably. 'What we want to know is how we find our way from the railway station to the Reichs Central Security building?'

Anna shot him an icy glance. 'I've enclosed a sketch map showing you where to go. You can get transport from the station if you contact the Duty Transport Officer. But I suggest you might choose to walk – it's not far to Prinz Albrechtstrasse. When you get there, just ask for the Duty Officer.'

She glanced at her wristwatch, crushed the cigarette she had been smoking and stood up.

'It's time for me to go,' she told them, replacing the forage cap on her head. 'I have to be back in Berlin tonight. I'm on duty in the morning. Don't worry about the body next door. Josef will have already had that removed.'

At the door she stopped and delivered her parting shot.

'If Stotz did manage to get a message through, they'll be waiting for you. If that's the case I'll get to know it as soon as I'm back to Berlin. If you are blown, I'll get to the railway station and stand on the platform. If you see me, then get the hell back onto a train, any train, and escape the best way you can. Otherwise, we can meet briefly in the Tiergarten tomorrow afternoon. I'll be waiting by the statue at the top of the Charlottenburger Chaussee, near the Brandenburger Tor at about three o'clock.'

Then she was gone.

16

SUNDAY, SEPTEMBER 27th

Early the following morning they were served breakfast in their room by a dark-haired woman in her mid-forties. She said little, simply introducing herself as Marthe, Josef's wife. A few minutes later she reappeared carrying a jug of hot water, which she placed by the bowl on the washstand, together with soap and towels.

'As soon as you are ready, Josef will take you to the railway station,' she announced. 'He says you must hurry. It is now 6.15 and the train for Berlin leaves in one hour.'

'We really do appreciate both your help and your hospitality,' said Thompson sincerely. 'I don't know what...'

'You have no need to thank me,' she interrupted curtly. 'You're Josef's guests, not mine. As far as I'm concerned, the sooner you have left the better for all of us. You're not the first people he's hidden here, and each time it becomes more and more dangerous. So please eat up and go.'

She left, closing the door behind her.

'Not very friendly,' observed Callendar, rolling out of bed and padding across to examine the contents of the breakfast tray.

'Are you surprised?' said Sinclair. 'How would you like to have three enemy agents under your roof, knowing it would mean the firing squad if you're caught?'

Callendar didn't reply. He was busy spreading margarine on one of the rolls.

After breakfast they quickly dressed themselves in the

uniforms provided by Anna, checking their appearance in the fly-blown mirror of the ancient wardrobe. Callendar was the first to be ready.

'Well, this is it. How do I look, chaps?' he asked, critically examining his image.

His dove-grey uniform carried a silver Death's Head on the right-hand collar patch, symbol of the Totenkopf Division of the SS, whilst the left collar patch carried the three silver pips of an SS Untersturmführer. As he stared at his reflection, he thoughtfully fingered the cold metal of the Death's Head badge, recalling Anna's words about the duties of an *Einsatzkommando*.

As soon as the others had finished dressing, Thompson adorned with his Knight's Cross at his throat, the three solemnly shook hands, picked up their canvas grips and made their way downstairs where Josef waiting for them.

After some discussion, it was decided that, with Josef in the lead, Callendar and Thompson would keep a distance of some fifty yards behind him, Sinclair following them at roughly the same distance. Josef led the way through a door at the back of the tavern into the small storage yard they had seen from the bedroom window. He opened the double wooden gates into the blind alleyway. They faced the worst and most dangerous moment of the journey next: being spotted emerging from the alleyway. It would be difficult to explain to a policeman, or other official, what they had been doing there. But few people were about at that early hour and they were soon in their pre-arranged 'order of march', wending their way through the busier main thoroughfares of the town.

They reached the railway station without incident and Josef stood to one side of the entrance, giving them each an almost imperceptible nod as they passed through. The station was crowded and there were a great number of military personnel milling around, which enabled them to mingle unnoticed in the mass of uniforms. Their confidence received a further boost when they were waved unchecked through the security barrier, the attention of the Feldgendarmerie Unterscharführer on duty, being taken up with making life uncomfortable for two young soldiers from an infantry regiment returning late from weekend leave. Jubilant at their good fortune, they made their way out onto the platform where Callendar and Thompson passed the time making conversation, Sinclair standing a few yards away.

Their train, like all those in Germany, arrived on time, a tribute to Nazi efficiency. Unlike British trains, with their separate compartments, the carriages were of open plan design, allowing the three men to maintain their agreed separation in the same carriage, yet at the same time, retain visual contact with one another.

The journey to Berlin took just over two hours. As the train pulled into the platform, they were relieved to see no sign of Anna on the platform. After disembarking they split up, leaving the station separately at specific intervals in order for them to arrive at Gestapo Headquarters at their suggested reporting times. Callendar went first, leaving both Sinclair and Thompson drinking coffee in the station bar.

He was glad he had followed Anna's advice and walked rather than commandeer transport from the Station Duty Officer. It gave him the opportunity to have a look at the German capital and recapture boyhood memories of visits to his parents at the British Embassy before the war. Anna's directions proved easy to follow as he made his way along Friedrichstrasse into Unter den Linden towards Brandenburger Tor where he could see the impressive Brandenburg Gate in the distance. Turning into Wilhelmstrasse, he passed the Reichs Chancellery where they would be carrying out their duties, then across Leipzigerstrasse, past Reichsmarshall Goering's offices and right into Prinz Albrechtstrasse.

He saw Gestapo Headquarters immediately, a sombre grey

building. He hesitated briefly, a last-minute preparation for what lay ahead, before marching, with a show of confidence he certainly didn't feel, towards the entrance. The *SS Rottenführer*[1] on sentry duty came smartly to attention, his Schmeisser machine pistol held across his chest, and snapped up his arm in a Nazi salute as Callendar approached. The Englishman acknowledged in like manner, accompanied by the requisite 'Heil Hitler'. He entered the building, looked around briefly, and made for a desk at the back of the reception hall where an SS Hauptscharführer sat, flanked by two more SS guards. After a further Nazi salute, the Hauptscharführer examined Callendar's papers, ticked his name off on a clipboard in front of him and entered the arrival time. Despite his situation, Callendar couldn't help an inward smile. It reminded him of his arrival at Blandford all those weeks ago – virtually the same check-in procedure, except that this time he wasn't late.

'*Danke*, Herr Untersturmführer. Please report to Room 145. Through that door and along the corridor.'

Pocketing his papers, Callendar picked up his grip and made his way towards the door indicated. Room 145 he found located halfway along the corridor, a notice on the door announcing it was the office of SS Sturmbannführer Otto Schiller – Officer in Charge, Reichs Chancellery Guard. Forcing himself to relax, he knocked firmly on the door.

'*Komm!*'

He pushed open the door and entered, to find himself in a fairly large room, approximately thirty feet long and fifteen feet wide, with a desk situated close to the door he had just entered. Behind the desk, another door presumably led to Sturmbannführer Schiller's office. A number of chairs had been placed against the walls, two of them already occupied by young SS officers reading magazines. Behind the desk

---

[1] Lance Corporal

194

sat a severe-looking woman in her forties, also wearing an SS uniform.

'*Heil Hitler.* Your papers please, Herr Untersturmführer.' Her voice was curt, officious. Her dark hair was pulled back in a tight bun; she wore no make-up – clearly a woman who would tolerate no nonsense.

Callendar echoed her greeting, placed his bag on the floor to retrieve his papers from his breast pocket. After a cursory examination, she too ticked his name on a list in front of her, before handing them back to him.

'Thank you, Herr Untersturmführer. If you would care to join the other two officers, there are some magazines and newspapers for you to read. Sturmbannführer Schiller will be with you as soon as the others have arrived.'

She glanced at the clock on the wall. It showed ten o'clock.

'In one hour's time, to be precise,' she added confidently.

Eleven o'clock, thought Callendar. That was the time Thompson was scheduled in, which meant he should be the last man. Sinclair was due to report in at ten forty-five. He seated himself next to the other two SS officers. After introductions, they talked quietly among themselves, comparing individual experiences; the other two impressed by Callendar's membership of the Totenkopfverbande. Callendar was thankful he had spent time reading up the notes on Hans Richter's military career.

By the time Sinclair reported in, two other men had also arrived, swelling their numbers to six. Callendar picked up a copy of *Das Schwarze Korps* from the chair beside him and began reading it. He couldn't help noticing that the woman at the desk kept glancing at the clock on the wall every few minutes, as though someone was overdue. He frowned thoughtfully. It couldn't be Thompson. He was certain about Thompson's reporting time of eleven, so it had to be the other man, the eighth member of the guard.

At three minutes to eleven came a further knock at the

195

door. All six men looked up expectantly as the woman called out, '*Komm!*' The door opened and in stepped the familiar figure of Thompson. 'Untersturmführer Dietrich reporting for duty,' he announced formally to the secretary. After she had checked him off the list, he went across and joined the rest of the group, avoiding looking directly at Callendar and Sinclair. He was in the middle of introducing himself when the telephone on the desk rang.

'No, Herr Sturmbannführer,' they heard her say. 'There is one still to come – Untersturmführer Schmidt. Time? He was due to report at ten-forty. No, there has been no message. Very good.' She replaced the receiver and looked up at the seven SS officers. 'Would you please stand up and form a single line. Sturmbannführer Schiller will be out now.'

The group rose smartly to their feet, busily adjusting their uniforms and straightening caps, ready to receive their new commanding officer. They had barely finished when the office door swung open briskly and out stepped a man in his early thirties wearing the uniform of an SS Sturmbannführer. Tall and lean, he looked the Nazi archetype: blond hair, pale blue, penetrating eyes and a cruel, thin-lipped mouth. He held himself erect, cap set at an almost jaunty angle, as if to give the impression of a devil-may-care character. But the eyes and the mouth belied this. He would be a tough one.

Sinclair, standing at the end of the line nearest Schiller, called the group to attention. Seven pairs of jackboots were brought together in unison, with a sound like a single pistol shot. At the same time, seven right arms shot into the air, each one at exactly the right angle, accompanied by a chorus of 'Heil Hitler'. Schiller drew himself to attention and responded smartly, his arm snapping up into the salute as though he were on the parade ground at Bad Tölz. He walked slowly along the line, inspecting each man from head to toe, looking for the slightest fault in their dress. Each man hoped he would not be the one to be found wanting. But their concern proved unnecessary. Sturmbannführer Schiller had already decided he would reserve his venom for a certain SS Untersturmführer Schmidt, who had committed the cardinal sin of reporting late for duty.

'All right, at ease. Sit down,' he said, removing his cap and placing it on his secretary's desk. 'My name is Schiller. I'm responsible for security at the Reichs Chancellery and for the next four weeks...'

His introduction was interrupted as the door from the corridor opened without warning. The figure that stepped into the room was unmistakeable. Schiller instantly grabbed his cap, slammed it on his head, called the group to attention and gave the Nazi salute. His visitor entered. Beady, shiftless eyes peered from rimless glasses, looking at everyone, missing nothing. He casually acknowledged the salute.

'Herr Reichsführer!' spluttered Schiller. 'I wasn't expecting you... No one phoned to say...'

Himmler held up his hand. 'No need to concern yourself, Schiller. It's a minor matter.' The cold eyes surveyed the seven men. 'Who are these officers?'

'They're the new guard for the Führer's office in the Reichs Chancellery, Herr Reichsführer,' he replied nervously.

Himmler nodded and began to walk along the line of assembled men. The room was deathly quiet; only the sound of his footsteps on the polished wooden floor broke the silence. He stopped in front of Callendar, who swallowed hard, struggling to maintain his composure. He stared straight ahead.

'So,' said Himmler, gazing at Callendar's right collar patch. 'You are with the Totenkopf Division. Your name?'

'SS Untersturmführer Hans Richter, Herr Reichsführer!' replied Callendar without hesitation.

Himmler nodded slowly as if digesting the information. 'And where have you been serving, Richter?'

'I have been serving with an *Einsatzkommando* in Riga, Latvia, Herr Reichsführer.'

A flicker of interest registered in Himmler's eyes. 'An *Einsatzkommando*? Tell me, Richter. Have you found your duties in Latvia ... arduous?'

'With respect, Herr Reichsführer. No duty is too arduous for an SS officer.'

Himmler gave a thin smile of approval. He moved along the line, looking at each man individually. He had just drawn level with Thompson when the door from the corridor burst open and a breathless, burly and dishevelled figure stumbled in.

'Untersturmführer Schmidt reporting for du ...' The big man froze in mid-sentence, suddenly aware there were other people in the room. His eyes widened as he met Himmler's icy stare. Swallowing hard, he promptly came to attention and saluted.

Schiller's face was a picture of evil. 'You're late,' he snarled at the unfortunate man. 'And you dare to enter this office without knocking! You're a disgrace to the SS!'

'My apologies, Herr Sturmbannführer... I mean... Herr Reichsführer... I...' Beads of sweat ran down his face as he stammered his apologies.

'Silence!' thundered Schiller. 'Stay where you are and keep your mouth shut.'

He turned to Himmler.

'My apologies, Herr Reichsführer. With your permission, I will deal with this wretch later.' Himmler stood staring silently at the shaking figure but, surprisingly, he said nothing and turned back to Thompson.

'Your name?'

'SS Untersturmführer Karl Dietrich, Herr Reichsführer.'

Himmler's eyes alighted on the decoration at Thompson's throat.

'I see you wear the Knight's Cross.' He turned to Schiller with a questioning look. 'The reason for this award?'

Schiller hurriedly referred to his file. 'Ah, yes! Dietrich was awarded the Knight's Cross for single-handedly destroying three Russian T34 tanks during the battle for Kiev. He was presented with it personally by the Führer at Rastenburg.'

'Good! I will speak to you later, Schiller,' he said, sending a final withering glance at Schmidt before disappearing through the door.

With the Reichsführer's departure, the atmosphere relaxed, sufficiently the errant Schmidt mistakenly thought to make his apologies to Schiller.

'Herr Sturmbannführer, I wish to...'

'Silence!' screamed Schiller, crashing a clenched fist on his secretary's desk, which caused the poor woman almost to jump out of her skin. 'I didn't give you permission to speak. Stand still and keep your mouth shut, until I've decided what I'm going to do with you.'

Schmidt froze rigidly at attention while Schiller turned to the rest of the group.

'All right. The rest of you, sit down and pay attention. During your time here you will be directly responsible to me. And I'm sure I don't have to tell you that, whilst you are here, you will come into contact with some of the most senior party members. Therefore you will conduct yourselves in the true tradition of the SS at all times. Any indiscipline, any infraction of the rules, will be severely dealt with.' He threw a cold glance at Schmidt. 'I don't need to tell you how much of an honour it is to be chosen to act as the Führer's personal guard.' He gave what passed for a smile, a thin stretching of the facial muscles. 'However, on this occasion, you gentlemen will probably be denied actually seeing our Leader during your tour of duty. He is at present, at Rastenburg and unlikely to return for several weeks. However, even when the Führer is away, his office is guarded twenty-four hours a day. Each guard duty lasts twelve hours, commencing at 0600 hours or 1800 hours, with two officers

199

forming the guard at all times. A duty roster will be posted on the notice board in your room, which you should check daily in case of any sudden changes. You will find you will be paired against a different officer for each duty and you are not permitted to leave your post for any reason *whatsoever!* So make sure you empty your bladders beforehand.'

Again he treated them to his sickly smile.

'Whilst you are on guard you will permit no one to enter during the Führer's absence, with two exceptions: Frau Christian, the Führer's secretary, and Frau Kemple, the cleaner. Frau Kemple arrives each night at midnight and departs at one o'clock, irrespective of whether the office has been used or not. While she is there, one of you will stand inside the door so that she is within your sight at all times. Is that clear?'

'Now, as members of the Chancellery Guard, you will be temporarily seconded to the Führer's Personal Guard, the *SS Liebstandarte Adolf Hitler*. New uniforms have been placed in your quarters, together with your ceremonial black uniforms, which will be worn only for guard duty, not for walking out! Which brings me to the more pleasurable aspect of your stay in Berlin. Whilst off duty, you are free to do whatever you wish with your time. You will have no other duties so, if you have not been to our great capital before, take the opportunity to have a look round and enjoy the sights. You will find the ladies of Berlin are very accommodating to members of the Liebstandarte. Enjoy yourselves whilst you are here. That is an order! Guard duties for your group will commence at 0600 hours tomorrow. Make sure you check to find out who will be on duty. That's all. Any questions?'

Everyone shook their heads.

'Good!' exclaimed Schiller. 'My secretary, Frau Graf, will show you to your quarters. Thank you, gentlemen.'

The seven men rose to their feet, came to attention, saluted and filed out of the room, following the austere figure of

200

Frau Graf. The door had barely closed behind them when Schiller's voice could be heard screaming invective at the unfortunate Schmidt.

'Glad it's him and not me,' muttered one named Lintz, as they began to climb a flight of stairs to the first floor. 'I've met the Sturmbannführer before, when I was attending a course at Bad Tölz. Believe me, they don't come any tougher. So be warned!' Callendar, Sinclair and Thompson exchanged glances. They were already in the lion's den; it didn't matter to them how vicious one particular beast was.

17

Despite the prestige of having been selected for the Führer's personal guard at the Reichs Chancellery, they found that the accommodation provided for them during their month's duty was surprisingly Spartan. It was a single room, approximately forty feet long and twenty wide, with four steel-framed beds regimentally spaced along the longer walls. Alongside each bed stood a tall wooden locker, with additional storage in the form of a metal footlocker situated at the end of the bed. Four small windows, two on either side of the room, allowed limited daylight to enter. In the centre, between the two rows of beds, stood a long wooden table, its top scrubbed white, together with six wooden chairs, which formed the only seating. Everything in the room – beds, lockers, table, chairs – was arranged in rigid uniformity, and with the strong smell of carbolic hanging in the air, mixed with the smell of floor polish, it was reminiscent of an Army barrack room back in England. In front of the wooden table, his tall thin frame held rigidly at attention, stood a young SS private.

'This is where you will sleep,' announced Frau Graf. 'The toilets and showers are through that door at the far end. Your meals will be served in the canteen, which is situated on the ground floor. Meal times are shown on the noticeboard. I am in the process of preparing the duty roster for your guard duties for the next seven days. This will be displayed on the noticeboard and updated at the end of each week.'

She indicated the gangly SS man with an imperious wave of her hand.

'Private Bauer will attend to all your needs whilst you are here. So if you require uniforms pressing, or laundry to be done, he will arrange it. Any questions?'

They shook their heads.

'Good! You are all off duty now and free to go sightseeing, but each time you leave the building for any reason, except when going on duty, you must sign out in the main hall. That is all.'

With almost military precision, she swung on her heel and disappeared through the door.

After she had gone, the seven men began searching for their respective bed spaces. These had already been allocated and were identified by a name card pinned on the door of each wooden locker. The three Englishmen discovered that by pure good fortune they had been allocated adjacent beds, with Sinclair having the first bed in the line, then Callendar and finally Thompson. The remaining bed on that side, next to Thompson, had been allocated to the absent Schmidt. The four on the other side accommodated the rest of the Guard.

'*Mein Gott!*' exclaimed a tall, blond-haired man named Strohm, glaring at his surroundings. 'Talk about recruits camp. I'd expected something far more comfortable for the Führer's personal guard...'

'Ach! This is typical Schiller,' replied Lintz, tossing his grip on the bed he had been allocated. 'He thinks we SS don't appreciate comfort.' He looked at the SS private still standing rigidly at attention in front of the wooden table. 'Well, Bauer? What do you say?'

'I do not have an opinion on that matter, Herr Untersturmführer,' Bauer replied, his voice as stiff as his body.

'Oh, for Christ's sake, Bauer,' snorted Lintz. 'Relax man. No need to stand at attention all the time. In fact, you can push off. There's nothing we need from you at the moment.'

The orderly visibly relaxed.

'Very good, Herr Untersturmführer. Thank you. If you do

require anything, you only have to ring this bell.' He indicated a bell-push fixed to the wall next to the notice board. 'My quarters are next door.'

He came smartly to attention, clicking his heels together, and gave a slight bow before making for the exit. But his intended departure coincided with Schmidt's arrival in the doorway.

'Out of my way!' snarled the burly German, pushing Bauer aside. 'Don't you know you make way for officers, you little worm?' He glared at the orderly. 'Who are you, anyway?'

'I am Bauer, Herr Untersturmführer,' replied Bauer, quickly resuming the position of attention. 'I am the orderly for officers of the Führer's guard.'

'Are you? Right then! You can start your duties right now by cleaning my kit.'

'But, Herr Untersturmführer,' protested Bauer, 'you have all been provided with brand new equipment and uniforms. They are hanging in your locker, ready for you.'

'Huh!' Schmidt frowned, disappointed at being unable to make life difficult for Bauer immediately. 'And which is my bed?'

Sinclair, sitting on his bed unpacking the contents of his grip, decided to come to the aid of the unfortunate Bauer. Like the others, he had taken an immediate dislike to the big bullying German.

'Yours is in the corner,' he said quietly.

Schmidt turned to face him, his eyes narrowing dangerously.

'Who says so?' he sneered.

'The card on the locker door says so,' replied Sinclair without bothering to look up.

Schmidt crossed to Sinclair's bed where he let his grip fall to the floor. Hands on hips, he rocked to and fro on his heels.

'Ach so!' he responded. 'Then the card's wrong. *This* is my bed, so you'd better shift your arse.'

Sinclair, in the middle of sorting out his socks, froze. Then, with exaggerated slowness, he carefully laid aside the socks and rose to his feet, his hands balling themselves into ham-like fists. Extending himself to his full six foot three inches, he looked down with contempt at the red-faced Schmidt.

'Make me.'

Schmidt stepped back in surprise. His face paled as he stared at the tall man. He hadn't expected this; most people backed down when he challenged them. Like most bullies, Otto Schmidt was mostly bluff and bluster. He became hesitant, realising he was up against someone who would doubtless better him in a brawl. Eventually he wordlessly capitulated, glaring hatefully at Sinclair before reluctantly reaching down for his grip and turning away.

He immediately made for the bed opposite, apparently considering this to be the next best option. Taking a leaf out of Sinclair's book, Lintz stood stolidly in front of it prepared to defend his territory.

'He isn't going to move either,' said Sinclair, going across to stand by the man.

Schmidt was beaten and he knew it. Turning away he stomped down the room to the empty bed in the corner, muttering under his breath.

It had been a bad day all round for Untersturmführer Otto Schmidt. It had started that morning when he had missed his train in Munich, owing to the fact that he had overslept on account of the amount of beer he had consumed the night before. He and a few cronies had spent the evening celebrating his enviable posting to Berlin by visiting almost every tavern in the Bavarian capital, with the result that he had missed his early morning call. The dressing-down he had received from Schiller, exacerbated by the fact that his late arrival had been witnessed by none other than Reichsführer Himmler himself and the rest of his colleagues, had done nothing to

205

improve his demeanour. On top of all that he had now been further humiliated by his colleagues. He was thus in bellicose mood and when he saw he would be sleeping next to Thompson he couldn't resist the opportunity to try once again to assert himself.

'Ho! So I'm to have the hero for company, am I?' He jabbed a stubby finger towards the Knight's Cross hung at the Englishman's throat. 'And what did you do to get that, old man? Chase some Russian tarts out of their houses?'

He guffawed loudly, expecting the others to join in. Instead he was met with a stony silence. He glared at Thompson.

'Well? I asked you a question, old man...'

Thompson knew Schmidt was still spoiling for a fight and only looking for an excuse to demonstrate his superior physical strength, so he chose to ignore him, continuing with his unpacking. But this didn't suit Schmidt at all. Having already lost face by backing down to Sinclair, he had no intention of letting this 'old man' ignore him. He stabbed his finger into Thompson's back. 'I won't ask you again. I want an answer. Or else...'

'Or else what, Schmidt?'

It was Sinclair. He had had enough and made his way down the room towards the two men.

'This is nothing to do with you,' Schmidt snarled, 'so clear off!'

'That's the second time you've tried to tell me what to do,' Sinclair replied softly, 'and, as I said before, make me!'

Schmidt looked at him sullenly. 'What's the matter? You his nursemaid? Can't he stand up for himself?' His face took on a crafty expression. 'After all, he's supposed to be a hero, ain't he?'

'Tell me, Schmidt. Where have you been serving our Führer and the Fatherland? On the Eastern front, fighting the Russians? Or perhaps North Africa, with Field Marshal Rommel, fighting the British?'

Suddenly Lintz was at Sinclair's elbow.

'Yes. Come on, Schmidt. Tell us about your war experiences. How many of the enemy have you killed? How many tanks have you knocked out?'

Schmidt scowled but said nothing; he turned away to begin his own unpacking.

Lintz glanced down at Schmidt's bed where the burly man had carelessly tossed his documents. Stepping forward he snatched up the buff-coloured Movement Order, scanning the contents before Schmidt could stop him.

'Ach so! I see the brave Untersturmführer Schmidt has been fighting the enemy in the taverns of Munich.'

This brought a burst of laughter from the others. Lintz tossed the document back on the bed.

'You're not fit to lick his boots, Schmidt, let alone be a fellow SS officer,' he announced contemptuously, then turned on his heel and made his way back to his own bed. After a few moments, Sinclair followed suit, leaving Thompson alone with Schmidt.

When he thought the others were out of earshot, the fat Nazi turned his head and hissed, 'This isn't finished, old man. Before long I'll have you licking *my* boots – or my name's not Otto Schmidt!'

Realising remaining silent had been a mistake Thompson knew he couldn't afford to ignore the challenge a second time. Dropping the items of clothing he had been unpacking, he summoned up his courage and suddenly whirled round on Schmidt who now had his back to him. Grabbing the fat German by the shoulder, he spun him around, seized hold of the man's tunic and, thrusting his face to within inches of Schmidt's, spoke clearly and loudly enough for the rest of the men to hear.

'I've had just about enough of you. Any time you want to try and make me, let me know. Any time... Any place... Got it?'

207

This unexpected outburst from the seemingly mild-mannered older man took Schmidt completely by surprise. The colour drained from his cheeks. Without waiting for a response, Thompson contemptuously thrust the fat German away and calmly resumed his unpacking.

'It would appear still waters run deep,' murmured Ströhm smiling.

'You surprised?' murmured Lintz. 'You don't get the Knight's Cross for nothing.'

At that moment Bauer reappeared through the doorway bearing a sheet of paper in his hand. He pinned it to the green baize notice board.

'Gentlemen, this is the Chancellery Guard duty roster for the next seven days. It commences at 0600 hours tomorrow. I have been asked by Frau Graf to draw it to your attention.'

With the customary click of the heels and slight bow, he departed.

Except for Schmidt, who elected to remain by his bed, the men crowded round the notice board. Callendar's name appeared for the first time against Thursday and, by sheer coincidence so did Thompson's. But what really caught his eye was that both he and Sinclair had been detailed for duty on the Saturday night. On the other hand, poor Thompson had been paired with Schmidt for the previous daytime duty. He risked a quick sidelong glance and caught the eye of Sinclair, who gave the slightest of nods to indicate he too had picked up on the weekend duty. It couldn't have worked out better.

'No late night for you, Schmidt,' chided Lintz loudly. 'You're on tomorrow morning with Kleist. Reveille 0500. And Schmidt, please don't make a noise. I'm a light sleeper.'

He grinned broadly, but Schmidt declined to respond.

'As for the rest of you lucky fellows,' he continued, 'the sooner we change our uniforms, the sooner we can enjoy the pleasures of Berlin. Who's for a visit to the Bierkellers of our great city?' He looked at Sinclair. 'How about you?'

'Another time, thanks. I've arranged to meet someone this afternoon,' Sinclair replied.

'Aha! Do I detect a female is involved?' enquired Lintz. 'If so, does she have a friend?'

Sinclair smiled. 'I'll see what I can arrange.'

The three Englishmen were deliberately slow in changing into their walking-out uniforms, in order that the others might leave before them. When they eventually did take their leave, they received a cheery farewell from Kleist but a sullen silence from the ill-tempered Schmidt.

Safely negotiating the checking-out procedure at the reception desk, they left the building and made their way towards the Tiergarten and their rendezvous with Anna.

'You're going to have to keep an eye on Schmidt,' Sinclair warned Thompson, as they strode along. 'He's got it in for you for some reason, so for goodness' sake, be careful.'

'I had noticed,' replied Thompson. '*And* I've got the pleasure of his company for twelve hours on Saturday.'

'Never mind that,' said Callendar excitedly. 'We shan't be here long enough for Schmidt to cause any trouble. That was a stroke of luck, two of us being paired off for night duty on the first weekend.'

Sinclair nodded. 'Being a Sunday everyone will have relaxed for the weekend. That should give us a good twenty-four hours' head start before we're missed, and by that time we should be in Switzerland.' He thought for a moment. 'We'd better get Anna to arrange for a car and some false papers. Even if it is a Sunday, we may get stopped in a routine check.'

As they got closer to the Tiergarten they found more and more people were about enjoying the warm sunshine, and their uniforms, with the *Liebstandarte SS Adolf Hitler* legend on the cuff, drew admiring glances, particularly young girls from whom they received friendly smiles.

'Schiller was right,' observed Thompson. 'With these uniforms, this is a bachelor's paradise.'

'Never mind that,' retorted Sinclair. 'Keep an eye out for Anna. She should be by that statue over there.'

He indicated a large bronze sculpture mounted on a stone plinth.

'There she is,' murmured Callendar. 'And she's alone.'

'Right. We'd better not all talk to her,' said Sinclair. 'You two carry on walking. We'll follow behind.'

He broke away from the other two and made his way to Anna, who had changed out of uniform and was now wearing a pretty floral dress.

'You're late, *Liebling*,' she greeted him, pouting for the benefit of passers-by. 'You've kept me waiting again.'

'Sorry. Got delayed.' He kissed her on the cheek. 'Everything OK?'

'Yes, fine,' she replied.

She slipped her arm inside his and they set off at a saunter, followed a few paces behind by Callendar and Thompson. Keeping his voice low, Sinclair passed on the news that he and Callendar would be on night duty on the coming Saturday.

'And the best of it is, with Hitler away in Prussia and not likely to be back for some time, we should be in England by the time the theft is discovered.'

'That's good news. For my part, I'll arrange for the cleaner, Frau Kemple, to have a night off on Saturday. No need for Schiller to know about it.' She stopped talking as two young girls in Hitler *Jugend* uniforms approached. 'Yes, *Liebling*,' she continued, 'and don't forget you promised to take me to the next Wagner concert...'

The two girls gave the Nazi salute as they passed, Sinclair responding.

'Frau Kemple should leap at the opportunity of a night off,' Anna went on. 'It'll be her first in a year.'

'What's the point?' frowned Sinclair.

'Simple. I'll take her place.' She smiled at him. 'Well, you've got to get the *Hakenkreuz* out of the Chancellery

210

somehow. And you can hardly stuff it inside your jacket, can you?'

'Hadn't thought of that, I must admit.' Sinclair gave her arm a squeeze. 'But how are you going to get it past the other guards?'

'Easy! I'll just stick it in my bucket of dirty water. They'll never look in there. And I can't think of a more appropriate place. Can you?'

'What then?'

'I'll arrange for a car to be available for six o'clock Sunday morning – there are always plenty in the motor pool and I'm often required to requisition them for SS officers. I'll meet you in the yard at the back of Gestapo headquarters at six-thirty. That'll give you time to get changed. I'll also arrange for an official movement order, which will authorise the four of us to get as close to the Swiss border as possible without attracting suspicion. How we actually get over the border is something we'll have to decide at the time. Once across, there'll be people waiting for us.'

'How...?'

'Don't ask questions,' she said tersely. 'Just take my word for it.'

They maintained their pretence of being young lovers until they reached one of the exit gates.

'We'll have to split up now,' said Anna. 'Better we don't see anything of each other until six-thirty on Sunday morning.'

'But what if we need to get in touch with you? Won't you tell me where you live?'

'That wouldn't be a good idea. Now I really must go.'

As he watched her hurry away he experienced an uncomfortable feeling. Why had she been reluctant to give him her address? He rejoined Callendar and Thompson, who had stopped to wait a few yards away and the three men continued their walk while Sinclair relayed the plans for the coming weekend, until Thompson interrupted

211

the briefing by stopping at a kiosk to buy picture postcards of Berlin.

'What on earth d'you want those for?' asked Callendar, as Thompson thrust them into his jacket pocket. 'Surely you don't intend to post them back to England?' he said jokingly.

'Something to show my kids when we get back. Otherwise they'd never believe I'd been in Berlin.'

Later that evening, as they prepared for bed, Thompson dug out his pack of postcards and flipped through them. There were ten in all: the Brandenburg Gate, the Tiergarten, the Reichs Chancellery and other famous sights, plus the inevitable photograph of the Führer himself. He slipped them back into their paper wallet and casually glanced round the room. Kleist and Schmidt had retired early in preparation for their five o'clock call, the latter snoring loudly. Callendar and Sinclair were talking quietly; Lintz and the remaining two men were still enjoying the Berlin nightlife. Satisfied no-one was watching him, he delved into his locker, pulled out a pile of socks and retrieved the photograph hidden in one. Cupping it in his hands he gazed at it fondly. It was the picture of himself, his wife and two children standing outside Buckingham Palace, the one he had shown around at the Jackdaw's Nest. He had secreted it in one of his gumboots during the search made by Ferguson and had got away with it. He gazed affectionately at the photograph for a few moments before slipping it between the postcards inside the wallet. Be safe enough there, he told himself. He opened the door of his wardrobe and pushed the wallet to the back of one of the shelves, placing the pile of socks on top. Then, with a contented smile, he climbed into bed.

18

ABWEHR HEADQUARTERS, BERLIN – ADMIRAL CANARIS' MORNING BRIEFING

'Is that it, Hans?' asked Canaris, closing the file in his hand and passing it back to his Chief of Staff.

Oberst Hans Oster, a studious-looking man, accepted the green manila folder and laid it neatly on the pile of files reviewed that morning, then picked up one he had left to last.

'There is just one other item which may be of interest, Herr Admiral.'

He opened the folder and removed a small sheet of paper. 'It's something which came in this morning from Rostock. The counterfoil of an *Ausweis* issued by Immigration Control to a Swedish seaman.' He passed it to Canaris. 'It's one of those evening passes issued to merchant seamen from neutral ships. This one refers to ... let me see...' He referred to his notes. 'Ah, yes. The SS *Hilversund*, delivering a cargo of mineral ore.'

'And?' frowned Canaris impatiently.

'It's what's written on the back of the form – just one word, "*Valkyrie*".'

Canaris turned the form over.

'*Valkyrie*,' he mused. 'Now why should a Swedish seaman choose to deface an official German document by writing the name of a mythological Norse maiden on the back? Does it mean anything to us?' He turned the piece of paper back over and read out the name of the Swedish seaman. 'Bjorn

213

Johannson.' He looked up at Hoffman. '*Valkyrie* sounds like a code name. Not one of ours?'

'No, Herr Admiral. It's a new one on us.' He thought for a moment. 'It is possible it could be one of Heydrich's people. You'll remember he set up his own espionage network before he took up that "dead end" job in Prague!'

Oster permitted himself a wry smile at his oblique reference to Heydrich's assassination by Czech partisans earlier that year.

'Careful, Hans,' Canaris cautioned softly. 'Someone may hear you and I have no wish to be compromised.'[1]

Canaris examined the *Ausweis* more closely.

'When did you say this came in? This morning?'

'Yes, this morning,' he confirmed. 'The vessel docked late Saturday afternoon. It was by pure chance that one of our people in Rostock happened to spot it when he happened to call into the immigration office. As you know, we've increased our staff there in an attempt to trace the source of coded radio transmissions in that area.'

'You'd better let the SD know about this ... just in case. But hang on to this piece of paper. You never know, might come in useful.' He reflected for a moment. 'See if you can find out if the name "*Valkyrie*" means anything to them. See what reaction you get.' He handed the document back to Oster. 'Let me know immediately if anything develops.'

'Very good, Herr Admiral.'

* * *

---

[1] (Hans Oster had secret connections with a resistance movement against the Nazis and came under suspicion from the Gestapo on several occasions. He was eventually suspended from duty in 1943 and arrested a year later. He was finally executed, along with Canaris, at Flossenbürg concentration camp on 9th April 1945, tragically, only a month before the war ended.)

Back in his office, Oster made a number of telephone calls. One such call was to an acquaintance in AmtVIB, of Reich Central Security Office, SS Hauptsturmführer Karl Bauer. Although their relationship could not be called friendly, the two men had cooperated successfully together on a number of previous occasions, Oster always being circumspect in the amount and quality of information he chose to pass on. Most of it was innocuous material, the nature of which did not compromise himself, Canaris or the Abwehr. On the other hand Oster, armed with skilful interrogation techniques, often found he was able to elicit far more information from Bauer without the other man realising what he was giving away. In less than twenty minutes he was again knocking on the Admiral's door.

'*Komm!*'

Canaris could see from his expression he had come up with something. He laid aside the file he had been reading and motioned Oster to sit down.

'*Valkyrie*?'

'Yes, Herr Admiral. I telephoned one of my contacts at Reich Central Security. It appears Valkyrie *is* one of theirs: an SS officer who managed to get to England back in 1940 when the British were evacuating their troops from Dunkirk. The story goes he dressed himself in a British uniform taken from a dead Tommy and got picked up by one of the evacuation boats. When he got to England he simply disappeared in the confusion. Since then he's been sending back intelligence information via one of their other operatives. Seems he's one of their top agents.'

Oster paused.

'Go on,' urged Canaris.

'Well, it seems the last message they received from him was sometime in July,' continued the Colonel. 'Reports indicate that, somehow or other, he actually managed to infiltrate British Intelligence – God knows how – and had

215

been selected for some secret work for the British. No precise details unfortunately, but they haven't heard from him since – that is until I made my phone call. And now they're hopping mad and want all details sent across to them without delay.'

The Admiral gave one of his rare smiles.

'You did well, Hans.'

He stood up and walked to the window. For a few moments he stared silently at the busy street below, endeavouring to analyse the situation. He turned back to Oster.

'What do you make of it? How do you interpret the message from *Valkyrie*?'

Oster withdrew the Immigration form from the file he was holding and stared at it for the umpteenth time.

'Valkyrie,' he said to himself. He looked up at the Admiral. 'I think we have to ask ourselves a number of questions. Firstly, why, when he's safe back in Germany, does he still use his code name and so cryptically? Why doesn't he declare himself openly? He obviously wants Reich Central Security to know he is back, hence the message. But at the same time he still wants to remain under cover. Why?'

'Go on,' murmured Canaris.

'We know he penetrated British Intelligence and we believe he's managed to get himself selected for some sort of secret work. If that's the case, then his presence in Germany would appear to indicate he's on some sort of mission – what that is we've yet to establish – but maintaining secrecy is obviously vital. Which could mean he's part of a team – say with a genuine British agent, or agents.'

Canaris returned to his seat behind the desk. 'All right. I'll go along with you thus far. What else?'

'Unfortunately, Herr Admiral, there's a stumbling block to my theory. You see, I also telephoned the Immigration Office at Rostock. They told me twelve Swedish seamen were issued with evening passes on that date, all requiring the bearer to

216

be back on board by twenty-three hundred hours. However, only eleven passes were handed back in.'

'Presumably the missing one is our friend Valkyrie?'

Oster nodded. 'Which does seem to indicate that he was alone. It doesn't make any sense.'

The Admiral sat back in his chair, a thoughtful frown creasing his face. After several moments of silent contemplation, he seemed to reach a conclusion.

'There's not a lot more we can do for the present. Send out a general instruction to all our people, telling them to keep their eyes and ears open. You never know, we might strike lucky.'

'Very good, Herr Admiral,' said Oster. 'If anything sinister *is* afoot, I hope Valkyrie, whoever he is, is able to frustrate the mission, otherwise Reichsführer Himmler will be distinctly displeased with the Abwehr.'

Canaris laughed hollowly. 'Anything but displeased, Hans. Little Heinie will be only too delighted to lay any amount of blame at my door.'

The telephone on Canaris' desk rang shrilly.

'Canaris,' he announced curtly. The conversation was brief, and ended with an assurance from the Admiral that the matter would be attended to immediately. He replaced the receiver, a whimsical smile on his face.

'Well, well. Fortune does favour us, Hans. That was SS-Brigadeführer Schellenberg. A very upset Schellenberg. He's demanded we pass the *Ausweiss* to his office without delay, and we are not to become involved in matters that are strictly the responsibility of Reich Central Security! Which tends to let us off the hook, so to speak.'

Oster allowed himself the briefest of smiles. 'So, if anything untoward should happen...'

'Precisely,' Canaris agreed. 'However, I think we would be neglecting our duty to the Fatherland if we didn't keep an eye on things ... unofficially, of course.'

217

'Of course,' agreed Oster.

'Good. We understand each other well, you and I.' He picked up a sheaf of papers from his desk, indicating the meeting was concluded. 'Let me know at once, if there are any developments. I've a feeling we've not heard the last of Valkyrie.'

19

TUESDAY, SEPTEMBER 29th

'Herr Untersturmführer! It is time for you to get up.'
Callendar sleepily opened his eyes to see the fresh face
of Bauer looking down at him.
'What?' he replied, rubbing his eyes. 'What time is it?'
'0500,' whispered Bauer, keeping his voice low not to
wake the others. 'You are on duty today, with Untersturmführer
Dietrich. Transport will be waiting for you at the rear of the
building at 0545 hours to take you to the Chancellery.'
'Thank you, Bauer. Have you woken Dietrich?'
'He is in the ablutions at this very moment, Herr
Untersturmführer.'
Callendar swung his legs out of bed, grabbed a towel and
washbag and padded barefoot down the room to join Thompson.
Half an hour later, having shaved and dressed themselves in
ceremonial black uniforms, they gulped down the breakfast
prepared by Bauer. After finally checking their appearance
in the full-length mirror, they picked up their MP40 sub-
machine guns, donned the polished black helmets and made
their way downstairs to the car park at the rear of the building
where they found a Kübelwagen waiting for them. Schiller
sat in the front seat alongside the driver and, after a brief
'Morgen', Callendar and Thompson climbed into the back
seats.
Leaving Gestapo Headquarters the Kubelwagen moved up
Prinz Albrechtstrasse, turned left into Wilhelmstrasse, past
the offices of Reichsmarschal Göring, and arrived at the

imposing buildings which formed the Reichs Chancellery. Alighting from the vehicle Callendar and Thompson followed Schiller to the main entrance where they each had their identity cards rigorously checked by one of the guards on duty – including Schiller, despite his being a familiar face around the building. It was obvious the highest state of security was maintained at all times, even in Hitler's absence. Entering the building, Schiller took them first to a brightly lit room where they were required to stand to attention and suffer the Guard Commander's critical inspection before he gave them a final briefing on their duties.

'Whilst you are on duty, Frau Christian, the Führer's secretary, is the only person you will allow to enter the Führer's office.'

He picked up a folder lying on a nearby table, opened it and showed them a photograph of a plain-looking woman in her thirties. 'That is Frau Christian. No one else is allowed to enter – not even the Reichsführer himself – and those are *his* orders. Is that clear? Good! Now follow me.'

He led them from the anteroom, along a short corridor and through a doorway into a vast hall, the size and grandeur of which was breathtaking. Oblong in shape, the huge hall extended some one hundred feet in length, lines of marble Doric columns supporting the thirty-foot high ceiling. Huge paintings and sculptures lined the walls interspersed with red white and black swastika banners. The few neatly laid out desks were unoccupied at this hour, as was the rest of the great hall, save for the two guards they were about to relieve. The sound of their highly-polished jackboots on the marble floor broke the silence as they goose-stepped in unison towards the pair of tall bronze doors at the end of the hall. These were twenty or so feet high, each bearing the inevitable swastika carved in relief; above the doorway, engraved in stone, the monogram 'AH'. On either side of the doorway guarding Hitler's office, stood Sinclair and Lintz. Callendar and Thompson came to a halt immediately in front of the other two guards.

'Guards change!' snapped Schiller.

Sinclair and Lintz side-stepped one pace inwards followed by one pace forwards, whilst Callendar and Thompson stepped one pace forward to occupy their positions then turned about to face down the hallway.

'Old Guard, anything to report?'

'Nothing to report, Herr Sturmbannführer,' announced Lintz.

'Old Guard, forward march!'

Callendar and Thompson watched Schiller, Sinclair and Lintz march off down the hall until they disappeared through the same door they had entered at the far end of the hall. Then they stood at ease, MP40s cradled across their chests, and settled down to their twelve long hours of duty.

They were not permitted to talk to each other, nor to anyone else, whilst on duty and time passed painfully slowly. The two men found their eyes frequently wandering to the gilded clock on the wall at the end of the hall. The first two hours dragged by, but at eight o'clock things began to happen. The few desks became occupied, one by a female SS Scharführer and another by a civilian female. Neither of these two women paid any attention to Callendar and Thompson, and quickly became engrossed in piles of paperwork.

As the day progressed there seemed to be a constant stream of people coming and going from offices leading off the hall, each carrying something – a bundle of files, ledgers or books. Anything to justify their existence, Callendar thought cynically.

Little happened to disturb their onerous duty until shortly before three o'clock in the afternoon. A short, fat and rather pompous Lieutenant General entered the hall from the far end and began strutting fussily down the hall heading in their direction. As he drew closer Callendar and Thompson could see he was carrying a heavy-looking leather briefcase.

221

He was also puffing slightly and his face was red with the effort of carrying it.

They suddenly realised he was heading directly for the door to the Führer's office. At a whispered command from Thompson, both men executed two steps sideways in perfect drill square fashion, effectively blocking entrance to the huge bronze doors. This move took the little General by surprise and forced him to stop abruptly to avoid colliding with the guards. He glared at them for a moment, then stepped back.

'Stand aside!' he declared, fussily waving his free hand. 'I have important reports for the Führer.'

Frau Christian, at her desk a few yards away, lifted her head at the sound of the General's raised voice. An experienced member of the Reichs Chancellery staff, she instantly took in the situation, quietly lifted her telephone and dialled a number. After a few brief words she replaced the receiver and tensely watched the scene in front of the Führer's office. Thompson, his face impassive, was responding to the General. 'I regret, *Herr General*, our orders are that no-one is to enter the Führer's office except Frau Christian, his secretary. I suggest you hand your reports to her.'

'Nonsense!' blustered the fat man. 'I'm a General officer of the Wehrmacht. How dare you block my path. I am required to place these documents on the Führer's desk personally. Now stand aside this instant.'

Both men's faces remained expressionless as Thompson started to repeat himself. 'I regret, *Herr General*, our orders are to prevent entry to the Führ...'

At this point the little General seemed to lose control.

'How dare you disobey me!' he yelled. 'I'm placing you both under arrest.'

His heavy briefcase fell to the floor as his hand moved towards the pistol holster on his belt. Thompson and Callendar reacted immediately. Swinging their MP40s from across their chests and dragging back the cocking handles, they pointed the muzzles at the diminutive General's midriff.

The General froze, his face paled and the great hall fell silent, as everyone present watched the astonishing scene. Nothing like this had ever happened in the Reichs Chancellery before. Seconds dragged by as the General's hand continued to hover over the flap of his highly polished leather holster whilst the forefingers of Thompson and Callendar wrapped themselves loosely around the triggers of their machine pistols.

General Helmut Schneider had never seen military action. In fact, he had never fired a weapon in anger. He had always been on the administrative side of the Army, one of the backroom boys, the 'unsung heroes', as he would have described himself, receiving promotion through length of service rather than by distinguished action. Yet he was no coward. His face ashen, he stubbornly stood his ground. Even so, there was a noticeable tremor in his voice as he spoke.

'For the last time, I am ordering you to stand aside,' he said.

His right hand slowly lifted the flap of his holster and grasped the butt of his pistol. Callendar and Thompson watched with mounting apprehension. Their orders were specific – they could not let him pass.

'I regret...'

'Put your gun away, General,' interrupted a quiet voice.

None of the three men had seen him arrive, but suddenly there he was: the close-cropped head, the rimless spectacles, the expressionless face. The little General turned to face the unmistakeable figure of Heinrich Himmler standing a few yards away.

'Reichsführer! Thank God you're here!' exclaimed the little General. 'These...'

'Put the gun away, General,' repeated Himmler.

Hastily the General thrust the half-drawn pistol back into

the holster and, after some nervous fumbling, managed to secure the flap.

'Reichsführer!'

'*Herr* Reichsführer!' snapped Himmler.

'Of course. My apologies, Herr Reichsführer,' blustered the General, his face a deep crimson. 'It's just that these men...'

'Were obeying their orders,' said Himmler icily. 'The Führer is surrounded by traitors. We can trust no one – not even General officers of the Wehrmacht.'

'Herr Reichsführer, I can assure you, the Führer has no more loyal an officer than myself!' protested the General, his small frame shaking visibly. 'I have just arrived from Paris with urgent reports for the Führer. I simply wanted to make sure he got them as soon as possible, and these men...' He pointed a trembling hand towards Thompson and Callendar. 'These men had the audacity to threaten me!'

'General, consider yourself fortunate. Had your pistol left its holster, they would have shot you.'

The colour drained from the man's face.

'Herr Reichsführer, I didn't mean to... You see, it's my first visit to the Chancellery. I didn't realise the procedures...'

'What do these reports cover?' Himmler interrupted, ignoring the man's protestations.

'The deficiencies of the French railway system, Herr Reichsführer – together with my recommendations. I understand the Führer takes a great interest in transportation in the occupied territories...'

'The Führer takes great interest in everything.' He pointed a finger in the direction of the SS clerk. 'Hand your reports to Frau Christian. She will make sure they are passed on to the Führer.'

The little General stood for an awkward moment, desperately trying to think of something to say to restore his dignity and save face. Eventually, mumbling a hurried apology to Himmler, followed by an equally hurried 'Heil Hitler' he hastily made his way across to Frau Christian. Now desperate to get out of the Reichs Chancellery as quickly as decorum would permit, he made his way down the hall conscious that all eyes were watching him. Himmler followed the diminutive figure's progress with unconcealed disdain. Then, without as much as a glance at Thompson and Callendar, he turned away and left the hall.

ABWEHR HEADQUARTERS THAT SAME EVENING

At five minutes to seven Admiral Canaris decided he had had enough for the day. As the grey-haired Naval officer strode along towards the flight of stairs leading out of the building, junior ranks he passed sprang to attention, each wishing him 'Good night.'

He paused at the door of Hans Oster's office and put his head in.

'I'm just off, Hans. I'll see you in the morning.'

Oster, in the middle of jotting down some notes, sprang to his feet excitedly.

'Herr Admiral! A moment, if you would. Something interesting has just come through.'

Canaris frowned wearily. 'What is it? What's happened?' he demanded, stepping into the office and closing the door behind him.

'We've just had some news in from Rostock. The Kripo* have found a man's body on the shore. He'd been shot twice – once in the head and once in the chest.'

'And?' queried the Admiral frowning.

Murders were not uncommon, even in Nazi Germany and could often be laid at the door of the Gestapo.

---

*Kripo – (Kriminalpolizei) Criminal police

'The body was naked,' continued Oster. 'And the face mutilated – probably an attempt to avoid identification. But the killer, or killers, were careless. Under the left arm they found a tattoo, a blood group number – exactly the same as those worn by the SS!'

Canaris' jaw tightened and the tiredness disappeared from his face in an instant.

'No prizes for guessing it's our friend Valkyrie, I suppose?'

Oster nodded.

'Have Reich Central Security been informed?'

'The Kripo informed both them and us at the same time. In fact, I've already been in contact with my source there. He tells me the blood group is quite a rare one and matches that of a certain SS Hauptsturmführer Anton Stotz – alias Valkyrie.' He permitted himself an amused smile. 'Apparently, Brigadeführer Schellenberg has gone berserk and dispatched a detachment of SS, plus Gestapo interrogation officers to Rostock, with orders not to return without the culprits.'

Canaris sneered. 'Then the man's a fool. Whoever's responsible is well away by now. He'd be better served by trying to find the reason why Valkyrie returned to the Fatherland in the first place.'

He paced the floor a few times, deep in thought. Suddenly, he turned and stabbed a finger in Oster's direction.

'If Valkyrie *was* part of a British espionage group, we could have a major problem on our hands.'

'But I thought we'd dismissed that idea. The numbers of the Swedish seamen – they didn't add up. Twelve came ashore, eleven returned. The missing one we agree had to be *Valkyrie*. The *Ausweiss* proved that.'

Canaris shook his head. 'I just don't buy it, Hans. Something's going on; I know it and I've a nasty feeling it's something big.'

He paced up and down the floor, hands clasped behind his back, brow furrowed in concentration. He stopped by the window and stared out, but took in little of what was happening in the street below. Suddenly, he wheeled round.

'The Führer. He's in Russia at present, touring the Eastern Front, isn't he? Do we know when he's due back?'

'The Führer?' Oster exclaimed incredulously. 'You don't think... That's impossible. No one could get anywhere near him. He's guarded too well by the SS.' He shook his head vigorously. 'It's not possible.'

'Isn't it?' Canaris observed dryly. 'Others have tried it.' He held up his hand as Oster was about to interrupt.

'All right, all right. I know they've all failed. But such attempts have always been made by disillusioned, or anti-fascist Germans. However, a professionally organised attempt by the British could have a very different result. As you so rightly pointed out the other day, you have only to look at what happened in Prague earlier this year. Four Czech soldiers parachuted by the British into Czechoslovakia succeeded in assassinating Heydrich, probably the second or third most important man in the Nazi hierarchy.'

'I understand what you're saying, Herr Admiral. But Heydrich was a fool, travelling in an open car without an escort. The Führer would never dream of taking such chances.'

'I agree,' responded Canaris blandly. 'Nevertheless, the British could be feeling flushed with success and consider a repeat performance a distinct possibility.'

He picked up the telephone and asked to be connected to the Chancellery. After a brief conversation he replaced the receiver with a thoughtful look on his face.

'It seems the Führer is still in Rastenburg, at the Wolf Lair, and he'll be there for some time. After that, he's off to Berchtesgaden for a few days' rest before returning to Berlin on the nineteenth.' He rubbed his chin. 'Which gives us a few days' grace.'

'Herr Admiral? Would it not be best to leave this matter

227

to Reich Central Security? You know how prickly Himmler can be.'

'Only too well, Hans. Only too well. He'd love to find a reason to have the Abwehr closed down. But we'll not tell him just yet. Let's continue our investigations – unofficially of course – and keep this to yourself. I'd be surprised if the Gestapo doesn't have eyes and ears planted in this building, so watch your step and be careful no-one is in earshot when you make any phone calls.'

'You really are convinced Valkyrie wasn't alone.'

'Until we have proof to the contrary, I don't believe we can afford to think otherwise.' Canaris made his way towards the door. 'Keep me updated on anything unusual, no matter how insignificant it may seem. If British agents did arrive with Valkyrie, and are now in Germany, then it's possible they may make a mistake.' At the door he turned to look at Oster. 'And my bet is, when that happens, it'll happen here in Berlin.'

20

THURSDAY, OCTOBER 1st

The following day found Sinclair on daytime guard with the amiable Lintz, whilst Callendar and Thompson, having spent the morning in bed following their own spell of guard duty the night before, were taking in the sights of Berlin.

After a couple of hours touring the streets, it was inevitable they would eventually find themselves back in the Tiergarten. As they strolled along a path, they were surprised to see Anna sitting on one of the benches fifty yards away. The two men changed direction and began making their way towards her, but they were suddenly halted in their tracks by the sight of Schiller approaching from the opposite direction. Having no desire to meet their senior officer, they quickly turned off onto another path but, after walking on for a few yards, they looked back to look back only to see Schiller had stopped where Anna was sitting and appeared to be engaged in conversation with her.

'What's that all about? D'you think she's in trouble?' murmured Callendar.

'It hardly looks that way,' responded Thompson, as he watched the couple laughing together as if they were old friends. Their astonishment increased when they saw Anna stand up and link arms with the SS officer, just as she had previously done with Sinclair.

Callendar became alarmed. 'What in the hell's going on?'

'I've no idea,' muttered Thompson as they watched Anna and Schiller stroll slowly along the path, appearing to all the world like a couple of lovers on an afternoon walk. 'But I don't like it. I suggest we follow them – see if we can find out what they're up to.'

Keeping a safe distance behind, to make sure they weren't spotted, the two men followed the couple along the path as they headed purposefully towards one of the exits.

'I can't believe she's double-crossing us,' said Callendar. 'Not after all she's done, for God's sake! I mean ... she killed an SS officer. She wouldn't...'

'Always assuming he *was* an SS officer,' replied Thompson.

'What? You don't think...?'

'I don't know what to think at the moment. Let's just keep an open mind, shall we?'

'But what if she is... I mean, what if she has betrayed us?'

'I don't think that's the case, otherwise we'd already be under arrest by now. But if it comes to it...' He grimly tapped the holster hanging from his belt. 'We follow her example for resolving problems.'

'But...'

'Shhh...'

A gefreiter in the infantry was approaching, arm in arm with his girl friend. As they drew closer he slipped his arm from his companion's and threw his right hand up to his feldmütze in the standard Wehrmacht salute. Absorbed with thoughts of Anna's possible treachery, Callendar barely noticed the man and it was an unconscious and automatic reflex when he raised his hand to his cap in response, something he had done so many hundreds of times back in England. But as soon as he had done it, he realised his mistake. It was impossible to remedy the error. Thompson muttered an audible 'Christ!' and both men hurried away, not daring to look back.

The gefreiter meanwhile, completely taken aback by the nature of Callendar's salute, stared in surprise at the backs of the two SS officers. Shaking his head in puzzlement and muttering something to his girlfriend, he dismissed the event from his mind and continued on his walk.

The Englishman might have got away with his faux pas, had it not been for an artillery major sitting on a nearby bench with his wife, who also witnessed the incident.

'That was damned strange,' he murmured to himself with a frown. 'I'd never have believed it, if I hadn't seen it with my own eyes. Damned strange!'

'What's that, dear?' replied his wife absently, as she rummaged through her shopping bag.

'Those two SS officers. The way that one of them saluted...'

'Why? Was there something wrong, dear?'

The artillery major closed his eyes in exasperation. 'It doesn't matter – forget it.'

But he was unable to forget it himself and his eyes followed the two officers until they had disappeared into the distance. Then he rubbed his chin thoughtfully, making a mental note to mention the incident to an old friend who worked in the Abwehr.

'D'you think anyone noticed?' questioned Callendar nervously, as they hurried along the path.

'That gefreiter certainly did,' answered Thompson, annoyed by his companion's carelessness. 'Let's hope he just forgets about it. We've got other things to worry about. Look, they've left the park. Quick, or we'll lose them.'

Still maintaining a discreet distance, the two men followed the couple along a number of streets until they disappeared together into one of the many apartment buildings in a street identified as Königstrasse. Callendar and Thompson stopped outside and gazed up at the building.

'What now?' queried Callendar.

'Well we can hardly follow them in,' said Thompson. 'But perhaps we can check the tenants – there's usually a list in the foyer. You wait here, I'll go and have a look.'

Unhurriedly he entered the building and, sure enough, on one of the walls he found what he was looking for. Running his finger down the list he quickly found a name he recognised – Anna Schenke. He rejoined Callendar.

'Let's walk,' he said, filling his companion in on what he had found. He looked around. 'Trouble is, we can't hang about until one, or both of them, comes out. Be too suspicious. Let's go across to that café.' He pointed to a small restaurant on the other side of the road some fifty yards or so away that had a number of tables arranged outside on the pavement. 'We can have a cup of coffee and keep an eye on the place. It's far enough away for them not to spot us.'

But when they crossed the street to the café they found every table occupied.

'Leave this to me,' muttered Callendar.

He cast his eyes over the scene. Dismissing those tables occupied by officers and civilians he continued his gaze until it came to rest on a table occupied by two Wehrmacht privates and their girlfriends. Unhesitatingly, he strode across to their table. Immediately, the two privates shot to their feet and stood stiffly to attention. Callendar gave them an imperious look, then gazed down at their almost empty coffee cups.

'You have finished, yes?' he snapped.

'*Jawohl, Herr Untersturmführer!*' replied one of the men nervously.

They quickly donned their *Feldmutzen*, saluted and rapidly vacated the table, almost dragging their girlfriends with them. Callendar flicked the seat of one of the chairs with his gloves, as if to remove any evidence of the Wehrmacht private, and sat down. Thompson followed suit and waved at the waitress hovering nearby. They ordered coffee and settled down to their vigil.

Almost an hour elapsed before Schiller reappeared at the

entrance of the apartment building. He stood outside for a moment then strode off in the opposite direction. Thompson glanced at Callendar.

'Time for a chat with a certain young lady, I think.'

He called the waiter over, paid the bill and the two men casually rose to their feet and retraced their steps in the direction of the apartment building. Entering it, they passed through an inner door and began climbing the stairs.

'Apartment two, second floor,' said Thompson taking the lead.

Outside the apartment door he withdrew his pistol. Callendar, after a moment's hesitation, followed suit. Thompson rapped on the door sharply. After a short delay they heard Anna's voice.

'Who is it?'

'Message from Sturmbannführer Schiller,' replied Thompson gruffly, attempting to disguise his voice.

'Just a moment.'

They heard sounds of the door being unfastened from the inside. Immediately it began to swing open Thompson threw his fourteen stone forward, sending the door crashing inwards and Anna flying backwards onto the floor. The white bathrobe she was wearing spilled open but Thompson ignored her semi-nakedness and stood over her, his pistol pointing at her head.

'Close the door,' he called to Callendar over his shoulder. A quick glance at the bed showed the bedclothes pulled back and the duvet trailing on the floor.

'No need to ask what's been going on here, is there, Fraülein?' he said bitterly.

Unfazed by Thompson's pistol, Anna scrambled to her feet, pulling the bathrobe around her.

'How dare you come here?' she stormed. 'What the hell d'you think you're doing? You fools! You could betray us all!'

Callendar stepped forward, his face white with anger.

'And how do we know you haven't already done that to Schiller?' he snarled, staring contemptuously towards the bed. 'You're Schiller's whore, aren't you?'

Her eyes blazed with anger as she stepped forward, hand raised to strike him across the face.

'Steady!' snapped Thompson, waving the pistol threateningly.

'Go on then... Shoot me!' she challenged. 'If you dare...'

Thompson's finger visibly tightened on the trigger. Only the slightest additional pressure would be needed for the room to resound with the noise of a pistol shot. They stared at each other for several seconds before she managed to control her temper and lowered her hand. She turned back to Callendar. 'How dare you?' she spat. 'What gives you the right to judge me? You've no idea what life is like under the Nazis. You live in the safety and freedom of England. What d'you know? Nothing!' Her eyes blazed. 'I'm supposed to be a junior rank in the SS. Do you really think I have the option of saying 'No' to a senior SS officer when he wants to go to bed with me? Do you?' Her tone made Callendar shift uncomfortably. He glanced towards Thompson, whose pistol was still pointed resolutely at the girl.

'Are you saying you haven't betrayed us?' he asked, a note of doubt creeping into his voice.

'Don't be a bloody fool! If I'd wanted to betray you, I would have done it in Rostock. Why would I bring you all the way to Berlin?'

'Then, this Schiller thing is...'

'Something about which I have no choice.' She closed her eyes, trying to hold back the tears. 'Do you think I like him touching me? I hate it. My flesh crawls every time it happens. Afterwards, I have hot baths and scrub my body, to erase the memory of his filthy contact.'

She sat on the bed and buried her face in her hands.

234

Callendar pushed Thompson's gun hand down and stepped hesitantly forward.

'Look. I'm sorry. You're right. I have no right to ... to judge you. I apologise. Forgive me ... please.'

She raised her head and stared towards the window as tears trickled down her cheeks.

'Dear God! How much longer must I keep this up?' She looked up. 'There's only one thing that keeps me going. D'you know what that is? Can you possibly guess?' She smiled weakly. 'No, of course you don't. How could you?'

She rose to her feet and moved towards a large portrait of Hitler on the far wall. Inserting her fingers behind the edge of the frame, she released a hidden catch and swung the picture outwards on concealed hinges. Behind it lay a hidden recess with two shelves. On the top shelf stood a gold, six-pointed Star of David, on the lower, a seven-branched candelabra. On either side of both objects were a number of silver-framed photographs. One depicted a man and a woman standing together with the Brandenburg Gate in the background. Then there were individual photographs of three young children – two boys and a girl. Finally, there was a photograph of the whole family, this time including a teenage girl, easily identifiable as Anna.

'My family,' she explained. 'Yes, I am Jewish, as is Josef.' She looked affectionately at the photographs. 'These give me the strength I need to keep going. Otherwise I know I'd go mad.'

Thompson holstered his pistol and placed his arm around her shoulder in a fatherly fashion.

'Where are they now, Anna?' he said softly.

She pulled away from the embrace and swung the portrait of Hitler back in place.

'Where I can no longer reach them,' she replied. 'These few things are all I have left to remember them by.'

For a few moments nothing was said. Then she laughed, a short, hollow, humourless laugh.

'Do you realise there's a certain irony in all this? Every time Schiller comes here, he's commits one of the greatest crimes an SS officer *can* commit. Having sex with a Jewess. Think of it! And under the very eyes of his beloved Führer.'

Thompson looked serious. 'Anna, you're playing a very dangerous game. If he ever gets to find out what's behind that picture...'

He didn't need to finish the sentence, the warning was all too obvious.

'Dangerous game?' she repeated. 'Of course it is. But it's the only way I have to keep me sane. Anyway, if all goes according to plan I shan't have to sleep with that bastard again. The game will be at an end. Thank God!'

Hans Oster was in the process of making his way back to his office at Abwehr Headquarters when his progress was stopped by a junior NCO.

'Excuse me, Herr Oberst. There is a telephone call waiting for you. It's a Major Schröder, of the 116th Artillery Regiment. He wouldn't leave a message. Said it was a personal matter.'

'Very well, Bock. Put it through to my office.'

Schröder had attended the same military college as Oster and the two men had become firm friends over the years, although they constantly kept losing touch with one another on account of their varying duties. As far as Oster could remember Schröder had been posted to the Russian front, a place from which it could be extremely difficult to get leave, particularly home leave. Arriving back in his office, he sat down and picked up the telephone.

'Oster,' he announced.

'Hans, you old dog! Is that you?'

'Hello, Karl. How are you?'

'Not bad, apart from a shrapnel wound in the leg. Got in the way of a Russian mortar. Still, it got me this leave, so I'm not going to complain too much. Anyway, how are you? How are things going in the spy world?'

They spoke for some time, swapping stories and experiences before Oster apologised and said he would have to cut the conversation short.

'Look, Karl. How about we meet for a few beers this evening. I'll show you the Berlin night-life.'

'Sorry, Hans. I'm only in Berlin for the day with my wife, keeping my promise to her of a day's shopping. We have to be back in Dresden tonight. But before I go, there is something else. It may be nothing, but I thought it worth mentioning to you in your official capacity.'

'Oh? And what's that?'

'You remember the Führer Order requiring all members of the Wehrmacht to salute SS officers? Well, I saw a gefreiter in the infantry salute two SS Untersturmführers in the Tiergarten this afternoon.'

'So?'

'Well, it's just that the gefreiter gave the normal military salute as you would expect, but here's the strange thing – one of the Untersturmführers responded with the *same* military salute. How about that? An SS officer not giving the Nazi salute!'

A frown creased Oster's face. 'Are you sure, Karl?'

'Sure? 'Course I'm sure. You don't think I'd imagine something like that, do you?'

'No. No, of course not. Sorry.' Oster's mind was racing. 'Tell me, what happened after that?'

'Well, the two SS officers must have realised what had happened because they both hurried off as quickly as they could – without looking too undignified, of course.'

'Did anyone else notice the incident?'

'Don't think so, though the Tiergarten was pretty crowded. I didn't see anyone else react at all.'

237

'All a bit strange,' commented Oster thoughtfully.

'Strange?' retorted Schröder. 'If you think that's strange, then how about this. I was close enough to see the legend on the cuffbands of those two officers: *SS Leibstandarte – Adolf Hitler* no less. How about that?'

'What?' exclaimed Oster, alarm bells ringing. 'Karl, I've got to go. Look, next time you're in Berlin, we'll have that drink. That's a promise.'

He hurriedly replaced the receiver giving Schröder no chance to reply. Less than sixty seconds later, he was in Canaris' office, not even having bothered to knock. The Admiral who had been on the telephone, glared at him, displeased at the unannounced intrusion.

'Not bothering to knock these days, Oberst,' he observed acidly, as he replaced the receiver.

'My apologies, Herr Admiral, but I think it's happened. The mistake you said they would make.' He briefed Canaris on the telephone conversation with Schröder. 'I'm convinced they weren't genuine. No SS officer would ever give a military salute.'

Canaris twiddled a pencil between his fingers, seeking to digest and analyse this piece of new information. Eventually he spoke. 'You're right. No genuine member of the SS would make such a stupid mistake.' He leaned back in his chair and nodded his head towards the telephone. 'There's been another development. That call I've just had – Hitler has cut short his visit to Rastenburg and cancelled his intended break at Bertchesgaden. He intends to be back in Berlin on Sunday morning and has called a meeting for eleven o'clock at the Reichs Chancellery.'

Oster raised his eyebrows. 'Is that a coincidence, or something singularly significant?'

Canaris responded with a shrug of the shoulders. Oster frowned at this non-committal response. 'What action do you wish me to take...? About these bogus SS officers, I mean.'

238

'None, my dear Hans. None at all,' replied the Admiral, sitting with his elbows on the arms of his chair and the tips of his fingers placed together and gazing steadily at the surprised Oster. 'Let's not forget, Reich Central Security Office is handling this matter and I certainly don't propose to offend Brigadeführer Schellenberg. Our relationship is already somewhat ... tenuous?'

'But, Herr Admiral, we could be charged with treason for not acting on such information.'

Canaris thought for a moment.

'Perhaps you've got a point. Don't worry, Hans, I'm not a fool. If I were, I wouldn't have survived these Nazi thugs for so long. All right, I will try and contact Himmler, although I understand he's out of Berlin for the day, visiting his beloved Wewelsburg Castle. If I can't get him, I'll speak to Schellenberg today, then simply pass the information onto Himmler at Sunday's meeting.'

Oster looked worried. 'If there are British agents in Berlin masquerading as SS officers, do you think they could gain access to the Reichs Chancellery?'

Canaris laughed. 'Come, come, Hans. You know as well as I do, entry into the Reichs Chancellery is impossible, unless you have the right security clearance. Why, even I have to show my pass every time I go to the damn place. And my face is well enough known. No, it's quite impossible.'

Oster remained unconvinced by the Admiral's assurances and his face showed it.

'Just think the situation through,' continued Canaris patiently. 'Let's accept there are two British agents in Berlin disguised as SS officers. But what better disguise? After all, the bigger the bluff, the more likelihood of it succeeding.' He sat down again at his desk. 'But you can relax, my dear Hans. They have no chance of gaining entry into the Reichs Chancellery in that disguise – none whatsoever. Absolutely impossible. The security measures there would expose them immediately.' He drummed his fingers on the desktop. 'If an assassination attempt is planned, it won't happen there. More likely when he's en route somewhere. I'll make a point to find out the Führer's itinerary for the next few weeks and discuss it with Himmler. Then he can take over and we'll drop the matter entirely. Now, I must prepare for Sunday's meeting. Let me know instantly if there are any further developments, even if it means interrupting that meeting on Sunday.'

Hans Oster left the admiral's office praying for the 'absolutely impossible' to happen.

21

The following afternoon, the three Englishmen decided to spend their free time sightseeing in Berlin and were about to leave Gestapo Headquarters when Schiller stepped out of his office.

'Ah, Richter!' exclaimed the Guard Commander, his eyes alighting on the three men. 'Just the man. Come with me.'

Callendar's heart missed a beat. 'Herr Sturmbannführer?'

'I want you to come with me. Someone I want you to meet,' replied Schiller curtly.

'Herr Sturmbannführer, will it not wait until later? I've arranged to meet someone.'

Schiller frowned with annoyance.

'If it's a woman, she'll wait for you. If it's anyone else, then they're not important. Come!'

It was unmistakeably a command and Callendar knew he had no alternative but to follow. He glanced helplessly towards Thompson and Sinclair.

'I'll catch up with you later,' he called, as Schiller led him to the top of a flight of stairs.

'May I ask where we are going, Herr Sturmbannführer?' he said, as they descended the stairs.

'I thought you might like to see how we carry out interrogation in Berlin and compare it with your methods in Riga.'

They reached the bottom of the stairs and began making their way along a dimly lit, stone-flagged corridor. The

241

whitewashed walls shone with moisture and a distinctly musty smell pervaded the air; their boots clipped hollowly on the flagstones. They passed heavy steel doors set into the stone walls at regular intervals on either side of the corridor. Each had a small sliding panel and Callendar guessed they were prison cells. Schiller came to a halt in front of cell number thirteen and pushed open the door.

The room was surprisingly large for a prison cell, about twelve feet square and, like the corridor, dimly lit, the only source of light coming from a shielded lamp on a bare wooden table in the middle of the room. A pile of filthy straw lay in one corner, presumably a bed for the unfortunate resident. Apart from Schiller and himself, there were three other people in the cell. The first was a man sitting on the only chair in the room with his hands tied behind his back and on whom the light from the table lamp was directed. He was groaning softly, head sagging forward, chin resting on his chest. His shirt had been torn open and was covered in a mixture of filth and blood. Callendar couldn't see the man's face, but it was obvious he had suffered a terrible beating.

Standing beside him was a huge brute of a fellow, his shirtsleeves rolled up, holding a length of metal bar in his hand. The third man, who could hardly be seen, stood against the far wall, his face hidden in shadow.

'Well? Has he talked?' asked Schiller, looking down at the wretched figure.

'Not yet, Herr Sturmbannführer. But he will. Müller here has only just got started.'

It was the man in the shadow who had spoken. As he heard the voice, Callendar froze. He knew that high-pitched tone; it was unmistakeable.

'Well, I've brought along one of my men to try his methods of persuasion. Richter here has been based in Riga, dealing with the Jewish problem. And as this spy of yours is also a stinking Jew, it would seem rather appropriate, don't you think?'

Without waiting for an answer, he turned to Callendar. 'By the way, Richter, this is Hauptsturmführer Kramer of the Gestapo.'

Kramer stepped out into the light and Callendar immediately recognised the man from Rostock. For a moment he panicked. What if Kramer should recognise *him*? What could he do? Thankfully, although Kramer stared at him for some time, he showed no sign of recognition. The Gestapo man pointed a gloved hand at the victim in the chair.

'Well? Let's see if *you* can make him talk, Untersturmführer.'

Callendar's blood ran cold. They clearly expected him to continue torturing this already terribly mutilated creature in an effort to extract information from him. He knew he was not capable of inflicting such suffering on a fellow human being. It was against everything he had been taught. But how could he refuse? He was supposed to be an SS officer, obedient to death. It was Schiller who inadvertently came to his rescue and provided a brief respite.

'Come Kramer,' he said, jovially slapping him on the shoulder. 'Let's leave Richter to practise his methods on his own. I've a bottle of schnapps in my office, and from the look of Müller he could do with a break too.' He looked at Callendar. 'We'll give you half an hour. That enough for you, Richter?'

'Of course, Herr Sturmbannführer,' replied Callendar, relieved the immediate pressure had been lifted. 'I'll make the swine talk, you can be sure of that.'

He must have sounded convincing for the three men left the cell, and he found himself alone with the groaning man. He had gained some thinking time but knew he would have to come up with a solution or risk being exposed and arrested himself. He stood in front of the chair and stared down at the man. There were massive bruises on the body: on the shoulders, around the rib cage, every part of his anatomy had been attacked. Poor wretch! And there was nothing he could do to help him. The man began to raise his head and when his face came into view Callendar felt physically sick. It was so bloody and swollen, it was hardly recognisable as the face of a man. Bruising around the eyes had almost closed them, leaving only narrow slits. Blood seeped from ruptures around the eyebrows and from his nose, which had clearly been broken. His mouth gaped open and Callendar could see bloody stumps of broken teeth through the split and swollen lips. Callendar stared closer.

'Josef!' he cried, recognising what was left of the features belonging to the landlord of *Das Wildschwein*.

The man tried to talk and immediately coughed blood. A broken rib had pierced one of his lungs. He tried again, but his words were unintelligible. His jaw, too, had been broken.

'What is it, Josef? What is it you're trying to say?' cried Callendar desperately.

Again Josef struggled to speak. This time Callendar could just make out the two words: 'Kill ... me!'

'What?' cried Callendar. 'What are you saying? I can't! I...' He dropped to his knees in front of Josef. 'I can't.'

'For ... God's ... sake ... kill ... me! Please! I ... beg ... you... You will ... be doing ... me ... a kindness. I'm done ... for!'

Callendar realised the man was right. He was finished. And he would die, but only after suffering further prolonged and sadistic beatings. People like Müller enjoyed inflicting pain and would make sure death did not come swiftly. For them, prolonging the agony was all part of the entertainment.

When he had been fourteen, during a foxhunt, his father had made him witness a veterinary surgeon putting a horse out of its misery with a pistol shot. The horse had broken a leg and it was considered the kindest thing to do. But he'd had trouble holding back the tears. But it had to be done,

244

he knew that – just as he had to help Josef now. But he had never killed another human being before. Could he do it? Could he deliberately place his pistol against Josef's head and squeeze the trigger?

'Please! For God's ... sake ... shoot me!'

Josef painfully raised his head, what could be seen of his eyes were full of pleading. Still Callendar hesitated. Josef closed his mouth and began moving his jaw around, groaning with pain as he did so. After a few seconds, he suddenly lunged forward and a large globule of spittle and blood shot from his mouth. Most of it landed on the front of Callendar's pristine light-grey uniform, but some landed on his face. Taken by surprise he jumped to his feet, automatically wiping the spittle from his face with the back of his hand.

'Now ... you'll ... *have* to ... kill me,' Josef croaked.

Callendar stood frozen to the spot for several moments, then his hand moved slowly towards his pistol holster. He knew what he had to do. He withdrew the Walther PP from its holster and moved to stand behind Josef's chair. Releasing the safety catch, he slid back the cocking mechanism and held the muzzle an inch away from the base of Josef's skull – just as he had been instructed back in England. His finger curled around the trigger, squeezing slightly to take the first pressure. There he froze, his finger refusing to move a millimetre further.

'Do ... it. Do it ... now,' whimpered Josef. But Callendar could not bring himself to apply the final pressure. The hand holding the pistol began to tremble and he was forced to use his other hand to steady it. Then that too began to tremble. The door of the cell had been left ajar and through the opening he could hear the others returning.

'For ... God's ... sake,' Josef almost screamed.

Closing his eyes tight, Callendar tightened his finger on the trigger. The force of the bullet sent Josef toppling forward, taking the chair with him while the noise of the shot

245

reverberated around the walls, sounding more like a cannon than a 9mm pistol. Callendar opened his eyes just as Schiller, Kramer and Müller came storming into the room.

'What have you done?' yelled Schiller.

Müller bent over the body. He looked up and shook his head.

'Dead,' he pronounced flatly.

'What in the hell prompted you shoot to him?' demanded Kramer, his eyes riveted on Callendar's face.

Callendar stood trembling. 'He... He...'

'Well? He what?'

Callendar still hesitated.

'Come, Richter,' interjected Schiller. 'What happened? What did he do to make you so angry. Angry enough to shoot him – and to make you tremble like that?'

Thank God he thinks it, anger, thought Callendar.

'Well?'

'He... He insulted the Führer ... and ... and spat on my uniform,' was all Callendar could think of by way of response.

'For God's sake, man! He's been throwing insults at every member of the Nazi Party,' snarled Kramer. 'That was no reason to kill him. Now we'll never get the information we want.'

'Forget it, Kramer,' said Schiller calmly. 'I doubt if he would have talked anyway. Tough old bastard.' He glanced at Callendar's tunic. 'You'd better get that cleaned up, Richter. There's some on your cap as well.'

Callendar removed the cap to see spittle and blood smeared across the silver Death's Head. He replaced the cap.

'With your permission, Herr Sturmbannführer?'

'Yes, all right Richter. You can go.'

Callendar threw up his arm in the Nazi salute and thankfully turned to leave.

'Just one moment, Untersturmführer.'

The sound of Kramer's high-pitched voice stopped Callendar in his tracks.

'Please remove your cap.'

Callendar complied and Kramer moved forward to stare closely at the Englishman's face.

'We have met before,' he announced with conviction.

Callendar turned icy cold. 'I don't believe so, Herr Hauptsturmführer.'

'Yes we have. I never forget a face. I have seen you somewhere before, I'm sure of it.' He continued staring at Callendar, who looked straight ahead to avoid the piercing eyes. 'Have you ever been in Rostock?'

Callendar knew if he instantly denied ever being in the town it would look suspicious. 'Yes, I have,' he admitted.

'Aha!' cried Kramer triumphantly. 'I knew it.'

'It was a long time ago. With my father. I was a young lad at the time. We visited one of his old comrades from the Great War.'

'This was more recent. Are you sure you don't remember meeting me? People have often said that I leave them with a lasting impression.'

'Perhaps it's your charming personality, Kramer,' guffawed Schiller, slapping the Gestapo officer on the back. 'But, in this instance, it appears your memory's playing you tricks. Richter here has been based in Latvia for the past... How long Richter?'

'Almost a year, Herr Sturmbannführer,' replied Callendar, grateful for the time he had spent studying Richter's records with such diligence.

'There you are, Kramer. It couldn't have been Richter. Someone else perhaps.' Schiller turned to Callendar. 'You'd better clean yourself up and go to meet that young lady of yours. Give her my apologies for detaining you.'

'Thank you, Herr Sturmbannführer.'

He quickly gave the Nazi salute, accompanied by a click of the heels and hurried out of the cell.

Kramer watched him carefully as he left.

'If I am wrong, then it will be the first time it has happened,' he said thoughtfully.

'Forget it,' urged Schiller. 'There's an unfinished bottle of schnapps waiting for us in my office. Get this mess cleared up, Müller.' He nodded towards Josef's body. 'And ... perhaps you'd better record the cause of death as a heart attack. Not that I anticipate any problems. After all, he was only a Jew.'

Callendar hurried along the dismal corridor, forcing himself not to run, despite the overwhelming urge to escape from the building. Making his way upstairs to the barrack room, he got Bauer to clean up his jacket and cap; the orderly made no comment about the blood and spittle, perhaps being all too familiar with such things. After quickly checking his appearance in the mirror, he hastened back down the stairs, past Schiller's office, from which he could hear raucous laughter, and out of the building.

Still trembling from the horrors of the afternoon, he made straight for the Tiergarten and began searching for Sinclair or Thompson, but without success. Desperately in need of friendly company, he headed for Anna's apartment in the hope she might be at home. He had to knock twice before Anna opened the door. She was wearing the same white bathrobe as on his previous visit with Thompson.

'What on earth are you doing here? I thought I made it clear you should *never* come here,' she demanded sharply.

'Please, Anna. You've got to let me in.'

He pushed past her, threw his cap on a chair and collapsed face down onto the bed, his body jerking with sobs.

After a quick glance down the corridor, Anna closed the apartment door. She crossed to the bed and sat beside him.

'Tell me what's happened. Quickly! Have you been discovered?'

'No,' he sobbed into the bed quilt. 'No. It's nothing like that.'

'Then what is it?'

Callendar raised his head. 'I've just killed Josef. I've just shot him.'

She pulled him into a sitting position.

'Josef? Josef who? You're not making sense.'

'Our Josef!' sobbed Callendar. 'Josef from Rostock.'

She stared at him in bewilderment. 'Look, calm down. Just tell me everything that's happened. Everything.'

Callendar related his recent experiences while she listened closely. When he had finished she took him by the shoulders and looked directly into the eyes, her own face pale and drawn.

'Think carefully. Did Schiller say anything, or this Gestapo man, that would indicate Josef had talked?'

Callendar shook his head emphatically.

'He didn't talk. I'm sure of that. That's why Kramer was so angry. He said something like ... "before we'd got a word out of the Jewish swine".' He looked at her through watery eyes. 'He didn't talk, Anna. I know he didn't.'

She stared at him for a few seconds then released her hold on his shoulders.

'No. You're right. Josef would never have talked. No matter what they did to him.'

She looked pityingly at Callendar, now sitting with his head in his hands and she slipped a comforting arm around his shoulders.

'You did the only thing you could,' she said softly.

'But he was a friend – and I killed him.'

'Tell me. What's your first name. Your English name?'

'James.'

'James,' she repeated. 'James, you've got to realise, Josef

249

was dead from the moment the Gestapo arrested him. What you did was a kindness only a true friend would perform. You prevented him suffering further. And if he were here now he would thank you for it. He knew the risks he was taking. He'd known for some time that the Gestapo had been watching him, but he wouldn't give up. He was fighting for what he believed in – freedom!' She gently placed a kiss on his forehead. 'There's nothing more any of us can do to help Josef.'

She stood up. 'D'you know where your two friends are right now?'

Callendar shook his head.

'You'd better stay here for a few hours. I'll make some coffee.' She disappeared into the small kitchen and began filling a kettle. 'Why don't you take off your jacket and boots? Lie down for a while,' she called out.

'You sure? There's no chance that Schiller will turn up?'

'No. He won't be coming around. I told him I wasn't feeling well. That's why I'm home this afternoon. You were lucky to catch me in.' She poked her head out of the doorway. 'And if everything goes according to plan tomorrow night then I shan't have to speak to that bastard ever again!'

Callendar removed his jacket, laid it over a nearby chair and placed his jackboots by the side of the bed. He had just made himself comfortable on the bed, his back resting against the wooden headboard when Anna returned bearing two cups of steaming coffee. He would have preferred brandy, but the strong, sweet coffee tasted like nectar at that moment. After a few sips, he lay back and closed his eyes for a few moments. When he opened them again, Anna was sitting on the bed next to him. The late afternoon sunlight streamed through the window, striking her long blonde hair. Suddenly, he realised just how beautiful she was.

'How did you get mixed up in all this, Anna?'

'It's a long story. You would find it boring.'

'I'd like to hear it nevertheless.'

She sighed. 'I suppose it really all started when I was at school in Switzerland. My father had sent me there to study music – he was one of Germany's leading concert pianists at the time. That was in 1938 – I was eighteen years old. By then the Nazi's intimidation of Jews was getting worse by the day and he felt I would be safer there. I would come home to Munich every holiday to see my parents and my younger brothers and sister, and we wrote to each other every week. I would often beg them to leave Germany and join me in Switzerland, but my father was stubborn. He said he was more German than any Nazi. Then, last year, in June I think it was, their letters suddenly stopped. I kept writing to them, but never got any replies.

'Eventually, after several weeks, I was so worried I had to come home to find out what had happened. We lived in a big house in a fashionable suburb of Munich but when I arrived there was no sign of my family. Instead, a blonde girl about my age, wearing the uniform of the Hitler Jugend, answered the door. She seemed suspicious of me, which put me on my guard, so I didn't reveal who I was. I told her I was a student studying National Socialism at the university and that I was looking for accommodation. She invited me in. She told me her family had been given the house as a reward for denouncing the Jewish family that had lived there. Her parents, both ardent Nazis, had been killed in an air raid by British bombers a few months earlier and she now lived alone in the house. But she had enlisted in the Algemeine SS and would be moving to Berlin shortly to join up.

'I asked her if she knew what had happened to the Jewish family. She just laughed and said they were now living in luxury in Buchenwald concentration camp. I'd heard stories about concentration camps and I knew I would never see them again – and all because of this girl and her Nazi parents. Something inside me snapped. I remember flying at her,

251

punching her in the face, scratching... She screamed and fought back – we were like a pair of wildcats... Then her foot caught in the hearthrug and she fell backwards, with me on top of her. There was a horrible crunching sound and her body went limp. Her head had struck the marble surround of the fireplace. At first, I thought she was just unconscious, but then I saw the blood – lots of it – and I knew she was dead.

'Initially I was afraid and my first reaction was to escape back to Switzerland. But that would have been pointless. With my father in Buchenwald and all our property confiscated, there was no one to pay my tuition fees. So I decided to stay, although at the time I wasn't quite sure what I was going to do. That night, I buried the girl's body in the garden at the back of the house – thick conifers surround the property so there was little risk of being seen. It was only after I had finished it suddenly occurred to me that someone might come looking for her when she failed to report for duty in Berlin. When I later found her enlistment papers I quickly realised that, apart from the difference in hair colour – I'm naturally dark – we could almost have been the same girl. So that's what I did – bleached my hair, took all her identity papers and reported to SS Headquarters in Berlin as Fräulein Anna Schenke. They accepted me without question. A few weeks later I wrote to an English girl I had made friends with at school in Switzerland. I knew her father was some sort of official at the British Embassy in Bern and he put me in touch with members of the resistance movement in Germany. From there we set up a communications system and I've been passing information back to England ever since.' She smiled. 'Now you know how your people got the information on the Chancellery guard. It's my contact at the Embassy who's helped with all the arrangements to get us across the Swiss border on Sunday so, with a bit of luck, in two days' time we shall be safe and sound in a neutral country.'

Callendar looked at her admiringly. 'You're quite a girl.'

'Am I?' she said. 'And how about your girl-friend back in England. What's she like? I take it you do have a girl-friend?'

'Well... Yes, I suppose so,' replied Callendar, with a little uncertainty. 'I mean ... there is Daphne.'

'And who is Daphne? She sounds terribly English.'

'She's... She's great. Both our families are great friends, have been for years.'

'Will you marry her?'

'I don't know... I suppose so. It's more or less expected of us.'

'Are you lovers?'

'What?' exclaimed Callendar.

'Have you slept together?'

'Good Lord, no! We... We don't do that sort of thing in England. Well... not before marriage, that is.'

Anna laughed at the look on his face.

'Oh, James! Have I offended you? I'm sorry.'

She reached out and touched his face.

'No. You haven't offended me,' he replied, clasping her hand. He held it for a while, for the first time appreciating the warmth and comfort of a woman's touch. He looked up at her.

'Have you never made love, James?' she asked.

He shook his head, his body trembling at her closeness. Her lips brushed against his mouth.

Anna lay in his arms, their naked bodies damp with perspiration from their lovemaking. She slowly traced a finger around his chest, whilst he gently stroked her hair.

'I think I'm in love with you, Anna,' he murmured softly, pressing his lips to the top of her head. She looked up at him smiling gently.

'Why, James? Because we've just made love?'

'It's how I feel. I've never felt like this before.' He squeezed her hand. 'When we get out of this, I want you to marry me. Please say you will. I want to spend the rest of my life with you.'

'James...'

'Don't say anything. Don't say "yes" or "no" – not yet. Just promise me this – when we get to Switzerland, you'll come with us back to England. Just promise me. Please!'

She closed her eyes.

'All right, I promise.'

22

SATURDAY, 3rd OCTOBER – 1800 HOURS

'Guards, change!'

Schiller's words of command echoed around the vast emptiness of the Chancellery hall as Thompson and Schmidt each stepped one pace sideways followed by one pace forward, whilst Callendar and Sinclair stepped one pace forward and turned about.

'Old Guard, anything to report?'

'Nothing to report, Herr Sturmbannführer!' responded Thompson and Schmidt in unison.

'Good!' He turned to the other two. 'I have some good news. All of you will be pleased to know there has been a change in the Führer's plans. He is due back in Berlin tomorrow morning and will arrive here at the Chancellery at eleven-thirty hours.' He gave what perhaps he considered was a sympathetic smile. 'Unfortunately you will be off duty by then. But there will be other opportunities for you to see our great Leader.'

He turned back to Thompson and Schmidt.

'Old Guard! Forward march!'

Sinclair and Callendar watched the three men march down the hall towards the exit. 'This is going to cut it a bit fine,' murmured Sinclair out of the side of his mouth. 'We're going to have to move fast once we get off duty.'

'*Very* fast,' agreed Callendar through clenched teeth. 'Let's hope Anna turns up OK.'

That night the hours seemed to drag even more than usual.

Being the weekend, there was even less activity in the great hall, which only served to worsen the situation, both men spending their time staring at the large clock, watching the hours slowly tick by. By seven o'clock the hall was completely empty of personnel, the last to leave being a couple of middle-ranking officers who had been making hasty preparations for the great man's unexpected return the following day. Eight o'clock came and went. Nine o'clock... Ten... Eleven...

Then, at midnight, one of the doors at the side of the hall opened and a figure appeared pushing a janitor's trolley. Their hearts missed a beat; this woman in a cleaner's overall with a dark scarf wrapped around her head was not Anna. But as she drew closer, they recognised their companion, heavily disguised – wearing no make-up and with strands of a grey-haired wig poking out from under the headscarf.

'Everything OK?' she whispered tensely.

Sinclair nodded. 'Let's get on with it.'

He turned towards the huge bronze doors and depressed both handles. Despite their weight, they opened easily, swinging inwards on silent hinges. Sinclair stepped inside and switched on the lights, illuminating the windowless room. It was the first time any of them had seen inside the dictator's office – like the rest of the building, it lacked nothing in size. Oblong in shape, its walls bore the usual display of Nazi flags and emblems, whilst at the far end hung a proportionately large oil painting of Hitler in flattering pose. Under this painting was his desk, an immense oak structure, grotesque in its dimensions but in keeping with the style of Nazi architecture created by Albert Speer. In front of this a conference table ran the length of the office, high-backed chairs ranged either side, with a larger chair at the head of the table dominating the scene. The dark mahogany surface of the table carried leather blotter pads, one in front of each chair; down the centre, miniature Nazi flags had been placed at measured intervals.

256

It all looked neat and business-like, but it was the object at the head of the table, directly in front of what was obviously the Führer's chair, which caught their attention. It was a small wooden cabinet, its highly polished surface gleaming in the artificial light.

'Is that it?' asked Anna.

'Must be,' affirmed Sinclair. 'Can't see anything else that meets with the dimensions we were given.' He turned to Callendar. 'You'd better stay outside just in case anyone comes. It'd be just like Schiller to pay us an unexpected visit. I'll check out what's in the box.' Callendar took up a position in front of the huge doorway, whilst Sinclair moved swiftly down the length of the carpeted office until he reached the head of the table. Was this it? he asked himself. Was this what they had come so far to steal – Hitler's beloved *Hakenkreuz*? He eyed the polished cabinet apprehensively. It looked the right size to accommodate the ancient swastika and its position in front of Hitler's chair seemed appropriate. There was only one way to find out.

He noticed a join in the polished walnut, running across the top and down two of the sides, with small brass hinges evident near the base of the other two sides. It seemed the cabinet would open in two halves from the top. Laying his machine pistol on one of the writing blotters, he reached forward with white-gloved hands and gently prised the cabinet open.

Their eyes widened and Anna caught her breath as the gleaming gold object came into view. Standing out starkly against the red velvet lining of the casket, it was exactly as Commodore Surridge had described – a solid gold swastika surrounded by an ornate wreath of laurel leaves and mounted on a plinth engraved with strange characters. Sinclair shivered slightly as he stared at the ancient object. It seemed to have a hypnotic effect, radiating a mixture of pagan beauty yet possessing an aura of terrible evil. He dragged his eyes away and closed the two halves of the cabinet together.

'It's horrible!' whispered Anna, staring at the closed box.

'You're right, it is. Look, you'd better not hang around. Make a token gesture of cleaning the place, just in case, while I stand inside the door as I'm supposed to. We'll leave the swastika in its box until you're ready to go.'

'All right. But I don't want to stay here too long. It makes me feel nervous.'

She pulled a cleaning duster and some polishing cloths from the trolley, together with a tin of wax polish and began working on the conference table, taking care to avoid any contact with the walnut cabinet. Sinclair picked up his machine pistol and retired to the doorway, where he stood just inside as they had been instructed. It was a good thing that he did, for less than ten minutes later the door at the far end of the Hall opened and in walked Schiller. Callendar whispered a warning of 'Schiller' as the Guard Commander strode purposefully towards them.

'Shit!' exclaimed Sinclair. 'Anna, keep your back towards the door. Let's pray he doesn't recognise you.'

Callendar came smartly to attention as Schiller drew close. 'Anything to report, Richter?'

'No, Herr Sturmbannführer. Nothing to report.'

Schiller nodded, stepped past Callendar and peered inside the office. 'Ah, good! I see Frau Kemple *is* here. Someone told me they thought she was having a night off.'

He watched the disguised figure of Anna industriously polishing the long conference table for several minutes, then turned to Sinclair.

'Make sure Frau Kemple does a thorough job. Don't forget, the Führer is holding a conference here in the morning.'

'*Jawohl*, Herr Sturmbannführer.'

'Good! I'll see you both in the morning. Good night.'

With that, he turned on his heel and marched back down the Hall towards the exit.

258

'Phew! That was close,' breathed Callendar. 'God knows what we would have done if he'd recognised Anna.'

'Killed him!' retorted Sinclair.

Anna rejoined them pushing her trolley.

'That wasn't good news – about Hitler coming here in the morning, I mean,' she said. 'Could make things difficult. Anyway, I'm going to get away. This place gives me the creeps.'

'Hang on! Aren't you forgetting something?' said Sinclair. Grabbing a large cleaning cloth from Anna's trolley, he hurried back to the end of the conference table, opened the walnut cabinet, withdrew the golden swastika and wrapped it in the cleaning cloth. Then he took something from his breast pocket and slipped it inside the cabinet before closing it and returning to the others.

'What was that you put in the box?' queried Callendar who had been watching closely.

'A little surprise for old Adolf!' he grinned and slipped the cloth-covered *Hakenkreuz* into Anna's bucket of water. 'Just to let him know who's got his precious swastika.'

'For God's sake, stop fooling around,' said Anna, nervously glancing down the Hall. 'Schiller might come back.'

'I doubt it,' replied Sinclair laconically. He turned off the lights and closed the huge bronze doors.

'Anyway,' continued Anna. 'I've organised the car and movement orders, and I'll see you both in the courtyard at the back of Gestapo headquarters at six-thirty sharp. For God's sake don't be late. We need to be well away from Berlin by the time Hitler gets here.'

'Don't worry, we'll be there,' Callendar assured her emphatically. 'And, Anna...' He gave her a brief affectionate smile. 'Take care!'

The smile didn't go unnoticed by Sinclair and when Anna had gone, he treated Callendar to a long quizzical look, but said nothing.

SUNDAY OCTOBER 4th – 0600 HOURS

The rest of the night had dragged by without incident. At three minutes to six the door at the far end of the great hall opened and Schiller appeared with Lintz and Kleist, the relief guard.

'Anything to report?' enquired Schiller when the guards had changed.

'Nothing to report, Herr Sturmbannführer,' replied Sinclair.

'Good!' He turned to Lintz and Kleist. 'Remember, senior Party members, including Reichsführer Himmler, will start arriving from about ten o'clock, so for God's sake keep your wits about you.' He paused, turning to face Sinclair. 'That reminds me... Did you make sure Frau Kemple gave the Führer's office a thorough cleaning?'

'Yes, Herr Sturmbannführer.'

Schiller hesitated, pursing his lips. 'I'd better give it a quick check. Come with me.' He opened the huge bronze doors. 'Wait here,' he told Sinclair, pointing to a spot just inside the doorway. Sinclair watched whilst Schiller made a few test wipes with his white gloves along the surface of the conference table, each time glancing at his gloved hand for evidence of dust. Seeming satisfied, he carried out the same examination on Hitler's desk, then turned to walk back down the office. Sinclair was about to heave a sigh of relief when Schiller suddenly stopped in his tracks. He was frowning at the walnut cabinet in front of Hitler's chair. The guard commander stepped forward and leaned over, his eyes only a few inches from the polished surface.

Sinclair watched closely, his jaw clenched. He knew if Schiller opened the cabinet, the game would be up and they would be forced to fight their way out of the Chancellery, killing Schiller, Lintz and Kleist and any other guards who got in their way. His hands tightened on the Schmeisser, thumb slowly easing forward the safety catch and finger

260

curling around the trigger. A bead of sweat ran down his brow. Schiller reached out, grasping the cabinet in his gloved hands. Sinclair began to swing the muzzle of his machine pistol in Schiller's direction. Thankfully, the guard commander was too intent on what he was doing to notice the movement, but outside, Callendar, who had been watching, tensed himself, ready to support Sinclair if necessary.

In the end their fears were not realised. The problem had simply been Schiller's paranoia for perfection – he had spotted the cabinet wasn't quite square in its position on the table. After twisting it a fraction and stepping back to view the alteration, he gave a nod of satisfaction and made his way towards the door, walking backwards in order to give the whole office one last general check. Sinclair used the opportunity to return his pistol to its normal position across his chest before Schiller reached him.

'Good! All is in order.' He closed the double doors. 'Old Guard! Forward march!'

SS Untersturmführer Otto Schmidt looked anything but an SS officer, as he slouched towards his bed after emptying his bladder in the latrines. Dressed in a pair of baggy, army issue shorts and a none-too-white vest, his appearance seemed more suited to a doss-house than the Reichs Chancellery. Overweight, with a beer gut acquired from too much time spent in Bavarian taverns, it was difficult to believe he was a member of the élite Nazi force. Nor did having an IQ well below the norm serve to justify such membership. Schmidt had been one of the original strong-arm men used by the NSDAP in their beer hall meetings to evict hecklers and communists. This had eventually gained him entry into Himmler's select Black Order. But Schmidt had always been aware of his shortcomings and envious of those around him – particularly such of his colleagues who had left him far behind in the promotion stakes. For Schmidt's greatest dream was to be a hero – a hero of the Fatherland. To be decorated by the Führer himself, to be admired, to be worshipped by beautiful young women. So far this had remained just a dream.

That Sunday morning he and Thompson were the only members of the Chancellery Guard in the billet. The two remaining members of the guard, Strohm and Möeller, had been up early to visit friends and family in Potsdam, and, being Sunday, the SS orderly, Bauer, had a day off. Schmidt stopped as he drew level with Thompson's bed and snorted at the Englishman's sleeping form. How could an old man like him possibly win the coveted Knight's Cross, he asked himself. Why, he looked more like a schoolmaster than a soldier. His eyes caught Thompson's jacket draped over a coat hanger hanging on the wardrobe door, the envied decoration looped around the neck. He stared at it jealously and, after a glance at Thompson to make sure he was still asleep, moved quietly towards the wardrobe and reached out to take the cross in his hand. How he wished it could be his. He would do anything, anything, to be the recipient of such an award. He swung open the door of Thompson's wardrobe and stared at the neatly laid-out clothing. Not like his wardrobe – that was a mess. But who cared? He wasn't at training camp now.

His eyes fell on the pack of tourist photographs poking out from between a pile of neatly folded socks. He sneered as he reached forward to grab them – typical of an old man, wanting photographs to take back with him. He went through them, one by one, hardly glancing at them – until he came to one that brought a puzzled expression to his ape-like countenance. Who the woman and children were, he hadn't a clue, but he recognised Thompson at once. What he couldn't understand was why an SS officer was wearing a British army uniform. Nor could he recognise the impressive building in the background. Curiously, he turned the photograph over

262

and stared at the writing, scrawled in Thompson's own hand: 'Buckingham Palace, London – May 1942'.

It took some time but realisation eventually penetrated the fat German's brain and with a yell of 'Englander swine!' he reached down, seized the side bar of Thompson's bed and heaved upwards, unceremoniously tipping the Englishman onto the floor.

'What the . . . !' exclaimed Thompson sleepily, as he struggled to extract himself from the blankets entwined around his body. Shaking the remnants of sleep from his head, he found himself staring up at Schmidt who stood over him waving the telltale photograph.

'Damned Englisher pig!' yelled Schmidt.

Fear gripped Thompson and he cursed his stupidity in bringing the photograph to Germany. There would be no point in denying his true identity. Schmidt just wouldn't believe him – he had the evidence in his hand. He also knew he had to silence the fat German for good.

He twisted his head, searching for his belt and pistol holster; they were lying on the floor three or four feet away. Rolling over he made a desperate grab for the leather holster but, despite his bulk, Schmidt was faster. He threw himself on top of the Englishman, knocking the breath out of him, at the same time looping a beefy arm around Thompson's neck.

'I'm going to break your neck, English swine!' Schmidt snarled, tightening his grip and twisting Thompson's head round.

Thompson struggled desperately, trying to break the big Nazi's grip, but Schmidt continued to tighten his arm, shutting off air to Thompson's lungs. The room began to swim as he slipped towards unconsciousness. Summoning up every last ounce of his remaining strength, he heaved upwards and at the same time twisted his body causing them both to roll over so Schmidt was now on his back. The suddenness of

263

this move took Schmidt by surprise and for a brief moment his grip around Thompson's neck relaxed. It was enough to allow the Englishman to break free. Quickly on his feet, he backed away, rubbing his bruised neck. He knew he stood no chance in a fight with Schmidt for the German was younger, far stronger than him. Half-crouched, he watched as his opponent got to his feet.

'So! English swine! You think you can fight Otto Schmidt, do you?'

Schmidt grinned evilly. Holding both arms low, his fists clenched into huge balls of bone and muscle, he began slowly circling Thompson, each waiting for the other to make the first move. Thompson's eyes flicked towards his pistol holster, now several yards away from him, wondering if he could make a dash for the weapon, have it out of its holster and shoot Schmidt before the German had time to stop him. But Schmidt saw the glance and quickly positioned himself between Thompson and his weapon.

'No you don't, Englishman. But I don't need your pistol. I'm going to kill you with my bare hands!'

Thompson made the mistake of glancing round the room for some alternative weapon. It was all Schmidt needed. With surprising speed, he launched himself forward and before the Englishman could move, he had him trapped in a crushing bear hug which pinned both arms to his sides. He gasped as Schmidt squeezed with all his strength and lifted him off the floor. Thompson twisted and turned, desperately trying to free himself but, though he managed to make the German take a few steps backwards towards Schmidt's bed, he could not break his crushing hold.

Suddenly, he spotted Schmidt's SS dagger hanging over the door of his wardrobe. With a supreme effort, he continued to twist and struggle, forcing Schmidt to again stagger back until they were close enough to the wardrobe for Thompson to reach out with one hand and grasp the handle of the dagger. Gritting his teeth against pain, he slid the dagger from its sheath, then forced his other arm round behind Schmidt's back to grasp the dagger with both hands. Guiding the point between Schmidt's shoulder blades and with his last remaining strength he drove the blade deep into the German's back.

Now it was Schmidt's turn to gasp as the keen-edged blade sliced into his flesh, severing an artery and penetrating one of his lungs. His grip loosened and Thompson fell to the floor. The Nazi sank to his knees, a look of surprise on his face. A sudden cough brought blood spurting from his mouth, after which he simply keeled over and collapsed onto the floor.

For a while Thompson just lay on his side, fighting to regain his breath and staring at Schmidt's motionless form. It was the first time he had killed a man, yet he felt strangely dispassionate about the whole thing – no remorse, no regret, just thankful he was still alive. He glanced at the clock on the wall. Nearly five past six. The others would be back from guard duty soon. Time he got ready. After a rapid wash and shave, he righted his bed and began to dress.

Absorbed in his preparations, he failed to see Schmidt open his eyes. Nor did he see the German's hand as it moved slowly towards the pistol holster still lying on the floor. His life ebbing away, Schmidt knew his opportunity to be a hero of the Reich had come at last. Struggling not to cough, though his lungs were filling with blood, he eased the Walther pistol from its leather holster and, with trembling fingers released the safety catch.

Thompson had almost finished dressing and was about to reach for his jacket, when Schmidt fired. At such short range, the nine-millimetre bullet struck the Englishman with considerable force, the impact first sending him sprawling onto Callendar's bed and then sliding onto the floor. At first he felt no pain, just numbness in his left shoulder where the bullet had struck but, realising he had been shot, he quickly rolled over in case the Nazi should fire again. He looked across at Schmidt lying a few yards away, to see his adversary cough more blood and collapse once more, the pistol falling from lifeless fingers as death finally overtook him.

Thompson's right hand went to his shoulder as pain began to register. But he had been lucky. Fortunately, the bullet had passed clean through, leaving him with only a flesh wound. As he pulled himself up into a sitting position, his eyes lit on the photograph that had caused his downfall lying a few feet away. He stretched out his good arm to retrieve it as the sound of jackboots could be heard running up the stairs. Someone had heard the shot.

Sinclair and Callendar could hardly believe their luck when Schiller, who would normally have returned with them to Prinz Albrechtstrasse, elected to remain at the Chancellery to ensure everything was in order for the Führer's return. This gave them a clear field for their departure from Gestapo Headquarters and obviated any risk of the Guard Commander spotting them climbing into the SS Staff car with Anna.

With this unexpected turn of events in their favour, Sinclair and Callendar were in buoyant mood as they made their way along the corridor. They had just reached the foot of the stairs leading to their billet when the sound of the pistol shot reached their ears. They dashed up the stairs and charged into the billet to see Thompson on the floor leaning against Callendar's bed, with the body of Schmidt lying a few feet from him.

Sinclair dashed forward and immediately spotted the bloodstain spreading across the back of Thompson's white shirt.

'Bill! What in the hell's happened?' he demanded, helping the wounded man to his feet.

Thompson clutched his shoulder, face etched with pain. 'Sorry... My own stupid fault... Brought this with me... Schmidt found it.'

Sinclair took the photograph from Thompson's hand. 'You bloody fool!' he muttered softly. 'You bloody fool.' Then he glanced across to Callendar who was kneeling down by Schmidt, checking for any signs of life.

'Dead,' announced Callender tersely, getting to his feet. 'How's Bill?'

'Don't worry about me,' insisted Thompson. 'It's only a flesh wound. You two had better hurry up and get ready. Anna will be here shortly... Mustn't keep a lady waiting...'

Sinclair frowned. 'You sure you're OK?'

'Yes, yes. I'm fine. As I said, it's just a flesh wound.' He pushed Sinclair away. 'I can manage. The sooner we get out of here the better.'

Ten minutes later, having applied some pads made from torn up sheets to Thompson's wound and changed from their black dress uniforms into the standard dove-grey, they hid Schmidt's body in his wardrobe and quietly made their way downstairs, supporting Thompson between them. Their luck seemed to hold, for they encountered no-one on the way and entered the courtyard just as Anna pulled up in an open-top, black Mercedes-Benz G5 staff car, SS pennants mounted on each of the front mudguards.

'What's happened?' she exclaimed, staring at Thompson with alarm.

'Had an argument with Schmidt,' replied Callendar shortly, as he helped Sinclair get the wounded man into the back seat.

Anna glanced towards the door leading back into Gestapo Headquarters. Callendar read her mind.

'Schmidt's dead. He won't be causing any more problems.'

'Come on,' snapped Sinclair, glancing at his watch. 'We've got between four and five hours before Hitler finds out he's been burgled. Let's hope we're well on our way to Switzerland by that time.' He climbed in the front passenger seat alongside Anna; Callendar sat in the back with Thompson. 'By the way, how are we off for petrol?'

'The tank's full and there are two twenty-five litre cans in the boot,' replied Anna. 'Along with four MP40s, spare magazines and a box of stick grenades. The *Hakenkreuz* is in a leather briefcase under my seat.'

Sinclair was impressed by the young woman's resourcefulness.

'Good! Now all we have to do, is to get past the guard on the gate without raising any suspicions. Incidentally, what important Reich business are we on, to justify a car like this?'

Anna nodded towards an official-looking form lying on top of the dashboard as she swung the big car around the corner of the building and headed towards the security gate. 'Believe it or not, we're acting on the personal instructions of Himmler and travelling to the Berghof at Munich – at least, that's what the movement order says. With any luck, we shouldn't need it.'

'Munich,' mused Sinclair, as Anna pulled up by the gate. 'Clever girl! That means travelling south, the same direction as Switzerland.'

'Heil Hitler!' greeted the SS guard, handing Sinclair the clipboard he was holding. 'Would you please sign out, Herr Untersturmführer.'

Sinclair signed the printed sheet recording the time and passed it back to Callendar to do likewise.

'And the other Untersturmführer?' queried the guard, looking at Thompson, who sat clutching his right shoulder.

'He's injured his shoulder,' Callendar hastily explained. 'I'll sign for him.'

He scribbled 'K. Dietrich' on the form, together with the time, and handed the clipboard back to the guard. As Anna

268

was about to pull away, he suddenly stepped in front of the Mercedes with his hand up.

'One moment!'

Sinclair's hand moved towards his pistol holster.

'I have to note the car registration.' He set about laboriously recording the number on his clipboard.

'Come on, come on!' muttered Callendar, impatiently drumming his fingers on the back of Sinclair's seat. At last the guard was satisfied and waved them on with a parting 'Heil Hitler'.

'How far is it to the Swiss border?' asked Callendar, as Anna steered the big convertible along Prinz Albrechtstrasse.

'About eight hundred kilometres. Say five hundred miles. With luck, we should be there by this evening.'

Callendar turned to Thompson, slumped, white-faced, in the corner of the Mercedes' leather-covered back seat.

'Did you hear that, Bill?' he said excitedly. 'We'll be safe in the British Embassy by tonight.'

Thompson responded with a painful smile, then closed his eyes in search of sleep.

23

SUNDAY MORNING, OCTOBER 4th
– THE REICHS CHANCELLERY

'Reichsführer! A word if I may.'

Canaris edged his way through the assembled senior Nazis in the great hall of the Chancellery building, carefully making his way towards Himmler who was standing by Frau Christian's desk. Himmler eyed his approach coldly through his rimless spectacles. He made little attempt to hide his dislike of the man and Canaris was fully aware of the Reichsführer's secret endeavours to persuade Hitler to merge the Abwehr with the SD, thereby giving Himmler total control of State Security and Counter Espionage. But his efforts had so far met without success. It was Hitler's deliberate policy to 'duplicate' functions within the Nazi hierarchical structure thus causing overlapping in departmental responsibilities and maintaining a degree of confusion and jealousy. It kept everyone on their toes.

'Yes? What is it, Canaris?' The unblinking eyes stared without apparent emotion at the elderly grey-haired naval officer. Canaris ignored the deliberate omission of his title, taking comfort from the fact that he shouldn't expect anything else from a former chicken farmer.

'I thought you ought to know, we received information which suggests there may be a couple of British agents in Berlin, masquerading as SS officers – Liebstandarte officers.' Himmler's expression barely changed.

'When did you receive this information?'

'Three days ago.'

'*Three days ago?* Why was I not informed before this?'

Himmler made no attempt to lower his voice and those standing close by turned to see what was happening. Canaris clenched his jaw muscles. He knew Himmler would seize the opportunity to attempt to belittle him, but he controlled his temper.

'I did make several attempts to contact you, Reichsführer,' he replied stiffly, refusing to be cowed by the man. 'Unfortunately you were not available. However,' he added, as Himmler was about to interrupt, 'in your absence I passed the information to Brigadeführer Schellenberg. I'm surprised he hasn't informed you.'

The implied criticism was not lost on Himmler but he chose to ignore it.

'And what was Brigadeführer Schellenberg's reaction?'

Again Canaris' jaw muscles clenched. 'The Brigadeführer chose not to give credence to the report, saying it was impossible for SS security to be breached.'

'Quite right!' replied Himmler with a sickly smile. 'You're a fool, Canaris. Do you really think anyone could penetrate the most effective security system the world has ever known? Go back to playing at spies and don't waste my time with such nonsense.'

He turned away, abruptly ending the conversation and leaving an embarrassed and offended Canaris standing alone. The Admiral turned and walked away. He had fulfilled his responsibilities. If anything went wrong now, he had a number of witnesses to confirm he had passed the warning to the Reichsführer.

Despite his offhand dismissal of Canaris' information, Himmler was no fool and would not fail to protect his own position. He stared thoughtfully at Lintz and Kleist standing guard in front of Hitler's office. Although, like Schellenberg, he placed little credence on Canaris' report, he remained a cautious man and leaned over to speak quietly to Frau

271

Christian. She immediately lifted her telephone, spoke into it, waited for a few moments, then handed it to Himmler.

'Sturmbannführer Schiller,' she announced.

Himmler took the phone from her.

'Schiller, I want you to check the personnel records of the SS officers currently on guard duty at the Reichs Chancellery. Yes, now! And phone me here at the Chancellery when you've done it.'

He replaced the receiver just as Adolf Hitler, entourage in tow, swept imperiously into the Hall.

'Erdmann! I know it's Sunday! Don't argue, just get over to your office in Personnel and I'll meet you there. We need to check the records of eight SS officers, immediately.'

Slamming down the receiver, Schiller grabbed his cap and hurried out of the building to his Kubelwagon. Less than ten minutes later, the two men were in the RHSA building, hastily sifting through SS personnel files. A further ten minutes later saw a white-faced Schiller using Erdmann's telephone and desperately trying to get through to the Reichs Chancellery.

Hitler gazed the length of the polished conference table at his assembled senior Party officials and military heads standing dutifully behind their respective chairs: Goering, Goebbels, Bormann, Raeder, Keitel, Canaris, the ever-faithful Heinrich Himmler... They represented his power. They were his tools, to be used to achieve his great Master Plan, a plan which was already well on the way to fulfilment. With Europe conquered – the British hanging on by their fingertips in North Africa, the Russian armies melting before his mighty Panzers like snow in the springtime – who could challenge his invincibility? He beamed at his audience.

'Gentlemen, please be seated.'

Everyone sat. He reached forward and placed his hands reverently on the walnut cabinet on the table in front of him. It was his habit to open such meetings by displaying the ancient *Hakenkreuz*, his legacy from the mighty Alexander. With a theatrical flourish, he opened the two halves of the cabinet.

Then he froze.

Instead of being greeted by the sight of his gleaming gold swastika, his gaze met with a photograph of his greatest enemy – a smiling Winston Churchill, an oversize Havana cigar in one hand and the middle and forefingers of his other hand held up in his famous 'V' sign.

For the briefest of moments a funereal silence fell over the room – a silence in which had the proverbial pin dropped it would have sounded like a thunderclap. Hitler's face went white. Then eyes bulging, nostrils flared, the Führer thumped the table with both fists.

'My *Hakenkreuz*!' he screamed. 'My *Hakenkreuz* – stolen! Thieves! Traitors! I'm surrounded by traitors!' He pointed a trembling finger at Himmler. 'You're in charge of security. Find my *Hakenkreuz*. Find the traitors who did this. Arrest them! Arrest them all! I'll have them shot. Every last one of them.'

Filled with the sort of terror he more commonly instilled in others, the normally dignified Reichsführer jumped to his feet, knocking over his chair in the process.

'At once, Mein Führer,' he gulped. 'At once!'

Hurrying from the room, he made straight for Frau Christian's desk, leaving the others to try and placate their infuriated Leader. She was already holding the phone out for him.

'Sturmbannführer Schiller for you.'

'Schiller! Quickly, what have you got to tell me?'

At the other end of the phone a trembling Schiller gave him the bad news.

'Herr Reichsführer, it appears that three of the men forming the Chancellery Guard are...' He hesitated, dreading Himmler's reaction.

'Are what?' yelled a panicking Himmler.

'... Are dead!' concluded Schiller, closing his eyes and clenching his fists.

'*Dead?*' echoed Himmler. 'Dead? What d'you mean "dead"? How can they be dead? What are you talking about, Schiller?'

'I'm sorry, Herr Reichsführer. But the records for Untersturmführers Richter, Dietrich and Steiner show that they have all been killed, either in action or murdered by partisans.'

'In which case, Schiller,' grated Himmler, striving to control his temper. 'Kindly explain how they were selected for guard duty at the Reichs Chancellery!'

'I... I have no idea, Herr Reichsführer,' stammered Schiller. 'Selection is made at random – by one of the Personnel clerks, SS Scharführer Anna Schenke.'

Schiller's relationship with Anna was instantly sacrificed, together with any sense of loyalty he may have had for her. He had no intention of protecting her from the wrath of Himmler.

'Find her,' snapped Himmler. 'Have her arrested and brought to Gestapo Headquarters. And arrest the Chancellery Guard.'

'All of them, Herr Reichsführer? How about those on duty now?' queried Schiller, hardly able to believe his ears.

'I'll deal with them. You find the others. Do it now, Schiller. I'm holding you personally responsible for all this.'

'All what, Herr Reichsführer?' demanded a frightened Schiller. 'I don't understand. What's happened?'

'What's happened? I'll tell you what's happened, Schiller. Last night, two of your men stole the Führer's gold *Hakenkreuz* and he's baying for blood, which at the moment means *your* blood! Find them, Schiller, and find them fast! Meanwhile

274

I'm ordering roadblocks on every road out of Berlin. Keep me up to date with any progress. Understood?'

'*Jawohl*, Herr Reichs...' He was cut off in mid-sentence by the sound of the receiver being replaced. White-faced, he turned to Erdmann. 'I want you to come with me. We'll pick up a couple of men on the way.'

'But where are we going, Herr Sturmbannführer?' exclaimed a puzzled Erdmann, as he hurriedly followed Schiller out of the office.

'To catch a traitor,' Schiller snapped angrily.

The Kubelwagen's tyres squealed in protest, as Schiller used both foot- and hand-brake to bring the vehicle to a stop in front of the apartment block in Königstrasse. First to leap out he sprinted up the steps into the building. He pointed at one of the two SS soldiers he had commandeered en route.

'You! Stay in front of this building and let no one in or out. Is that clear?'

'*Jawohl!* Herr Sturmbannführer!' replied the man, clicking his heels together.

Schiller turned to Erdmann and the other SS soldier. 'Both of you follow me!'

Drawing his pistol, he entered the building and raced upstairs to Anna's apartment. He turned to the other SS man, a big brawny individual, and pointed at the door.

'Break it down!'

The man threw himself at the pine door, splintering it with his massive weight. Schiller was first to enter. His eyes swept the room. At first everything seemed normal; then his eyes turned towards where the portrait of Adolf Hitler usually hung. Panic struck him for the second time that day. The picture frame had been swung back to reveal the alcove containing the Jewish Star of David and the seven-branched candelabra. The photographs were missing, but in their place

275

a message was scrawled on the wall in bright red lipstick. *'How did you enjoy sleeping with a Jewess, Schiller?'*

'What does it mean, Herr Sturmbannführer?' exclaimed Erdmann.

'Nothing!' snapped Schiller, stepping forward and sweeping the contents of the alcove onto the floor. 'It means nothing! Now check the bathroom. Find the bitch!'

Erdmann hurried into the bathroom only to emerge shaking his head.

'Right,' snapped Schiller, endeavouring to regain his composure. 'Then it's Gestapo Headquarters next. We've got arrests to make.'

Schiller leading, the three men hurried downstairs, collected the other SS soldier and piled back into the Kubelwagen. Schiller drove like a madman, ignoring everything in his path and almost knocking over the SS guard on duty at the entrance to the yard at the back of Gestapo Headquarters. The man glared at the Kubelwagen as it disappeared round the corner of the building. Then he picked up his clipboard and laboriously noted the vehicle's registration number and time of entry. He was a very fastidious man.

Schiller, the three others following, raced up the stairs to the billet, his pistol at the ready. After briefly checking Bauer's room, he crashed open the door of the billet and rushed inside – only to be disappointed once again. The room was empty.

'Check everywhere,' he ordered. 'Search all the lockers. Find me something. Anything!'

The sound of wardrobe doors being opened and slammed shut filled the room until Erdmann arrived at Schmidt's bed space. As he stepped forward to open the door, it swung open of its own accord and Schmidt's bloodstained corpse toppled onto the floor, the SS dagger protruding from his back. At the sound of Erdmann's exclamation, Schiller dashed forward and gazed down at the body.

'Schmidt!' he murmured and turned away. 'Come on. We've got to find the rest of them.'

The four men raced back downstairs and once more piled into the little jeep. Not quite sure where to search next, Schiller stopped at the gate and spoke to the sentry.

'Have any SS officers signed out this morning?' he demanded.

'Yes, Herr Sturmbannführer.' He reached inside his sentry box and referred to his clipboard. 'Untersturmführers Strohm and Möeller left on foot at 0600 hours. Going to Potsdam, they said. And Untersturmführers Richter, Dietrich and Steiner left in a staff car at 0630.'

'A staff car you say? Was there anyone else with them?'

'A female Scharführer was driving, Herr Sturmbannführer.'

'That bitch Schenke!' Schiller swore to himself, angrily smashing a balled fist into the palm of his hand. 'Let me see your clipboard,' he snapped.

The SS guard handed it over.

'Is this the registration number of the car?' demanded Schiller, pointing with his finger. The man stared at where Schiller was pointing.

'No, Herr Sturmbannführer. That's the number of *your* car. The number of theirs is this one, a Mercedes G5.'

He indicated further up the page. Schiller ground his teeth, annoyed at his own faux pas.

'I don't suppose they told you where they were going, by any chance?' he added sarcastically.

'I happened to see a movement order lying on the dashboard, Herr Sturmbahnführer. It said Munich,' replied the guard.

'Münich?' repeated Schiller. 'Why Münich?' he mused. 'That means they're heading south.' Then realisation dawned. 'They're not going to Munich! They're heading for Switzerland! Quickly, back to my office. We need a bigger car, one with a radio – and we need to concentrate road blocks on all roads leading south.'

277

Back in his office he made a series of frantic telephone calls, including one to Himmler advising him of the fugitives' intended route. Then it was back to the courtyard to rejoin the others and climb into a Mercedes G5, complete with radio, which had just arrived. Within minutes they were heading south, threading their way through the streets of Berlin at the highest possible speed.

'It can't be helped, it was just bad luck,' sighed Sinclair as he climbed back into the Mercedes. 'It's just a pity it had to happen at this particular time.'

Despite his outward display of stoicism, inwardly he nursed bitter disappointment. Had it not been for the breakdown, they could have been another two hundred miles further on, over half way to the Swiss border. As it was they had travelled just over a hundred and twenty miles when the engine of the Mercedes had suddenly died on them ten miles the other side of Leipzig. From his pre-war experience working with the giant German car manufacturer, Sinclair had quickly diagnosed the fault as a fuel blockage but, having no tools, he had been unable to rectify the problem. Consequently, it had taken almost three hours from the time they managed to contact the nearest Wehrmacht transport unit, some twenty miles further on, and arrange for the car to be towed into their workshops and the repairs to be effected. Sinclair glanced at his watch as Anna re-started the engine.

'Eleven thirty. I think we can expect the balloon to be going up right at this minute. Everyone keep their wits about them. I'd be surprised if we don't encounter a few roadblocks from now on. Thank God it's Sunday and little traffic about.' He turned round in his seat. 'How are you feeling, Bill?'

Thompson forced his pallid features into a grin.

'Don't worry about me. I'm only sorry I'm such a burden.'

'Don't talk rot!' exclaimed Callendar, as he tried to make

his companion more comfortable. 'I'm doing the same as you, just sitting here enjoying the ride. So stop apologising.'

'James! There is something you can do,' said Anna. 'There are some maps in the pocket behind my seat. See if you can find any alternative routes, just in case we do come across road blocks and have to make a sudden diversion.'

'And as a precaution,' added Sinclair. 'I think we'd better get those MP40s ready, together with the grenades.'

Once they were out in the country again, Anna pulled over to the verge for Callendar to fetch the Schmeisser machine pistols and grenades from the boot. Then they spent a few valuable minutes checking and preparing the weapons.

With the other Mercedes in hot pursuit, Schiller maintained a breakneck speed, Hauptsturmführer Erdmann sitting in the front passenger seat holding on for dear life, with the two SS soldiers in the rear doing likewise. They had left Berlin an hour ago and were fast approaching the northern outskirts of Leipzig when the radio mounted in the dashboard crackled into life.

'Reich Security calling SS Sturmbannführer Schiller. Reich Security calling SS Sturmbannführer Schiller,' the voice repeated.

'Take it, Erdmann,' snapped Schiller, concentrating his attention on overtaking a convoy of Waffen SS troop carriers, horn blaring. Erdmann picked up the handset.

'Receiving you, Reich Security. This is Hauptsturmführer Erdmann. I am in company with Sturmbannführer Schiller.'

'Message for Sturmbannführer Schiller,' the voice continued. 'The vehicle you are pursuing stopped for repairs at the eighty-second Motorised Infantry unit thirty miles south of Leipzig.'

'Why the hell didn't they stop them?' yelled Schiller over the sound of the engine.

Erdmann posed the question.

'Apparently they only received instructions to be on the look-out for the fugitives *after* the car had left.'

'All right,' said Schiller irritably. 'What time did they leave?' The SS Hauptsturmführer again spoke into the handset, listened for a few moments as the information was passed, then restored it to its cradle.

'They left the depot at eleven-thirty hours.' He glanced at his own wristwatch. 'That was twenty minutes ago. But they won't get far. Road blocks are being set up at fifteen kilometre intervals, starting from the transport depot where they stopped, all the way to Munich.'

'Good!' exclaimed Schiller. 'Now get back on that radio and tell whoever's co-ordinating the road blocks the car is simply to be stopped, the occupants arrested and held until I arrive. They are not to be interrogated by anyone other than myself. Is that clear? And if anyone queries those instructions, you can tell them I'm acting on the personal orders of Reichsführer Himmler himself.'

'Damn!' exclaimed Anna, easing her foot off the accelerator and staring at the road ahead. 'Road block.'

Sinclair and Callendar followed her eyes. Sure enough, two hundred yards ahead, they could see a military vehicle had been pulled across their half of the road, effectively stopping all traffic heading south.

'What now?' she asked. 'We can hardly turn round ... look too suspicious.'

Sinclair pursed his lips and stared at the roadblock. Being a Sunday, there was little traffic on the road and the only other vehicle in sight, a civilian lorry, had stopped at the roadblock whilst being checked by a member of the Field Police. He glanced behind them. The road was clear as far as he could see.

'Any turn-off ahead?'

'No, nothing,' replied Callendar. He grabbed one of the Schmeissers from the floor of the car and passed it to Sinclair. He took one for himself, loaded a magazine and applied the safety catch. Thompson watched him.

'Better let me have one of those,' he grunted sitting forward painfully.

'Forget it. We can manage. You lie back and rest, save your strength. You'll need it later.' He looked at Sinclair. 'I'm ready.'

Sinclair nodded. 'OK. Now we're not sure it's us they're looking for, but I'd be surprised if it was anyone else.'

They were now less than fifty yards from the roadblock. He turned to Anna.

'Slow down as if you intend stopping. If it's us they're looking for, we shall soon know. So be ready to put your foot down and go like hell. James, you'd better let me have a couple of grenades.' Callendar passed over two of the stick grenades and made two available for himself.

They were now close enough to see there were a total of four soldiers operating the road block, a gefreiter wearing the silver gorget of the Feldpolizei around his neck and three privates. The gefreiter and one of the privates were standing in the road to stop and check each vehicle, a second man sat in the cab of the Steyr truck and the fourth soldier manned an MG34 heavy machine-gun mounted in the open back of the lorry. They could see the gefreiter peering intently at their vehicle. He seemed to be paying particular attention to the number plate.

'I think they're on to us,' said Sinclair. 'Get ready.'

As he finished speaking, the gefreiter suddenly let out a cry of alarm and swung his Schmeisser machine pistol round to cover them.

'Let them have it!' shouted Sinclair, heaving a stick grenade into the back of the lorry. Callendar was instantly on his feet in the back of the open car, blazing away with his MP40. His first burst struck the gefreiter in the chest, killing the man before he had chance to fire his own weapon. Quickly adjusting his aim, he dispatched the private in the same manner, the man's Mauser rifle slung uselessly from his shoulder. The explosion from the grenade killed the machine gunner and the man in the vehicle cab received a burst of fire from Sinclair's machine pistol.

'Let's go!' Sinclair yelled, slapping his hand onto Anna's shoulder.

Letting in the clutch, she slammed the accelerator to the floorboards and, tyres screeching in protest, veered round the now blazing vehicle and tore off down the road at breakneck speed.

'Well, there's no doubt about it now. We know they're onto us,' announced Sinclair, gripping the dashboard to steady himself. 'We can expect more road blocks ahead. James, get those maps out and see if you can find a road off to the right. That'll take us westwards. We can resume travelling south to Switzerland once we're safely out of the area.'

Callendar urgently scanned the map, desperately searching for a suitable route.

'There's a minor road about two miles ahead, but it doesn't seem to lead anywhere. Apart from that, the next junction's a crossroads about five or six miles from here.'

'No point in getting lost on a side road. We'll make for the crossroads and hope we get there before they get a road block in place.' He glanced round at Thompson and saw the older man's face white with pain from being thrown about by the careering vehicle. 'Sorry about this, Bill, but it can't be helped. We'll slow down again as soon as we can.'

Thompson forced a smile.

'I told you,' he said through clenched teeth. 'I'm fine. Just get us to Switzerland. I'm dying for a cup of tea.'

Anna proved a skilful driver, overtaking the few vehicles

on the road without once slackening speed. After about two miles they passed the turning to the right Callendar had mentioned, looking just as he had described, not much more than a track. Anna did not slacken speed as they passed, but concentrated on reaching the crossroads as quickly as possible.

'Shouldn't be far now,' advised Callendar, looking up from the map spread across his knees. 'There's a bend coming up; it should be just around there.' Sure enough, just as they came out of the long curve, the crossroads swept into view, barely a hundred yards away.

'Shit!' exclaimed Anna, braking furiously.

Ahead of them, a number of vehicles, including an armoured personnel carrier, lay stretched across the road, effectively blocking any way through. Troops had spread themselves amongst the vehicles and on both grassy verges, weapons pointing menacingly in their direction. Immediately Sinclair reached down and yanked the handbrake upwards, sending the vehicle skidding into a one hundred and eighty degree turn. The sudden manoeuvre caught Anna unawares and in her eagerness to get moving again she stalled the engine. Whilst she frantically tried to get it started, both Callendar and Sinclair seized their MP40s and sent streams of bullets towards the troops occupying the barricade, together with a couple of well aimed stick grenades. In response a surprisingly limited amount of fire was returned, although they heard, and felt, several rounds strike the Mercedes. Suddenly the engine roared into life again. Anna put her foot to the floorboards and they very quickly regained the protection of the long bend.

'What now?' she demanded, as they retraced their route at high speed.

'We haven't got much choice,' shouted Sinclair above the noise of the screaming engine. 'We'll have to try that side road, wherever it leads. Let's hope they haven't beaten us to it and blocked it off.' He looked at Thompson lolled to one side, his eyes closed. 'Is Bill OK? That must have shaken him up quite a bit.'

Callendar slid an arm behind his companion to pull him into an upright position. As he did so, he felt a warm stickiness at the back of Thompson's head. He pulled his hand away and stared at the blood smeared on his palm. He leaned the man forward and at once saw the gaping wound in the back of his head. He knew there was no point checking for any pulse. The bullet would have killed him instantly.

'He's dead!' he announced, trying to swallow the lump in his throat. 'A bullet ... in the head.'

'Damn!' exclaimed Sinclair, thumping the dashboard with his fist. 'Damn! Damn! Damn!'

They drove on in silence, stunned by the unexpectedness of Thompson's death.

'Turn off coming up,' said Anna. Sinclair's eyes searched the road ahead. It was empty. He looked behind and saw a motorcyclist had been tagging them, some two hundred yards distant. The rider would see them making the turn, but they had no choice – it would hardly make any difference.

'Go for it.'

Anna swung the car off the metalled roadway onto the stony track. Trees and thick bushes grew on either side, their leaves coated with a fine grey dust thrown up by passing vehicles. The track went on for a hundred and fifty yards before ending at a set of metal gates. A sign hanging from one of them announced they had reached Mannheim's Quarry and that entry to unauthorised personnel was strictly forbidden.

'Looks like the end of the road,' said Sinclair.

24

'We can't give up now!' exclaimed Callendar in desperation, as he leapt from the car. 'Not after all we've been through. There's got to be some way, perhaps we can escape on foot. At least let's give it a try!'

Sinclair took a deep breath. 'You're right! We're not beaten yet.' He glanced back down the track. 'But first we've got an inquisitive motorcyclist to deal with. You two get to work on that lock. See if you can smash it open. I'll deal with the motorcyclist.'

Whilst Anna and Callendar set to work on the padlock with a large hammer, taken from the boot of the Mercedes, Sinclair tossed his peaked cap onto the back seat of the car, picked up a length of heavy metal tubing he found lying nearby in the grass and made his way back along the track. Quite what he intended doing he wasn't too sure at that stage, but one thing he knew for certain: he had to stop the motorcyclist from rushing back and reporting their position. Nearing the first bend, he heard the sound of the motorcycle's engine and dived into the bushes, taking cover behind the thick trunk of a fir tree.

The motorcyclist approached cautiously, driving at not much more than walking pace. From his hiding place, Sinclair watched closely as the man approached. He was dressed in the standard grey-green, long waterproof coat used by Wehrmacht motorcyclists and the customary steel helmet, and appeared to be concentrating solely on what lay directly ahead and paying scant attention to the trees and bushes at the side of the track, which suited Sinclair's intentions. The

Scots-Canadian glanced up. The lowest branches of the fir tree were well over ten feet above his head, allowing him to hold the six foot long rusty tube aloft. This would give him a clear field to swing the heavy pole firstly downwards, then horizontally, much as a baseball player swings his bat. Timing would be crucial. He decided to wait until the man had negotiated the bend and could see Anna and Callendar at the quarry gates; his attention would then be entirely focused on them. Sinclair gripped the tube and held his breath.

Sure enough, as he rounded the bend, the motorcyclist stopped and stared. It was the perfect moment. Using all his upper body strength, Sinclair swung the pole down and around, striking the German across the throat. The force of the blow sent the man flying backwards off his machine and he landed heavily, the back of his head striking the stony ground first. The motorcycle meanwhile had run on into the bushes where it stalled. Sinclair rushed forward, pistol drawn, ready to deliver the *coup de grâce*. But it was unnecessary. The angle of the man's head reminded him of how Bob Nicholson had looked when they had found him below the sabotaged ropewalk. A quick examination confirmed the man's neck was broken. Not without difficulty, he concealed the corpse in the bushes. He stared at the tail end of the motorcycle protruding from a tangle of brambles and an idea formed in his mind. Hurrying back to where he had hidden the body, he removed the man's full-length waterproof coat and helmet. Then, pulling the machine back onto the track, he pushed it towards the now open gates and into the quarry, the coat and helmet balanced on the seat.

Meanwhile, after successfully opening the gates, Anna and Callendar had driven the big Mercedes into the quarry and parked it at the side of a solidly built, single-storey building at the foot of one of the quarry's sheer walls. Sinclair found them trying to see inside the building through a couple of long, narrow apertures set high up in the front wall of the concrete structure.

'What've you found?' he asked, propping the motorcycle onto its stand.

'Explosives store, I think,' responded Callendar, nodding his head towards the sign on the heavy metal door in the middle of the structure. Sinclair glanced at the red lettering: '*Achtung! Explosiv – Rauchen Verboten!*'

Callendar went across to examine the motorcycle, then looked questioningly at Sinclair.

'Dead!' announced the big Canadian. 'I've hidden the body in the bushes at the side of the track.'

His gaze swept the quarry, taking in the steep cliffs on three sides and the numerous plateaux formed by the various stages of excavation. Opposite the explosives store stood a huge stone-crushing machine, with mountainous piles of broken stone close by. A tall crane sat on one of the lower levels, together with several battered vehicles evidently used for transporting the huge boulders to the crushing machine. Being Sunday, the place was deserted – much to Sinclair's relief. He didn't relish the idea of taking on civilians in a one-sided gun battle.

'I can't see an obvious way for us to get out of here,' said Callendar, his eyes following Sinclair's gaze. 'Unless it's possible to scramble up there.'

He pointed a finger towards the left-hand side of the quarry where what looked like a little-used path ran up the hillside, parallel to the quarry rim.

'That'll do,' responded Sinclair, sounding almost off-hand.

He went to join Anna, who was unloading the weapons from the Mercedes.

'I'll give it a quick reconnoitre,' suggested Callendar, moving towards the start of the path.

'Don't bother,' replied Sinclair, lifting the box of stick grenades from the boot.

287

'But we need to see where it leads. It'll be OK. I've done a bit of mountain climbing...'

'You won't be going.' He stacked the box by the door of the explosives store. 'See if you can get this lock off, Anna, while I finish unloading the car.'

Anna again took the heavy hammer from the boot and began attacking the padlock and chain on the door.

'What d'you mean, I'm not going?' demanded Callendar.

Sinclair reached behind the driving seat of the Mercedes and withdrew the leather briefcase containing the *Hakenkreuz*.

'This has got to get back to England, it's the reason we came here, remember? And the best chance of doing that, is if we split up.'

Callendar stared at him in surprise then shook his head firmly.

'No! We can't. We've got to stick together. We'll stand a much better chance that way.'

'Sorry, James, but that's the way it has to be,' insisted Sinclair. He took the hammer from Anna, who had been so far unsuccessful with the lock, and smashed it with one hefty blow.

'Who says so?' demanded Callendar angrily. 'Who put you in charge anyway? I say we stick together.'

'He's right, James,' said Anna. She took his hands in hers and gave him a warm smile. 'It'll be better for all of us if we split up. They're looking for four people in a car, not one man on a motorcycle and a young couple taking a Sunday walk in the country.'

'But why me?' Callendar turned on Sinclair. 'Why don't *you* take the bloody motorcycle?'

'Because I've never ridden one and you have,' came the quiet response. 'Remember? You once told me you used to ride one at home. So here's your chance. You dress up as a dispatch rider, take the *Hakenkreuz*, get back on the road and carry on heading for Switzerland. My bet is you won't even be stopped at the checkpoints.'

The logic of Sinclair's plan was unassailable. Desperately he turned to Anna.

'I'm not going. I'm not leaving you, Anna. I love you.' He took her in his arms and held her tight against him. 'I'll never, never leave you.'

Sinclair, embarrassed by Callendar's emotional display, disappeared into the explosives store.

Anna pulled away from him and tenderly cupped his face in her hands. She kissed him tenderly on the mouth.

'James, it's for the best. We won't be separated for long. A few days – perhaps a week at the most – then we'll all meet up again in London and you can buy me the most expensive dinner imaginable.'

He looked at her searchingly, desperate to believe what she was saying.

'You promise? A few days, that's all?'

Anna kissed him again and smiled reassuringly.

'Yes. I promise. Within a few days I'll be in touch with a resistance contact and they'll get us out on one of their escape routes.'

Callendar breathed a sigh of relief.

'All right,' he murmured.

At that moment Sinclair emerged from the store carrying some workmen's overalls draped over his arm.

'These might be useful as a disguise. Shouldn't think they'd be too interested in a couple of farm workers tramping across the countryside.'

As he handed a pair to Anna, the sound of a light aeroplane could be heard in the distance. Shading his eyes with his hand, he searched the skies.

'There it is!' He pointed away to the north, where a Feisler Storch could be seen carrying out a sweeping search pattern. 'No prizes for guessing who they're looking for. Come on,

James. Let's get you dressed up and on your way.'

'How about you and Anna? Shouldn't you go first? After all, you'll be on foot.'

'We'll be on our way as soon as you get on the road. Now come on, there's no time to lose.'

'How about Bill? We can't just leave him,' said Callendar, as he donned the voluminous weatherproof coat.

'I'll pin a note to his body, stating he was a British soldier and giving his name and rank. I'm sure they'll give him a decent burial, no matter what we've done.'

'I suppose there's not much else we can do.' He looked into the big man's rugged features. 'You won't try anything heroic, will you?'

'We'll be on our way as soon as you disappear down that track. Now get that helmet on and be off,' urged Sinclair. 'You'll find the German dispatch rider's papers in the right-hand pocket. And don't forget this!' He stuffed the leather briefcase containing the gold *Hakenkreuz* into one of the canvas panniers mounted at the back of the motorcycle.

'How much petrol is there in the tank? Never mind...'

He hurried across to the Mercedes and pulled one of the jerry cans from the boot. A couple of minutes later and the tank had been filled to the brim. Anna, looking comical in a pair of overalls far too big for her, handed him one of the route maps and gave him a final lingering kiss.

'One other thing, James,' interrupted Sinclair. 'I've been thinking. Schiller will be expecting us to continue south for Switzerland.' He rubbed his chin. 'Why don't you do the exact opposite – head back north, first for Berlin then on to Rostock. Try and contact Josef's wife at the tavern. Maybe she can help you get on a ship back to Sweden.'

'That's not a bad idea, James,' urged Anna. 'Her name's Marthe and if she can't help you I'm sure she will know someone who can.'

'OK,' Callendar agreed. 'I'll head back north.'

He turned reluctantly away, mounted the motorcycle and kick-started the engine which fired at the first attempt.

'Don't forget, you two! Dinner at Claridge's, my treat.'

Swallowing the lump in his throat, he waved, revved the engine and set off down the track.

'Right!' said Sinclair. 'Now it's your turn. You'd better be off at once. The sooner you're out of the area the better chance you stand.'

'And what about you? Aren't you coming?'

He shook his head. 'Not straight away. I'll hang around for a while, see if I can delay them a bit longer.'

She forced a smile. 'We both know I'm not going anywhere. Schiller won't give up until he's found me... And with that search plane overhead, that won't take long. Besides, the longer we can delay Schiller here, the better chance James will have.'

'Are you in love with him?'

Tears filled her eyes as she picked up one of the Schmeisser machine pistols together with some spare magazines.

'Why the hell d'you think I'm staying with you?' she snapped. 'It's the only way he'll stand any chance of getting through!'

Nothing further was said, as they hurriedly moved all the weapons inside the explosives store. Finally, with great care, Sinclair carried Thompson's body inside and set it down reverently.

About the time Callendar left the quarry, Schiller, together with Hauptsturmführer Erdmann and the two SS soldiers, had arrived at the first roadblock. The wrecked truck and bodies of the dead German soldiers had by this time been removed and an armoured personnel carrier now took their place, with a squad of ten men manning it.

'Give me a situation report!' snapped Schiller, leaping from the car.

The young officer in charge, a lieutenant in the infantry, snapped smartly to attention and saluted.

'Herr Sturmbannführer! I have to report the fugitives are trapped between two road-blocks, this one and the one commanded by Hauptmann Thurmann located six kilometres further on.'

'Yes, yes,' retorted Schiller irritably. 'I'm already aware of that.' He looked keenly at the young officer. 'You're absolutely sure they haven't slipped through?'

'Impossible, Herr Sturmbannführer. Each vehicle has been thoroughly checked and searched before being allowed to pass.'

'And there are no roads where they could have turned off?'

'No, Herr Sturmbannführer. Only two tracks, one leading to a farm and the other to a quarry. Both dead ends.'

'Very well.' He looked at the soldiers gathered around the roadblock. 'We're going to need more men than this.' He turned to Erdmann. 'That Waffen SS convoy we passed a few kilometres back – I'll take one man as driver and go back to meet them.'

He pointed at one of the two SS troopers who had accompanied them from Berlin. The man immediately slipped into the driver's seat and started the Mercedes' powerful engine. Schiller climbed into the back before turning to Erdmann.

'You stay here. Make sure no-one slips through, and get in touch with the spotter plane, just in case they try to get away on foot.'

'Yes, Herr Sturmbannführer.'

'And another thing. Get on to Thurmann at the next roadblock. Tell him to stop all further vehicles from coming through – get them diverted onto other routes. From now

292

on I want this road kept clear of all traffic.' He tapped the driver on the shoulder. 'Drive fast!'

The SS trooper revved the engine, let in the clutch and, tyres squealing in protest, the big car roared off to meet the approaching convoy. They spotted them ten kilometres further on and at Schiller's command, the trooper slewed the Mercedes across the road effectively blocking their route. The Nazi officer leapt from the car and strode towards the lead truck where he was greeted by a young and handsome SS officer, elegantly dressed in what was clearly a tailor-made uniform and accompanied by a Hauptscharführer wearing a camouflaged combat smock. Schiller inwardly sneered, guessing the officer was a member of the German aristocracy who fancied himself as a member of the SS elite. His suspicions were well-founded. As he approached, the young officer came to attention, clicked his heels smartly, threw his arm up in the Nazi salute and introduced himself.

'Heil Hitler! Obersturmführer Klaus von Teussen, commanding Number Two Company, SS Panzergrenadier Regiment Number One, Das Reich Division, en route to Erfurt for military exercises.'

Schiller returned the salute with military correctness, at the same time critically eyeing the smart dove-grey uniform.

'Do you always dress this way for manoeuvres, Obersturmführer?'

Von Teussen smiled apologetically. 'You must forgive me, Herr Sturmbannführer. I received my orders somewhat belatedly and had no time to change – I was having coffee with some young ladies at the time. I shall of course change when we arrive at Erfurt.'

'Well, your plans are changed. You're no longer going to Erfurt. I am acting on the direct orders of Reichsführer Himmler and I'm commandeering you and your men to help me catch three spies and a traitor we've got cornered about twelve or thirteen kilometres up ahead. Just follow me as fast as you can.'

Von Teussen clicked his heels and gave a snappy salute. 'Very good, Herr Sturmbannführer!' With a broad grin, he turned to address his senior warrant officer. 'Pass the word, Zimmerman. Manoeuvres are cancelled. We're in for an enjoyable afternoon's sport instead!'

Von Teussen swung himself back into the cab of the leading vehicle and slapped his hand enthusiastically on the dashboard.

'Let's go!'

25

At the same time as Schiller's Mercedes pulled away from the roadblock, heading north to locate the SS convoy, a lone Wehrmacht dispatch rider approached from the opposite direction. Erdmann stepped into the road and held his hand up, bringing the motorcyclist to a halt.

'Papers!' he snapped, holding out his hand. Callendar slipped off his right-hand glove, retrieved the dispatch rider's papers from his pocket, and handed them to Erdmann. Whilst the SS officer was examining them, Callendar looked around warily, half expecting to see Schiller and prepared to drive off at breakneck speed if recognised.

'Where are you heading?' demanded Erdmann.

'Berlin, Herr Hauptsturmführer.' He tapped the pannier containing the briefcase. 'I have urgent documents to be delivered to the Reichs Chancellery.'

For an uncomfortable moment Callendar thought the SS officer might ask to examine the contents, but Erdmann merely nodded and handed back the papers, obviously satisfied with his story.

'Have you seen any sign of a Mercedes bearing an SS registration, between the last road-block and here?'

Callendar thought quickly. Obviously they knew they had trapped their prey between the two road blocks and to deny having seen anything might seem a little suspicious, albeit a genuine passing motorist would hardly have spotted it hidden in the quarry.

'Yes, Herr Hauptsturmführer. There was one a few kilometres

295

back, pulled off the road.' He tried to look puzzled. 'Why? Is it important?'

'Never mind,' snapped Erdmann irritably. 'Get on your way.'

He turned and waved to the troopers, indicating the motorcyclist should be allowed through. Callendar opened the throttle, eased in the clutch and pulled smoothly away. He did not hurry. In fact, he had already decided to drive at a fairly comfortable speed all the way to Rostock, not necessarily to avoid drawing attention to himself, but because he wanted to delay his arrival until dusk.

Several kilometres along the road he came across the Waffen SS convoy heading in the opposite direction. An open-top Mercedes was in the lead with the unmistakeable figure of Schiller standing in the back, urging them on like the American Sixth Calvary. He gave the briefest of glances at the passing dispatch rider, not that he would have recognised Callendar, his face masked by helmet and goggles. The sight of the convoy, however, made the young Englishman's heart sink. He knew that unless Anna and Sinclair were already well away from the quarry, with a company of crack troops now chasing them, their chances of escape were dramatically reduced.

On his arrival back at the roadblock, Schiller found an excited Erdmann waiting for him.

'Herr Sturmbannführer, the pilot of the spotter plane has radioed in. He has spotted a car similar to the one we're looking for, in the quarry about two kilometres down the road. He also says he saw at least three people, possibly four, one of them injured, moving about inside the quarry.'

Schiller punched the back of the car seat with clenched fist. 'We've got them! Get in the car and contact the pilot on this radio. Tell him to stay up as long as he can and keep a lookout in case they try to make a break for it across the fields.'

Leaving the roadblock in place, the Mercedes again set off together with the convoy of SS troops and headed towards the quarry. As soon as they reached the turn-off, the trucks halted on the roadside and the hundred or so men disembarked, lining up in two ranks facing the track entrance. Schiller wasted no time in getting things organised.

'Von Teussen! Send six of your men up the track to reconnoitre and report back. I don't want any shooting. The Reichsführer wants all the fugitives alive. Is that clear?'

'*Jawohl*, Herr Sturmbannführer!'

The young officer selected five men and an NCO and dispatched them.

Reaching the quarry gates, they quickly dragged them open and, with a typical disregard for personal safety, charged through into the quarry where they were met by a withering hail of machine-gun fire from one of the ventilation slits in the concrete blockhouse. Four were killed instantly. Of the other two, one sustained serious chest wounds and was dragged back into the cover of the bushes by the remaining trooper who had been lucky enough to receive only a slight flesh wound in the arm.

'First blood to us,' commented Sinclair, calmly changing the magazine of his machine pistol.

Anna gazed carefully through the other ventilation slit and saw the four bloodstained corpses lying in the quarry dust.

'I wonder how many more there are,' she murmured, more to herself than to her companion.

'Does it matter? Let's just make sure we take as many of them as we can.'

Leaving Sinclair on lookout, Anna peered round the dim interior of the concrete blockhouse. There was no electric light, but her eyes had already adjusted to the darkness and she looked at Thompson's body, propped against the back wall where Sinclair had placed him, and thought how peaceful he seemed, almost as if asleep. Then her eyes swept over the stack of yellow-painted wooden boxes which took up most of the floor space, each one stencilled with a skull and crossbones and bearing the legend *'Achtung – Dynamit! (25 kilos)'*. They were neatly stacked and it wasn't difficult for her to count the number of boxes and do some rapid mental arithmetic.

'Do you realise we're sitting on nearly two tons of dynamite, complete with fuses and detonators?'

Sinclair merely nodded, refusing to take his eyes away from the ventilation slit.

'Could prove useful later on when the grenades run out.' he said laconically. 'By the way, how many do we have left?'

Anna went across to the box lying by Thompson's body. 'Three.'

'All right. Better keep our eyes open. I've a feeling it won't be long now.'

Meanwhile, the sound of gunfire had sent Schiller, Erdmann and von Teussen scurrying towards the quarry, followed by the troopers who now lined both sides of the track. They met the man who had been slightly wounded on his way back to report.

'Get some help and get him back to the trucks,' commanded Schiller, on hearing what had happened. 'The rest of you follow me.'

Now more aware of what they were up against, Schiller approached the quarry entrance with greater caution, stopping short of the gates and using the undergrowth for cover. Von Teussen handed him a pair of binoculars with which he peered through the bushes, sweeping the whole of the quarry and finally coming to rest on the concrete building.

'Well, it seems we've got them trapped. It looks as though they're holed up in an explosives store on the far side of

298

the quarry. Trouble is, there's a lot of open ground between here and the store.'

'What d'you propose?' asked Erdmann.

Schiller looked thoughtful. 'They can't have a lot of ammunition that's for certain. And if they keep firing as they did earlier they'll soon use it up. Then it'll be a simple matter of walking in and arresting them. So that's what we're going to do – make them waste their precious ammunition by sending our men into the quarry and getting them to keep running from cover to cover to draw their fire.'

'You can't be serious!' protested Erdmann. 'They won't stand a chance. Think of the casualties!'

Schiller eyed him coldly. 'They are SS, sworn to die for their Führer, just like you, Erdmann, or had you forgotten your oath?' He turned away contemptuously and resumed peering through his binoculars. 'You've spent too long behind a desk. It's about time you saw some real action.'

Erdmann blanched and closed his mouth.

'Von Teussen, have a look at the layout inside the quarry. There is plenty of cover for your men, don't you think?' Schiller handed the binoculars to the young officer. 'Apart from the natural cover, there are those piles of stones and those big machines.'

Von Teussen carefully swept the ground inside the quarry and, from what he saw, quickly realised Schiller's plan would result in heavy casualties. He lowered the glasses.

'Herr Sturmbannführer, might I respectfully suggest an alternative? We have a supply of smoke grenades and some tear gas canisters on one of the trucks. If we create a smoke screen, perhaps a couple of men can get close enough to lob tear gas inside the building. That would soon bring them out.'

Schiller approved. 'Good idea. See to it!'

Von Teussen dispatched a man back to the trucks. He returned minutes later carrying a canvas rucksack. Von Teussen examined the contents.

'Is this all we have? Six smoke grenades and two gas canisters?'

'That was all we were allocated, Herr Obersturmführer,' interjected Zimmerman with a shrug.

'Damn! Well, it'll have to do. Right, who's got the best throwing arm?'

Zimmerman looked behind him back down the track.

'Hartmann! Berger! Get yourselves up here.'

Two men left the ranks and hurried forward.

'I want you to take a smoke grenade each and lob it as close to that concrete building as you can,' explained von Teussen. He pointed through the bushes towards the explosives store. 'When you've got a good build-up of smoke, take a gas canister each, run like hell to the building and drop them through those ventilation slots. Leave your weapons here – there must be no shooting. The place may be full of explosives.'

The men laid down their rifles and armed themselves with the smoke grenades and gas canisters. They had seen the bodies of their four comrades lying in the grey dust a few yards away, their uniforms bloodstained from the fusillade of bullets that had struck them and knew they too would come under the same vicious fire as soon as they left the comparative cover of the bushes. But they didn't hesitate. Lighting the fuses of the smoke grenades, they nodded their readiness to one another and dashed out into the open, the grenades already belching thick clouds of white vapour.

'Look out!' yelled Sinclair, as he saw the two men suddenly appear from behind the bushes at the end of the track.

He immediately opened fire with his MP40, Anna following suit a split second later. The hail of bullets found their mark, but not before both men had successfully tossed the belching smoke grenades. Both missiles struck the ground only yards in front of the concrete building, bouncing forward and coming to rest a few feet from the thick steel door. The area in front of the building was soon shrouded in a thick fog.

300

'Watch out!' warned Sinclair. 'They're going to attack under cover of the smoke. Just fire short bursts in different directions.'

Back at the entrance, von Teussen dispatched two more of his men to pick up the tear gas canisters dropped by the first two when they were hit, with instructions to continue the attack on the building. But the hail of bullets pouring from the ventilation slits created a curtain of death and both men were quickly brought down, wounded in the legs, making it impossible for them to continue the assault.

'More men!' yelled Schiller, a note of desperation in his voice. 'Send more men this time. Someone's bound to get through.'

Von Teussen detailed ten men this time, urging them on into the smoke. The sheer increase in numbers might well have worked, had Fate not decided to take a hand. An unexpected gust of wind sprang up, swirling down into the quarry and sweeping the smoke away from the building in the direction of the charging stormtroopers. The leaders were only ten yards from the building when they suddenly lost the smoke cover. Sinclair and Anna fired ruthlessly. At such close range it was impossible to miss. Of the ten men, nine were killed outright. However, the tenth man suffered only a slight wound and lay still feigning death. He was one of those who had managed to pick up a tear gas canister. This he kept concealed against the side of his body whilst he stared at the ventilation slits through narrowed eyes. When he could no longer see movement, he leapt to his feet and charged towards the building, at the same time activating the canister. The sudden movement caught Anna's eye and she instinctively fired, hitting the man in the chest. It was a fatal wound, but in the few seconds before he died, the soldier managed to reach the building and push the hissing canister through the ventilation slit. The grey-green canister rolled between the boxes of explosives, belching out its acrid fumes. The building quickly filled with noxious fumes. Hardly able to see, Sinclair dropped to his knees and felt desperately among the wooden cases.

'I'll deal with this,' he coughed. 'For Christ's sake, keep a lookout!'

It was sound advice. Through the quickly dissipating smoke, Schiller had seen the partial success of the attack and wasted no time in sending more men charging towards the building. It took two stick grenades tossed through the partly open door and a full magazine from her Schmeisser to fend off the attack and send the survivors scurrying for cover. Meanwhile, eyes streaming from the effects of the acrid fumes, Sinclair had managed to locate the hissing canister. Carrying it at arm's length, he stumbled towards the door and tossed it out into the open.

'That was close,' he gasped. 'I wonder what other tricks Schiller's got up his sleeve?'

'Why aren't they shooting back at us?' said Anna.

Sinclair jerked his thumb towards the yellow boxes.

'Probably afraid a stray bullet might set off this lot. Which, if it happens, would take Schiller and his pals with us!'

Suddenly Anna shouted a warning and fired a short burst, quickly followed by another.

'What's happening?' Still unable to see properly, Sinclair peered myopically through the slit.

'I'm not sure,' she replied. 'More and more men seem to run into the quarry, take cover, then charge across open ground to another point of cover. I've just hit two of them, but it doesn't seem to deter the others. There! There they go again...' Her comments were punctuated by the staccato sound of her machine pistol as she fired at more running figures, felling a burly Rottenführer before he could gain sanctuary behind the huge crane. 'They're mad! They're just getting killed.'

'And we're wasting a lot of ammunition,' snapped Sinclair,

eyes still streaming. 'That's what he's up to. Deliberately sacrificing the lives of his men to make us use up ammunition. How many magazines have we got left?'

Anna did a quick check. 'Four. Two each.'

'All right. From now on, we fire only in single shots – and only when we're sure of a hit.' He again peered out through the slit. 'My guess is that Schiller thinks he's got all four of us trapped in here and is concentrating his efforts on this place. In which case, the longer we can hold out, the more chance it'll give James.'

Back at the entrance Erdmann was expressing his concern to Schiller at what he considered the unnecessary losses suffered by the SS troopers.

'This is madness! Sheer madness. Look!' He pointed a finger towards the bodies lying around the quarry. 'There must be at least twenty, or even thirty, men lying out there, either dead or wounded. What's the point?'

'The point, Hauptsturmführer Erdmann,' replied Schiller coldly, 'is that we are acting on the orders of Reichsführer Himmler. We are instructed to catch these spies alive so the Gestapo can interrogate them. Now don't question my orders again!'

Von Teussen shared Erdmann's concerns – after all it was his men being killed – but he had been wise enough to remain silent. Now, however, he felt he must do something to stop the slaughter.

'Herr Sturmbannführer! I've just been talking to one of my men who once worked in a quarry. He tells me the building is typical of many he has seen. The narrow apertures are ventilation slots and are usually positioned on two sides of the building to allow air to pass through so avoiding any build-up of heat and keeping the explosives cool.'

'So?' snapped Schiller.

'Well, if there are similar openings on the other side, the one facing the quarry wall, it might be possible for one man

303

to climb the rim of the quarry, then climb down the other side without being seen from inside the building. The occupants wouldn't be expecting an assault from that direction; a few carefully aimed shots and it could all be over fairly quickly.' The idea immediately appealed to Schiller. Despite his remarks to Erdmann, he was conscious of the excessive losses the men were sustaining.

'D'you think you can do it?' he asked, assuming von Teussen was himself volunteering for the mission.

'I don't see why not, providing you can keep them occupied and divert attention away from me.'

'All right. But remember! Shoot only to wound. We want them alive.'

Von Teussen nodded and calmly checked the magazine of his Walther PPK. Erdmann stared at the handsome young officer and shook his head.

'You're mad!' he exclaimed. 'You'll never make it. You'll be cut down before you get halfway.'

'Shut up, Erdmann!' snarled Schiller. 'If he thinks he can do it, then it's worth a try.' He turned back to von Teussen, his eyes burning, and slapped the young man on the shoulder. 'Succeed in this, Obersturmführer and, I promise you, you'll get the Knight's Cross!'

'Or a coffin,' muttered Erdmann tersely.

Schiller glared at him, but Von Teussen remained unabashed. He brushed some dust from his impeccable uniform and gave Erdmann a sardonic smile. 'If it is to be a coffin, Herr Hauptsturmführer, would you be kind enough to make sure it's a good fit? I should really hate to offend my tailor.'

With a wave of his hand, he turned, slipped into the bushes and began to move upwards between the trees towards the quarry rim. Schiller watched von Teussen as he made his way among the trees. He was still watching when he spoke in a voice dangerously soft voice.

'Erdmann, when we get back to Berlin, I suggest you

spend the day enjoying the sights of our great city, because within twenty-four hours, you'll be on your way to the Eastern Front. Perhaps there you'll learn what it means to be an officer in the SS.' He turned and sneered at Erdmann's ashen face. 'Meanwhile, you can get back to the car and man the radio. You're no use to me here.'

Erdmann rose to his feet. Several men close by had both heard and seen what had happened and he felt their stares on him as he walked back down the track. One of them watched him all the way until he disappeared round a bend.

'Ivan will teach him how to fight!' he muttered, turning back to his comrades with a grin.

Von Teussen made good progress ascending to the rim of the quarry, and reached the point immediately above the building after only a few minutes. From his vantage point he could see his men sheltering behind piles of stone or large boulders, or finding sanctuary behind the huge machinery. They also saw him and he prayed they wouldn't keep staring up and give his position away. He saw too the bodies littering the quarry floor and swore silently that they would be avenged.

Heights had never bothered the young German. A skilled mountaineer before the war, with the Matterhorn among his conquests, he viewed the drop of fifty feet or so unperturbed and confidently swung himself over the edge. As he began his descent, several troopers dashed from cover to cover, deliberately drawing fire from the blockhouse, and keeping the attention of the defenders away from what was happening above. One man stumbled and paid the ultimate price for his bravery, two bullets from Anna's machine pistol finding their mark.

Three and four at a time, the SS soldiers kept up their suicidal game of hide and seek until they saw von Teussen reach the base of the wall behind the building. Taking care not to disturb the loose stones at the foot of the quarry, the young SS officer covered the dozen or so metres to the back

305

of the building without being heard. Drawing his pistol, he pressed himself against the wall of the concrete structure and edged his way along to one of the ventilation slits. He peered inside. It took a few seconds for his eyes to adjust to the dim interior before he made out the shapes of Sinclair and Anna standing at the slits on the far side. Both had their backs to him and were clearly unaware of his presence. Von Teussen's eyes quickly scoured the rest of the interior. He knew from Schiller's briefing that there should be four people inside. Then he saw Thompson's body propped against the wall and concluded that the fourth individual, though he was unable to see another corpse, must have suffered a similar fate.

Thinking the man's reactions would be faster than the girl's, he decided to take out Sinclair first, with a shot aimed at the right-hand side of his back – a disabling wound – to be rapidly followed by a similar shot at the girl. He took aim and gently squeezed the trigger. The bullet struck Sinclair precisely where it had been aimed, passing through his right shoulder blade and then his lung before lodging itself in the rib cage. Its impact thrust the big man against the wall. He gave a gasping cry as his knees buckled and he sank to the floor.

But von Teussen's assessment of Anna's reaction time proved sadly at fault. She heard the pistol shot almost before Sinclair was hit, whirled round and, with her own pistol, snapped off two shots in rapid succession towards the ventilation slit. Once again, the many hours she had spent on the firing range paid off. One of her bullets found its way through the narrow aperture and struck von Teussen just above the right eye, ending his life instantly.

Hearing the three pistol shots so close together, Schiller immediately assumed von Teussen's mission had been successful and, with a cry of triumph, jumped to his feet and excitedly waved his troops forward. Although Sinclair

306

was out of action, Anna was ready for them and burst after burst of machine-gun fire sent them running for cover, not before several more had paid with their lives. Cursing, Schiller withdrew to the comparative safety of the track.

Back inside the building, Anna was on her knees hurriedly examining Sinclair's wound. He pushed her away.

'Forget it. It's only a flesh wound. Give me a hand to get to my feet.'

But as he tried to rise, he was overtaken by a fit of coughing; blood and spittle spurted from his mouth and ran down his chin.

'Sit still,' ordered Anna. 'You'll only make it worse.'

His face betrayed the pain he was suffering, though he tried to mask it with a brave grin.

'It's OK. I wasn't planning to go anywhere special this afternoon.'

Anna rose and peered outside. Seeing little movement from the scattered troops, she used the opportunity to check the ammunition status, tossing one empty magazine after another onto the floor. Sinclair could see from her expression that their stocks were exhausted. He coughed, and brought up more blood.

'How about your pistol?' he croaked.

He felt for his own Walther, only to find the holster empty. She checked the magazine and shook her head. The last two rounds had been expended on von Teussen. They had both known they would arrive at this situation sooner or later.

'Guess that's it then. Still, James should be well on his way by now.' He looked around and saw the grenade box lying near his foot. He pushed it towards her. 'You know what to do?'

'Yes,' she replied calmly.

He smiled. 'Best get on with it then. No point in hanging around.'

'Not quite yet... There's one thing I still have to do...'

307

Rummaging through her jacket pockets, she withdrew a white handkerchief and tied it to the muzzle of one of the MP40s. She stepped up to the steel door, eased it slightly open and poked the machine pistol through the gap, waving it as a flag of truce. Alarmed, Sinclair tried to protest but a further fit of coughing overtook him.

'There's no need to worry. I know what I'm doing.'

She waved the 'flag' again.

'What are they up to?' muttered Schiller suspiciously.

'Perhaps they've used up all their ammunition, Herr Sturmbannführer,' suggested Zimmermann.

'Perhaps,' replied an unconvinced Schiller, continuing to stare suspiciously at the white handkerchief fluttering in the breeze.

Stabsscharführer Zimmerman had liked and respected his company commander. He took his death personally, as well as that of his men whose bodies now littered the quarry. He had a score to settle with those responsible.

Rising to his feet he announced grimly, 'With respect, Herr Sturmbannführer. There is only one way to find out. With the Herr Sturmbannführer's permission...'

But he didn't wait for Schiller's permission. Machine pistol at the ready, he waved to the troops still on the track to follow him and purposefully moved into the quarry, the men fanning out behind him. Seeing what was happening, those troops already in the quarry left their cover and joined their comrades as they advanced towards the building.

Momentarily taken aback, but seeing no reaction from the fugitives, Schiller recovered himself and dashed out into the quarry to take the lead and resume command. Slowly, they approached the explosives store. Sweat broke out on Schiller's brow and he gripped his pistol tighter to mask his trembling hand. Twenty yards ... fifteen ... ten... Suddenly, Schiller signalled the troops to halt. Zimmerman stepped forward.

'Do you wish me to go in first, Herr Sturmbannführer?'

Not daring to take his eyes off the rusty steel door now only a few yards away, Schiller shook his head.

'That particular pleasure is going to be mine.' Taking a deep breath, he marched forward, pistol at the ready. The door was standing just wide enough for him to enter. He slipped inside, immediately placing his back against the wall. As his eyes grew accustomed to the dimness of the interior it was Anna he saw first. She was casually leaning against the far wall, both hands behind her back, the baggy overalls gaping open to expose her white blouse, now grey with quarry dust. She wore an odd smile on her face.

Schiller's eyes flicked towards Sinclair propped up against the wall next to Thompson, the front of his uniform covered in blood from his haemorrhaging lung. Frantically, he sought for the fourth member of the group.

'Where's Richter?' he demanded angrily.

'Long gone,' she announced with a satisfied smile. 'Gone with your Führer's precious *Hakenkreuz*. You'll never catch him.'

'We'll see about that,' snarled Schiller. 'As for you, you Jewish whore, you'll cause no further trouble. Die, bitch!'

The bullet struck Anna in the chest, hurling her back against the wall. She looked down, almost with curiosity, to watch the red stain gradually spreading on the front of her blouse. Before oblivion claimed her, she looked up with a smile and pulled the cord of the stick grenade clutched behind her back.

'You too, Herr... Sturm... bann... führer.'

Then, with her last scrap of energy, she made her final gesture. Schiller gazed in fascinated horror as the grenade prescribed a graceful somersault through the air before disappearing behind the boxes of explosives.

'*Nein!*' he screamed and raced for the door.

26

Schiller never made it. The reinforced concrete and steel structure had been designed to withstand minor explosions outside the building, but not the instantaneous blast of two tonnes of dynamite from within. The blast ripped it apart, delivering death and destruction to everyone and everything trapped inside the quarry walls. None of the SS troops stood a chance of survival; they were swept up like autumn leaves in a gale, the huge shockwave lifting them from their feet and smashing them against the rocky walls of the quarry. Two were impaled on the same branch of one tree, whilst the body of another was shredded by the metal latticework of the crane's jib. The crane itself toppled majestically, killing another five who had remained in their refuge behind the stone-crushing machine. Contained on three sides by towering walls, the explosion reverberated around the quarry and sent clouds of dust and smoke hundreds of feet into the air. All in all, the explosion killed almost a hundred crack Waffen SS troops in an instant, the few who escaped the mercy of instant death soon succumbing to the effects of their horrific injuries.

Back on the road, a hundred yards away, the sound of the explosion had sent Hauptsturmführer Erdmann and the two troopers left in charge of the vehicles fleeing for cover, as a hail of stone came crashing down out of the skies. It seemed to go on forever, yet in reality lasted only a matter of seconds. As the patter of falling debris ceased, Erdmann crawled coughing from beneath one of the trucks. Signalling the two men to follow, he set off along the track, running as fast as the uneven surface would allow.

Nearing the quarry, he found the area littered with larger boulders and rocks, some weighing several tons. Negotiating these made progress difficult. Eventually, he arrived at the entrance to be greeted by a scene of horror and devastation. Clenching his teeth, he made his way into the quarry. Bodies and the remains of bodies lay everywhere. Clouds of fine dust still hung in the air, but he could see the explosives store had completely disappeared. The top section of the crane's jib stuck out from a pile of rubble, like an up-thrust finger of defiance, whilst the huge stone crushing machine now rested at the foot of the quarry wall, tossed aside by the explosion like a toy relinquished by a spoilt child.

'Madness!' whispered Erdmann. 'Sheer bloody madness!'

'Should we see if anyone is still alive, Herr Hauptsturmführer?' ventured one of the young troopers.

'Still alive?' said Erdmann absently, unable to drag his eyes from the scene of devastation. 'Do you *really* think anyone could have survived that?'

'Well... You never know. Someone might just...'

Erdmann closed his eyes tight, trying to shut the scene from his mind and thinking coherently.

'Yes... Yes, you're right. We should check. Come on.'

He stepped forward, then stopped, holding up his hand.

'Wait! Can you hear something?'

'Hear what, Herr Hauptsturmführer?' said one of the troopers. 'I still have the sound of the explosion ringing in my ears.'

'Listen!'

At first it was just a murmur, accompanied by small quantities of loose rock scampering down the quarry walls. Then the murmur became a rumble. Soon the rumble became a roar as whole sections of the quarry walls, weakened by the force of the explosion, began to break away, loosening thousands of tons of rock and creating major landslides all round the quarry.

311

'Back!' yelled Erdmann.

He turned and pushed the two men towards the relative safety of the track. The three tore down the track, pursued by huge boulders which bounced along behind them like monstrous rubber balls. Fear gave impetus to their flying feet.

Gaining the relative safety of the road they remained still for a few moments, panting for breath and listening as noise of the landslides gradually diminished. When all seemed quiet again and the clouds of choking dust had begun to settle, they gingerly made their way back to the quarry.

When they reached the entrance they beheld a great transformation. The quarry had taken on the shape of a saucer, its sheer walls now gentle slopes, its floor covered to a depth of several metres with hundreds of thousands of tons of rocks. Of the human remains that had been visible only minutes earlier, nothing could be seen. A sea of rubble had engulfed everything.

For a while none of them spoke a word. Erdmann felt strangely calm. Then, nearby, a thrush began to sing.

'I have to radio a report to Berlin,' he said quietly. 'You two may as well come back to the trucks with me. There's nothing more to be done here.'

'No, Herr Reichsführer, there isn't the slightest possibility of any survivors. Sturmbannführer Schiller, the four fugitives and over a hundred SS troops have been killed, either in the explosion, or crushed to death under the landslide that followed.'

Erdmann listened as the line crackled with Himmler's response.

'Gold *Hakenkreuz*? No, Herr Reichsführer, not a sign of anything like that. And if one of the fugitives were carrying it, then I'm afraid it's buried under thousands of tons of rocks, impossible to find.'

'Impossible?' retorted Himmler acidly. 'To an SS officer,

Erdmann, it should be only a minor difficulty. You seem to forget the massive resources we have in the German Reich. I will have several hundred Todt workers there within an hour, more if necessary, together with sufficient transport to move these rocks of yours. You see, Erdmann, it will be found, because the Führer has ordered it. Meanwhile you will remain there until you are relieved. Is that clear?'

'*Jawohl!* Herr Reichsführer.'

He replaced the handset.

'Madness!' he murmured to himself. 'Sheer madness!'

The theft from the Reichs Chancellery, together with the associated breach of security and the escape of the perpetrators from Berlin, had created uproar among the Nazi hierarchy; it was as if the whole of the Wehrmacht and police forces had been jointly mobilised. The roads which had been so empty earlier that day were now crowded with military and police traffic. Although most of this was heading south, Callendar's journey in the opposite direction had been slowed by the sheer volume of oncoming vehicles. In fact he had travelled less than five miles and had stopped at one of the numerous control points when the sound of the explosion reached his ears.

All heads turned southwards to see the column of smoke and dust lazily climbing into the air. Immediately a knot formed in Callendar's stomach and his heart sank, for he knew it could mean only one thing. He removed one of his gauntlets to lift his goggles and wipe the unbidden tears from his eyes.

'Something the matter?'

A burly member of the *feldgendarmerie* stared at him suspiciously from the roadside.

'N ... no. Nothing,' he replied. 'Some dust in the eye, that's all.'

313

'Teach you to wear your goggles then, won't it?' the military policeman responded unsympathetically.

It was dusk by the time the young Englishman reached the outskirts of Rostock. He had made good progress since passing through Berlin. His guise as a Wehrmacht dispatch rider had ensured he was briskly waved through, past the columns of waiting traffic. The further he had travelled from Berlin, the fewer road blocks he encountered.

He deliberately slowed as he entered the town, not sure what direction he should take. He had already decided to follow Anna's suggestion to try and make contact with Marthe at The Wild Boar, despite Josef's arrest by the Gestapo. He also realised he would have to get rid of the motorcycle fairly soon. With the light Sunday evening traffic, it would look suspicious if he were to be seen riding aimlessly. But where could he leave it without attracting unwelcome attention?

As he followed Anna's directions through the town, he began to recognise a few landmarks and soon found himself heading for the railway station. He decided this could be a place to dump the motorcycle. When he arrived a fair amount of military traffic was moving in and out of the station approach and he spotted a number of unattended motorcycles already parked in front of the entrance. Blessing his good luck, he pulled up alongside the last machine, switched off the engine, dismounted and set the machine on its stand. Retrieving the leather satchel from the panniers, he glanced around to see if his arrival had attracted any attention, but it seemed everyone was too busy, or in too much of a hurry, to notice just another dispatch rider.

Praying his luck would hold, he made his way towards the station, passing unchecked by two members of the *Feldgendarmerie* on duty at the entrance and threaded his way through the crowd, heading for the public toilets. A stream of people, mostly military personnel, was passing in and out of the conveniences and no one gave him a second glance as he searched for an empty cubicle. Finding one, he quickly slipped inside, closed the door, slid home the bolt and breathed a sigh of relief. He took a few moments to compose himself, then he peeled off the waterproof coat, together with his steel helmet and hung them on the hook behind the door. Opening the brief case, he checked the *Hakenkreuz* was still safe and retrieved his peaked cap. He spent the next few minutes using toilet paper to brush the accumulated dust and mud from his normally highly polished boots. Satisfied he had done as good a job as possible, he tossed the paper into the bowl, donned his peaked cap, straightened his uniform and, pulling the flush, left the cubicle.

Again, no one paid any attention to the young SS officer with a briefcase, as he made his way back along the platform and through the busy entrance hall. He returned the military salute of the two field police with a snapped up Nazi salute, accompanied by an equally crisp 'Heil Hitler', as he marched past them onto the station concourse.

Fighting the urge to walk quickly, he turned onto the main thoroughfare and headed in the direction of *Das Wildschwein*, retracing the steps all three of them had taken barely a week earlier, but which now seemed years ago.

It was dark by the time he reached the alleyway leading to the back of the tavern and he hurriedly approached the green-painted wooden gates to the tavern's yard. Praying they would not be locked, he turned the handle and gently pushed . . .

Ten minutes after Callendar had left the station, an imposing Nazi staff car drew up in before the entrance. At the same time four Wehrmacht motorcyclists emerged from the station building. Mounting their machines, they took up position, two in front and two behind the staff car, and, with engines

315

running, waited the arrival of Generalfeldmarschall Keitel from Berlin.

Callendar's motorcycle, now left standing alone and covered in quarry dust, stood out like a sore thumb. Its presence and its appearance attracted the attention of one of the motorcyclists, who stared at the dirty machine with a puzzled frown. After a moment's hesitation, he drew out a notebook and pencil from his waterproof and hastily scribbled down its identification number.

As he finished doing so, the Generalfeldmarschall swept imperiously from the station entrance, accompanied by his ADC, and stepped into the waiting staff car. The motorcyclist hurriedly slipped the notebook and pencil back into his pocket, just in time to pull away in unison with the other escorts, as the convoy set off.

On return to his depot some twenty minutes later, the German motorcyclist produced his notebook to his duty officer and, after a brief conversation, the officer put a call through to Central Vehicle Registry in Berlin.

'This is Hauptmann Schröder, thirty-fourth Motorcycle Unit, Rostock. Has a motorcycle been reported missing from the Sachsen region? One of my men has spotted a machine bearing the symbol of the eighty-second, which I happen to know is located near Leipzig. What? Yes, I have the number. WH-IM6434.' He repeated it to ensure accuracy. 'All right, I'll leave it to you. Meanwhile, if it's still at the railway station, I'll get it brought here. *Gute Nacht!*'

The records clerk who took Hauptmann Schröder's call, happened to be a fastidious individual whose greatest fear was the build-up of an unmanageable workload. Accordingly, he wasted no time in telephoning the transport officer of the 82nd Motorcycle Unit at Leipzig. Less than ten minutes after that call was made, the telephone rang on Oberst Oster's desk at

Abwehr headquarters in Berlin. Although it was almost eight o'clock in the evening, Oster was still working hard.

'What? Are you sure?' he demanded. 'All right, all right! Have you informed Reich Central Security? No? Then do so at once, otherwise you'll have Reichsführer Himmler down on your head!'

He pressed his forefinger on the bar of telephone handset to terminate the call and rapidly dialled a number.

'Herr Admiral! My apologies for disturbing you at home, but I thought you should be aware of the latest developments in the Reichs Chancellery fiasco.'

'Go on,' invited Canaris, suddenly alert. 'What's happened?'

'You'll recall, Herr Admiral, that the last report we received, at fourteen-thirty hours, indicated that the enemy agents were all killed in an explosion at a quarry on the outskirts of Leipzig, together with a number of SS personnel?'

'Yes, yes,' replied Canaris impatiently. 'Get on with it, Hans.'

'I've just received a report from CVR, that a motorcycle based south of Leipzig, and used in the pursuit of the enemy agents earlier today, has been found abandoned, over four hundred kilometres away, outside Rostock railway station.'

'So... Rostock again,' murmured Canaris. 'Well, well! You'd better inform Reich Central Security right away.'

'Already in hand,' replied Oster.

'Good. I rather suspect they'll be issuing similar orders to their people, but get on to the Feldgendarmerie and military headquarters in Rostock. I want that town sealed. No-one gets in or out without my permission – or that of Reichsführer Himmler. Is that clear?'

'Perfectly, Herr Admiral. I'll get onto it at once!'

No matter how hard Callendar pushed, the solid wooden gates refused to budge. He glanced desperately back along the alleyway, hoping no-one had spotted him. There was no moon and the alleyway was pitch black; even if a pedestrian crossing the entrance on the main road had glanced in he would not have been seen.

He stepped back and looked up. The wall was solidly built, standing some ten feet high with a row of rusting spikes set into the coping stones on top. There was no way he could reach the top, not without something to stand on. He glanced around and his heart leapt. The tavern must have had a delivery that afternoon because, on the other side of the alley, a large wooden beer cask stood against the wall of the adjoining building. Callendar studied it for a moment. If it was full, he knew he wouldn't have a hope in hell of moving it. Leaning his briefcase against the gate, he crossed over, took hold of the rim with both hands and pushed. It was empty. Probably missed by the driver of the delivery vehicle, Callendar thought, blessing the man's oversight.

He tilted the cask on its edge and, not without some difficulty, managed to manoeuvre it across the alley to the yard wall. Breathless from his exertions, he retrieved the briefcase and clambered on top of the cask. From this elevation he found he could grasp the iron spikes with both hands. Balancing the briefcase on top of the wall, he gripped two of them and began to haul himself up. When he was high enough, he looked over into the yard. It was deserted. Hauling himself a little higher, he looked down and saw that a number of casks had been conveniently stacked against the wall on the inside.

Taking great care not to impale himself on the rusty prongs, he began to ease himself over the wall. Just as he was precariously perched on top of the wall, his peaked cap slipped from his head and tumbled down between the stacked beer casks inside the yard. Cursing, he reached down with one leg until his foot located the top of a cask then, transferring his weight, began to slide his other leg over. It was at this point one of the spikes decided to hook itself into his jacket and he heard the unwelcome sound of tearing cloth. He carefully disengaged himself, but the damage had been done. Clambering down from the stack of casks, he stood in the cobbled yard and examined the torn jacket. He shook his head in despair. It had suffered a rent from just below the armpit down to the bottom edge. Not even the most skilful tailor could repair the damage. This, with the loss of his cap, meant it would be impossible for him to go back onto the streets. The die was cast. If Marthe refused to help him, he would be finished.

Making his way to the back door of the tavern, he put his ear to the panel but all he could pick up was the muffled sound of voices emanating from the bar. He knocked tentatively – no response. He tried again, this time a little harder – again no response. He tried a third time. It was no good. No one could hear him. Deciding he would have to wait until the tavern closed before trying again, he settled down behind a stack of smaller casks and prepared for a lonely vigil.

He hadn't been waiting long when he noticed a marked increase in the sound of vehicle activity from the main road, accompanied by the sound of foot patrols marching up and down past the alley entrance. Clearly something was afoot and he huddled closer to the casks, praying fervently that whatever was happening was nothing to do with him.

Then it began to rain.

27

It was only drizzle at first but, as the minutes ticked by, the rain grew worse until it became a heavy downpour. Callendar's uniform soon became saturated and he began to shiver. Mercifully, the shower was not prolonged and he was soon able to move around the yard, flapping his arms around him, in an attempt to regenerate body heat. He was still doing this some two hours later when the noise from the bar gradually abated. Shivering, he again rapped gently on the back door. No response. He repeated the action and this time he was rewarded with the sound of footsteps on the stone passageway.

'Who's there?' a voice called out. 'What d'you want?'

Callendar heaved a sigh of relief. It was Marthe.

'Marthe! Open up, please,' he begged.

'Who are you?'

'One of the men who stayed here a week ago. One of Anna's friends.' He heard the sound of bolts being withdrawn and the door opened a fraction. Marthe's worried face appeared in the gap.

'What d'you want?' she demanded fearfully.

'Please. You've got to help me.'

'I can't help you. It's too dangerous! Can't you hear the polizei vehicles? They know you're here in Rostock. They're setting up roadblocks across the town and it's rumoured they'll soon be starting house to house searches. You must go!'

'I have nowhere else *to* go. Please let me in!' Callendar begged.

'I can't. I'm sorry. You must go away. They've already arrested Josef.'

'I know,' Callendar responded tiredly, not realising what he was saying.

The door suddenly swung back and the stout figure of Marthe filled the doorway. She held a spluttering candle in her hand.

'What d'you mean, "you know"?' she asked. 'How d'you know? Have you seen him? Have you seen my Josef?' Her voice trembled as she held the candle up to Callendar's face.

Mentally kicking himself for his unguarded response, he nodded. 'Yes... Yes, I've seen him, Marthe.'

'Oh! Thank God!' she exclaimed with relief. 'Is he all right? Where have they taken him?'

Callendar averted his eyes, not knowing what to say.

'What's wrong? Why don't you look at me?'

'I'm sorry, Marthe...'

The candle shook in her hand.

'He's dead, isn't he?'

Callendar nodded. 'Yes. I'm afraid he is.'

'No! Please God, no!' she cried, tears filling her eyes. She raised a hand to her mouth, stifling her sobs.

'I'm sorry, Marthe.'

Callendar laid a sympathetic hand on her arm.

'How... How ... did it happen?'

'He was shot... Firing squad. It was very quick. He didn't suffer.'

She stared at him with tear-filled eyes. 'Did they ... torture him?' .

'No!' he lied. 'I ... happened to be present at the interrogation. They threatened to torture him, but he just laughed in their faces. So they decided it would be a waste of time. I guess they knew he wouldn't talk.'

Marthe dried her eyes on her apron. A look of pride appeared on her face.

'That's my Josef!' she declared. 'He would never have talked. He was a man! He was *my* man!'

'Yes. Yes, he was,' agreed Callendar. 'A very brave man.' He hesitated. 'Look. I'm sorry, Marthe. I should never have come here. I've put you in enough danger. If you'll open the gate, I'll disappear.'

'You'll do no such thing!' she declared vehemently. 'Josef would never forgive me. Come inside and let's get you out of those wet clothes.'

'What about the Gestapo?'

'If Josef can handle them, so can I. Now come in, before you catch pneumonia.'

Gratefully Callendar entered and followed her into what must have been the living room. A fire blazed cheerfully in the grate and he immediately crouched down in front of it, holding his hands out towards glowing coals. Marthe disappeared for a few moments, returning with a couple of large towels.

'Come on, now. Get those wet things off and dry yourself. Later, I'll hang your clothes in front of the fire, though looking at your jacket I don't suppose you'll be wearing that again! I'll see if I've got anything upstairs that'll fit you.' It seemed she had momentarily dismissed all thoughts of Josef from her mind, and was concentrating her attention on making her visitor comfortable. 'Now don't be shy. You'll not be the first man I've seen naked.'

Callendar stripped off his clothing and wrapped one of the towels around his waist.

'Now. Hot soup and bread I think.'

Callendar realised he hadn't eaten for twenty-four hours.

'That'll be wonderful,' he sighed eagerly.

As she made to go to the kitchen, a thought struck her. 'I'm sorry. I don't know your name.'

'James. Please call me James,' he smiled.

'James.' She repeated it with difficulty, pronouncing the

322

'J' as a 'Y'. 'How are your two friends – and Anna? Will they be coming too?'

Callendar stared into the flames.

'No, Marthe,' he replied softly. 'They won't be coming.'

She looked at the whiteness of his back. 'You mean . . . ?' Her voice faltered.

'I'm afraid so.'

'All of them?'

He nodded.

She covered her face with her hands and left the room. They both knew there was nothing more to be said.

After he had wolfed down a bowl of beef stew and several chunks of coarse bread, Marthe led him upstairs. She didn't take him into either of the two rooms he had visited a week earlier, but to one at the far end of the passage which was almost completely empty. No bed – just a threadbare carpet, a pair of faded curtains hanging at the window and, set against the far wall, a dilapidated-looking wardrobe with one of its doors missing.

Marthe walked across to the wardrobe, took hold of one side and pulled it towards her, as if she were opening a door. And, just like a door, it swung open, gliding on unseen, well-oiled hinges, to reveal a secret room. He followed Marthe inside.

'We've used this room a number of times to hide people,' she explained with a little smile. 'It's quite safe. Both the polizei and the Gestapo have searched the premises a number of times, but they've never discovered this place. You can stay here as long as you want. No-one will betray you.'

Callendar glanced at his surroundings. The space measured about ten feet by six. A single camp bed was set against one wall. Apart from the bed, there was a chair, a large trunk and a commode stool. There was no window. The only light came from a low-wattage, naked bulb hanging from the ceiling.

'It's not much,' she said with a shrug, 'but at least you will be safer here than on the streets.'

'Please... It's fine. I can't thank you enough,' he stammered, sitting on the edge of the bed. For the first time since arriving in Nazi Germany, he felt safe. But he couldn't shut out the day's events. Anna.... Sinclair... Thompson. He knew they were dead. He closed his eyes to prevent Marthe seeing the tears which welled up. But she was a perceptive woman and possessed that motherly instinct all women seem to have. She sat on the bed next to him and took his hand.

'Do you want to talk about your friends?' she asked.

Callendar stared at the floor. A tear splashed silently on the bare floorboards.

'They died for me, you know, Marthe. They gave their lives so that I could get away. So I could get away with that.' He pointed at the leather satchel beside him. 'To get it back to England. Not that there's much hope of that now, is there? I can't even get out of Rostock.'

'Is it important? Whatever it is you've got in there?'

'That's what they told us. It's the reason we came here.'

Marthe looked at the satchel then she began to stare into space. She stared for a long time, before seeming to arrive at a decision. She stood up.

'It has to be very important, this package of yours. Important enough to have the whole military garrison of Rostock, plus the polizei for miles around, on the streets trying to find you.' She turned to him. 'I wasn't involved in the resistance work Josef was doing. He wouldn't allow it. But I will see if it is possible to find the wireless operator he used. Perhaps he can contact London.'

'No, Marthe. You mustn't. You're putting yourself in too much danger already. Let me rest here for a few days, then I'll see if I can find a way out of Rostock. If I'm lucky, I'll revert to the original plan and head for Switzerland. They won't expect that.'

'Switzerland? Across the whole of Germany? With everyone looking for you?' she smiled benignly. 'No! You are better off here. Leave it to me.' She pointed to the trunk at the foot of the bed. 'There are some old clothes in there which might fit you. Now try and get some rest. I will see you in the morning.'

She walked through the hole in the wall and began to swing the wardrobe back into place.

'When it is closed, push home these bolts,' she instructed, indicating two bolts fixed to the back of the wardrobe. 'And don't open up unless you hear this signal.' She gave three double knocks on the inside panelling of the wardrobe. 'That will tell you it is me. Goodnight. Sleep well.'

She closed the wardrobe fully and Callendar thrust home the bolts.

The following morning he was awakened from a deep, refreshing sleep, by a loud knocking. For a moment, he couldn't remember where he was. Then it all came flooding back to him. Grabbing a blanket to cover his nakedness, he leapt from the bed, his heart thumping. Again came the knocking.

Knock, knock! Knock, knock! Knock, knock!

He recognised Marthe's signal and gingerly slid back the two bolts. Pushing the cupboard open slightly, he saw her pale, strained face.

'The Gestapo and the polizei are carrying out a house-to-house search,' she announced. 'They're in the premises next door, turning the place upside down. We shall be next. Don't worry, they won't find you. But you must be absolutely quiet. Don't make a sound, or we're all done for.'

Callendar nodded. His mouth dry, he pulled the cupboard back into position and pushed home the bolts. Then he crouched down and waited. As he did so, his eyes fell on the torn and soiled SS uniform he had been wearing. Something was missing. His cap! He had forgotten to mention it to Marthe. It was probably still where it had fallen, behind the beer barrels stacked in the yard.

The sound of loud voices reached his ears – official sounding voices, shouting orders and instructions – followed by the sound of boots running up the wooden stairs. Too late! There was nothing he could do. He could only offer up a silent prayer. Doors banged as noisy troopers began searching each room. The din grew louder as they approached the end of the passageway leading to the room where he was hiding. He closed his eyes and crossed his fingers.

Bang! The door of the outer room was suddenly thrown open and he heard the clumping of feet of a trooper. He held his breath, the remaining door was dragged open, then slammed shut again.

'Nothing here! This room's empty,' the trooper announced loudly. Callendar breathed a sigh of relief as he heard the heavy boots clump out of the room. Then another voice spoke, the sound of which made his blood run cold.

'Just one moment!'

Callendar froze. There was no mistaking that voice. It was Kramer.

'Bring the woman here.'

Callendar heard the trooper calling for Marthe to be brought upstairs. What could be wrong? Had Kramer spotted something? He heard footsteps on the stairs again. Lighter this time, a woman's tread.

'Yes. What is it? What is the problem?' he heard her ask.

'I am curious,' the Gestapo agent replied. 'You have eight or ten rooms here. Why is this the only one that is virtually empty? No furniture, no bed, only a broken wardrobe?'

The true purpose of keeping it empty had simply been to convince any searchers that nothing could be hidden there. But had Josef been too clever? Its very emptiness

326

seemed suspicious to Kramer. But Marthe proved equal to the crisis.

'It is empty because we used to use it as a storage room,' she explained. 'It contained mostly rubbish, not worth hanging on to. So it was cleared out last week.'

A period of silence followed, broken only by the sound of someone walking up and down the room. Probably Kramer, Callendar thought, wishing he could see what the Gestapo man was up to. Whatever it was, Marthe's answer seemed to satisfy him, because the next thing Callendar heard, was Kramer ordering everyone downstairs. The sound of heavy boots receded down the wooden staircase and he wondered if it was safe for him to move. Perhaps owing to the drenching he had received the evening before, he began to suffer cramp pains in both legs and needed to exercise the muscles. Yet some sixth sense told him to remain still, despite his discomfort. Five minutes elapsed and the pain in his legs had become almost unbearable. He began to slowly ease himself upwards. Suddenly he heard the faint sound of footsteps in the outer room.

Could it be Marthe? No. They were the same as he had heard earlier. Kramer was still in the room! Sweat formed on his brow as he tried to imagine what the Gestapo officer was up to. A sharp knocking on the cupboard almost made him jump out of his skin. Then came the sound of someone trying to move it. Heart in mouth, he prayed for a miracle. Then Fate took a hand. One of the troopers rushed upstairs and breathlessly announced that a man answering the description of the fugitive had been detained at one of the checkpoints leading out of town.

'Excellent!' replied Kramer, his high-pitched voice tinged with rare excitement. 'Get me there at once.' Callendar heard the sound of the two men pounding down the stairs. The roaring of an engine and screeching tyres confirmed Kramer's hasty departure.

It was a further ten minutes before Marthe's signal was again rapped out on the wardrobe. Her face was pale and drawn, but she managed a brave smile.

'It is all right. They have gone,' she assured him.

Callendar seized her by both arms.

'Marthe, my SS cap. It fell behind some of the barrels in the yard when I climbed over the wall, last night. I'd forgotten all about it. I hope to God they didn't find it!'

She smiled and waved her hand. 'Don't worry. My barman, Rudi, found it last night, when he went to get fresh barrels in. He burnt it straight away.'

Callendar hung his head in abject contrition. 'Marthe, I'm sorry. That was stupid and careless of me not to have remembered it. Look, this is crazy – I've put you in great danger by coming here. I'll stay here for the rest of the day and tonight I'll slip away. I should be able to find somewhere to hole up until the panic dies down. Then I'll get out of Rostock.'

'And if you do, where will you go? Switzerland?' She shook her head. 'No. You must stay here. Today, I will start making some enquiries among Josef's friends. I cannot promise anything. But I will somehow try to get word to London.'

Callendar again opened his mouth to protest, but Marthe ignored him.

'Meanwhile, perhaps you'd better get some clothes on,' she continued. 'You look rather foolish with that blanket wrapped around you. I will bring you breakfast shortly.'

The following day she confirmed she had managed to make contact with a member of the German resistance movement. She told Callendar a message could be sent, but it would have to be very brief owing to the increase in Nazi radio detection vehicles patrolling the area.

Elated by the news, he immediately set to work drafting a message. He knew if he could make it short enough, it could perhaps be transmitted several times, thereby increasing its chances of it being received in London. It was no easy task but, after several attempts, he settled for:

'Jackdaw successful. One fledgling needs help back to nest.'

Hoping that reporting the success of a mission sponsored by Churchill himself would bring a swift response, he handed the minute slip of paper to Marthe, who promised it would be actioned immediately. The message was sent the following day, Tuesday; however, it wasn't until Thursday that a reply was received. Marthe brought it to him late in the evening. It read:

'Jackdaw. Mother hen coming. Next same day, same route.'

'Mother hen?' Callendar frowned. He presumed it meant someone was coming to meet him. But who? It wouldn't be Surridge – he'd never risk it. Perhaps Ferguson? He dismissed it as relatively unimportant. What mattered was the sentence 'Next same day, same route'. 'Same route' could mean they were coming by neutral ship, possibly even the *Hilversund*. But 'Next same day'. Same day as what? The same day they had arrived in Rostock? A Saturday? That meant the next day would be a Sunday. Or did it mean the next Saturday? The day after tomorrow?

'It makes sense to you?' queried Marthe anxiously.

'I think so... Marthe, would it be possible to find out if the SS *Hilversund* is due in to Rostock the day after tomorrow?'

'The docks have been sealed off. No-one is allowed in or out, except for the regular dockers and they are double-checked each time they enter and leave.' She looked dubious. 'It will be very difficult, but I will try.'

The following evening, Marthe's knocking on the door sounded urgent and when Callendar slid back the bolts, he saw her face was filled with excitement.

'We are in luck!' she announced, her eyes shining. 'I had forgotten. Rudi, my barman. His son works on the docks and today he was told he will be working late tomorrow night, unloading timber from a Swedish ship, the *Hilversund*.'

'What?' cried Callendar, joyously throwing his arms around her. 'That's fantastic news! By this time tomorrow, I could be on my way home.'

Marthe withdrew his arms and looked at him soberly.

'But how will you get on board? You will not get past the guards on the gate and Rudi's son said that the docks are alive with both the military *and* the polizei. They patrol constantly, day and night. Besides that, each ship has a guard posted on deck and only selected workers are allowed on board.'

Callendar sat down, fists clenched, his expression desperate.

'It's my only chance, Marthe. Somehow I've got to get on board the *Hilversund* tomorrow night. I've got less than twenty-four hours.'

'I will see what I can do,' she replied softly.

28

The following day found Callendar pacing the small room with increasing impatience as he watched the hours slipping by, eager for Marthe to reappear with news that might aid his escape. In the end he had to wait until nearly six o'clock in the evening before he heard the now familiar knock on the wardrobe panelling. Marthe was holding a tray of food. She also had two men with her, their clothes wet from the rain pouring down outside.

'This is Rudi,' she explained quickly, indicating the older of the two men, a small man in his late fifties, with thinning grey hair and a weather-beaten face. 'And this is his son, Viktor.'

She indicated the younger man. Viktor was tall and lean, fit-looking and much the same age and build as himself which immediately made Callendar wonder why he hadn't been conscripted into the armed forces.

'Rudi and Viktor think they have an idea which may get you on board the *Hilversund*,' continued Marthe, 'but it will not be easy.' She set the tray down on the small chest and turned to leave. 'I will leave you to talk alone. It will be much better that way.'

The two men entered the small room and settled themselves on the bed, Viktor moving with a pronounced limp. The young German noticed Callendar's gaze and glanced down at his leg.

'English anti-personnel mine,' he explained. 'One of your British Tommies left it lying around in a field near Dunkirk two years ago. Took my leg off just below the knee.'

'I ... I'm sorry,' faltered Callendar, feeling he should somehow share the guilt for Viktor's disability.

'Forget it. At least I survived ... and it got me discharged from the Wehrmacht. Thank God! Not like the rest of my platoon. They were completely wiped out by your retreating artillery.' He stared at the floor. 'I lost a lot of good friends that day, but then...' He looked up. 'I expect you too have lost a lot of friends.'

Callendar nodded.

'It will not be easy to get you on board,' said Rudi. 'I expect Marthe has told you the whole town is swarming with troops, as well as Gestapo and polizei. You would be picked up the moment you set foot on the streets.'

Callendar, about to take a bite out of a thickly-cut sandwich, looked at them puzzled.

'Then how...?'

'We will become *Maulwurfen*,' Viktor replied grinning. 'Moles, burrowing underground. In the alley at the back of the tavern there is a manhole which gives access to a storm water drain. The drain runs under the streets and empties into the River Warnow, about five hundred metres away. From there you should be able to swim down river into the harbour where the *Hilversund* is moored.'

'How do you know about this drain and how can you be sure it runs to the river?'

'Before the war, I was employed by the *Wasserstrassennetzamt*, the inland rivers authority,' Viktor explained. 'It was part of my job to inspect all the storm drains in this area to make sure they didn't become blocked. Don't worry. I don't expect you to make the journey on your own. I shall come with you as far as the outfall. I know the layout of those drains like you know the streets of your home town.'

'And how far is it from the outfall, to the harbour?' asked Callendar, still munching his food.

'To the harbour? About eight hundred metres. To the

Hilversund? I'd guess another ... seven, maybe eight hundred metres. She's moored at the seaward end of the harbour.'

'God! That's... That's over a mile! I've never swum that far before.'

Viktor looked at his father. 'We thought that might be the case. So my father came up with a possible solution.'

'At first we thought of using a lifebuoy, the sort you'd find on board ship,' explained Rudi. 'Trouble is, they're always painted white, to show up in the dark – just what you don't want. And as there was no time to get hold of one to paint it black, we settled on an alternative – the inner tube from a lorry's tyre. It's black, lightweight and will easily support your weight. When you reach the ship, you can simply puncture it and let it sink to the bottom of the harbour.'

'Obviously we can't take it through the drain while it's inflated,' Viktor pointed out. 'Too big. So we'll have to carry a hand pump and inflate it when we get to the outfall.'

'Just how big is this drain?'

'One metre in diameter,' replied Viktor. 'Yes, we shall have to crawl all the way on our hands and knees.'

'And what about the rain?'

Viktor laughed. 'You will get wet anyway, when you swim to the ship. So why worry?'

'I was thinking more of the water level in the drain. Surely it's going to be pretty full now?'

He nodded at their wet clothes.

'Marthe said it was important you get on board tonight.' The young German shrugged nonchalantly. 'We will just have to take the risk.'

'But that's not fair on you. I can't possibly expect you to take...'

Viktor silenced Callendar's protest by rising to his feet and glancing at his watch.

'It's almost seven-thirty. With all the additional rainwater, it will take us about half an hour to get through the drain.

333

Then we must allow another half an hour for you to get downriver into the harbour.' He looked at Callendar with concern. 'The difficult part for you, will be making your way through the harbour to the *Hilversund* without being spotted. Don't forget, there will be lookouts on every ship, plus the dockside patrols. If you are seen, they will shoot first...' He left the sentence unfinished. 'I suggest you allow another half an hour to be on the safe side. That makes it an hour and a half in total, which means we must leave here by eight thirty.' He walked to the open doorway, followed by his father. 'Finish your meal and I'll get Marthe to bring you some hot coffee. It's going to be a cold night.'

'Just a moment,' Callendar called. 'Why is the time we leave so important?'

'Oh, yes! I forgot to tell you. The ship's mate is Erik Carrlson – you'll remember him. I managed to get myself on board this afternoon and we had a quick conversation. He is going to hang a rope over the side and will wait on deck for you for one hour, between nine-thirty and ten-thirty. It would be dangerous for him to stay any longer than that. So you must not be late. OK?'

Viktor and Rudi took their leave, promising to return within the hour.

Left alone with his thoughts, Callendar experienced mixed emotions: elation at the thought that he was at last going to escape, but also fear. He had never been a strong swimmer and the thought of the cold water brought back memories of the lake incident at the Jackdaw's Nest, when Nicholson had practically saved his life. It wasn't surprising he viewed his forthcoming immersion in the River Warnow with concern. But he had no choice; he had to take the risk.

After finishing his supper he rummaged through the chest for suitable clothing. The choice was limited – in the end he opted for a pair of thick woollen trousers, even though these could prove cumbersome in the water, a coarse shirt and a sweater. Woollen socks and a pair of stout, if oversize, shoes completed his ensemble. Then he pondered on the best method of carrying the *Hakenkreuz*. Its weight prevented its being thrust under his sweater; it would simply fall out and be lost forever in the river. At first, he experimented with tying the briefcase to his back, but realised this would pose problems when crawling through the storm drain. In the end, he took one of the coarse shirts and tore it into long strips, about an inch and a half wide. These he carefully plaited to form quite a strong and reliable rope which he used to tie the cross to his bare chest. He donned his shirt and sweater just in time to hear the signal being rapped out on the wardrobe panelling. He opened the door.

'Ready?' smiled Viktor.

The young German looked relaxed and confident, and his demeanour put Callendar much more at ease.

'Come on, let's go.'

They found both Marthe and Rudi waiting for them in the yard. Thankfully it had stopped raining and the moon was peeping out between scudding clouds, its pale light reflecting off the wet cobblestones of the yard. Callendar inhaled the fresh air. It smelt clean and pure, a welcome change after his confinement in the dingy room. The gate to the alleyway was already open and through it he could see the open manhole waiting to receive them. Marthe threw her arms around Callendar and gave him a big hug, as well as a kiss on both cheeks. There were tears in her eyes.

'God go with you,' she murmured. 'I will pray for you every night.' She touched the side of his face with her hand. 'You must go now, James. You cannot be late.'

Quickly, Callendar turned away and he and Rudi strode purposefully out of the yard into the alleyway where Viktor was waiting. The old man was holding a large coil of thin rope, about the thickness of a clothes line, as well as a deflated inner tube and an object which Callendar assumed was the pump.

Viktor knelt by the side of the opening, torch in hand. He pointed the beam down into the open manhole for Callendar to have a look. Peering into the shaft, he heard the sound of flowing water before he saw it, swirling along some ten feet below. It didn't appear too deep, only coming a third of the way up the side of the drain – he guessed about a foot. Nor did it seem to be flowing particularly fast, despite the heavy rain.

'Doesn't look too bad,' breathed Callendar.

'Don't be fooled by that,' said Viktor. 'This is only a primary drain. There are lots like this and they all link up to empty into the main drain that eventually leads to the river outfall. When we hit that, it'll be a very different story. That's what the rope is for. When we arrive at the main drain I'll tie it to one of the metal footholds inside the drain, then I'll go first with the rope tied around my waist. When I reach the outfall I'll give three strong tugs to signal I'm OK, then you follow behind, holding on to it with one hand. OK?'

Callendar nodded.

'The rope will also help me make my way back. I'm afraid you'll have to carry the inner tube and pump,' Viktor went on. 'I'll need both hands to feel the way as the torch won't be much use to us once we hit the main drain. So I suggest you wear the inner tube like a coat – slip it over your shoulders. That way it'll leave your hands free. As for the pump, probably be best to stick it inside your shirt.' Callendar slipped his arms through the big inner tube, so that it came behind his neck, then over his shoulders and round behind his rear end. He forced the pump, which was quite slim, under two of the plaited shirt ropes which held the *Hakenkreuz* securely to his body.

'Ready,' he announced.

'One more thing before we go,' said Viktor, handing him a small flat tin. 'Black boot polish – for your face. It'll help prevent you being spotted.'

Callendar gave his face a liberal coating of the greasy substance, receiving a nod of approval from Viktor.

'Let's go.'

After a solemn handshake with Rudi and a final wave to Marthe who was standing in the gateway to the yard, Callendar eased himself into the open hole and began climbing down the iron ladder into the murky depths. As he descended, the smell of the drain entered his nostrils and he shivered as his hands came into contact with the slimy surface of the walls. He gasped as he reached the final rung and lowered his feet into the water. He had expected it would be cold, but nothing like this! He gasped again as he dropped down on all fours and began following Viktor along the dark tunnel.

At first his mind was totally taken up by the effects of the chilling water sweeping along the underside of his body. Then his old problem manifested itself once more. It had been bad enough in the submarine but now, in the close confines of a tunnel barely three feet high, the feeling of claustrophobia became almost unbearable. Closing his eyes, he gritted his teeth and tried to concentrate his mind on anything but his present situation. He paddled on relentlessly, following Viktor's shape silhouetted by the light of the torch some five yards in front.

Progress was painfully slow, the sound of rushing water making it impossible to speak to Viktor, and thus hold a conversation which might act as a distraction against his claustrophobia. At times it became so bad, he wanted to scream. He tried to think of Daphne, of home, of his family. But his brain played tricks on him. These memories had somehow become distant and, in place of Daphne, visions of Anna filled his mind – beautiful Anna whom he would

337

never see again. He closed his eyes and tried to shut out the painful images.

Preoccupied with his thoughts he hadn't noticed Viktor had stopped and he suddenly collided with his rear. Viktor turned towards him, still pointing the torch ahead. By its light he saw their drain was about to join another one, some five yards ahead of them. He could also see the water was deeper, almost to the top of the drain itself, and flowing much, much faster.

'The main drain,' shouted Viktor, above the noise of the torrent. 'This is going to be more difficult than I thought.'

'Can't we wait until the level drops?' Callendar shouted back.

'Could be several hours before that happens and you'd be too late arriving at the ship.'

'What can we do?'

'Well, we're about a hundred metres from the outfall and, from the look of it, the water is going to be above our heads for the rest of the way. So there's only one thing we can do.'

'What's that?'

'Forget the torch, take a deep breath, dive in and let the flow of water take us the rest of the way.'

Callendar looked at him horrified. 'You're not serious?'

Viktor shrugged. 'No other way. Look, the water in the main drain is flowing pretty fast. I'd guess about twenty kilometres an hour. But let's say it's only fifteen kilometres an hour. At that speed it should take less than half a minute to reach the outfall. You can hold your breath for that long, can't you?'

'I suppose I could,' responded Callendar cautiously. 'But what if it turns out to be more than a hundred metres?'

'Then you hold your breath that bit longer,' grinned Viktor, handing him the torch.

Close to where they had stopped metal rungs had been

set into the wall leading up to another inspection cover, similar to the one by which they had first entered the drain. Viktor uncoiled the rope and tied one end to one of the steel rungs.

'When my father and I made up this rope, we made sure it would be long enough. We know its length is exactly one hundred and twenty metres – twenty metres longer than we need. When I reach the outfall, I'll give three tugs on the rope to let you know I've made it. Then you follow. OK?'

His claustrophobia helped Callendar come to terms with the situation. Anything was better than being stuck there doing nothing.

'Well, here goes!' said Viktor.

He moved further along the pipe, until he reached the brink of the faster flowing water, Callendar following close behind with the torch. Viktor barely hesitated. He plunged feet first into fast flowing water and vanished in an instant.

Callendar watched the length of rope rapidly disappearing as it was dragged into the main drain and counted off the seconds.

Whether he was counting faster than he should, it was difficult to tell, but he reached an alarming forty-three seconds before the rope suddenly went taut. He desperately grabbed hold of it with both hands, carelessly dropping the torch, which fell into the water and immediately went out, plunging him into Stygian darkness. An image arose in his mind of Viktor on the other end of the rope, struggling to get free and slowly drowning... He began to panic.

Then came the signal. Three unmistakeable tugs. He almost cried with joy, his fears forgotten, as he prepared to launch himself into the maelstrom. Taking a number of deep breaths and then exhaling, he drew in one last great breath and, following Viktor's example, rolled feet first into the plunging water. He was instantly swept along, bounced from side to

339

side by the racing water, occasionally bumping his head as it collided with the concrete sides of the drain.

The bitter cold temporarily forgotten, his mind was completely dominated by the passage of time as he counted the seconds one by one. It seemed the journey would never end. Then, suddenly, he found himself flying through the air, as if shot from a cannon, as he exited the outfall to plunge into the waters of the River Warnow.

Lungs bursting, he struggled to the surface, and gratefully gulped in the life-giving air. Despite the recent rain, the river flowed quite slowly and Callendar was easily able to swim the dozen or so yards to the bank, where he saw Viktor sitting on the concrete foundation supporting the outfall pipe. The German reached out his hand.

'You OK?' he asked, as the Englishman sat panting at his side.

Callendar nodded.

'You mustn't hang about too long. There's a path just above us and you can bet your life it's being patrolled.'

The fitful moonlight enabled Callendar to take in his surroundings. The river looked about thirty feet wide at this point, with mud banks on either side. Above the opposite bank, he could make out the dark shapes of buildings etched against the skyline which, he concluded, were probably warehouses and factories, although they were all now in total darkness to comply with blackout regulations. A glance behind him revealed a row of similar structures, although these were set back from the riverbank, the path that Viktor had mentioned running between them and the river.

'What are you going to do?' he managed to shout, still breathless from his prolonged immersion. 'It's impossible to crawl back through there.'

'Don't worry, about me. It'll slow down now it's stopped raining. Give it half an hour and I'll be able to return. You'd better get the inner tube inflated and be on your way. It's

340

dangerous to hang about here. As I said, there may be a foot patrol on the path above us.'

Callendar peeled the inner tube off his shoulders, retrieved the pump from inside his sweater and set to work pumping air into the rubber ring. Within a few minutes he judged it sufficiently inflated to buoy him up and, after profusely thanking his German guide, he slipped back into the cold waters of the River Warnow.

He allowed himself to drift out into the middle, where the current was strongest and began to gently paddle his way downstream towards the harbour.

As he turned to give a final wave to Viktor standing upright on the concrete block Callendar saw the patrolling sentry – a dark shape, with the unmistakeable outline of a coalscuttle helmet on his head and the silhouette of a rifle and bayonet slung over his shoulder. He was walking slowly down the path towards Viktor's position. It was obvious from his leisurely gait, that he couldn't yet see Viktor, but as he grew closer it would be impossible to miss him. It was equally obvious that Viktor was completely unaware of the man's approach, any sound he was making being drowned by the noise of the water pouring from the drain.

Callendar looked back helplessly, praying Viktor would sit down again, out of sight of the sentry. But he didn't; he continued waving farewell. Callendar turned and swam, hoping this would encourage Viktor to conceal himself. Not daring to look back, he carried on swimming, the sound of water gushing from the drain gradually diminishing, as he moved farther away from the outfall. It grew quieter, only the murmur of the slow-moving river and the distant sound of traffic breaking the tranquillity.

Suddenly he was aware of rifle shots coming from behind him and he knew it could only mean Viktor had been spotted. For a few insane moments he considered turning back to see if he could help his friend, but the river's current and his own helpless position meant any such attempt would be wholly futile. Praying Viktor would manage to evade the sentry and get safely away, he concentrated on swimming as fast as he dared towards the distant harbour.

29

Drifting downstream, Callendar found he was becoming more and more affected by the cold. He had already lost the feeling in both feet and the numbness was slowly migrating upwards. He began moving his legs rapidly up and down, as if he were performing the crawl, in an endeavour to improve the blood circulation to his legs and feet. But this made far too much noise, as well as creating waves that caught the reflection of the moonlight and risked betraying his presence.

To make matters worse he saw he was approaching a bridge. One of the main road bridges in the town, it carried a heavy volume of traffic and was an obvious point for a roadblock. As he drew closer, he could see torch beams wavering in the darkness where armed police, or maybe soldiers, were stopping traffic to carry out identity checks. He could also see one of the soldiers leaning over the parapet of the bridge, idly flashing his torch on the flowing waters below. He would surely spot Callendar as he floated past.

At this point, the mud banks alongside the river had been replaced by stone walls against which a number of small craft were moored. He gently manoeuvred himself to the right-hand side and took refuge between two rowing boats.

As he remained there absolutely motionless, the cold became more and more intense. His teeth were chattering uncontrollably and the numbness in his legs had now reached his thighs. He realised that if he didn't get out of the water soon he would die from hypothermia and he prayed for the soldier to tire of his game and rejoin his colleagues. But he seemed happily occupied and showed no sign of giving up.

Callendar realised he couldn't stay still much longer and, in desperation, decided to take a chance. Waiting for the moment when the soldier had his torch pointed towards the boats moored on the other side of the river, Callendar eased himself away from between the two rowing boats and continued his journey, keeping close to the craft in case he needed to gain sanctuary quickly.

He had travelled only a few yards when he bumped into something else floating in the river, something soft. For a moment he mistook it for a bundle of rags but, turning the bundle over, he saw Viktor's sightless eyes staring at him, a bullet wound in his head.

At that moment there was a commotion on the bridge – the sound of a vehicle braking sharply and a number of raised voices. Quickly he swam back to the relative safety of the moored craft, pulling Viktor's body with him. He had just made it when a powerful beam of light struck the water and began methodically sweeping the surface. The vehicle that had just arrived carried a searchlight and it was this that was now waving its finger of light over the river. He heard the sound of booted feet running along the wall above him and voices shouting. It became apparent from what he could make out, that the 'secret agent' the whole of Germany was looking for had been shot further upstream and his body had fallen in the river.

More and more soldiers began moving along the riverbank, shining torches down on the dark waters, looking for anything that might resemble a body. Peering around one of the moored vessels, Callendar spotted a small rowing boat, caught in the beam of the searchlight, moving slowly upriver in his direction. He could see the silhouettes of two armed soldiers on board, one busily shining a torch between the moored craft as they passed. Callendar realised he would be spotted and knew he had to do something fast. He looked at Viktor's dead face.

'You helped me once, old friend. Now I've got to ask you to do it again.'

He thrust the body away from him, pushing it out into the sluggish current.

His actions were just in time. The soldiers on the bank had drawn level with his position and were in the process of searching around the boats near him, when one of them let out an excited shout.

'There! What's that?' yelled the soldier, directing his torch beam into the centre of the river. His companions added their torches to his and the searchlight on the bridge swung round to join them. The dark shape of Viktor's body became bathed in light and the two soldiers in the small boat rowed frantically towards it.

'*Ja!*' one of them yelled, as they drew level. 'It's a body all right.' He turned Viktor's corpse over in the water. 'And it's been shot. It's him all right.'

Then came a voice of authority, possibly an officer, ordering the men in the boat to take the body along to a landing stage by the bridge. One of those in the boat pulled away on the oars, whilst the other hung on grimly to Viktor's body, unable to drag it into the boat for fear of capsizing the vessel. At the same time the shore party also began to move off towards the bridge.

Callendar swam quietly away from the riverbank to observe developments on the bridge. Things happened quickly. As soon as the body was lifted from the water at the landing stage, it was carried up a flight of stone steps onto the road and unceremoniously dumped in the back of a police van. Sirens wailing the van set off, escorted by motorcyclists. A few minutes later, the vehicle with the searchlight also departed, followed by the rest of the soldiers in an open-backed truck. Callendar could hardly believe his luck. Traffic on the bridge immediately began to move freely, unhindered by the presence of military or police personnel. The way was clear for him to resume his journey.

Realising he had lost a considerable amount of time, he swam as quickly as he dared, keeping always in the shadow of moored vessels. Twenty minutes later, he entered Rostock harbour.

Erik Carrlson stubbed out his umpteenth cigarette and glanced impatiently at his watch. Eleven-fifteen. He had been on deck for almost an hour and a half, awaiting the arrival of the Englishman. He dared not risk moving far from the deck bollard around which was secured the knotted rope hanging over the port side of the *Hilversund*, the side away from the quay. At first his presence hadn't drawn any attention, but now the German sentry, posted by the gangplank, had started casting curious glances in his direction. He had no reason to be on deck, the watch on the bridge being all that was required when in port – the sentry was becoming suspicious.

He glanced up at the night sky. The earlier rain had gone and the clouds were now beginning to break up, allowing the moon to shine through intermittently. Carrlson muttered under his breath and clenched his fists in frustration. The moonlight was a curse and would only serve to increase the chances of the Englishman being seen as he climbed aboard. He also couldn't help wondering if the commotion he had heard some twenty minutes earlier had anything to do with his expected visitor. Had he been caught? If so there was little point in staying on deck. He glanced across at the German sentry still staring in his direction and looking as though he might at any moment cross the deck towards him. Knowing he couldn't allow this to happen, Carrlson himself sauntered over to the sentry, at the same time drawing out his packet of cigarettes.

'Cigarette?' he smiled, offering the open packet to the German.

The man glanced nervously down onto the quayside.

'It is forbidden. I mustn't,' he replied, gazing longingly at the packet.

'Go on,' encouraged the Swede. 'No-one's going to see you. It's too dark.'

The man looked tempted, but shook his head.

'Better not. My officer is due on his rounds soon. He's a stickler for discipline, especially since the special alert started. Still, that should die down soon, now they've caught him.' He gave another yearning look at the packet. 'Perhaps later, after he's done his rounds?'

'Sure thing.' Carrlson frowned. 'You said they'd caught him. Caught who?'

'Some spy,' the guard said off-handedly. 'Fished him out of the river about half an hour ago. Dead, of course – shot by a Waffen SS sentry. Always trigger-happy the SS. He looked quizzically at the Swede. 'Something's been puzzling me about you.'

'What's that?' replied Carrlson.

'I've been wondering why aren't you down below with the rest of the crew, keeping warm, instead of spending your time up here on deck?'

Carrlson was ready for the question and already had an answer prepared. Stubbing out his cigarette, he tossed it over the side and heaved a big sigh.

'Ah, it's just that I've got a few problems,' he explained. 'It's the wife. Keeps nagging me about the time I spend away at sea. You know what women are, they want you home all the time.'

The sentry gave a sympathetic snort.

'Don't I know it! I get two or three letters a week, asking when my next leave's going to be. Women? They just don't understand. She thinks I can jump on a train and travel home

347

to Dusseldorf any time I please. Stupid woman!' He gave Carrlson an envious look. 'Still, it's all right for you merchant sailors. You get home a lot more often than us soldiers. But then, your country's neutral. You don't have a madman in charge, who wants war with the rest of the world.'

As soon as he had said it, Carrlson could see the man regretted it. Fear appeared on the German's face. He glanced furtively around and laid a hand on Carrlson's arm.

'You didn't hear me say that. Did you?' he entreated.

'Say what?'

'Thanks,' breathed the sentry. 'We Germans, we've got to be so careful these days. One wrong word and...' He drew a finger meaningfully across his throat and gave a nervous look over the side onto the quay. 'You'd better go. Wouldn't do either of us any good to be seen talking together.'

Carrlson smiled.

'Sure, OK. I think I'll just take stroll on deck before turning in. If your officer's been round by that time, I'll let you have that cigarette.'

Nodding to the sentry he made his way unhurriedly across the deck to the port side, his brain working rapidly. What if the Englishman were dead? What if it had been his body pulled from the river – it would certainly explain his failure to appear. He removed his cap and ran his fingers through thick curly hair. Was he wasting his time and drawing unnecessary attention to himself? He walked along the deck and peered over the side, looking for any tell-tale movement in the water. But there was none. He reached the bollard with the knotted rope secured and again peered over. Nothing. Nothing save the moonlight dancing on the ripples. He reluctantly turned away and walked towards one of the companionways to join his shipmates in the warmth below decks.

* * *

Callendar had never imagined it was possible to feel so cold. He had been in the water for almost three hours and his body temperature had dropped dangerously low. He couldn't feel his legs as he forced them to drive him through the water. His hands too, particularly his fingers, shared the same lack of feeling and he wondered how he was going to climb up the rope when he reached the *Hilversund*. His body was also tired and he was finding difficulty in thinking rationally. He knew that if he didn't find the ship soon, they would be fishing another body out of the water in the morning.

He moved through the bitterly cold water, his progress becoming slower and slower. Always keeping in the shadow of the moored ships to avoid detection, he worked his way along the row of rusty hulls, eyes sore from the polluted water, searching the stern of each ship, desperately hoping the next one would be the *Hilversund*.

Suddenly his heart leapt. There she was! He could just make out the faint lettering on the stern: *Hilversund – Göteborg*.

The steel sides towered frighteningly above his head; then he found the promised rope dangling down to the water. Offering up a silent prayer, he painfully wriggled his way out of the inner tube and slashed the rubber with the small penknife given to him for the purpose by old Rudi. Holding on to the rope with one hand, he forced the air from the inner tube with his free arm, before releasing it to sink below the surface of the murky waters. Then, taking a firm grip of the rope with both hands, he began the painful task of heaving his exhausted body up the sheer side of the hull. He had progressed only a few feet before he was compelled to stop. Despite the knots in the rope, his numbed fingers could not grasp the hemp line and he was soon became in danger of falling back into the water. Supporting his weight by standing on one of the large knots and wrapping his arms around the rope, he looked up towards the deck. He could see it, some fifteen feet above his head. It was fifteen feet that might as well have been a hundred.

Carrlson had almost reached the bottom of the companionway, when he realised he had forgotten to remove the rope hanging over the side.

'Blast!' he muttered. Knowing he couldn't leave it hanging over the side to attract attention, he turned on his heel and quickly climbed back up the steep stairway onto the deck. Striding across to the rail, he had a quick look around to make sure the sentry wasn't in sight, then dropped to his knees to untie the rope from around the bollard. But something was wrong; the rope was too taut. He peered over the rail to see Callendar's pale face peering back at him. For a moment they stared at each other. Carrlson was the first to recover.

'Quick!' he called out softly. 'Get up here as fast as you can. I'll go and keep the sentry occupied.'

'I c...c...can't,' gasped Callendar, his teeth chattering. 'I c...can't m...m...move. T...t...too cold. No strength left.'

The Swede thought quickly.

'Can you hang on for a few more minutes?' Callendar nodded painfully.

Swiftly Carrlson ran back to the door of the companionway. Using both handrails, he leapt down the stairway in one bound. A few strides took him to the crew's mess. Throwing open the door, he quickly looked round the room. A giant of a man was among those at the table playing cards.

'Sven! No questions. Just follow me up on deck, now. The rest of you stay put.'

Without a word, the big crewman tossed his cards on the table and was on his feet in an instant. With a nimbleness that defied his bulk he was out of the cabin in seconds and

350

hard on the heels of Carrlson as he climbed the staircase three at a time. When they reached the top, Carrlson motioned Sven to stay where he was, then leaned out of the doorway to peer along the deck. Satisfied it was all clear, he moved and looked round the corner of the superstructure to where the sentry stood at the top of the gangplank. He could see the soldier talking to an officer who had arrived on deck. Probably making a report, Carrlson thought.

Returning to the companionway door, he beckoned Sven to follow him and moved towards the rail. He was relieved to see Callendar still clinging to the rope.

Carrlson glanced at Sven. 'Think we can pull him up?'

'No problem,' grunted the big man, immediately dropping to his knees and taking hold of the rope in his huge hands.

Throwing their combined strength into the task, they were soon rewarded with the sight of Callendar's head appearing level with the deck. But as they were about to reach down and heave the Englishman up onto the deck, a voice called out and the German sentry came round the corner of the superstructure. Thankfully, the moon had disappeared behind a thick bank of cloud, making it difficult to see clearly. Nevertheless, he peered curiously at the two men.

'What are you doing?' he demanded.

Leaving Sven to support the whole of Callendar's weight on his own, Carrlson released his hold on the rope and turned round. Keeping himself between Sven and the German, he walked quickly towards the sentry, at the same time withdrawing a packet of cigarettes from his pocket.

'Ready for that smoke now?' he asked cheerfully, holding out the open packet and carefully blocking the sentry's view of Sven. The sentry glanced down at the cigarettes, then looked up again, nodding towards the big Swede.

'What's he doing?'

'Doing?' echoed Carrlson, giving a brief glance over his shoulder.

In the darkness, it looked as though Sven was simply leaning over the rail staring at the water. Any sign of Callendar's head was obscured by the deck bollard. He turned back to the German. 'He's... He's... well, to tell the truth, he's a bit upset. Ship's cat died today. Silly really, big man like that. You wouldn't think it would affect him.'

The sentry nodded sagely. '*Ja, ja.* I know what you mean.' He helped himself to one of Carrlson's cigarettes.

'Strange how some people like animals the way they do. I'd better smoke this round the other side, so I can keep a watch on the gangway. My officer's done his rounds, but he's young – a keen swine. Likely to come back at any time.'

'Sure thing,' agreed Carrlson, flicking the wheel of his petrol lighter to light the German's cigarette.

'You not joining me?' the sentry asked, as he turned to walk back towards the gangway.

Carrlson glanced back at Sven, wondering how long the big man could support Callendar's weight on his own. The German saw him.

'*Ach!* Don't worry about him,' he said. 'Best left on his own. He'll get over it. Come and join me in a smoke.'

'I expect you're right,' rejoined Carrlson, reluctantly following the soldier over to the starboard side of the vessel.

He smoked his own cigarette quickly, puffing away nervously, half expecting at any moment to hear the sound of a loud splash, announcing Callendar's unwelcome re-entry into the harbour. But he heard nothing, save the sentry's continual moaning about how hard it was in the army. Eventually, he could stand the suspense no longer. Crushing out his half-smoked cigarette, he mumbled an apology, saying it was time he turned in, and made his way around to the port side. When he rounded the corner of the superstructure, there was no sign of the big Swede and a quick glance over the side revealed Callendar had also disappeared, together

352

with the rope. He hurried below decks and made straight for the crew's mess where he threw open the door. Sven stood with other members of the crew, massaging his arms. He looked up as Carrlson dashed in.

'It's OK. I got him on board, but he's in a bad way. I've put him in your cabin. Jan is with him.'

Carrlson nodded his thanks, then quickly made his way along the corridor to his own cabin, thankful that the ship's medical orderly was already with him. He found Callendar wrapped in thick blankets, occupying his bunk, a pile of wet clothing on the floor. Jan was leaning over his shivering body, holding a glass of brandy to his lips.

'Is he conscious?' Carrlson demanded anxiously.

'Just about,' replied Jan. 'But he's not good. Suffering from hypothermia. I've got hot-water bottles inside the blankets, trying to get some warmth back into his body, but I can't get a bottle onto his chest. He's got something tied to it, which he won't let me move.'

'Let me see,' said Carrlson, sliding a hand under the blankets onto Callendar's chest. 'Christ! What is it?' he muttered, as his probing fingers located the bundle.

He picked a pair of scissors from Jan's medical chest and, pulling back the blankets, snipped away at the wet plaited rope. Callendar protested weakly and feebly tried to stop the Swede as he removed the bundle and began peeling away the saturated cloth covering the *Hakenkreuz*. The gold swastika glinted dully as it was exposed to the ship's dim lighting.

'What the...!' exclaimed Carrlson, as he and Jan stared at the ancient artefact. 'No wonder you nearly drowned, carrying this great lump strapped to your body. What the hell is it? Is it gold?'

'Please ... give it to me,' whimpered Callendar, reaching out feebly. 'They ... must not ... get it. Too ... many ... died...'

'OK! OK! Don't worry,' Carrlson assured him. 'You're

safe now. They won't get you, or this. Look. I'll put it under your pillow.' He lifted the pillow and slipped it underneath. 'There, it's safe now. I promise you, none of the crew will try to take it from you. Now you must get some rest.'

He turned to Jan.

'Where are we going to put him? In the locker?'

'Can't do that. Already occupied, remember?'

'Damn! Of course it is.'

'Anyway,' the medical orderly continued, 'he needs to be kept warm. He'll have to stay here. I've got some hot soup coming along from the galley soon. That should help.'

'OK. You'll stay with him?'

'Of course. I'll keep working on him. Don't worry, Erik. If I leave, I'll lock the cabin and bring you the key.'

'Thanks.' Carrlson turned towards the cabin door. 'I'd better check on that sentry – and our other passenger. I'll see you later.'

Jan returned his attentions to his patient, whose eyes were now closed. He placed a hand on Callendar's forehead, feeling for any sign of improving body temperature.

'Well, my friend,' he said. 'What are you going to do? Are you going to live ... or are you going to die?'

30

Callendar opened his eyes slowly, awakened perhaps by the sound of the *Hilversund*'s engines throbbing deep in the heart of the vessel as the Swedish ship ploughed its way north-westward across the Baltic Sea. For some time he lay there staring at the ceiling, unable to remember where he was. He closed his eyes again, enjoying the warmth and comfort of thick woollen blankets and hot-water bottles, the latter having been continually replaced by the ship's medical orderly during the night. Gradually memories seeped back: the bitter cold of the River Warnow, the sight of Viktor's dead face, the struggle to climb the rope hanging from the *Hilversund*.

Then he remembered the *Hakenkreuz*. Turning onto his side he quickly thrust his hand under the pillows and was rewarded by the reassuring feel of cold metal. He withdrew the gold swastika from its hiding place, held it up and stared at it. It was the first time he had had an opportunity to examine it closely. Yes, it was beautifully carved, and made of solid gold – the weight confirmed that. But had it all been worth it? All the lives that had been sacrificed...

Would what they had done make a difference? Denying Hitler its possession? It was hard to believe it could, but then it always had been.

His thoughts were interrupted by a knock on the door and he quickly thrust the gold swastika out of sight back under the pillow. The ship's cook entered with a tray bearing a plate of bacon and eggs and a steaming mug of coffee.

'The mate thinks you will be hungry,' he announced, setting the tray down on the bunk.

'Thanks very much,' Callendar responded, suddenly realising how hungry he was. He had eaten little during the past few days.

'Where are we?' he asked, as the cook was about to disappear through the door.

'We leave Rostock two hours ago. When you have finished eating, you can come up on deck. One of your countrymen, a major, is waiting to see you there. It is quite safe now.'

He closed the door behind him and Callendar, eager to find out who had come to meet him, wasted no time in tucking into the cooked breakfast.

It was a crisp, cold morning when Callendar emerged on the deserted afterdeck. He looked up at the clear blue sky, screwing up his eyes against the bright sunlight. Screaming seagulls circled the ship. A stiff northwesterly was blowing, bringing white caps to the tops of the waves as they rolled past the ship's hull. He inhaled the keen air relishing the sense of freedom.

Reaching inside his reefer jacket he withdrew the *Hakenkreuz*.

'So you managed it after all. Well done!'

The voice had come from behind. He recognised it immediately. Heart leaping with excitement, he whirled round.

'Major Ferguson! Thank God! I guessed it would be you. I can't tell you how marvellous it is to see an English face.'

Ferguson was standing a few feet away, wearing a reefer jacket, thick corduroy trousers and with a woollen hat on his head. His hands were thrust in his pockets, hiding them from the chill wind. He gave a welcoming smile, withdrew one hand and held it out expectantly.

'Well? Are you going to let me see it? Or are you intending to keep it as a personal memento?'

Callendar smiled and stepped forward. 'Sorry, sir. Yes, of course . . .'

'Stand perfectly still! Both of you.'

The words were barked with authority by another voice he recognised. Whirling round, Callendar saw the familiar figure of Keppler emerging from behind one of the ship's ventilators. He too was similarly dressed much the same as them, only he had a pistol in his hand and it was pointed in their direction.

'Keppler!' breathed Callendar, taking a step back towards the rail.

'I said "stand still"!' snarled Keppler, moving the pistol to cover both of them. 'That includes you, Major.'

Ferguson had begun to withdraw his other hand from the pocket of his reefer jacket. Callendar watched in fascination as the scene developed in front of him, like watching a film being run in slow motion. He now saw Ferguson also had a pistol and, as it cleared his pocket, he began to raise it to point it at Keppler. But Keppler's Walther suddenly spat flame and Ferguson's body jerked. The bullet had struck him in the chest. Keppler fired a second time, this time hitting Ferguson in the forehead; his body fell backwards onto the deck. It twitched a few times, then lay still.

Keppler now pointed the Walther in his direction. He had his other hand extended towards Callendar.

'Let me have the swastika,' he ordered.

Callendar shook his head.

'No! You'll not have it,' he yelled defiantly. Swiftly, he turned towards the rail and with one tremendous sweep of his arm, sent the *Hakenkreuz* spinning up into the azure sky. The sunlight glinted on the golden cross, as it described a lazy arc before plunging with a barely audible plop into the Baltic and disappeared forever beneath the waves. He heard Keppler scream and tensed himself for the expected bullet in the back. But it never came.

He turned round to see Keppler calmly slipping the pistol back into his pocket.

'That was a bloody daft thing to do,' he snorted.

'What?' replied Callendar. 'What d'you mean?'

Keppler walked over to join him and peered into the sea, as if hoping to see the *Hakenkreuz* somewhere below the surface. Callendar backed away, puzzled, and wary of the other man's presence.

'What a pity! You went through enough trouble stealing the damn thing and it would've been something to show for all the effort.'

'Just who are you?' demanded Callendar, glancing quickly at Ferguson's pistol lying on the deck a few yards away and wondering if he could make a dive for it. 'And why did you shoot Major Ferguson?'

Keppler saw the glance towards the pistol, but made no effort to retrieve it.

'Because he was about to shoot you, laddie,' he replied quietly.

'Nonsense!' retorted the younger man. 'He came here to help me safely back to England.'

'He came here to meet you all right – after he had received instructions from his bosses in Berlin. They were to recover the Führer's swastika at any cost.'

'What on earth are you talking about?' demanded Callendar.

'Ferguson was a spy, an enemy agent. So was "Walters", only that wasn't his real name...'

'No. It was Anton Stotz,' interrupted Callendar.

'If you say so. The real Walters was murdered by this man Stotz, as you call him, on Ferguson's instructions, simply to take his place as an instructor at the Jackdaw's Nest. You see, Ferguson had been working at Military Intelligence for some considerable time, passing any useful information that came across his desk back to Germany. When he heard about a hush-hush operation being set up by Surridge, he tried to get more information and by doing so drew attention to himself. We knew information was getting out from Ferguson's department, but we couldn't prove anything. And because of the intense security Surridge had managed to draw over his operation, Ferguson came up against a brick wall. Realising something "big" was on, and desperate to find out more, he managed to persuade the dear old Commodore to take him on his staff. Of course this set warning bells ringing and I was also selected for operation, with orders to watch Ferguson.'

He paused.

'Incidentally, Churchill was under the impression the object of the mission was to assassinate Hitler. He knew nothing about stealing any swastika! As your training progressed, Ferguson got more and more desperate for information. But the Commodore continued to play his cards close to his chest, because he was scared the real purpose of the mission might get out, which was the last thing he wanted to happen. Ferguson gleaned nothing and by the time the final selection was made he knew he had to do something desperate. That's when he got Walters to apply acid to the tree-bridge ropes.' Keppler shook his head. 'It was my fault, hounding young Nicholson so much about that damned bridge. It gave them the ideal opportunity to put him out of action and replace him with Walters. Whether or not they actually meant to kill him, I don't know – but then I don't suppose they were bothered.

'As you found out, Walters was genuine SS. To avoid exposing the fact that he already had a number tattooed under his arm he had to kill the Italian barber, Capaldi, to keep him quiet. After the dinner party, when they knew the true purpose of your mission, their course of action became simple. As soon as you'd arrived in Germany and made contact with our agent, Walters would expose the lot of you, then make his escape and come back to England, report the mission was a failure and carry on his espionage activities with Ferguson.

359

'By the time the real Walters' body was found it was too late to do anything and, until your message came through a week ago, we thought you had all been betrayed and shot.'

He turned round with his back to the sea and rested his elbows on the rail.

'When we did get your message, it all began to happen. Ferguson quickly disappeared, killing the sentry on the compound gate in the process, and somehow got back to Germany. Meanwhile, the Commodore broke down completely and told Whitehall all about Hitler's swastika. Poor old sod was immediately relieved of duty and put in a padded cell somewhere – quite crazy apparently. Seems he wanted the swastika for himself – believed it would bring him unquestionable power.'

He looked at Callendar.

'Anyway, I volunteered to come along and meet you. Flew out to Stockholm, then by car to our friends here on the *Hilversund*. When Ferguson appeared on board just before we left this morning, I nearly had a fit and decided to lie low until he made his move. The rest you know.'

For several long moments, Callendar stared at Keppler with incredulity. He struggled to speak, but could not find the words.

'Do you realise what you've done?' he burst out at last. 'You bloody fools! You stupid bloody fools! This is just a game to you, isn't it? A stupid game. My friends are all dead just because a crazy old man was allowed to play games with people's lives.'

He gripped the rail.

'Nicholson, Thompson, Sinclair, Josef, Anna. . .' He repeated her name softly. 'All of them dead, and for what? Nothing, absolutely nothing! What a bloody awful waste!'

'I'm sorry, lad,' said Keppler, laying a comforting hand on Callendar's shaking shoulder. 'I know you won't think it now, but maybe it wasn't such a total waste. Between you,

you successfully penetrated the most efficient security system in the world and, from the reports we're getting back, you certainly stirred up a hornet's nest amongst the Nazi hierarchy in Berlin. I know it's cost the lives of your friends and I can guess how you're feeling... I too have lost friends. That's the worst thing about any war – the waste of human life. But, you know, freedom is the most precious thing we possess and whenever that freedom is threatened by madmen like Hitler, there will always be people – quite ordinary people like your friends – who will be prepared to fight to preserve it and to sacrifice their lives in doing so.'

He gazed out over the blue-green sea.

'The price of freedom is never cheap.'

EPILOGUE

It was on the morning of Sunday 11th October, 1942 when Lieutenant James Callendar consigned Hitler's *Hakenkreuz* to its final resting place in the depths of the Baltic Sea.

Its loss, together with the audacious nature of the theft, had an overwhelming effect on the Nazi leader. Flying into one of his uncontrollable rages, he immediately ordered the arrest of the remaining four SS officers who made up the Chancellery Guard. Lintz, Kleist, Möeller and Strohm were executed by firing squad in the grounds of the Chancellery, their fate echoing that of Alexander's personal guard some two thousand years earlier.

Despite this and other vengeful acts, the Nazi leader could not be mollified and the theft was something to which he could never be reconciled. It has been suggested that it was also at around this time that his reasoning and judgement, up to then the source of his unprecedented military success, began to fail him and his mental stability became questionable. However, it would be unreasonable to conclude that this deterioration in his health and the change in his fortunes were due simply to the theft of the ancient *Hakenkreuz*. Or, indeed, that the theft had any bearing on the fact that within six weeks of its loss the Nazis were to lose two significant and decisive battles: El Alamein on October 23rd and Stalingrad on November 19th. Although these defeats are generally recognised as marking the turning point in the war, their proximity to the disappearance of the Führer's revered artefact has to be considered a matter of pure coincidence.